H.E. Spencer

bert.spencer@btinternet.com

ISBN 978-1-8380634-6-7

Cover design by dom@candco.co.uk

Proofreading by Catherine Timmons

Printed by Sarsen Press, Winchester. info@sarsenpress.com

Chapter 1. Chronicler

My concentration had drifted. I was watching the smoke curling from the logs in the fire, the flames reflected on people's faces, when at the end of the Sunday meeting, Martin suddenly said, 'Oh, and I want someone to be recorder for the Group. Keep our diary. Gerry should do it.'

Other than a sneer from Craig, nobody commented. Everybody seems to accept Martin's suggestions as orders nowadays, to be carried out without debate. Which is good because nobody else seems prepared to give them. But he surprised me; there had been no consultation whatsoever. He has not mentioned it since.

The more I have thought about it, the more the idea appeals. Not sure how to fit it in ... but I am tempted. Listening to the others tell of their experience has made me realise that mine was wider-ranging and revealing. I saw and experienced things they had not. Apart from the military, I am the only one of us who went outside the London Cordon. So here I sit, making a start before the light fades.

I suppose I am the obvious choice. Ex-teacher, not the most robust specimen, unprepossessing, some might say detached. Odd to have become the Chronicler: the Bede or the Matthew Paris of our Group. Also, oddly appropriate that we should have a Chronicler, given where we have landed up. Maybe that is what gave Martin the idea.

It has been a challenge to get the horrifying events into perspective; there is a paralysing, nightmarish quality about it. I keep hoping I will wake. We have all been traumatised. On more than one occasion, I have come across people crying quietly. Some will never recover from it. Not that we would be able to tell since none of us knew any of the others before we became, The Group.

I do not relish trying to commit the last sixteen months to paper; remembering the detail will be painful. It will take many sittings. But the Chronicle of The Group will be incomplete without describing the catastrophe. The story of how we came together and ended up here would have been unbelievable just two years ago, but I shall try. Our existence is totally beyond anything any of us would have foreseen.

A skein of Canada Geese is dropping low to land in the field across the river, honking as they come, black silhouettes against the sunset. Can't help wondering where they last landed; birds have been one of our few contacts with the outside world since we settled here. I wonder if geese can carry the virus. As usual, I am still hungry after supper.

From the outset, I am determined to be objective and honest about what happened. That applies to whatever I record of our future lives. My Chronicle will be the facts of happened to us as a Group; of what we individually know of the catastrophe that overtook humanity rather than speculation.

It is, of course, impossible to remember exactly what was said at any given point, but I will strive to reproduce the gist of what I heard personally. I can do no less. But it must ... and will be ... a document about humanity, not just a list of dates; not only a record of the government's heroic if futile policies as the fabric of society unravelled. As far as possible, I will recount the past chronologically.

I am sure my mind will dally and drift into the, why, or ... if only ... or how could they? The questions are endless and, I fear, now largely unanswerable ... at least for us. Maybe future historians will try to piece it together ... if there are any future historians. I suspect my Chronicle will also split into two parts; one for Martin and The Group to read; the other my personal thoughts and meandering. I have always had a good memory, so the incidents described will be as accurate as possible. Nothing embellished, nothing omitted.

So, to begin. My name is Gerald Morris. I am forty-seven years old and until sixteen months ago, taught science and history at a sixth-form college in Norwood, South London. Rose and I had been married for nearly twenty-four years, and both our children were at university. Nick was taking his final year in software engineering at UMIST; Julie was beginning her economics degree at Warwick. We lived in a pleasant, detached house on Norwood Hill, in South London, which afforded us a glorious view towards Central London.

My God, how easy it is, to sum up one's old life: just four sentences! And it's all gone. Unbelievable!

Rose and I first met at a party at Loughborough Uni when we were taking teaching degrees. She was a vivacious, petite, freckled, bubbly, extrovert with what seemed like dozens of friends. I, as usual, was on the edge of the action, looking in. There were other parties and at one of them, being even more drunk than usual, I asked her for a date. That was it; one of those life-defining moments; the die was cast. But I was shocked when I realised she wanted a proper relationship. A few weeks later, she looked straight at into my eyes and simply said, 'I want you to be a major part of my life.'

I have sat thinking of Rosie for the last half-hour and been close to tears.

From the start, we were comfortable with each other, although I was never sure how long it would last. On graduating we were both offered places at schools in London, but Rose, who taught English in Camden Town, only stuck it for two years.

'Too boring and the kids in Camden are doomed to be louts.'

After some temping, Rose got a job with a broadsheet newspaper: nothing grand, just fetching and carrying. But she seemed to enjoy it and made some useful contacts.

I, on the other hand, enjoyed teaching and after a few different schools, settled at Norwood. We lived in a flat in Streatham for three years before she became pregnant with Nick, then we married. Sometime after Nick was born, Rosie started sending articles to magazines and was surprisingly successful. Gradually she became a full-time freelance journalist. By a combination of good luck and a knack for getting to the heart of a subject, she developed quite a reputation for the 'in-depth' interviews much loved by the weekend supplements and women's magazines.

When her mother died, Rosie inherited enough money to buy our house on Norwood Hill. It was ideally situated; Rose had easy access to Central London, and the school at which I taught was only three miles away. It also had a largish garden which allowed me to indulge in my occasional hobby of vegetable gardening. This was almost an extension of my interest in science. I dabbled with different soils, fertilisers, and seed strains. All very innocuous and utterly dull when I try to explain it.

Our relationship was placid; we rarely argued, just got on with things, although there had been one period of concern for me. Rose occasionally needed to spend time away from home researching and interviewing, and during the 1990s these became more frequent. Then one evening, she returned late looking as if she had been crying. When I asked what was wrong, she said it was just an argument with an editor. But I suspected that it was more than that; I suspected that she had been 'seeing' someone. I didn't push it. I didn't really want to know the truth and had weeks of anxiety dreading the prospect of arriving home to find a letter saying she had left me. But it never happened. One of them must have broken it off; I persuaded myself it had been Rosie.

It was because I was half watching football on TV and half listening to Rose taking a phone call late one evening that I can pinpoint the time I first heard of the disease.

Rosie had been scheduled the next day to have an interview with Professor Norman Foster, who some years previously had been a joint winner of the Nobel Prize for biochemistry. Not that Rose was focusing on anything scientific. Foster had recently married a woman younger than his daughter and Rosie was putting together a series of interviews on marriages where the partners had wide age differences. It had the salutary title, *"What counts, Age or Blessings?"*

It had taken Rose weeks of persistent wheedling to get the interview, but now, at eleven o'clock in the evening, Foster's secretary was phoning from Cambridge to cancel the appointment scheduled for the following morning.

'Well, when can he do it? .... But surely, he can fit it in one day this week! ... Well, when will he be back? ... OK, please ask him to as soon as possible.'

She tossed her mobile phone onto the settee.

'Shit, after all that!'

'Stood you up?'

'God knows. Some tale about an outbreak or something. Unexpectedly summoned to some meeting of a government committee. Pathetic. If he doesn't want to do the bloody interview, why did he agree in the first place!'

'Outbreak of what?'

'I don't know! Who cares!'

'At least you've got Judge Thompson in reserve ...'

'Foster married a girl he had taught ... a girl who went on to gain a doctorate in his own field. Reasonable basis for a relationship; good potential for a revealing interview. Thompson … who God knows ought to have known better … married his chambers' bicycle!'

There was no consoling her.

But as the days went by, we realised that Norman Foster was one of the government's leading advisors on biotechnology and biological warfare. The night Rose had received the call postponing her interview, Foster was attending the first meeting of an Advisory Committee hastily formed by the government, in fact, a sub-committee of Cobra.

Chapter 2. Pandora's Box

Science has been a lifelong fascination. Before opting for teaching, I had considered a career in mathematical physics. Each month I spent happy hours at the Dulwich Library reading 'New Scientist', 'Nature', and any other scientific journals to hand. That was before the internet revolutionised access to information. Perhaps my interest in science made me more aware of certain aspects of the world around me than others in the Staff Room; perhaps it allowed me a better understanding of how events evolved.

It was a time of promise, a time of unprecedented progress in virtually every branch of science and technology. Not the least of these being research into microbiology and biochemistry.

Almost every month came announcements, many stemming from the Genome Project; new insights that would enable targeting illnesses caused by mutant genes. And after initial public resistance, trials of genetically modified crops became commonplace. The potential to banish starvation globally was a genuine possibility. At the same time, the medical and pharmaceutical professions were pioneering procedures, techniques, and drugs of huge promise. The prospect of a healthier world, free of famine was within our grasp.

Alas, as ever, the progress and promise ran in parallel with national posturing and suspicion that led to the development of new weapons. While weapons have always been a part of the human condition, certain aspects of this new weaponry caused concern, biological and biochemical weapons. Added to which nature itself continued to evolve its myriad lifeforms indifferent to the wishes of humans; continuing to surprise and puzzle Homo sapiens … just one species in many million … but a species that considered itself omnipotent. For the sake of this Chronicle, I feel it incumbent on me to at least try to identify the recent milestones on the road to our present catastrophe; both those man-made and those wrought by nature. Of course, these are merely the milestones in the public domain; undoubtedly, there were others known only to scientific and government 'inner-circles'.

1992

In 1992 one of Russia's leading scientists, the deputy chief of their Biopreparat organisation, Colonel Kanatjan Alibekov, defected to the USA. During lengthy debriefings, he chillingly reported that Russia possessed no less than 52 different biological agents that could be used as weapons. They had developed over 2,000 strains of Anthrax, many of which were stockpiled in their Sverdlovsk installation. These included a 'battle strain' Anthrax with up to 90% mortality rate, and a genetically modified Super-Plague with a 100% mortality rate if not recognised and treated quickly. It was clear that Russia held vast stocks of weapons-grade biological agents. Soviet scientists had also experimented with making these bacteria resistant to antibiotics, as well as genetically modifying existing viruses by splicing into them genes from other deadly strains. This was to develop what they called a Chimera Virus. Similar work had been undertaken with the Smallpox virus, a disease responsible for more deaths in the last century than all of man's wars and natural disasters put together.

Personally, I found these revelations incomprehensible. But I do not recall reading anything about stocks of biochemical weapons held by the USA or UK.

1995

A report to a US Senate Sub Committee in 1995, listed Libya, North Korea, South Korea, Iraq, Taiwan, Syria, Israel, Iran, China, Egypt, Vietnam, Laos, Cuba, Bulgaria, India, South

Africa & Russia as all possessing biological and biochemical weapons. The UK was not mentioned, probably because we were regarded as allies. Also in 1995, a terror attack took place in Tokyo when Sarin gas was released into the underground railway system. Twelve people died, and fifty were seriously injured.

2001

The cases of anthrax in America that following the 9/11 attack in 2001 provided a strident wake-up call. It was of little comfort when this was eventually proved to have been the work of an unbalanced mind of U.S. origin. But it came as a shock to learn that such a disease could be sent through the post and that there were organisations, governments or individuals prepared to unleash scourges which humanity had struggled for centuries to eliminate.

2002

But at least the wake-up call had positive results in the USA. The government tripled its bio-defence budget from $2Bn to $6Bn. It also ordered 120 million doses of Smallpox vaccine. The UK government ordered 20 million.

And in 2002 it became possible, via the internet, for any organisation to obtain the genetic code of the Ebola virus.

The release of a UK government report that year outlined what research into biochemical weapons had been undertaken here. And it was considerable! Many of the experiments conducted were to investigate how biochemical agents would spread if released over England.

2003

The possibility that Saddam Hussein's Iraq was manufacturing biochemical weapons predicated the Gulf War of 2003.

There had been several other harbingers for those perceptive enough to recognise them; some natural, others man-made. One was Severe Acute Respiratory Syndrome, (SARS) that erupted in China in February 2003. Caused by a so-called Corona Virus … usually benign to humans (the common cold being one of them). The SARS virus is endemic in poultry or pigs; by infecting humans, it had jumped species. It rapidly spread to a dozen countries infecting about a thousand people and killing over a hundred before being contained. One cause of the delay was that the Chinese authorities would not admit they had a problem.

Of course, there are about twenty or so other viruses lethal to humans, of which Ebola, Lassa, Rift Valley and Hantavirus are the most commonly known.

To me, the most alarming aspect came from reports of research aimed at identifying those genes which defined race; those which determined whether a person was black, white, Caucasian, Mongoloid, Aboriginal, Middle Eastern, Polynesian or Oriental. Clearly, if such genes could be identified, then bioweapons could be targeted at specific races.

Perhaps those responsible for defence against such weapons were lulled into complacency by the pragmatic theory of Mutually Assured Destruction (with its appropriately black acronym, MAD) that had evolved when considering the proliferation of nuclear weapons. After all, humanity had possessed the capability to eliminate itself with nuclear weapons for the past seventy years. Miraculously it had refrained from using them. We had also been incredibly lucky that none of the hundreds of accidents that had occurred with nuclear weapons, had been catastrophic.

But for biological weapons, the MAD theory did not necessarily apply. For a start, virtually any nation could produce them; it did not need an expensive infrastructure. Not for nothing had someone called biological weapons 'The poor man's atomic bomb'. Secondly, unlike nuclear weapons that need costly missile delivery systems, with biochemical weapons, it would be difficult to pinpoint the enemy. If a biological agent was released into a city's underground railway system, undetected, silent, slowly infecting travellers who would carry it outside the city, where does one begin to look? So relatively small nations could develop and deploy germ weapons against an enemy with far less chance of direct retaliation.

2011

Alarming reports began to emerge about maverick scientists; people carrying out bio-weapon research at universities. Apparently, these people were genetically modifying deadly viruses ... with the excuse that once we knew their DNA, vaccines could be developed.

The first I recall reading of was in about 2011. A team of Dutch scientists had mutated the H5N1 avian flu virus ... just five mutations in two key genes. Previously this virus could only be passed between humans by close personal contact. Their leader was reported as saying.

'In the laboratory is was possible to change the H5N1 virus into an aerosol-transmittable virus that can be rapidly spread through the air.'

What made H5N1 so dangerous is that it killed about 60% of the people who contracted it. Even the US government reacted to this work fearing that if published, it could fall into the hands of terrorists. But as usual, the world shrugged indifference.

2014

In 2014, *The Independent* newspaper revealed that a research team in America had been working along similar lines. They had genetically manipulated the 2009 strain of pandemic flu that had killed 500,000 people. Before that, they had attempted to recreate the 1918 flu virus. Following publication on their work, another scientist said ... and I quote:

'He took the 2009 pandemic flu virus and selected out strains that were not neutralised by human antibodies. He repeated this several times until he got a real humdinger of a virus. He left no doubt in my mind that he had achieved it. He used the flu virus that is known to infect human beings and then manipulate it in such a way that it would effectively leave the global population defenceless if it ever escaped from his laboratory. He has basically got a known pandemic strain that is resistant to vaccination. Everything he did before was dangerous ... but this is even madder.' Unquote.

The saner minds in the scientific community castigated such people, but somehow the mavericks retained their funding. One assumes some of this work was government-funded.

Probably the Ebola outbreak in West Africa in March 2014 was the most severe warning. The virulence of this apparently natural strain that killed thousands before it was brought under control had shaken the WHO and all the health workers who tried to contain it.

2015-2016

The Zika virus, carried by species of mosquito and previously confined to a narrow belt in equatorial Africa and Asia, spread eastwards eventually causing an outbreak of Zika Fever in

South America. It was estimated that in 2015-2016, 1.5 million people were infected in Brazil alone with 3,500 babies born with brain and other organ abnormalities. Again, nature had confounded humans in its ability to evolve and adapt.

But to my mind the most both amazing … and disturbing … facet associated with such research was the whole CRISPR scene; an acronym for (CLUSTERED REGULARLY INTERSPACED SHORT PALINDROMIC REPEATS). From when it was first accidentally performed in 1987 right up until today, the development of this methodology of manipulating genes has been phenomenal. For both good and bad causes, it was going to be used no matter what regulation was introduced.

One way or the other, I felt a growing concern about two things; the proliferation of manufactured bio-chemical weapons and the ability of nature to surprise us with new organisms; and thus to challenge our undeserved complacency.

And for the past twenty or so years, one other lethal ingredient was stirred into this toxic mix. Intelligent, well-educated, well-prepared Islamic fundamentalists seeking martyrdom. There were real fears about what would happen if they acquired nuclear or bio-chemical weapons. With their appearance came the recognition that humanity had entered a far more unstable era. In retrospect, all the ingredients for a catastrophe were poised … just waiting.

But as it turned out, any security processes to counter bioterrorism would probably have been ineffective. Because the individual who unleashed the plague was a calm, rational insider with detailed knowledge of how the systems worked. Not religious in the accepted sense, he marched to a different drummer, but also a drummer that demanded the life of its acolytes. It was not a virus that emerged from some primordial swamp or rain forest … or one that accidentally escaped from a laboratory. It was deliberately engineered before being unleashed.

The first time anything appeared in the media about Brazilian Flu was two days after Professor Foster had cancelled Rosie's interview.

Chapter 3. Outbreak

BBC1 10 o'clock News, 15th March.

As I recall, it was not even the lead story of that night's BBC news; it appeared towards the end of the bulletin.

'An outbreak of a severe strain of influenza is being reported from Sao Paulo, Brazil. Dozens of cases have been reported over the past few days. Our Political Correspondent, James Munro, who is currently in Brazil covering the G8 Global Environment Congress, sent us this report earlier today.'

'Bet this is why Prof. Foster blew you out!' I said helpfully.

Rose was tapping away on her laptop. 'Big deal. Flu in bloody South America. Drop the dead donkey!'

James Munro was standing outside a sign stating that the solid-looking edifice behind him was The Albert Einstein Hospital. Patches of dampness stained Munro's beige shirt; one could sense the humidity. Some of the people entering the hospital behind him appeared to be wearing handkerchiefs over their mouths and noses.

'The Sao Paulo health authorities are being pretty tight-lipped about this outbreak, and so far, they have refused to confirm or deny whether they have actually identified the cause of the illness. But this sprawling city covers about a hundred square miles and is home to some 20 million people. Sao Paulo is a city of both extreme wealth and extreme poverty, and a high proportion of the Paulistanos live almost at subsistence level. Shantytowns here are called Favelas, and these are as bad as anything I've seen in Africa, India or the Far East. They consist of crude shelters built on any open space; they have no running water and the sewage runs down the muddy tracks between the dwellings. Food poisoning is common and has not yet been ruled out as the cause. But the flu-like symptoms are affecting rich and poor, young, and old alike.

Earlier today, I spoke to Dr Hererra-Alvarez, spokesperson for the hospital, and she expressed some concerns'.

Dr Hererra-Alvarez's soft Portuguese accent had the hint of Brooklyn about it.

'We have just over one hundred cases so far at The Einstein. The initial symptoms appear as a particularly nasty dose of flu, although there have been no reports of anything unusual from the WHO regarding new strains. And new strains of flu usually surface in Asia first. Basically, we are telling people to go home and go to bed. Take some aspirin for the headache and try to sleep it off for a few days. But we're aware that many of the people affected can't afford to visit hospitals, clinics or doctors, so it's impossible to know the true extent of the outbreak.'

'Is the outbreak concentrated on the Einstein Hospital catchment area?'

'No, it seems to be widespread, with many of the cases coming from the poorer areas of the city.'

'How long before you can identify the illness with any certainty?'

'Hard to predict. We have biochemists and forensic specialists working on it in the four big hospitals in Sao Paulo ... and samples have been flown to both the WHO in Geneva and CDC in Atlanta. I'm sure we'll know exactly what's causing it in a few days. Then we will be able to act accordingly.'

'Has anyone died of this illness?'

There was a moment's hesitation. *'We have had a couple of deaths of people who had the symptoms, but these were elderly people who were also suffering from other ailments.'*

This is James Munro reporting for BBC News, in Sao Paulo.

'In tonight's European Cup quarterfinals, Newcastle United lost to Anderlecht by two goals to nil, and in the other....'

Switching off the TV, I put away the exam papers I was marking and aided by my walking stick, hobbled towards the kitchen.

'I thought we'd escaped the flu for this winter.'

'Take a long time for it to get here,' Rosie said, closing her laptop.

'You're kidding. No city on earth is more than about two day's air travel away.'

'Well, I'm not having any more flu jabs. They didn't do a thing for me last year.'

I had explained ad nauseam about the efficacy of flu jabs, and that they are designed to combat the strains of any virus circulating at the time. But my explanation had fallen on deaf ears.

'Heard any more from Prof. Foster?'

'Nope. Tried him again today, but his secretary said he was still away, and she didn't know when he'd be back. Perhaps he's laid up with flu somewhere,' Rosie said brightly.

'Are you intending to interview his nubile young wife?'

'Of course, but not much point until I know I can get him as well.'

Next day, *The Times* reported possible cases of Brazilian Flu in Rio de Janeiro and Mexico City. For that is what the disease became known as, Brazilian Flu; innocuous, anodyne, Brazilian Flu. For me, it had a nasty resonance with Spanish Flu that had killed an estimated 100 million people between 1917-20, a high proportion of them fit and healthy young adults. Nearly half the population of the world had been infected, one-third seriously.

Another TV report I also saw sticks in my memory. It occurred a few days later, and many of the Group also remember seeing it. It was on ITV's Early Evening News, again reported from Sao Paulo. This time it was the lead story. ITV's urbane Karen Bloom sent to Brazil to cover it had a slight edge to her voice. It was videocam and not good quality, but according to the screen logo, it was live.

'There are now reported to be over five hundred cases of the so-called Brazilian Flu in Sao Paulo with many of those earliest infected now seriously ill. The symptoms of the early sufferers have evolved into respiratory infection and other unusual side effects. It is rumoured that there have been over one hundred deaths attributed to it.

Officials from the Brazilian Health Ministry have imposed travel restrictions to prevent the disease from spreading. But there have already been unconfirmed reports of cases from Rio de Janeiro, Buenos Aires, and Santiago. There are also unofficial reports that this is not a new strain of an influenza virus at all, but something new. Experts from America's Centre for Disease Control in Atlanta have flown to Sao Paulo to help track the source of the infection and advise on treatment.

Sao Paulo is one of the world's largest cities, sprawling across a vast area. It is home to both the very rich and to the poverty-stricken. Today, we have driven to the outskirts of the city, to one of the many impoverished areas, the favelas. We are in the Municipality of Sao Bernardo do Campo to see how the smaller hospitals, like the Clinique Santa Domingo, behind me, are coping.'

She was outside a dilapidated building, where about two hundred people had gathered in the heat. As usual, many had clustered behind the reporter, some with crude facemasks covering their mouths and nose. Beside Karen Bloom stood a woman in her mid-50's, a nurse, who appeared to belong to a religious order; she looked exhausted.

'This is Sister Emanuella Grace, who runs this clinic. Sister Grace, can you tell me how many people have the flu in this area?'

'Many, many. There are more each day.'

'And are your staff able to treat those affected?'

'Most of my helpers have left. They are poor people who are afraid of infecting their own families. And none of the medicine we have seems to do any good. The antibiotics we tried had no effect. We are waiting for the health authorities to send us the proper medicine.'

Bloom was about to ask her next question, when Sister Emanuella Grace began to cough, a racking, spasm of coughing, which shook her whole body. Coughing so severe it made her retch. It seemed to go on for minutes but was probably less than one minute. When she finished, her handkerchief was bloodstained. Karen Bloom involuntarily stepped backwards, wide-eyed, and shocked, clearly realising that she was much too close for comfort. Sister Emanuella Grace seemed to start to apologise, then collapsed. The camera stayed on her prostrate body, as she went into a violent convulsion, with blood running from her nose and mouth. Nobody went to assist her; those standing near backed away. Then the picture lurched and ended up looking at a blue sky as people scrambled to get clear of the area.

Before Bloom could speak again, the editor had cut back to the ITV News studio in London. Even the unflappable news anchor-man, Bill Henderson was stunned into momentary silence, before clearing his throat.

'Well, it appears we have lost Karen for the moment. She was reporting there on the flu outbreak that seems to be sweeping Sao Paulo.'

The camera pulled back to reveal two men sitting close to Henderson.

'I am joined now by Dr Hamid El-Mallah, from the London School of Tropical Medicine, who is an expert in tropical diseases, and Professor Norman Foster, Nobel Prize-winning biochemist from Cambridge and a member of one of the government's Cobra sub committees. Dr El-Mallah if I may ask you first. Those worrying pictures did not look like normal flu to me.'

'No, they certainly did not. There has been a lot of communication with Sao Paulo, and we think we can rule out any of the normal influenza viruses. CDC and the WHO have confirmed this. Blood and tissue samples from patients have been sent to various centres, and many people are trying to identify the DNA. Of course, we have to face the possibility that it may be something we have not encountered before.'

'So, it's not influenza as we know it?'

El-Mallah hedged. 'Too early to say. There are hundreds of strains of what is commonly known as influenza, and it's a virus that has proved to be extremely proficient at mutation. Its eight genes have a history of complex adaptation.'

Henderson let that sink in for a few seconds.

'Professor Foster if I can bring you in. Does the fact that this may be a new disease cause you any particular concerns over how the Brazilian authorities need to fight this epidemic?'

Foster was composed. Mid sixties, well-dressed, his dark wavy hair streaked with grey at the temples, he reminded me of a stereotypical Tory MP. I sensed women found him attractive. Rosie was riveted.

'Well, yes and no. It's premature to start talking about epidemics. Undoubtedly, they have a pretty virulent virus on their hands, if indeed it is a virus, but there is a whole armoury of weapons available to modern medicine, once we are certain what this is. But you are right in saying that a new disease poses new problems, if only from the viewpoint of natural immunity. If it is something man hasn't encountered before, then we may not have any natural immunity; that means we would have to depend on the expertise of modern medicine. But we shouldn't get too worked up about it. The media gets hold of some outbreak or another about twice a year and blows it out of all proportion. For example, there was an outbreak of an undefined fever in Nigeria a few years ago that proved to be insignificant. Then there was Severe Acute Respiratory Syndrome in early 2003, spread to about a dozen countries and claimed about a thousand lives worldwide because the Chinese tried to cover it up. The hysterical media christened it, "Killer Pneumonia" and if the Second Gulf War had not been raging at the time, it would have been front-page news for days … if not weeks.

Then there was the Asian Bird Flu. Most people who become infected with these diseases are treated with modern drugs and make a full recovery. Unfortunately, it required some intensive hospital treatment. It's worth remembering that about ten thousand people die of influenza each year in the UK alone, yet that doesn't make headlines. So, I think it's really unwise to jump to conclusions as far as this outbreak is concerned.'

Bland, condescending stuff.

'I understand that you have just come from a meeting of a group set up to advise the government on this disease.'

Foster looked slightly surprised. 'Not quite true. I have been attending a meeting of a group that discusses health issues of all kinds. Not particularly connected with this outbreak.'

'Was the Brazilian Flu discussed?'

'Yes, briefly. Part of the group's remit is to monitor all reports of abnormal manifestations of disease.'

'And you rate the Brazilian Flu as no more than that, an abnormal manifestation?'

'At the moment, yes, that's how I would describe it.'

'Dr El-Mallah, how do you interpret the fact that there have been reports of the disease from Mexico City, New York, Los Angeles, and today I understand from Jakarta?'

‘Jakarta! I hadn’t heard that.’ he paused. ‘Well, as Norman said, we should not jump to conclusions. So far, these are unsubstantiated reports. We must wait until we receive confirmation that this is the same disease before we can make any analysis of the epidemiology.’

Henderson persisted. ‘Frankly, I’m astonished that with all the technology and analytical tools available … all the DNA analysis and genome knowledge, and so forth … the scientists have been unable to identify it, even though it has been rampant in Sao Paulo for over two weeks!’

Foster answered carefully. ‘It really is not that easy to identify new strains of a disease. It can take weeks, sometimes months. We are getting a clearer idea of what it may be. But we are waiting for confirmation from other medical institutes before we can finally confirm it.’

‘And what might it be?’

‘As I said, we need to wait a few more days.’

Realising he was getting nowhere Henderson brought the discussion to a close.

‘Professor Norman Foster and Dr Hamid El-Mallah, thank you for your time.’

Chapter 4. Interview at Cherry Hinton

18th March

To her surprise, the next morning, Rose was invited to interview the Fosters. It was more of a summons than an invite. She was brusquely informed by his secretary that the Prof had found an hour in which he could fit her in ... if she could meet them at his home at Cherry Hinton, on the outskirts of Cambridge. Not one to miss an opportunity, Rosie the Journalist began to envision a whole different interview with a man in the limelight. She was quite bubbly as she left for Liverpool Street Station, twittering on about these sorts of breaks sometimes happening in journalism! But when she returned that evening, she was uncharacteristically pensive.

'It was totally chaotic; not at all what I'd expected. We hardly got started. The whole thing was so rushed. Foster spent most of his time answering 'phone calls. Then he had to rush off after about twenty minutes, even though I'd been promised an hour. Left me with the wife. Their bloody phones didn't stop ringing!'

'Man in great demand.'

'Very guarded about this Brazilian Flu. All he seemed interested in was playing down any talk of an epidemic and how quickly my article would be printed. Apparently tomorrow, they both fly off to some conference on genetic engineering in Ottawa. He's giving the keynote speech, and she's giving a paper too.'

'But did you get the interview you went for? Older men and Trophy Wives? You do remember that?'

'Yes, no problem there. Glenda Foster and me sort of clicked. Really easy to talk to. She's an attractive thirty-something. Highly intelligent, no-nonsense scientist without a romantic bone in her body. Obviously adores Foster ...'

Rosie paused.

'And?'

'Well, two things really. As I said, he took a call on his mobile and went into the next room. Then another phone started ringing somewhere in the hall, and she went to answer it. But I could overhear some of what he was saying in the next room. Very agitated. Something about someone from a laboratory...'

'From the university?'

'No, I don't think so. According to his CV, he doesn't only hold the chair in biochemistry; he's also a director of a couple of biotech companies. Sounded more like one of them. They were trying to get hold of someone, and something about someone called, Pefles or Tefles or Kefles, something like that. I couldn't quite hear.'

I smiled at the thought of her trying not to overhear.

'Must have been difficult for you.' She didn't bite.

'Second thing was as I was leaving. Glenda said something rather odd. Asked whether I have any children. When I said they are both at university, she said she envied me; wished she and Norman had had time to have children. Odd phrasing; oddly, past tense. I was wary of stepping on sensitivities about his age and was just about to say something about IVF being a wonderful thing when she suddenly asked if we were planning a holiday.'

'So? Even no-nonsense scientists probably resort to social chit-chat occasionally.'

'No, it was more than that. She said that with all this threat of flu, it might be a good time to be on holiday somewhere very isolated. When I asked her if she was worried about the outbreak, she said quietly that she didn't think it was flu. I asked her if she knew what it was, and she got very embarrassed and muttered something about she shouldn't have said anything. I asked her if she was planning a holiday, and she said Norman would consider it a dereliction of duty at a time like this. Although it doesn't seem as if he's got any qualms about flitting off to Canada! We'd reached their front door by then, and I didn't have time to follow it up. I got the impression she was trying to warn me.'

'Of what?'

'I don't know, can't put my finger on it. But I think it had something to do with this disease in Brazil.'

Naturally, the Group have talked about their own experiences. I have concluded that, through the pure fluke of Rosie's contact with the Fosters, I am the most knowledgeable among us about what went on behind the scenes. None of the rest of The Group has any anything to add. In fact, when I told them our story one evening, Craig inferred that I was making it up. God knows why he should think that! But that's Craig.

When I arrived home from work the next day, I had a shock. Rosie had been on The Mother of All Shopping Sprees. She must have made a significant gap on the shelves of our local Sainsbury's. There was tinned and packet food and bottled drink everywhere; it must have been five hundred pounds worth. Astonished, I asked her why and how much it had cost, she simply said she been unable to sleep last night and had a nasty feeling; put it down to woman's intuition. She also said that the woman on the checkout counter told her that she was the third person that day to have had such a binge!

Rosie's action that day undoubtedly saved my life. But to my lasting sadness, not her own. That evening she rang the kids, just wanted to say Hi, you understand. But not wanting to worry them during their run-up to end-of-term exams, she did not mention Brazilian Flu or holidays.

Next day there were unconfirmed reports of possible cases of Brazilian Flu in New York and Los Angeles. Again, TV news reporters appeared standing outside major hospitals speculating on the spread and pathology of the disease. The usual clutch of 'experts' were wheeled into the CNN studio, either to say that not enough was being done to combat the disease or alternatively, why there was no cause for concern.

I do remember being surprised at how fast it had spread. But in a way, I also felt oddly comforted by the fact there were now cases in the USA. Because I was sure that the Americans ... the most technically advanced nation on earth and experts in disease control ... would soon pin it down. The Americans had established rigorous procedures for dealing with infectious disease, and I was confident that these would come into full force if there were any real threat to them.

Chapter 5. Deepening crisis in Brazil

29th March, BBC 6 o'clock News. Lead item.

'The news this evening is dominated by the escalating health crisis in Brazil. There is unrest in Sao Paulo where cases of the unidentified illness continue to spread. Luis Sedano of Agencia Meridonal reports from Sao Paulo.

'There was a major development today when during a television interview Dr Antonio Vega, Brazil's Minister of Health, said that the authorities had eliminated influenza as the cause of this outbreak. But he added that the actual virus had not yet been positively identified. Dr Vega reported that seven hundred and eighty people have now died of the disease.'

The scene switched to a large square. Lines of police in riot gear and gas masks occupied one end and a few thousand demonstrators milled around at the other. Most wore crude face masks of some sort. Some held placards, most of which carried slogans in Portuguese. But one or two were in English calling for the resignation of the Minister of Health.

'There have been ugly scenes at hospitals, clinics, and pharmacies over the past few days as people have been demanding medicine to combat the outbreak. Several pharmacies have been looted. The police report that several people have been killed or injured in these incidents. There are also reports of medical staff abandoning their posts.

Experts from America's Centre for Disease Control have so far failed to identify the source. But there is speculation that it's been caused by contact with a virus unknown to man. And the location of suspicion for Brazil is inevitably the Amazonian rain forest, about 1,000 miles north of here. Earlier today, I spoke with Dr Walter Carmichael, who is a member of the CDC's Incident Investigation Team from Atlanta.' Luis Sedano stood inside a laboratory. People wearing full biohazard suits were visible through a glass panel behind him.

'Dr Carmichael, what do we know about how this disease attacks people?'

Carmichael was a short man, weary but tense and alert: a surgical face mask hung loosely around his neck.

'Those affected exhibit flu-like symptoms in the initial phase that can last for anything between 8 to 15 days. The patient then lapses into the second phase where their respiratory systems break down, with blood entering the lungs. The third and final phase shows symptoms similar to some of the haemorrhagic fevers; the skin appears to be bruised, and blood leaches from multiple organs of the body.'

For a moment, Sedano seemed shocked by this brutally frank description; then he recovered.

'What lines are the CDC team investigating?'

'We are trying to trace the initial victim, the so-called Index Case, and all of the earliest cases. We need to identify what they have in common. Where they had been, what they had eaten, what they had been exposed to. That sort of thing.'

'What's the progress on that?'

'The earliest cases we have identified so far all seem to have lived in the Brecos and Los Alandda districts. Now we are trying to track their movements over the days before they first showed signs of illness. But this is not proving easy.'

'Why is that?'

'All of the earliest cases have died. This disease is deadly. It has an exceptionally high mortality rate. We think we have isolated the virus that's causing it, but it's not something we've encountered before.'

'Do you know how the infection passes between people?'

'Not 100% proven, but the initial tests suggest airborne transmission, sneezing, coughing, breathing.'

'As you're probably aware, there is speculation that this is something which originated in the Amazon rain-forest and has been carried to Sao Paulo by one of the logging workers coming home for leave. Do you think that could be so?'

Carmichael sighed. His team had also speculated endlessly on this possibility.

'It's possible … so it's one of our lines of investigation. After all, western medicine hadn't encountered Bolivian Hemorrhagic Fever until 1962 or the Ebola Virus until 1976. Ebola probably originated in the Congo, another rain forest, but we still haven't identified its source. And that's after nearly 40 years of research and thousands of deaths.'

'Do we know what the incubation period is?'

'Not for certain. The first cases were reported over three weeks ago, but we don't know when the initial contact was made. The person could have been incubating the disease for weeks.'

'What treatments are proving successful?'

Carmichael was silent for a moment, and then quietly said.

'At this moment, we know of no patient who has recovered once infected.'

The interview ended there.

The BBC anchorman in London then said that the first suspected case in Europe had been reported from Lisbon. It was believed that the man had recently been on a business trip to Sao Paulo. The patient was being kept in isolation. Two days later, there were reports of a sick passenger being taken off a plane at Heathrow. He was a man in his sixties who had arrived on the BA flight from Rio de Janeiro. He was taken to Hillingdon General Hospital and placed in isolation. As were the other passengers and crew of the plane. The suspect passenger turned out to be the first case of Brazilian Flu in the UK. He died three days later.

Chapter 6. Meltdown in Brazil

15th April

Sao Paulo became the benchmark against which other cities would measure their fate. With little in the history of modern civilisation to assist them during the critical decision phase, the Brazilians made desperate efforts to control the disease. By the end of another two weeks, over seven thousand deaths had been reported. There were probably hundreds more unreported where people had died alone or where families had contracted the disease while nursing a relative.

In a further two weeks, the number of deaths had risen to over twenty-one thousand, and the number of people infected was estimated to be nearly two hundred thousand. Hospitals, clinics, and doctor's surgeries were overwhelmed. The Brazilian Government declared a state of emergency in Sao Paulo as people were ordered to stay at home to try to slow the rate of infection. By then, hundreds of cases of the disease were being reported from other locations in Brazil. From Recife and Salvador in the north and Porto Alegre in the south, the reports flooded in.

As the situation worsened, the Brazilian Government suspended airline flights and railway traffic to and from the stricken city. Soon after that, all roads into the city were blocked and guarded by police or army. From then on, only authorised vehicles were allowed through the cordon and only then if the occupants wore bio-hazard suits. Alas, the measures to quarantine this sprawling city were too little and too late. It proved impossible in a city of twenty million people. There were several riots by citizens demanding action. After losing a vote of No Confidence in their handling of the crisis, the Brazilian government resigned. Due to the deteriorating situation and realising there was little time for the niceties of elections, The President appointed a Military Committee to take control. Predictably the fragile Brazilian economy went into free-fall with the inevitable knock-on to other world markets. The value of the Brazilian cruzado crashed.

The new Military Council imposed a regime of strict internal censorship and tried to expel foreign news agency staff. Initially, any media correspondent whose reports implied that the disease was out of control, found themselves under house arrest. But in the days of global mobile phones and social media, with servers and hubs in different countries, imposing a news blackout proved impossible. For a while, news found its way out via emails, chat rooms and blogs. Eventually concluding that a world which knew of the scale of the catastrophe would be more likely to send assistance, the Military Council lifted all reporting restrictions. And via a global media insatiable for bad news and indifferent to good, the world watched with growing alarm.

Inevitably the UK media played its part in 'exposing' the difficulties faced by the Brazilian health community. The British tabloids ran 'exclusive' interviews with spurious experts and reports from their journalists in South America. I regarded them as the usual tabloid hype.

Then a very alarming fact was confirmed. *"The Times"* quoted a confidential CDC report giving the disease a staggering 99.9% Mortality Rate: only one person in a thousand had survived once infected! This was coupled with an unusually high Spread Rate. The potential for even greater catastrophe loomed larger every day. No vaccine was available, and there was no news as to whether any regular medicines worked. The whole of the medical and pharmaceutical world was desperate to take samples from anyone who had survived to try to produce a vaccine. If anti-bodies could be isolated and manufactured, then this at least would be a start at stemming the rate of infection. But by then, the number of doses needed probably made that task impossible.

Even then, we Brits remained typically phlegmatic. Brazil might have been on another planet. Conversations on the topic in the Staff Room at college displayed vague indifference. After all, floods, famine, and pestilence happened in the less developed countries; it was a part of the human condition in such countries. Whereas in developed countries, we ordered things differently. We will have sufficient medicines to prevent these irritations from getting out of hand. So what if an aircraft had brought someone carrying the disease to London? People regularly came back from foreign travels with Malaria or Hepatitis or even Green Monkey Fever. We isolated them, treated them, and they either recovered, or they died. But we contained it.

It was after listening to one such puerile conversation in the Staff Room that I spoke to Colin Jefferson, the Head of College. Jefferson had been appointed Head only a few years previously, and he and I had never really hit it off. Our relationship had worsened since my accident, an event that he had found oddly amusing.

Educated at Stowe and Cambridge, he enjoyed lording it over those of us who had attended "lesser universities" as he was pleased to call them. I suspected that he dreamed of becoming Head of one of the great public schools and was disillusioned to find himself at a sixth form college in London. As a result, he had a condescending manner that many found irksome. This manifested itself yet again when I asked what he thought we would do if the disease affected the UK in the same way. Smiling in that oily way of his, he said, 'I rather think my old Latin tutor would rebuke me sternly for loose translation, but 'Ex Africa Semper aliquid novi,' seems appropriate. The rest of us probably looked blank, so he enlightened us,

'Funny things happen in other places.'

He then suggested that rather than panicking over something I could do nothing about, I should focus my efforts on improving the A-level results from the science candidates! Feeling publicly humiliated, I remember walking away thinking, Arsehole! But it is not kind to speak ill of the dead.

By then the suspect cases in Mexico City, New York, Los Angeles, Honolulu, Jakarta, Tokyo, Hong Kong, Bombay, Lisbon, and London had all been confirmed as being caused by the same virus. It was assumed the disease had spread at such an alarming rate due to the sheer volume of air travel. Some ominous news broke for the UK. It was announced that twenty-eight of the two hundred and fifty passengers and crew put into isolation at Hillingdon and Slough Hospitals from the BA flight from Rio de Janeiro were now showing flu-like symptoms. Two baggage handlers who had been on duty at Heathrow when the plane landed had fallen sick. One of them had been taken ill while visiting his parents in Walsall. Also, the driver who had ferried the passengers to isolation had collapsed after complaining of flu-like symptoms. He was rushed to the same hospital. Up until that point, my colleagues in college had been right; it had been all very remote, very distant. But now it was real; now it was in our own back yard. From then on, we all became more concerned about what was happening in our own country than the situation in Sao Paulo. Or anywhere else in the world.

The last TV report I recall seeing from Sao Paulo was from a Spanish reporter from Sky News standing on a hill with the city lying far behind him in the late evening haze. I was struck by how few lights burned in the city.

Chapter 7. Accident

28th April

Anil and Nalini Patel had been our next-door neighbours for nearly 10 years. Anil was a consultant for a computer company; Nalini worked part-time as a receptionist in the Orthodontic Department of St. George's Hospital in Tooting. Both had arrived in England as children after their parents had fled Idi Amin's purge of Ugandan Asians in the '70s. They were good neighbours; our two kids played with their two kids in whichever garden took their fancy, and there were often drinks and barbeques in each other's homes. There had been a surprising and unplanned addition to their family the previous year when Nalini gave birth to a third child, Sherida.

Our next-door neighbours on the other side were the Brabourns. They were a retired couple in their early seventies: Alex had been an accountant: Marjorie had worked in Harrods for some years and never tired of name dropping which of the great and good had had the privilege of being served by her. We always had the impression that the Brabourns were dubious as to how we could afford to live in Newbury Crescent … me being only a teacher … as Marjorie delicately phrased it. Rose and I took some pains never to reveal to them that, thanks to Rosie's inheritance, we were quite comfortably off.

It was Nalini Patel who came to my assistance following my stupid accident. I had been putting up Christmas lights outside the house when the ladder slipped on a frosty lawn. It was this aspect of my misfortune that Jefferson found so amusing.

Scrambling to hang onto the ladder I landed heavily on the rockery breaking the second metatarsal bone in my right foot and cracking the navicular bone in my left. The break was compound; I almost fainted when I saw the bone sticking out, and the bloody patch slowly spreading on my sock. Nalini heard me fall. She promptly drove me to the hospital, where the broken bone needed an operation. It had to be pinned. I then spent a miserable and quite painful month in a wheelchair followed by some weeks on crutches. My walking stick was the symbol of the final phase of recovery.

The accident and operation proved to be both good and bad news. In the short- term, bad news, because the wound became infected. I spent weeks as an outpatient taking large doses of antibiotics to stem the infection. In the long-term, it may have saved my life. Viruses are not themselves treatable by antibiotics, but the damage inflicted can sometimes be limited by substantial doses of certain antibiotics. I have often wondered whether it was because I was stuffed full of antibiotics that the virus was not fatal when eventually I caught it. Such are the vagaries that decide one's survival.

Towards the end of April, Nicholas brought his girlfriend, Lindsey, home for the weekend. We had not met this one before, and as soon as we saw them together, it was clear that Nick was smitten. Lindsey was a bright, sparkly, charmer who knew instinctively that flirting with her guy's father would do her no harm; and she very quickly established a great relationship with Rosie. For her part, Rosie found my suggestion that this precocious handful was flirting with me absolutely hilarious.

The four off us were walking together on Wimbledon Common on one of those gloriously cold misty mornings when the dew magically covering every branch, leaf and cobweb is a work of art. Out of the blue, Rosie suddenly said,

'How about us all taking a cottage in the Highlands for the summer?'

Ever one for subtlety, Nick's response was, 'Yeah, right!'

'I'm serious …'

'The Highlands! To do what exactly?'

'Just to enjoy ourselves … and take in nature.'

'Mum give us a break. You're a sun worshipper! The Highlands?'

'I was looking at some brochures the other day. There are some beautiful cottages available. Not too expensive. And I'm sure Julie and Matthew would come.'

'Oh, goody. Not only can we go cavorting in the heather, we can also be bored witless learning about macro-economics.'

'That's unkind, Nicholas. Matthew means well.'

Matt was Julie's latest relationship and a seriously self-centred yawn.

'Have you actually asked Julie?' I ventured since the whole suggestion had come from left field as far as I was concerned.

'Not yet, but I'm sure she'd love it,' Rosie persisted.

'Mum, Jules and I have not been on holiday with you and Dad since we were fifteen. What on earth makes you think we could survive such an event without invoking physical violence in some form?' Nick liked to wind Rosie up.

'It would be nice. Don't you think so, Lindsey?'

'Yeah, great.' One could detect sarcasm in Lindsey's voice.

That was about as far as Rosie got in trying to gather up her brood and whisk them away to a safer nest site. Julie had already made other plans for the summer; so had Nick and Lindsey.

Looking back, it is almost unbelievable that the disease declined in interest for the UK media for a while. But it did. The sudden possibility of a potential - if highly unlikely - Royal Engagement and its implications for the Monarchy and the Church of England produced the predictable media feeding frenzy. As usual, the story involved Prince James. The "happy couple" had met while at university and ... incredibly ... managed to pursue some sort of clandestine relationship before a "friend" of the Prince tipped off the press. After that, they had no chance of a normal relationship.

True to form, Prince James was hounded to distraction by the media, and in a fit of sheer exasperation rounded on them and publicly declared his love for Lubna Iman, a fellow student on his land management course at Oxford. The word ballistic appeared in most reports about the reaction from Buckingham Palace. Prince James was unrepentant and the paparazzi with their lenses that could photograph the far reaches of the Milky Way, caught the couple holding hands about two miles away.

Some of the headlines were memorable.

'Will she give up Islam?' yelled The Mirror.

'Love may be blind, but Jamie knows his duty,' pontificated The Mail.

'Lubna's Wiltshire Oasis,' was billed as a 'Hello!' magazine exclusive.

'Another Bad Heir Day!' from The Sun

'Im-Shalla', The Express.

Maybe it was a ruse; if it was, it was a commendable one, because it gave the health authorities breathing space out of the spotlight. But not entirely. The spread of infection around the world was still being reported on about page 4 for those who were interested. And I was.

It soon became public knowledge that we had not contained the spread in the UK. Several new cases were reported from the Hillingdon, Slough, Feltham, and Windsor areas, most of them being people who worked either at Heathrow Airport or at one of the nearby hospitals. Cases also started to be reported from Salford and Glasgow.

Chapter 8. Epidemiology

3rd May

When teaching science classes, I always made a point of finishing the part of the lesson required by the National Curriculum 10 minutes early. Then I would give the class a flavour of advances that were taking place. My "Futures Sessions", I called them. It was surprising how many pupils responded to those sessions rather than to the turgid stuff in the textbooks.

(In truth, not all students took kindly to them; some referred to them as "Hannibal's Happy Hour", Hannibal being the rather unkind nickname I had acquired because of my slight resemblance to the actor, Anthony Hopkins. Teenagers can be cruel.) But I was gratified when one or two former pupils confided that those sessions had inspired them to follow careers in science or technology.

At about that time, I began to think about the mathematics of epidemics to use it in one of my "Futures Sessions". I felt sure it would interest a few of the better pupils. As I recall, it ran as follows.

'There are some sophisticated mathematical models which take account of all sorts of variables, but the basics are relatively simple as far as humans are concerned. In its search for a host, a new virus inevitably infects a single person first. Depending on how it is genetically programmed, it installs itself in one or more organs of the body. In the case of airborne viruses, this is usually the respiratory system. In common with all living organisms, a virus's main objectives are to survive and reproduce …'

'Just like Colborne,' came a voice from the back of the class invoking the inevitable sniggers; I ploughed on.

'The period during which the host human is incubating the virus also tends to define the period during which they are contagious. The longer the incubation period, the longer the host is capable of infecting others, often without the host even realising they are infectious. That is how the common cold works and that is how more dangerous pathogens work.

The number of people we encounter varies from individual to individual. For some, like ourselves attending this school, it's many hundreds a day. For others, for instance, older or infirm people confined to their homes, it could be less than 5 per day. But let us assume that on average we come into contact with between 20 to 30 people per day. Thus, if an infected person infects only 10% of those they came into contact with, this means they infect 2 or 3 people a day.

The maths are impressive. If a single person carrying the disease infects only **2** other people and within 3 days these 2 have incubated the virus to a point where they too can infect another 2, and so on, then within **20 days over 500** people will be infected.

If they infect **3** new victims per day, and these three, in turn, infect 3 others every 3 days and so on, then within 20 days **a surprising 19,000** will be infected. If the infection rate per individual is **4** people, then within **20 days over 250,000** could be infected. As I said, and I think you will agree, the sums are impressive!

Then there is the Mortality Rate to consider. On TV the other evening, a doctor from America's Centre for Disease Control, suggested the disease had a terrifying 99.9% Mortality Rate. Thus, once infected, only one person in every thousand would survive! Now that is a seriously lethal disease.'

I suddenly realised that the class had become completely silent and that I might be scaring some of them. I switched tack.

‘Fortunately for us, viruses are fragile organisms. In general, they do not survive more than 4 or 5 hours once exposed to the ultra-violet present in normal sunlight. But the other critical factor which defines the scale of an epidemic is the degree to which it penetrates the host population. In sparsely populated areas the disease could effectively burn itself out as long as the vector on which the virus was carried could not jump from one host community to another. Certain viruses also appear to be able to transfer between host species. It is thought possible that the HIV virus originated in monkeys.’

‘We thought it started in Colborne…’

‘In previous ages, when there was more limited interpersonal contact, there was more chance of the infection stalling; although the Black Death and Plagues of the Middle Ages proved the exception to this basic rule.’

At which point, the exit bell sounded. One or two pupils in that class asked questions, but as usual, most had been waiting for the bell before clamouring off.

Sadly for humanity, the Brazilian Flu Virus had a combination of the worst of the characteristics I outlined to my class that day. Being airborne the virus is highly mobile; it has an unusually long incubation period during which time the person infected is infecting others without even realising they are carrying it. And lastly, it is horrendously lethal. We did not know then of course that it had also been genetically engineered to survive many weeks in a normal atmosphere and to lay dormant for long periods. If swift cauterising action had been applied, who knows what might have happened. But humanity had not encountered this phenomenon before. Regrettably, humanity … and the risk-averse politicians they had elected to rule them … could not contemplate taking any measures that might affect business. Until it was too late.

Chapter 9. Questions in Parliament

3rd May

The demands in the UK media for prompt and decisive action had been growing from the start of the Sao Paulo outbreak. By now, it was a clamour. The Opposition in Parliament pressed the government to reveal its contingency plans in the event of the virus taking hold in the UK. This simply invoked banal statements from Health Ministers.

'What measures are the Government taking regarding the cases recently reported in Huddersfield?'

'The Department of Health is monitoring the situation closely.'

'Supplementary question, Mr Speaker. Will the Minister confirm that there are now twenty-three cases in the Manchester Royal Infirmary, and tell Honourable members what his department is doing to contain this latest escalation?'

'We see no need for hasty measures at this juncture.'

'Mr Speaker, the way the government is dithering with this health crisis, reminds one strongly of the way a previous British government dithered with the Foot and Mouth crisis in 2001. That dithering resulted in the slaughter of millions of cattle and almost caused the elimination of our livestock industry. Judging by what is occurring abroad, we will have another potentially devastating health crisis on our hands unless urgent and firm action is taken. I ask again! Will the Minister tell the House what is being learned from other countries regarding containment of this threat to public health?'

'We are in regular communication with other nations regarding the preventative measures they are taking. The government will give a comprehensive statement on its plans shortly.'

All standard straight-bat responses conveying absolutely no information of value. It was the job of the civil servants to devise such answers for their minister, and they were adept at it. I remember watching these sessions in Parliament on TV and feeling nothing but contempt for these mandarins and their lackeys. Later events proved just how hard those people were working behind the scenes for the good of the country.

It was apparent from the media that the situation in the UK was becoming as bad as everywhere else. Outbreaks of the disease were being reported from about fifteen different locations in the UK, and people were starting to get twitchy.

I recall someone sneezing in class and noticed most of the students were anxiously looking at him as hard as I was.

On Tuesday, it was announced that a Prime Ministerial Broadcast would take place the following evening. The media had been speculating on the actions the government might take. In the event, even they must have been surprised, especially the newspapers. It seemed odd that in an era of 24/7 instant global news, "as it broke" there should be a twenty-four-hour build-up to a broadcast by the PM.

Rosie had been in town visiting the offices of Hello!
magazine and arrived home early bursting with gossip.

'I had lunch with Joanne, and we met a guy she knew from the BBC. He said there's a lot happening behind the scenes. Apparently, the government's seriously worried. He said even the Americans are struggling and they haven't managed to contain it. And they have much better infrastructure for dealing with outbreaks of disease than we have.'

I commented, 'That figures. According to CNN last night, their much better infrastructure isn't helping them too much. But they've been preparing for this sort of crisis for some time.'

'Joanne's friend reckoned that Carlsen will announce some pretty strong measures tonight. He said the troops were already being flown home from abroad.'

'Looks as if word has already leaked out. I had to queue for petrol on my way home.'

Rose was suddenly anxious. 'Do you think we should tell Nick and Julie to come home?'

'Why?'

'Obviously, they'd be safer here!'

'How do you work that out?'

'We could all stay in the house. Not risk catching it….'

'I think Colin Jefferson, M.A. would regard that as deserting my post.'

'Who cares what Jefferson thinks! Aren't you worried?'

'Not unduly,' I lied. 'These things have a habit of burning themselves out.'

To our surprise, was not the Prime Minister, Oliver Carlsen, who appeared on our TV screens that evening, but the Deputy Prime Minister, Richard Preston. Despite the best efforts of the make-up artist, Preston looked grey, strained, and tired. He had by then been Deputy PM for three years, and I remember being struck by how suddenly he had aged.

There was no preamble. Preston simply launched in.

'I have come straight from a meeting of the Cabinet and want to bring you up to date with the health threat being posed by what has come to be known as Brazilian Flu. Firstly, the international scientific community has established beyond doubt that the illness is not caused by any strain of the influenza virus. Even as I speak, disease control experts from the World Health Organization are making strenuous efforts to track down the original source of infection.

But I must be honest with you; what this virus is and where it has originated it is not too important at the moment. What is important to Britain, indeed to humanity, is that this disease is highly contagious and that it has an extraordinarily high mortality rate. Therefore, the most important thing is to contain it and stop it from spreading.

Like you, I have watched it cross the countries of South America with growing concern. I must pay my respects to the Brazilian people, who had the misfortune to be the first nation to be afflicted. Every nation is deeply indebted to the government and medical community in Brazil. They have stuck to their task and sent out priceless information about how the disease develops and what steps they have taken to control it. But despite their superhuman efforts, it is estimated that over a half million people are infected in Sao Paulo alone and that over twenty thousand people have now died.'

I had an awful sinking feeling in my stomach.

'However, it's encouraging to know that some of the steps taken were successful at a local level. Regrettably, we have been less successful in containment at an international level. I can tell you tonight that outbreaks have now been confirmed in many other countries. These include, the United States of America, Canada, Mexico, Japan, Indonesia, China, Taiwan, Australia, India, The UAE, Spain, Portugal, France, Germany, Italy and today the first cases were confirmed in Russia. Humanity has paid a grotesque penalty for the privilege of cheap, mass air travel because clearly, this is how the disease has spread so rapidly.

As you are aware, we already have a growing number of cases in the UK. As of today, there are over eight hundred confirmed cases in twenty-two different locations. There are also suspected cases at seven other locations. This disease has now killed sixty-seven people in the UK.'

I can still picture Rosie putting her hand to her mouth.

'I can state these facts clearly and knowing that the citizens of Britain will not panic. That is not our way. We will fight this as we have fought every other would-be invader of our islands for the last thousand years.'

Very Churchillian.

'No, the reason I am telling you these facts is so that you will understand and support the emergency measures the government is taking. The key to success is containment!

I will now ask the Government's Chief Medical Officer, Dr Brian Donaghue, to tell you something about the symptoms and practical precautions you can take.'

The camera switched to Donaghue, a robust Scot in his late forties.

'As the Deputy Prime Minister said, we must contain this disease. Put quite simply, this means stopping the virus from spreading from person to person. We have established that the virus is airborne. That means it can spread when an infected person coughs or sneezes or even as they talk or breathe. So the less we are in contact with others, the less chance it has of spreading, and the more chance we have of containing and eradicating it.

The early symptoms are similar to influenza: headache, sore throat, coughing and aching limbs which gradually gets worse over six to seven days. Unfortunately, the evidence points to the fact that people are initially infected by the virus about 8 to 10 days <u>*before*</u> *the onset of the first symptoms and that they are contagious from about the fourth day of being infected, even though they don't know they're incubating it. This is what makes early containment so vital! As the infection progresses, the lungs become heavily congested, and breakdown of some blood cells starts to occur.*

Just to complicate matters, as you are no doubt aware, there is already a nasty strain of Asian Flu going the rounds which has been causing illness since January. This is adding difficulties to the task of early diagnosis of the Brazilian Flu.

What I want you to do is this. If you believe you have the flu, do all the usual things your doctor would prescribe. Get a hot drink, take something to ease the symptoms, aspirin, Paracetamol or the like and get yourself into a nice warm bed for two or three days! That is always the best way of dealing with the flu. If you are infected with Asian Flu, you will feel better after about four days.

If on the other hand, you have reason to believe that you have been in contact with the Brazilian Flu, if a member of your family, a friend or a colleague has been taken ill with it, then I want you to telephone the Brazilian Flu Helpline. There will be different telephone numbers depending on the area you live in, and these will be displayed on the TV screen following this programme. You will be asked a few questions and then depending on your answers, you may be invited to attend an Emergency Assembly Centre in your area.

As of today, there are no known vaccines to treat the virus. But as you can imagine, nearly every medical laboratory, every medical research establishment and every pharmaceutical company in the world has switched its resources to finding methods of combating it.'

The cameras switched back to the Deputy PM.

'To start the containment process, the government, with the full support of the Opposition Parties, is tonight voting through an Emergency Powers Bill which will enable us to take unprecedented measures. Some of these measures are based on what proved to be effective at a local level in Brazil, and I will now outline them to you.

Firstly, all forms of public gathering are to be prohibited for one week. This means the closure of all places of business, education, entertainment, sport and regrettably churches. The only exceptions to this will be for those engaged in public services, like hospitals, clinics, doctor's surgeries, police, fire, and ambulance services. The armed forces and those providing electricity and water supplies are also excluded, as will be those employed by local authorities in delivering emergency services.

Therefore, from midnight tonight, all shops will be closed. And I mean all shops. As soon as possible, basic food will be delivered on a street-by-street, road-by-road basis. Local authority employees who are required to help to provide additional emergency services will be contacted during the next 24 hours. As I say, this is for one week only. At the end of one week, the government will re-assess the situation.

From midnight, all public transport will be suspended. No trains, undergrounds, buses, coaches, or taxis will operate. The Channel Tunnel will be closed. No commercial aircraft will be allowed to land in the UK that has not already left their departure points. No passengers will be allowed to disembark from any ships docking at British ports. These measures are also being put into effect by all European countries. UK citizens who find themselves abroad will, regrettably, have to remain where they are for the duration of this emergency.'

There was just a hint of a smile when Preston said,

'I suspect that we in these islands may yet again regard ourselves fortunate that we have a substantial physical barrier between us and the rest of the world. Most other countries no longer have the means to isolate themselves quite as readily or comprehensively as we British.

From midnight, no petrol or diesel fuel will be delivered to petrol stations or garages. All fuel will be reserved for use by the Emergency Services.'

Undoubtedly he was reading from an autocue since this statement must have been scrutinised by many spin-doctors. But

Richard Preston then did something totally unscripted; in normal times a human, if unpredictable occurrence; in these times, a PR nightmare. He sneezed. Struggling for his handkerchief, he blew his nose and looking somewhat shocked, recovered himself sufficiently to carry on.

'The bottom line is stay at home. Close all windows and doors. Settle down with a book or two ... or watch television ... but stay indoors!

I can hear many of you saying that these extraordinary measures will cripple the UK economy. Well, just let me just assure you by telling you that since other countries are putting into force similar measures, the damage to the UK economy will be relative in global terms. Besides, this is only for a week, and as we all know, the Christmas and New Year holiday tends to stretch for a week nowadays.'

Another slight smile.

'I repeat again that these measures are for one week only. This disease must be contained. And quickly. We have a finite window of opportunity, and your government is determined to use it to maximum effect. Despite what you may have read or heard to the contrary, the Brazilian medical authorities reported that catching the disease is not always fatal. People have caught it, fought it with their natural immune systems and survived. That also means that the scientific and pharmaceutical communities now have samples of antibodies which they can synthesise.

That is all I can tell you this evening. Again, I urge you to follow the government's instructions to the letter. Stay at home. To do otherwise is to unnecessarily risk the health of your friends, your colleagues and most importantly, your family and loved ones.

The measures I have just announced will be repeated on all news channels for the remainder of this evening. There is also a

Web Site that will show the information. I will speak to you again at the same time tomorrow, and there will be further Ministerial Broadcasts as necessary during the coming week. In the meantime, stay indoors and stay well.'

With that, Richard Preston faded from our TV screen.

Rose and I looked at each other in stunned disbelief.

Chapter 10. Aborted journey

3rd May

'Jesus, they must be shit scared!' I muttered.

'Well, he's certainly managed to scare me!'

Stiff brandies were called for, so I poured two.

'Who would have thought a British government would have the balls to bring in such draconian measures. And where the hell was Oliver-bloody-Carlsen? A statement of that importance and he leaves it to dithering Preston!' I commented.

'I wonder how the Brabourn's will get back. Their cruise only set sail last week.'

'Sounds as if they'll be quarantined for the duration.'

Rose quickly got out of her chair. 'I'm going to ring Julie and Nicholas, get them to come home.'

'Rose didn't you hear what he said. Public transport is suspended.'

She was fumbling in her handbag for her mobile.

'No, he said it will be suspended from midnight. If Julie can get on a train this evening, she can get home. Or we can drive to Warwick and pick her up. If Nicholas can get as far as Birmingham, he could meet Julie, and they could travel together.'

She had the phone to her ear.

'Rosie, stop, think. This is exactly what they are trying to prevent, people rushing around the country coming into contact with hundreds of others…'

'So what do you suggest, just to leave our kids?' She was getting angry now, I could tell.

'They're no safer here than where they are…'

'Of course, they are. They're mixing with hundreds of other undergrads.'

She had a point.

‘When they get back here, we shut ourselves away for the week and let it blow over! Christ, why isn’t this stupid phone working!’

‘Probably because thousands of people are doing exactly what you’re doing. Swamping the networks. Anyway, Nick and Julie are sensible enough to stay in their rooms, the same as everyone else.’

She tried our house phone with a similar result.

‘We can’t just sit here!’

‘We can and we will. Let’s calm down.’

‘If we left now we could be in Warwick by eleven!’

I tried to deflect her thinking.

‘These measures are draconian. Totally unprecedented. More extreme than anything done in wartime I’ll bet.’

‘Well, as you said, the government must be bloody scared.’

‘There must be a lot they’re hiding. Didn't somebody say that in war, the truth is always the first to suffer.’

She was still prodding at her mobile.

‘I can’t get Nicholas either …’

‘I’ve just told you; the networks will be swamped. They can’t cope with instant peak traffic.’

We bickered back and forth for the next hour while the BBC & ITV replayed the Preston and Donaghue broadcast. Sky News was reporting identical measures being announced by other European governments. CNN was showing a similar statement from US President Boyne. Obviously, the announcements had been co-ordinated, and if any of the media had got wind of the story, they had been ordered not to leak it. During that time, Rosie repeatedly tried to raise both Julie and Nick, but always with the same strange tone as an answer. She grew quieter – which was always a bad sign.

‘The logistics of what they’re proposing are mind-boggling. How on earth do they plan to feed people!’ she asked.

'I'd bet most people have enough in their house to last about a week. Anyway, Preston said they're organising deliveries of food. But it will be a bloody huge task. How do you even begin to plan it, and where do you get the labour? And if this virus is so contagious, how do you protect the helpers?'

'This'll bring this country to its knees. Treat it like a Christmas holiday, what bullshit! What do they think we are, fucking cretins!' Rose rarely swore, which made it particularly disconcerting when she did. After trying to reach Julie and Nick for over two hours more, she gave up.

'Let's hope they're already on their way home!' she fretted.

It was palpable anxiety; I felt powerless to help. At about midnight I went upstairs to look out of our bedroom window. Down the hill, I could see the main road. The traffic seemed heavy. The lights of London were twinkling away, and I could clearly see the aircraft warning beacon flashing on Canary Wharf. I wondered how many people in London were still unaware of the government broadcasts; unaware that their lives were about to change forever. I closed all the windows; it seemed the sensible thing to do. When I came downstairs, I tried several radio stations only to find that they too were broadcasting the government message.

But one local radio station was running a phone-in on the crisis, and the questions were pretty much those Rose, and I were asking ourselves. I wondered how their listeners were getting through and concluded that the station staff were probably generating the questions themselves. Suddenly Rose was putting on her coat and picking up the car keys.

'Whoa, whoa. Where do you think you're going?'

'Gerry, I must. Don't try to stop me. Please come with me. I'm feeling sick with worry. And you know how much I hate driving in the dark.'

She was begging, and I knew she would not be deflected. We were just leaving the house when our phone rang. It was Nicholas.

'I've been trying to ring you all evening,' he said tersely. 'Who's Mum been rabbiting to? As if I can't guess!' Rosie virtually snatched the phone out of my hand.

'Nicky, darling. Thank God you've phoned. I've been going out of my mind. Are you feeling OK? Dad and I are just leaving to pick up you and Julie…'

'What on earth for? Mother, you stay right where you are. I am perfectly safe here. I'm at Lindsey's parents. We were visiting here when the news broke, and her Mum has insisted we stay. Really looking forward to a week of Scrabble,' he said dryly.

I recalled Lindsey telling us that her parents lived in a small village about twenty miles north of Manchester - which in the circumstances was comforting - but I could not remember its name. Rosie paused.

'Are you sure you're feeling OK? No signs of flu?'

'Mum, I'm OK, honest. Now I'm going to ring off because they are trying to contact Lindsey's Nan. I rang because I knew you'd be panicking. I'll ring you tomorrow. G'night.'

He rang off.

'Phew. At least we don't have to go as far as Manchester.'

'But we must fetch Julie.' Rose insisted. I sighed.

It was no good arguing. But as soon as we pulled out of Newbury Crescent onto the main road, it was clear it was a forlorn quest. It seemed likc half the population of London were trying to collect someone or other. Or get out of the city. I wondered if the government planners had predicted this.

It usually took us about an hour to get onto the M40 when visiting Julie, but as we tried to pull onto the main road, it was clear that this was no normal night. We spent most of our time either stopped in traffic or crawling along. The traffic bulletins on the car radio were reporting massive congestion and several serious accidents. After two hours, we had not even reached Hammersmith. It was stop-start. I was glad that I had filled the car with petrol earlier that day because just after midnight I noticed that the entrances to petrol stations were blocked by police waving traffic on. We crept forward for what seemed like hours, with Rose plaintively asking why we could not try the back streets. One glance down one gave me all the answers I needed to that question.

Rose kept on sporadically trying to phone Julie when suddenly she was answered by a sleepy voice.

'Mum? What's the matter? It's three in the morning?'

'Thank God I've got you at last. I've been ringing all night. Haven't you heard the news? We are on our way to pick you up.'

'What!'

'We should get clear of London soon, although we've already been stuck in traffic for five hours …'

'No, don't worry, I'm OK. The six of us heard the news. We rushed out to the local Co-op and got some provisions. We're OK. It'll be fun.'

The six referred to the other students who also had rooms on Julie's floor in Broderick Hall. There was a quiet mumbling in the background, Matt, no doubt. Julie shushed him.

'It would be better if you came home, love. Much safer….'

'Mum, no, I'd prefer to stay here. This will force me to stay in my room and concentrate on my studies.'

'No, Julie, please listen to me ….'

A policeman tapped on the window of the car. He had a face mask covering his mouth and nose. I wound the window down just enough to hear him.

'Where are you heading, sir?'

‘Warwick, via the M40 to pick up my daughter at Warwick University.’

‘Well, I should forget it for tonight. Traffic’s been snarled up like this for hours. And we're hearing about bad accidents on the motorways. Total gridlock.'

Rose looked at me, the phone still pressed to her ear. She shrugged.

‘Honest Mum, I’ll be fine. All my friends are staying.’

‘Julie, promise me you won’t go out?’

‘I promise. Now you get back home and stay indoors.’

So that was what we did.

Many, many times have I cursed myself for not pressing on that night; how deeply I have regretted it. Rose never forgave me.

Chapter 11. Call-up

4th May

It must have been nearly half-past five in the morning before we got to bed. And it seemed as if we had just dropped off to sleep when the phone rang.

'Is that Gerald Morris, a teacher at St. Michael's College, Norwood?'

'Speaking,' I mumbled.

'Good morning, Mr Morris. This is the Emergency Co-ordinator's Office for Lambeth Borough Council. As a local government employee, you are conscripted to assist during the current health emergency. A vehicle will collect you at about seven o'clock this morning.'

Suddenly I was awake.

'What … Is this some sort of wind-up?' I waited for the tell-tale giggle of school kids; it had happened before.

'No joke, I'm afraid. Under the Emergency Powers Act, all government and local government employees may be required to undertake duties as the government directs. As I said, a vehicle will collect you at about seven this morning. By my watch, that's in about one hour.'

'But I've only just got to bed!'

'Then just think yourself lucky, mate. I've been up all night.' He rang off.

'Who was that?' Rosie mumbled from under the duvet.

'Something about Emergency Co-ordinator's Office. Apparently, they want me to help.'

She turned to squint at me. 'Why you?'

'Because I'm a local government employee.'

'Don't like the sound of that. You might be exposed to people when we should be staying isolated.'

'Hmm. I'm not that keen myself.'

Rose turned over and pulled the covers over her ears. 'Tell them about your feet. That'll get you excused.'

But as I reflected on the situation, I became curious. How would this be handled? I decided I would do my bit. After all, it couldn't be that dangerous compared with yesterday when I was exposed to over five hundred people at the school. Now at least I would have limited contacts.

By the time my lift arrived, I had decided not to take my walking stick. The man who knocked at the door was carrying a prosaic looking clipboard. But the mask that covered his mouth and nose looked anything but prosaic.

'You Gerald Morris?' I could just about understand him through the mask.

''Fraid so!' He handed me a sheet of paper.

'Are you suffering from any of those symptoms?' The sheet held a comprehensive list of flu symptoms.

'Thankfully not.'

'Might you recently have come into contact with anyone with those symptoms?'

'Christ, I teach in a college of 530 kids. I should think it highly likely!'

He sighed, 'Yeah, that's what all you teachers say. Come on, we're running late.'

He handed me a mask similar to the one he was wearing.

'Put this on. You've got to wear it at all times from now on.'

The mask was a light, flimsy article, little better than the sort sold at a DIY store; it smelled of rubber and something else that I could not identify. But I was comforted that I had some protection. As I climbed into the school bus, I waved to Rose, who was watching from an upstairs window. She waved forlornly back.

I must have been the last person to be picked up since there was only one empty seat. Nodding to the other people, I recognised Carol Millard, a colleague from the history department at St. Michaels. Her mask gave her attractive face a pinched appearance. She was hemmed in by a large, overweight man but fluttered her fingers in response.

It was a bright, cool May morning. The cherry trees were in full blossom, making it the sort of morning that put a spring into one's step. It felt like a Sunday. There was significantly less traffic than normal, but there were pedestrians about. At the end of our crescent, our window-cleaner was cleaning windows, a handkerchief tied around his mouth. A well-dressed elderly woman, without any semblance of protection, walked her poodle.

'So much for staying indoors,' muttered the big man.

'Wonder if they heard the broadcasts?' Carol said.

'Well, they can only advise people to stay indoors. Can't force them,' the driver chipped in.

The big man was growing irritated. 'Bet they'll be forced to before this lot's over. If Brazil is anything to go by, this is nasty! And these idiots are just endangering everyone else. Ought to lock all the daft buggers away immediately. Look at that idiot pushing the pram with kids in it! Stupid Cow.' He shook his fist at a young woman. The prospect of having to spend time with this ray of sunshine did not fill me with joy.

After a journey of a couple of miles, the car stopped in the car park of a church hall, and we piled out. There were several cars already parked, and another two pulled in behind us. We followed the driver into the hall to find about fifty people standing around in groups, trying to master the new skill of conversation through face masks. The building had a cheerless, ill-lit and damp atmosphere.

Carol sidled up to me, 'Lucky us.'

'Something to tell your grandchildren about.'

'Looks as if some of them have coffee. Can you see any?'

'Should be fun to try to drink with this mask on.'

'I've a feeling we'll have to learn the knack.'

'Over there.' Carol indicated a table with an urn on it. Behind it stood a matronly figure wearing a WRVS uniform, complete with hat and mask. She pushed two polystyrene mugs filled with coffee and two straws towards us.

'All there is, for now, love. Mind, it's hot. You have to wiggle the straw under your face mask. Bit awkward at first but people seem to be getting the hang of it.'

Thanking her, we turned our attention back to the gathering.

'See anyone else from St. Mikes?' Carol asked.

'Not yet. Anyway, only you and I live in this neck of the woods. They've probably been dragged off in their own patches.'

Suddenly a man was trying to make himself heard above the assembled groups. He was on the stage at the end of the hall. Speaking into a microphone, he was trying to gain our attention, but it was proving difficult through his mask. Gradually the murmur of conversation subsided, and we edged towards him. He was in his 60's and looked to be of West Indian descent, balding, slight and nervous. Standing close to him was a police sergeant, two constables and a woman in civvies.

'Thank you for coming, ladies and gentlemen.'

'Can't hear you,' I glanced around; it was the big man from the Scenic. The man on stage held the mic closer to his mouth and turned up a knob on the amplifier beside him.

'Is that any better? Good. My name is Clayton Teague, and I am Emergency Co-ordinator for this area. I'm assuming all of you heard the Ministerial Broadcast, so there is no need to elaborate on why we're here. Briefly, our job is to get the wheels in motion for this area. I'm appointed by government warrant for the duration of the emergency. Normally, I'm employed by Lambeth Borough Council, as are many of you.

Others here are employed either by the Local Education Authority, government departments or other public services. Apart from our WVS ladies, none of us is a volunteer.'

He tried to smile at his attempt to lighten the proceedings, but it does not have the same effect in a facemask.

'However, we do not yet have any powers to force you to help during this emergency. So, I guess you are free to leave if you wish.'

That was a surprise. Many people started to look around, but nobody made any move to leave. The big man chimed up again.

'But what exactly have we been brought here for?'

'Put quite simply, to assist the government in any way required.'

'I thought we were supposed to be doling out food.'

'That may be so in a few days. Until then, our task is to deliver leaflets to every home in the area and to start to survey the health of the people living here. Look, instead of me trying to tell you via questions from the floor, perhaps it would be better if I pass out the information document we've received. It's headed, Emergency Planning Directive Number One. Once you've had the chance to digest it, we can take questions. I'll give us ten minutes.'

Photocopies of a single sheet document began to be distributed. We waited for one to reach us.

Carol said quietly, 'Emergency Planning Directive has a distinctly Soviet ring to it.'

'So did most of what Preston announced last night. Such measures are unprecedented in Britain. There's got to be stuff they're not telling us.'

'Wasn't there some talk of Emergency Plans in about 2002 when there were threats of Islamic terrorists using bio-chemical weapons?'

'God knows. Maybe that's what they've brought into force. It's certainly not like we Brits to be ready for an emergency.'

I could sense Carol smiling. 'Restricting petrol supplies to emergency vehicles is neat. Do you remember how fast the country ground to a halt when the farmers and lorry drivers blockaded the oil refineries over fuel tax a few years back? About three days, flat!'

'Yup. Our modern lifestyle is dependent on the car, that's for sure.'

I told Carol about our petrol wasting exploits of the night before. She smiled and shrugged. Then she was serious again.

'I've been logging on to one or two of the Sao Paulo chat-rooms. It's looking grimmer every day in Brazil.'

'I looked at a few when all this first started, but most of it was Portuguese. I haven't looked recently.'

'A few of the locals are using English, especially the undergrads. There was one yesterday who estimated that well over a hundred thousand have died. Scary stuff!'

'God. Preston said over twenty thousand last night.'

'Like the man said, in war, the first casualty is the truth. And this is looking more and more like a war scenario.'

Emergency Planning Directive Number One contained much of what had been announced the previous evening, but with a few additional bits of intriguing information.

Firstly, the document confirmed Teague's point about our involvement being voluntary (although it had not sounded like that at six o'clock in the morning!) Secondly, the boundaries of each area were defined by the electoral wards for local government; our area contained five. This meant nothing to me since I had no idea where or how large such wards were. Thirdly, and most surprisingly, those who chose to help could only do so if they signed the Official Secrets Act. I did not like the sound of that one.

Carol read it at the same time. ‘Hmm. What precisely does that mean?’ she queried quietly.

‘Not much probably. Rosie has a brother-in-law who used to work for the GPO. He had to sign it as part of his terms of employment. God knows why.’

Teague resumed his address. ‘I’ll try to answer any questions, but actually having read that document, you now know about as much as I do. Questions please?’

‘Are we going to get paid for this?’

Someone behind me tutted loudly.

Teague responded, ‘I can’t confirm that, but since we are being asked to record the amount of time worked by each of you, it may be that you are.’

‘How much protection are we getting from these dozy masks? You can get better than this at B&Q’, the big man contributed.

‘I’m advised they have been impregnated with a chemical which repels most viruses. We can expect to receive more substantial masks in a few days.’

‘Clayton, you mentioned something about surveying the health of the local community,’ asked a woman near the front.

‘Yes, that’ll be our priority task. The authorities are anxious to know how far the virus has spread, and, if it has, what the incidence of infection is.’

This produced a predictable reaction from about fifty masked mouths.

‘But we’re not trained, medical people! That’s their job.’

‘I don’t mind helping out, but I’m not doing that!’

‘What happens if we catch the bloody disease while we’re doing this? Preston said it was highly dangerous.’

‘Who’s going to compensate us for any time we have to take off work because we’re down with it?’… and so on.

Teague answered. ‘From what I'm told, it will be a very brief and straight-forward Q and A session which we are advised to conduct standing well back from the householder. And you are protected by your masks.'

'But that's ridiculous. They can phone their doctor if they think they've got this bloody flu!'

'Is this being done everywhere?'

Teague paused slightly before he replied. 'No, not everywhere. Only in areas where there's reason to believe there are already cases.'

There was silence as the implications of his answer sank in.

'You mean there are cases near here?' someone finally asked.

Teague motioned to the woman standing behind him to step forward.

'This is Doctor Amanda Jarvis of the Communicable Disease Surveillance Centre at Hendon. She will be our area liaison on medical matters. Will you respond to the last question, please, Doctor Jarvis?'

Dr Jarvis, who looked to be in her mid-forties, was brief and to the point.

'To answer the last question. There are eight confirmed and twenty-two suspected of Brazilian Flu in St. Georges Hospital, Tooting. Five confirmed and twelve suspected in Mayday Hospital, Thornton Heath, six suspected at King's College, Dulwich and twenty-nine confirmed and sixty-three suspected in Kingston Hospital.'

There was an eerie silence as this information sank in.

Each of those hospitals was within a five-mile radius of where we stood.

Chapter 12. Emergency duties

4th May

Looking back, I have an inexplicable feeling of pride that nobody left that dismal church hall right there and then. And nobody did. But the full implications of that bland announcement left us stunned. The disease was already on our doorstep! I was shocked, and for the first time, alarmed.

Gradually on that first awkward morning, we began to understand what was expected of us. We would be divided into teams, and each team would focus on an area of a concentrated area. A particular point was made that we should not be working in the ward where we lived. I could not really understand this precaution at the time, but as things progressed, we all became very thankful that someone had had some foresight. We were given maps and copies of the electoral register for the streets where we would deliver. We were also given copies of the leaflet to be posted through the letterbox of every premises. Entitled, "How to protect yourself and your family from the Brazilian Flu," it re-stated what Preston had said in his broadcast and with some ringing phrases again exhorted everybody to stay at home.

'Stay indoors until advised otherwise … The very best protection is to avoid contact with anyone infected. If you think you have already contracted flu, ring the Brazilian Flu Help-line for your area.' A local telephone number was given. 'Watch the news bulletins on BBC and ITV or listen to BBC Radio 4 on VHF for further updates. Watch for new information provided by the Emergency Teams for your area. It may contain specific instructions. Help us by talking to the Emergency Teams that call on you from time to time. And again … Stay indoors … and stay healthy.'

Carol and I had been assigned to the same team of six people. By about 10:00, we had signed the Official Secrets Act and were being driven to where we would deliver leaflets. Our area turned out to be diverse. It included a couple of six-floor blocks of council flats, a section of a high-street with mixed shops, a small industrial estate, and a few roads of leafy suburbia.

Nobody had been appointed to manage the group, so we just divided up the leaflets and road lists. We agreed to meet back at the car at four o'clock come what may and got started. I suggested to Carol that we should stay together; neither of us knew the area and wandering about alone did not seem to be a good idea. On that first day, we simply delivered leaflets.

When we started, the streets were quiet, but by mid-day, more people were about, completely ignoring the government's pleas. They were engaged in everyday activities; a few wore some sort of protection across their mouth and noses, but most did not. Our facemasks were definitely noticed! In retrospect, right from the outset, they were regarded as a badge of authority. I remember one man asking where we had bought them and seemed quite impressed when Carol told him that they were, "Government Issue." I didn't tell her I regarded them to be of psychological value only. As a precaution against the virus, they were probably useless.

A couple of people opened doors as we put leaflets through the letterboxes; obviously, the occupants had been watching from windows. One old dear wanted to know which shops were open so that she could get food for her Alfred. I tried coaxing her to stay indoors and promised to report her need when I returned to the centre. But she insisted that Alfred was starving and had to be fed. Puzzled, I looked at Carol.

'How old is Alfred?' Carol asked.

'Oh, I'm not sure. Mrs Bradshaw gave him to me years ago.'

The penny dropped. 'Is Alfred your cat?'

‘Of course, love. You didn’t think I had a man in here, did you? I should be so lucky!’ She grinned broadly. We couldn’t help smiling as we left.

By four in the afternoon, we were out of leaflets, and I was knackered. My left foot was aching like hell, and I was famished. I literally limped back to the car.

‘Tomorrow, we bring a flask!’ Carol commented, tersely.

I felt obliged to tell Teague about my accident and that I would not be able to be on my feet for another day delivering leaflets. He eyed me suspiciously.

‘It’s true.’ Carol chipped in. ‘He and I teach at the same school.’

‘Look, I’m not trying to get out of anything. I’ll come down here and do any admin work you need sitting down.’ Teague seemed placated.

Most of the teams arrived back by five o’clock, and Teague held a de-brief. None of us had encountered any difficulties, although one team did ask if it could swap areas. When Teague asked why they looked sheepish and said it was a pretty rough neighbourhood. Teague thought for a moment, then suggested that the team should be men only … and that they should stay in sight of each other when delivering. His final comment was to remind us that the vehicle would collect us at eight o’clock the next morning.

It was gone six when I arrived home. It was good to get that damned mask off! Rose poured gins and tonics while I put my feet up. She had prepared a Shepherd’s Pie which really hit the mark. I told Rose about my odd day, although I decided to leave out the part about there being confirmed cases at nearby hospitals. But she seemed distracted. I asked if she’d heard any more from Nick or Julie and she said she had phoned them both this morning and that they were OK. I surmised it wasn’t the kids she was worrying about. I got her to tell me about her day.

She had spent most of it in front of the television. Not surprisingly, the TV channels had carried programmes about The Emergency all day long.

The measures taken worldwide were being reported at some length, and there seemed to be no slowdown of the spread of the disease in South America. There were scenes of deserted rail tracks and air terminals. Businessmen were predicting significant job losses in the travel and tourism industries and the potential threat to the global economy. The usual suspects from the political parties fronted their party's positions, all from the studio in the Palace of Westminster. There had been some worrying interviews with managers in the retail food industries where there was a lot of background work going on regarding distribution. Sports fanatics had been trying to argue that certain events, like snooker, should still be allowed to go-ahead, but with no live audience. Various church dignitaries had provided their views, via telephone links.

Great play was being made of the fact that TV news staff would be spending all their time at the studios, and not returning home to their families each night. I smiled when Rosie told me that the newspapers were furious that they were being prevented from printing while the TV & radio companies were stealing the limelight. It made sense though; papers need to be delivered or collected, and the government wanted to minimise contact between people. The papers would have to make do by publishing on the internet.

As he had promised the day before, the Deputy Prime Minister appeared on all domestic TV channels that evening. If anything, he looked more haggard.

'Where the hell's Carlson again?' Rosie asked aloud.

'Today many of you will have received the first government leaflet telling you how to avoid being exposed to Brazilian Flu. Teams of volunteers have been at work in every community

delivering these leaflets. On your behalf, I must thank them for their work and their excellent show of public duty.

I must also inform you of one further development that has taken place today. The Prime Minister, David Carlson, was admitted into St. Thomas's Hospital late this afternoon with suspected influenza. So far, we do not have any further information. I have the Prime Minister's and his family's full agreement to advise the nation of his temporary incapacity, and the statement has been made to prevent the spread of any malicious rumours. On the nation's behalf, I wish him a speedy recovery.'

'That explains where Carlson is,' Rose muttered.

'It has therefore been decided that for the duration of his unavailability, I will chair all further meetings of the Cabinet and that these will be held by closed-circuit television thus minimising personal contact.

I must also tell you the latest figures we have of the disease. As of this evening, there are just over fourteen hundred confirmed cases in the UK. Regrettably, there have now been a total of 112 deaths attributed to it. Again, I am telling you this, not because I wish to cause alarm, but because of the need to reinforce the message of how crucial it is that you stay in your homes.

There have been reports today of people ignoring the government's request to stay at home. We stress our determination to enforce it. If it is not done voluntarily, the government will use whatever measures necessary to impose it. Please be assured that it is being done in the best interests of the community at large.

Meanwhile, we are doing all in our power to ensure that the disease is contained. Hospitals, clinics, and doctor's surgeries have specific instructions to immediately report all new suspected cases to the Department of Health.

I will be honest with you and tell you that there are areas where we are particularly vigilant. Some of these areas are in our major cities. Therefore, the authorities will be resolute in enforcing the "No Contact" policy. From tomorrow, some of you will start to receive visits from the Emergency Support Teams. These teams will be inquiring about the health of those in your household. They will be wearing official armbands and wearing protective masks. They will not infect you. Please assist them in identifying all possible clusters of infection. We believe that there are only a few of these clusters and we think that we know where they are, but we need to be certain. Please do not give misleading information, just tell them the truth about your own household. They are there to help you.

Now, some of you may be getting worried about the food you have available at home. Well, from the day after tomorrow, Friday at the latest, food supplies will start to be delivered to your streets. I will tell you more about the procedure we have for food distribution tomorrow evening.

That is all for this evening. I wish you Good Night.'

'I don't like the sound of any of this. If they can't protect Carlsen, they can't protect anyone,' I said.

'That's' awful. God, his wife must be terrified.'

'Didn't he attend some sort of economic summit meeting in South America last month? Yes, that's right. Wasn't there a fuss in the press about the size of the British delegation. Over eighty people went.'

'And hundreds of delegates from all around the world.'

'What if he's caught this Brazilian Flu? What if they all caught it?'

'Doesn't bear thinking about.'

Rosie was quiet for some minutes.

'Joanne rang me today,' she eventually said.

'Oh, yes.'

'You remember me mentioning meeting that guy she knows in the BBC? Well, he's been onto her. Seems he overheard me talking about Norman Foster when we met him in Brady's Bar the other day. She said he'd asked for my phone number, and would I mind if she gave it to him. Which of course I didn't; he could be another useful contact. His name's Clive Mortimer. He rang me almost immediately and started asking about that interview I did with the Fosters a few weeks back. All very intense. Had I asked Foster about the lines of research he was following, or about his interests outside the university? I ask you as if I would! I was there to do an interview on their marriage for Christ's sake!'

'Did he say why he was asking you?'

'Something about the BBC had been following up a rumour in the States that this Brazilian Flu is not flu at all but the result of some biological weapon trials.'

I was curious. 'What's that got to do with Foster?'

'Well, the rumour is that it may have come from a laboratory he's connected with.'

'In Brazil! Bit far-fetched, isn't it?'

'That's what I thought at first. Then I remember those odd comments Glenda Foster made as I was leaving; you remember, I told you. And I must have said something because Mortimer asked me if I know where they are now. I told him I remembered her saying they were due to attend that biochemistry conference in Ottawa.'

'Weird!'

'I thought I'd got rid of him. But he rang again about an hour ago. Wants to see me this evening. Apparently, Mortimer's doing a piece on Foster for the BBC, and he wants to interview me. He's bringing a cameraman.'

Chapter 13. Concern over the Fosters

4th May

'Is that a good idea? We're supposed to be staying isolated! And I'm knackered.'

'Oh, for God sake, Gerry! Two days ago you were in a school with five hundred kids.' She was tetchy, but she calmed.

'Besides, when I mentioned about staying isolated, Mortimer laughed and said he would be sure to wear his new face mask. He also said something about having had the tests, and he wasn't infected.'

'What tests? I didn't know there were any tests!'

'Neither did I, but that's what he said.'

'Well, let's hope he isn't infected.'

Rosie was upstairs changing when the doorbell rang. I looked out of the window to see two men standing at our front door, one carrying an impressive video camera. Both wore serious-looking facemasks, not the toy articles we had been issued. I answered it, and Clive Mortimer introduced himself and his companion, whose name I did not quite catch through the facemask. I ushered them into the lounge, and Rosie joined us, wearing a little black dress that I had always considered to be far too short.

Feeling ill-at-ease with two characters who had strayed from, *"Dr Who"*, I asked if they wanted to remove their masks. They did so with some relief. Then the penny dropped; this was the Clive Mortimer who presented BBC TV science programmes.

It's odd that even after all the government's dire warnings and my personal knowledge that we were living in one of the Hot Cluster Areas, we were still convinced that the disease was something caught by others, not by us.

After asking if we were OK about the cameraman shooting everything, Mortimer got straight to the point. He said the BBC wanted to get this piece screened ASAP. He asked Rosie to go through the interview with the Fosters right from the start. And being in the spotlight, Rosie was happy to oblige. She covered the whole bit including the things Glenda Foster had said as she left. Mortimer then asked Rose whether they had mentioned their research; they had not. He then asked her whether they had mentioned a man called Kevles, Douglas Kevles. Rose thought for a moment and said it sounded like the name she had overheard Norman Foster say on the phone. But she could add nothing further. Mortimer then thanked her, and they stopped recording.

'What's all this about?' I asked.

'Well, I can't say much, all a bit sketchy really. We must be going.'

'Fancy a drink?' asked Rosie.

Mortimer glanced at the cameraman. 'Oh, OK, just the one. Scotch if you have it.'

'You do the honours please, Gerry. I'll have a G and T.'

I knew my place.

Rosie waited until Mortimer and friend had packed up their equipment and then invited them to sit down; make themselves at home. She sat opposite Mortimer, leaning forward, hanging on his every word, and showing far too much cleavage.

'So, is Professor Foster tied up in all this Brazilian Flu stuff?'

'Like I say, it's all a bit sketchy and rumour prone at the moment. We're trying to fit the pieces together. I'm not allowed to say too much.'

'Oh, come on now. Fair's fair, I'm in the business. And I have just added a piece to the puzzle!'

Rosie actually pouted, and I suddenly realised that I had never watched her working before; I was quite impressed. It amuses me to remember the little "exchange" we had after they had gone. She accused me of being churlish, just because she had fluttered her eyelashes to make them stay. Otherwise, we would not have learned anything. It looked more than that to me.

Mortimer smiled at Rose and concluded she was not a competitor.

'We're not absolutely certain how ... or even if ... he is involved yet. As you know, Foster is one of the movers and shakers in the biochem world. Nobel Prize when he was in his forties. Chair in Biochemistry at Cambridge. Managing Director of a biotechnology company he founded himself. Government Advisor of biological weapons. Consultant at Porton. High-flyer if ever there was one.'

'Which sort of makes his involvement somewhat improbable,' I ventured.

'That's what we all thought at first. But there's word in the States that one of his labs is involved in producing a vaccine against this virus everyone is calling Brazilian Flu. Except that it's not a simple flu virus.'

'What is it then?' I asked.

There was a noticeable pause, before Mortimer said, 'The word is that it's some biological weapon that's been developed. It's said to have been genetically engineered.'

'What does that mean, precisely?' Rose asked, totally focused.

'That it's a highly infectious virus in its own right. And it's had genes from other pathogens added to its DNA, essentially to make it more lethal.'

'By Foster?' asked Rose incredulously.

'We're not sure, but we don't think so.'

'So, by whom?'

'That's the big question. You'd be amazed at how many people are trying to find the answer.'

'Then what's the interest in the other guy, Kevles, was it?'

'As far as we can make out, Kevles was working on a vaccine for this virus at Foster's company and liaising closely with Porton Down. That's the government's biochemical defence establishment on Salisbury Plain.'

It really irritated me they way this condescending git talked down to us.

'Something of an oddball by all accounts. He went AWOL in February and hasn't been heard from since.' Mortimer emptied his glass. Rose immediately took it and refilled it without asking him; then she did the same for the cameraman. I estimated them to be treble whiskies at the very least. I had to refill my own.

I commented, 'Comforting to think we have "oddballs" involved with a place like Porton Down.' Mortimer ignored me.

'I still don't get the Foster connection.' Rosie said.

'We believe that Foster's company was one of three which hold government contracts to produce a vaccine against this virus, Kevles was liaising with Porton about how an enemy, or a terrorist group, could best deploy it.'

'I thought we Brits gave up all this biochemical warfare stuff years-ago!' I chipped in, determined not to be sidelined.

'No. A common misconception. The UK announced it had given up developing and stockpiling biochemical weapons. But not our ability to produce defensive measures against such weapons. No country did.'

'Then how did we get hold of this virus in the first place? Genetically engineered viruses don't just appear! Who the fuck developed it?'

'That's another part of the mystery,' Mortimer shrugged. 'Obviously, nobody's admitting it. We're doing all we can to find out.'

'Jesus, you seem pretty calm about it. There are thousands dead in Brazil, and the thing's spreading all around the world with absolutely no sign of a slowdown. We've now got hundreds of confirmed cases within five miles of this house!'

Mortimer's mouth tightened. 'Take it easy, chum. I didn't develop the bloody thing.'

Dismayed at what I had just said, I took a big swig of my scotch.

Rose looked at me hard, then turned back to Mortimer.

'But why Brazil! What's made it appear in Brazil? Surely Foster's got no labs there?'

'Not that we're aware of.'

'Well, what does Foster say about it?' Rose asked.

'We'd love to ask him. So would the security agencies. Trouble is, we don't know where the Fosters are. Apart from their immediate staff, you were probably the last person to talk to them. They never showed up at the conference in Ottawa. As far as we can make out, they never caught their flight.'

Rosie's mouth hung open in a very unladylike way.

'You are kidding!'

As I stood at the door, waiting for my lift the next morning, I felt decidedly hung-over. Carol soon noticed. There seemed to be fewer people in the hall than there had been on the previous day, but perhaps it was my imagination. But sporting their new armbands and checklists of Health Questions, the Emergency Support Teams soon left. Carol fluttered her fingers at me as she went through the door. As good as his word, Mr Teague had consigned me to a drab anti-room which contained two dilapidated tables. On one of these stood a computer. He asked me if I knew how to use a computer and showing considerable restraint, I answered, yes, very politely. Looking unconvinced, he gave me a pile of electoral registers and told me to make lists of the numbers of houses and residents that could be sorted by road. I sat at the computer and got on with it.

Later in the morning, Dr Jarvis came into the office wearing the same sort of serious-looking facemask that Mortimer and friend had worn the previous evening. Barely acknowledging me, she sat down at the other desk, pulled a laptop out of her case, and booted it up. Initially, I thought she would make enlightened company, but it soon became apparent that she wanted to work in peace. So, wearing my DIY deluxe facemask, I got on with my lists.

After about ten minutes, I remembered what Rosie had said about Mortimer.

'I understand that there are tests we can have to see if we're infected.'

Dr Jarvis glared at me. 'Who told you that?' I seemed to have touched a nerve.

'A man from the BBC.'

'That's not been made public.'

'Tell him that.'

'How many of the others here know?'

'I've no idea. I haven't discussed it with them …'

'Well, for heaven's sake, don't. We're trying to make sure all of the priority personnel are tested before it becomes too public.'

I paused before commenting on this earth-shattering piece of information.

'Who gets to play God?'

'What?' I could see that her eyes were hard even through the mask.

'Who decides which are priority personnel and which are virus fodder?'

'It's not like that. Hundreds, probably thousands of people are working extremely hard to set up critical emergency services. We need to be certain that they're not already infected. Otherwise, it could be so much wasted effort.'

'Have you been tested?'

She absolutely glared at me. 'Yes, I have as it happens.'

'Bully for you! When's my turn?'

'You're a real smart arse. It's not a vaccine against the flu, it's a test to see if I'm a carrier, whether I could be infecting others. Have you any conception whatsoever of the danger we're facing?'

'Sort of. It started in Sao Paulo ... which has now been abandoned because the Brazilians couldn't control it ... and now it's meandering its way around the world. Oh yes, and there are probably hundreds of cases within five miles of where we sit. That's about as much as I need to know, thanks.'

'Really. Well, how about showing an adult approach to helping solve the problems. Now if you don't mind, I've got work to do even if you haven't.'

I turned back to my computer, feeling something of a jerk. Perhaps it was the tension. But people in authority sometimes bring out the worst in me. I have an insatiable urge to burst their bubble.

'What do you think of this rumour about Professor Foster?'

She sighed and turned towards me again. 'What rumour? And who's Foster? I don't know anything about any rumour.' But by now, she was wary of me; I seemed to know things. I looked back at her and gave her my best smile. It failed to transmit through my mask.

'Oh, can't be anything in it … or you'd have heard,' I said continuing to type.

Her icy look turned into a glare; then she turned back to her laptop and continued her work. But a few minutes later she got up and left the room. I could see her in the corridor using her mobile.

I finished compiling my list at about 2 pm and went to tell Clayton Teague. He came to see what I had produced and seemed surprised. He said I had done well. I expected him to rumple my hair, but he refrained. I learned later that my lists would be used to provide the initial estimate of food to be distributed in our area.

On the Ministerial Broadcast that night, Preston revealed that during the last 24 hours the number of deaths in the UK due to Brazilian Flu had been 303. The total deaths since the start had increased to 415. The number of suspected cases was nearly 4,000. One of the dead was Prime Minister, Richard Carlsen. Three other Cabinet Members had been hospitalised with flu symptoms.

Chapter 14. Hot Spots

5th May

Preston announced that the first food deliveries would start on Saturday. He again stressed that the government intended that the 'No Contact' period would be short. However, since the number of deaths and confirmed cases had risen more sharply than anticipated, it might have to be extended.

'The manufacture of protective facemasks is another of the government's priorities. The government's Chief Medical Officer has already told you that the disease spreads by droplet infection; that means it's airborne. We can catch it when someone who is already infected simply coughs or sneezes or even breathes. Quality facemasks will prevent this. Nearly four hundred thousand such masks have been produced over the past week, and the production plants are working around the clock. The Emergency Teams will be the first people issued with these new masks as will those distributing food supplies. These Teams will be assisted by personnel from the local authorities, police, fire services and armed services. The government has also invoked its power to call-up all military reservists and the territorial army. Also, all army, navy and air-force personnel who have left the services during the last ten-years are being recalled for the duration of the emergency.'

Preston stated boldly that the food ration per head would be small due to logistical difficulties. He also said it would be applied rigidly. To avoid people coming out of their homes, mingling, and risking spreading the infection, the Emergency Teams would initially place the ration on the doorstep of each dwelling, according to the number of people listed at that dwelling on the latest electoral registers. Emergency Ration books would be delivered shortly. To simplify the procedure ... and presumably, reduce contact ... no money would be collected; people would be billed for the rations they received when the Emergency was over.

In retrospect, it was worth a try. Government policies did seem sensible at the time. What else could they have done? In the absence of any vaccine, the 'No Contact' policy was crucial. Despite the logistical nightmare, it had to be tried. And, according to the TV & radio news bulletins, most other countries were taking similar measures. That night I dreamt of hauling sacks of food up a tower block that had an Escher like-staircase on which I made no progress. As things turned out, I never did get hands-on experience of food delivery.

When we arrived for duty the next morning, there were two large haulage vehicles loaded with emergency food packs parked in the road. The Hall seemed to be heaving with people, at least double the number present on the two previous days. Several were in uniform. Carol and I had just collected our coffee when Clayton Teague brought everyone to order.

'May I have your attention please, ladies and gentlemen. Thank you. I would like to start by welcoming our new colleagues who will be helping us with food deliveries. As you can see, most of them are army personnel under the command of their officer, Lieutenant Creen. However, I am sure we will all co-operate splendidly.'

Master Creen looked about 17 years old.

'Now, just to bring you all up to speed, Dr Jarvis spent all last night analysing the answers to the Health Questions the teams asked yesterday. I'll let her fill you in.'

Amanda Jarvis stepped forward. Hearing that she had been up all night gave me a pang of guilt about the hard time I had given her yesterday. It also struck me how quickly we had become accustomed to understanding people talking through facemasks.

‘I won’t waste too much time. Just to advise people who were not involved yesterday, a few simple questions were asked of each household, one being, "Is any member of the household currently showing signs of or complaining of flu-like symptoms?" Remember we are looking for clusters. Thankfully, several wards are clear. But there are a few with a higher than normal incidence reported. And disturbingly, some real hotspots where there is a significantly higher incidence. I’ll be visiting those hot-spots today and asking follow-up questions. That’s all.’

Dr Jarvis then handed the mic back to Teague.

‘Thank you, Amanda. Right, today the Teams stick to their usual rounds and start to deliver the food ration. Our first job is to unload those lorries outside and load it into the five Transits. Now, you may encounter difficulties when delivering. There's sure to be discontent at the size of the ration ... and a hundred and one other possibilities. Wherever you can, ignore them. Just concentrate on delivering the food. If difficulties are encountered, please ring them in on this number, and we will try to help you.’ Teague pointed to a phone number written on the whiteboard behind him.

‘It’s going to be a long day. Good Luck!’

People started to chatter as they gather into their teams.

‘Got any interesting - if sedentary - activities planned for the day?’ Carol chided as we walked towards our team.

‘No, the foot seems easier today, so I thought I’d join you again.’

‘Mr Morris!’ I turned to see Teague and Dr Jarvis approaching.

Teague said, ‘Since you are still ‘hors de combat’, I wonder if you’d mind assisting Dr Jarvis today. A job you can do sitting down.’

I was astonished. With Jarvis eyeing me coolly, what could I say!

'Sure, if you think I can help. What do you need me to do?' I assumed she would have me carrying out some mind-numbing computer routine.

'I need someone with me when I visit the hot spots. Do the driving while I check the addresses and data.'

So much for assumptions! I probably stood open-mouthed for some moments; not that anyone could see that through the facemask. Carol winked and gave her quirky finger wave. 'Have a nice day.'

Within ten minutes, I was driving Amanda Jarvis's Volvo towards Thornton Heath; she sat next to me studying her lists. I estimated her to be in her mid-forties and rather an attractive woman. Still feeling guilty, I decided to offer the olive branch.

'Look, I apologise for yesterday. I was a right pain in the arse. No excuse ... except perhaps anxiety.'

She continued studying her lists. 'It's OK, Mr Morris. Thanks anyway. And we do have something to be stressed about.' She turned and smiled.

'It's Gerry by the way.'

'Amanda,' Phew, ice melted.

There were still a few pedestrians about, but it was comforting to see that most of them now had some sort of cover over their mouth and nose. As always, a few morons were oblivious to all warnings. The roads were virtually deserted, and we drove along smoothly.

'Frankly, after yesterday, I'm astonished that you asked for me to help you.'

'I didn't. It was Mr Teague's idea. He was so impressed by your computing skills that last night he had to show me what you'd done.'

‘Really! It was nothing. Only an Access database and a spreadsheet.’

‘Yes, I know. But Clayton was impressed, and it seemed a shame to disillusion him.’ Ouch.

I turned and saw her smiling slightly. I laughed and decided I liked Amanda Jarvis.

As we neared our destination, I asked her what the drill would be.

‘I’d like you to accompany me on the calls. If you don’t mind. You may pick up something I miss. To be honest, I don’t really know what to expect, so we’ll have to play it by ear. If you find it all too much, just say.’

‘I’ll do what I can.’

If I were honest, I did not like the idea at all! Rose would have gone bananas had she known. But what else could I say without seeming a total wimp?

‘Good,’ Amanda paused.

‘This first one’s worrying. Mr & Mrs Prabandra and four children. They reported three people in the house suffering from flu.’

When we stopped at the address, she opened the car boot and took out her medical bag. She also handed me a facemask like her own, an armband on which was printed, **‘Emergency Team’**, and a light green plastic overall. I took off my Micky Mouse mask and pulled on the new one. It smelled of rubber. But I felt better protected. And wearing my green overall and my bright yellow armband, I felt important. Pathetic really.

The address was in a terrace of houses on Raymead Avenue, Thornton Heath. Probably built in the 1860s as the railway boom drove London's sprawl; the houses now looked drab. Amanda rang the bell three times before it was opened slightly by a boy of about nine years of age. His jaw literally dropped as he saw two people in black facemasks. His lower lip started to quiver.

'Hullo, I'm Gerry. What's your name?' I asked gently.

'Majid.' the boy answered timidly.

'Are Mummy or Daddy in?'

'Yes, but they're in bed … sick,' the boy said, virtually hiding behind the door.

'Can you tell them a doctor's here to help them?' Majid disappeared into the house, leaving the door open. In a minute or so, he reappeared.

'They're up here.' We followed him up the stairs.

The parents were in bed, and just one glance was enough to tell that the man was seriously ill. Of Indian descent, he appeared to be asleep, and there were dark purple blotches on his face. The pillow beside him was spattered with droplets of blood.

Amanda spoke to the woman.

'Hullo, Mrs Prabandra. I'm Dr Jarvis. How are you feeling?' The woman looked blankly at the boy and muttered something I couldn't understand. The boy handed his mother a glass full of water which she drank ravenously. When she had finished, she muttered something else to the boy.

The boy said, 'Mama says Dada needs the hospital.'

'I don't think she speaks English,' I muttered. Amanda felt the man's pulse, took his temperature, examined his retina, and listened to his breathing through her stethoscope. 'He's unconscious and very sick.'

She then examined the woman. 'How long have you been like this?' Again, there was a brief exchange between the mother and son.

'About five days. Dada got worse yesterday.'

Amanda left the room, and I could hear her talking on her mobile.

‘Have you got any brothers or sisters, Majid?’ I asked the boy. He nodded.

‘Where are they?’

‘Uncle Khalid collected them last night after Mama rang him.’

Amanda came back into the room. ‘I’ve called for an ambulance.’ She turned to the boy.

‘Now Majid, can you tell me where your father works?’

‘In the shop.’

‘Does your mother work there too?’ Majid nodded his head.

‘Is the shop near here?’

‘It’s just around the corner in London Road.’

‘What do you sell in the shop?’ I asked.

Majid shrugged, ‘Everything.’

‘Do you ever help Daddy in the shop?’

‘Sometimes.’

‘Do you get lots of customers in the shop?’

He shrugged again. ‘Sometimes.’

Mrs Prabandra muttered something, and Majid again fetched her water from the bathroom.

‘Does your mother keep asking for water?’ Amanda asked.

‘All the time.’

I told Amanda about the siblings but could not read her expression through the mask.

While we waited for the ambulance, I found out that Uncle Khalid lived in Croydon, and although Majid had been there, he did not know the address. He was not even sure of the uncle’s family name. Meanwhile, Dr Jarvis was looking at a street map. I heard her mutter, “Shit!”

She pointed to the street we were in then moved her finger to London Road. In it stood Mayday Hospital.

'I bet their shop is where visitors buy chocolates and magazines for people they're visiting in hospital,' she said, 'And where the staff buy their snacks for work.'

It was nearly an hour before the ambulance arrived. The mother insisted that Majid went in the ambulance with them, which was just as well because we would not have known what to do with him.

Before we headed anywhere else, we found the Prabandra's shop in London Road. It was firmly locked. We peered through the window and confirmed that it was one of the typical and ubiquitous grocery-cum-newsagents, run by a hard-working Asian family. Open from 6am to 10pm they had become an indispensable feature of all British cities. As Amanda suspected, the shop was within 200 metres of the main entrance to Mayday Hospital.

Back in the car, Amanda told me to head for Streatham. We were quiet for a while.

'You were good back there; good with the boy.'

'Put it down to years of dealing with kids. I'm a teacher.'

'Oh, dear.' she said. 'Big school?'

'St. Michael's, a Sixth Form College.'

'How many pupils?'

'About five hundred and fifty.'

'Ah.'

'What's the, Ah for?'

'I'd have preferred you to have been a ... lighthouse keeper ... or a hermit who saw about six people a day, instead of five hundred. We need to get you tested.' I did not react. We were silent for a while.

'Were the Prabandras typical of the symptoms?'

'From the photos I've seen, yes. He's the first case I've had where the disease is that far advanced.'

'What are their chances?'

She sighed deeply. 'If the Brazilian experience is anything to go by, very few people recover once they've got it. About one in a thousand. By the sound of it.'

'Jesus!'

We made eight more calls to infected cases that day. Three were people who worked in hospitals, one was a bus driver, and two were shop assistants. I was unnerved to learn that the final couple we visited – a husband and wife - were schoolteachers. Amanda called ambulances for each case.

Our drive home was sombre. 'We've got a problem, haven't we,' I sighed.

'You've got that right. If we don't contain it during the next few weeks, it will be a catastrophe for humanity.'

The Ministerial Broadcast that night was given by Home Secretary, Ann Freer. Preston had collapsed and been rushed to St. Thomas's. Mrs Freer announced that the death toll in the UK had risen to nine hundred and sixteen. Five hundred and eleven people had died during the past twenty-four hours.

Chapter 15. BBC Panorama: Douglas Kevles

7th May

A BBC Panorama Special followed the Ministerial Broadcast. The first part gave a stark global update on the epidemic, with BBC correspondents in various cities providing input. Significantly, there was no slow-down in Brazil. The news from Sao Paulo had become scarce, simply because there were few newsgathering teams still there. CNN, NBC, Fox, CBS, BBC, ITN, Sky and everyone else had pulled out.

The exception was the Brazilian, Agencia Meridonal. Luis Sedano, their reporter was stilted in his report, as if he could hardly bring himself to speak of the infection or mortality rates. Eventually, he hazarded a guess of more than a million people were infected in Sao Paulo alone and over a quarter of a million dead. He reported people trying to flee the stricken city but being blocked by the army. There had been several incidents of soldiers shooting into crowds, forcing the majority to turn back. Some of Sao Paulo's hospitals had been abandoned as the disease had scythed through its medical staff. Other South American countries also seemed to be losing the fight.

The report from North America told of a situation similar to Europe; desperate measures being taken to slow the spread. The conditions in New York, Los Angeles, Dallas, Chicago, and San Diego were regarded as particularly critical. Many city dwellers and some would-be survivalists had headed for the hills before travel restrictions were fully imposed. This had effectively spread Brazilian Flu to the Mid West, Idaho, Oregon, Montana, and The Dakotas. Canada had its share of cases, particularly Montreal, Ottawa, and Vancouver. The disease appeared to be absolutely ravaging Mexico City.

In the Far East, Jakarta and Tokyo were badly infected, as were Hong Kong, Soul, Beijing, and Singapore. Bangkok and

Kuala Lumpur reported that cases were on the increase. The major cities in Australia and New Zealand had imposed severe travel restrictions early on, which appeared have been useful and given them more chance of containment. But the disease was rampant in Delhi, Bombay, Bangalore, Calcutta, and Islamabad.

Oddly, the situation in the Middle East seemed less severe, although increasing numbers of cases were being reported from Beirut, Riyadh, Dubai, Cairo, Damascus and particularly Tel Aviv. Istanbul, Ankara, and Athens were severely hit. In Africa, cases were starting to be reported from Cape Town, Johannesburg, Nairobi, Lagos, and Algiers.

All major European cities were now reporting hundreds of cases. Frankfurt, Munich, Rome, Amsterdam, Copenhagen, Paris, Madrid, Moscow, and Stockholm were all suffering. Panorama's presenter made the chilling observation that it was significant that virtually all the cities initially infected were major airline hubs.

But the most depressing news was that the UK was one of the worst affected countries in Europe. Cases were being reported from virtually all major cities with London, Birmingham, Manchester, and Glasgow being the worst. Dublin also had hundreds of cases. Globally, there was nothing of comfort in anything Panorama reported.

The second part of the programme I found intriguing but worrying in a subtly different way. It was presented by Clive Mortimer and both Rosie, and I stirred at the prospect of seeing her interview screened. But we were in for a surprise. Without preamble, Mortimer cut to the chase.

'It is a shock to recall that less than two months have passed since we first heard the term, Brazilian Flu. It first appeared in early March in Sao Paulo in Brazil and, thanks to the

convenience of modern air travel, it has spread around our planet with devastating speed.

But what exactly is this disease? It is certainly not any strain of influenza experienced in our lifetimes. But it does have some striking similarities to the so-called Spanish Flu epidemic that swept the world between 1917 and 1920. Modern analysis has concluded that the Spanish Flu outbreak probably infected half the population of the planet, about one-third of them seriously, and resulted in 100 million deaths. In those days travel between continents was either by ship or train and therefore much slower.'

He was doing it again; he was talking down to us!

'But the Panorama Team has learned that this current outbreak may have been caused by something more sinister. We have been unable to confirm all the details, but the story emerging is as follows.

In July1919 a Danish fishing boat ... the Anders Nyquist ... left Copenhagen to fish the Denmark Strait. But a week later it called in at Longyearbyen in Spitzbergen to drop off one of its crew who had fallen ill. Before it could be quarantined, the Anders Nyquist slipped its moorings and sailed again ... and no sign of it was seen for over seventy years. But in 1998 a wreck was found by Danish soldiers on winter manoeuvres in a remote fiord in Greenland ... a fiord that in living memory had been permanently iced over. The wreck was on a beach, and part of it was still covered in ice. The ship may have been deliberately beached. Markings found on the wreckage confirmed that it was the remains of the Anders Nyquist. But significantly, the frozen remains of three of the crewmen were discovered on the ship. These were later buried in the fiord, but not before tissue samples were taken, particularly from the lungs. Subsequent analysis confirmed that Spanish Flu ... or a variant of it ... had been the cause of death. Importantly, it was realised that the strain that had killed the fishermen had been a mutated form of Spanish Flu, a form probably more virulent than the original.

Such was the interest in the Biological Warfare community that samples of the DNA were passed to Porton Down in the UK and Fort Detrick in the USA so that vaccines could be developed.

The BBC has learned that analysis of the so-called Brazilian Flu has revealed that it was based on the sample recovered from Greenland. But of more concern is the realisation that the virus had been genetically re-engineered. It has had genes of other pathogens grafted onto it to make it even more lethal and more robust. The analysis estimates that the virus would have a 99.9% Mortality Rate to humans once infected. From that point on in late 2004, there has been a desperate search to produce a vaccine against the virus.

Under government funding, three laboratories in the UK have been working on the project.

The principal stakeholder at one of these is Dr Norman Foster, who is also Professor of Microbiology at Cambridge University.

An employee from Professor Foster's laboratory at Cambridge was seconded to Porton Down to research likely methods an enemy, or as importantly, a terrorist group might use to deploy the virus. The man is Dr Douglas Kevles, and this photograph of him was taken three-years-ago when he addressed an international conference on bioterrorism.

The fuzzy picture on the screen was of a man standing at a rostrum; stocky and bearded he looked to be in his late forties to early fifties. His face reminded me of someone, but at the time, I could not quite place who.

Chapter 16. Kevles continued

7th May

Mortimer continued.

'Dr Kevles has an international reputation in the molecular biology of infectious diseases. He also has an interesting background.

His father was Dr Rastislav Kevlesnovic, who graduated in medicine from Belgrade University in 1935. He served as a doctor with Tito's partisans in Yugoslavia but became disenchanted with Communism soon afterwards. He and his wife Dragana, fled from Yugoslavia to Austria in 1949, finally settling in England in 1952.'

The black and white photograph was the sort taken in the studio of a professional photographer. It had a potted plant and a backdrop of a distant scene of Italian hills and forests. It was of a moustachioed man in his forties with smile lines around the eyes, standing behind a slim, attractive woman who was seated. He had one hand on her shoulder, and she was touching it with her hand; overall, it was an awkward but affectionate composition.

After obtaining the appropriate license allowing him to practice in Britain in 1954, Rastislav set up shop as a G.P. in Lower Edmonton, North London. His wife, Dragana, who had graduated from Belgrade University with a degree in modern languages, taught English to refugees from Central and Eastern Europe. Their only child, who we know as Douglas Kevles, was born in London in 1953. Rastislav died in 1982 and Dragana in 1995.

This picture was of a family group with a boy of about four years of age standing with his parents. It reminded me of a photo of my parents and myself at that age taken by a photographer on Margate promenade.

Dr Douglas Kevles' birth certificate records his name as Dujan Milos Kevlesnovic, which he later Anglicised to Douglas Kevles. Encouraged by his parents, the academically gifted Dujan did well at school, and in 1971 obtained a bursary to Cambridge. It was while studying at Cambridge that he first caught the attention of Norman Foster, who was at that time a Reader there. After graduating with first-class honours in biochemistry, Douglas Kevles was employed briefly in a laboratory of a food processing company in Bedfordshire. In 1974, he was accepted by Stanford University in California to study for a doctorate in the molecular biology of viruses. His brilliant doctoral thesis entitled, "Viruses of Epidemic Haemorrhagic Fevers", is still required reading for students in this field.

This must have been Kevles formal photograph taken as he received his PhD. He appeared gaunt, as if uninterested in food.

Kevles returned to Britain in 1978, where he took up a post with a pharmaceutical company in Birmingham involved in anti-viral research. While there, he met Georgina Wallace, who was employed as a research assistant, and the couple married in 1984.

Outside a registry office; Douglas still slim, Georgina in a pale-yellow suit; shorter, thick-set, intelligent looking.

In 1986, Kevles joined the UK's Nuclear, Chemical and Biological Defence Directorate at Porton Down as a Senior Scientist. The couple moved to Laverstoke, near Salisbury. On two occasions over the following years, he was seconded to the United Nations Biological Weapons Inspectorate. He visited both Russia and Iraq as a member of inspection teams and spent time in America at Fort Detrick, the US version of Porton Down, on an exchange programme.

He was highlighted as being third from the left in a posed group of about 20 people.

By 1992, the now Professor Norman Foster had recognised a niche market in the need for treatments to counter the threat of biological weapons, including bacterial and viral agents. The intelligence agencies and Dept of Health had perceived this to be a matter of growing national importance. Using his contacts in academia, industry and government, Foster managed to get the funding to build an advanced research facility. He did not intend to produce drugs or vaccines, just to develop and patent them and gain income by allowing the major pharmaceutical companies to manufacture them under license.

Neither did Foster have any intention of giving up his prestigious and comfortable chair at the university. The plan was for him to be a major shareholder and occasional public face of the organisation; someone else would head the research team and managed the day-to-day operations. He would, of course, take a keen interest in any work being undertaken and visit the labs regularly.

Foster had watched Kevles' career develop since his student days. They had also met occasionally on the conference circuit, and Foster carefully monitored his field of research. Deciding that Kevles would be the perfect choice for the job he had in mind, Foster offered him the post of Research Director of Foster BioTech Ltd. Douglas Kevles jumped at the opportunity. The family Kevles thus moved from Wiltshire to Little Thetford, in Cambridge during March 1993.

By this time, Douglas and Georgina had two children, Rasti aged 8 and Marie aged 5. Colleagues and neighbours all tell of the Kevles' enjoying a happy family life. They had a pleasant house in the country, two cars, the children went to private schools, and the family took an active part in the social life of the village.

Kevles seemed to have been blessed with a photographic memory and was a voracious reader on a wide range of topics.

The evolution of life on earth, palaeontology, and the early development of man were topics holding a particular fascination for him. Once settled in Cambridge, he was also able to pursue his lifelong interest in wildlife and natural history by becoming a volunteer with the Cambridge Wildlife Trust.

A quick succession of pictures. Douglas and a very pregnant Georgina with the 3-year old Rasti holding a toy lorry. Then a recent shot of an imposing detached house standing in its own grounds with paddock view across fields. Finally, a picture of a motley group of people wearing anoraks and Wellington boots, carrying axes, saws, and shovels. A smiling Douglas was in the centre: the only photo in which Kevles smiled.

But shortly after the move to Cambridge, a dissonance started to creep into Kevles's life. Possibly triggered by issues raised in his research work coupled with the topics that interested him deeply, he became increasingly concerned over environmental and conservation matters, particularly global warming. Colleagues recall increasingly animated conversations at mealtimes examining the ethical issues surrounding man's treatment of his environment and fellow creatures of the planet. After a while, colleagues found reasons to be elsewhere when Kevles got started on such topics. He noticed this and did not raise them again.

But what began as mere concerns, gradually escalated into an obsession.

Kevles joined Greenpeace in 1996. He actively campaigned for an organisation called Compassion in Farming, and for a reduction of what he regarded as the excessive use of pesticides. Given his standing in the scientific community, his voice was one to be reckoned with; and he found growing support for his views from like-minded scientific contacts worldwide. He became an increasingly influential and vociferous opponent of trials of GM crops, some of which took place near his home.

A regular contributor to learned journals he also wrote newspaper and magazine articles roundly condemning "irresponsible" farming practices. He castigated the role of the big supermarkets, business ethics in general and government and UN policies on the environment, conservation, pollution, factory farms, fish farms, cloning and numerous other issues which impacted the living environment. On one occasion, a magistrate gave him a suspended sentence for causing public disorder because of his persistent barracking of a representative of a GM crop company at a public meeting.

The strain began to show. It is common for activists to become frustrated when their voices and passionate beliefs go unheard. And so it was with Douglas Kevles. He began to write of 'ineffectual and intellectually bankrupt humanity unable to see beyond self-interest' of 'the institutional deafness of big business' of 'flawed mechanisms for dissent', and of 'the irresponsibility of rational men not prepared to act.'

A couple of grainy looking newspaper photographs; one next to a caption saying, "Local man a signatory on a letter to Downing Street." The other showed Kevles standing next to Dr Martin Ryle.

Then tragedy struck. In February 1998, while Douglas attended a conference in Prague, Georgina went to pick up the children from a school friend's evening party. It had rained after a freezing day, and on the return journey, their Range Rover hit a patch of black ice and skidded into the path of an oncoming lorry. Georgina and the children were killed.

The mangled wreck was almost unrecognisable as a car. Nobody could have survived that. God knows what the combined speed on impact was.

In one of those strange ironies the ancient Greeks would have recognised, the lorry had been delivering pesticides to a local farm. Douglas Kevles was inconsolable.

After the funerals, Douglas spent weeks away from work, and colleagues grew concerned over his well-being and whereabouts. It later transpired that he had been walking in the Scottish mountains. When eventually he returned, Kevles threw himself into his work, often working late into the night and over weekends. As the Research Director of the laboratory, nobody questioned anything he did. About six months later, Foster BioTech Ltd, was one of those given a sample of the Greenland virus and a government-funded contract to develop a vaccine against it.

Dr Douglas Kevles was last seen in February this year. Again, his whereabouts are unknown. But this time a quantity of the modified Spanish Flu virus is also missing. And during the last 24 hours, it has been confirmed publicly that the disease we know as the Brazilian Flu is in fact caused by a variant of the virus recovered from the wreck of the Anders Nyquist. A variant that has been genetically engineered to contain elements of haemorrhagic viruses.'

Chapter 17. Body Work

8th – 11th May

Next day, I saw my first dead victim.

To my surprise, Amanda Jarvis had asked Teague if I could be her permanent assistant, and he seemed happy to get me out of the way.

Amanda was quiet in the car. I glanced down at the list of addresses we had to call at. It looked twice the length of yesterdays. We were nearing Kingston before I spoke.

'Do you think the government will extend this 'No Contact' period?'

'They'll have to. According to the data my department is getting, the infection rate hasn't slowed one iota.'

I was surprised. 'But surely it must slow if people are not in contact!'

'It's beginning to look as if there's a wide variation in the incubation period. Carriers are probably spreading the disease well before they realise they're infected.'

For the first time, I noticed she was wearing a wedding ring.

'Is your husband in the medical profession?'

'David's a surgeon; specialises in paediatric heart surgery.'

'How are hospitals coping?'

'They're not. They couldn't possibly cope. David says that all NHS Trusts have all been instructed to identify buildings that could be used as Isolation Hospitals. Top Priority, straight from Number 10. They've got emergency powers to commandeer any building they need. Everything except emergency cases have been cancelled at normal NHS Hospitals … for the duration ... I think the circular said.'

'I suspected it might be getting hairy.'

'Anyway, we may have to resort to quarantining people to their own homes, the way the Chinese did in the SARS outbreak in 2003. That proved effective for a while.'

'What, just tell infected people to stay at home? That'll go down well. What about their relatives?'

'They'd become Carers ... if there's to be any care. If the Rate of Infection doesn't slow soon, we have no choice. Besides which, the First Responder Paramedic Teams are taking a big hit.'

'What, being infected?' I asked anxiously.

'That, and scared.'

'Aren't they wearing these industrial-strength masks?'

'Yup. And being bloody careful ... and some have still caught it.'

'But I thought the virus was airborne.'

'It is. But it's also been detected on people's clothes, in urine and faeces, on door handles, on spoons, pens, money, in fact on anything people touch.'

'Oh, Great!' We were silent for some time while I reflected on the fact that we too were First Responders.

'Did you see Panorama last night?' I asked, for the sake of something to say.

'It was ending when I got home. David watched it.'

'What do you think about this Kevles bloke?'

She shrugged, 'For the last decade, people in my field have been saying that Pandora's Box is sitting there unlocked. It was only a matter of time before someone opened it. Now some lunatic has done just that. They've unleashed a virus that can actually threaten the survival of our species.'

This time I was really shocked. 'That's a bit strong, isn't it!'

'No, that's my expert opinion.'

I sat remembering the myth of Pandora's Box when after the evils of the earth had been released, the only thing left ... was hope. Amanda stirred me from my depressing thoughts by saying, 'We want the next turning on the left.'

A young, scared-looking, policeman let us in. Amanda estimated that the woman, who was about 24 years old, had been dead for four days. I tried not to get too close. But I could not help noticing the blotches on her skin and the dried bloodstains on the pillow and around her mouth and nose. We spoke to her neighbour - who covered her mouth with her hand all the time she was with us. She had become suspicious because her dog would not stop barking. She told us that the dead woman worked as a checkout assistant in the local Lidl. Amanda and I glanced at each other, both realising she had probably been in contact with hundreds of people every day, touching their food and handing them money.

'Ring the mortuary to have the body picked up,' she told the PC.

'I'll let the Coroner's Office know. Come on, Wandsworth next.'

I contributed nothing on that call. Driving along, Amanda said quietly, 'Quite soon there will be no niceties like Coroner's Offices. It'll be the army collecting the corpses for burying or burning somewhere. Just like the Black Death and Foot and Mouth.'

'Christ, for a doctor, you're a real comfort!'

'It's my defence mechanism. I'm terrified.'

And so it was for the next two days. Call and confirm; call and confirm. Occasionally I felt that maybe it helped Amanda my just being there to support her, but mostly I felt helpless. I did my best to comfort distraught relatives, which she said I was good at. Their fear was tangible. Amanda confessed that her lack of bedside manner was one of the things that stopped her becoming a GP.

She was right about the government extending the "No Contact" period. On the next Ministerial Broadcast, it was announced that it had been extended for a further month.

The news from abroad was grim, and there was much wringing of hands over the prospects for the world economy. Shaky at the best of times for most countries, the financial gurus were predicting an economic meltdown for even the G8 countries from which it would take decades to recover.

I was utterly unmoved by these predictions. Not being a shareholder myself, I held a blissfully uninformed view that monetary gloom and doom affected only people whose personal fortunes were tied up in airlines, shipping, tourism, hotels, gilts or whatever. Basically, the people on television who were wringing their hands.

It was as if there was an official clampdown on news from Brazil. By then, little was coming directly from Sao Paulo and what there was, appeared to be third hand and speculative. Whether all news agencies had departed, it was impossible to tell. The few English language web sites, chat rooms and blogs I logged onto painted a worsening situation. Power supplies had failed in some areas and with it the water pumping stations and telecoms infrastructure.

The Americans were flying their servicemen and women home to help with Homeland Security. There had been rioting in New York, Chicago, Los Angeles, and Washington when people trying to leave those cities had been turned back by National Guardsmen. CNN reported severe travel and food supply restrictions in the USA for 'Non-essential personnel'. That had gone down like a lead balloon in the Land of the Free. Any hint of restriction brought an outcry against the Federal Government and appeals to state laws. But this time to no avail. The Federal Government was implacable.

The first comparable incident reported in the UK was from Sheffield. In the early hours of the morning, a police roadblock had been overwhelmed by people intent on leaving the city. A policeman had been struck by a vehicle and killed.

Next evening, Home Secretary, Ann Freer informed the nation that the government had declared a State of Emergency. A curfew was imposed between 8pm and 6am. All Territorial Service personnel were to report for duty and cordons manned by the armed services were being placed around each major city. All main roads would be blocked, and only authorised vehicles allowed to use them. Any driver trying to cross these cordons not carrying an appropriate pass would be subject to immediate imprisonment. Passes would be issued from Government Departments, Metropolitan, County and District councils, but only under strict guidelines.

The TV news showed roads barricaded by large container lorries positioned across the carriageways to impose chicanes negotiable only at slow speed. The soldiers, wearing full bio-chemical protection, were armed. The main roads were obviously a no-go. The traffic jams on feeder roads made road travel impossible anyway. Mission accomplished.

Freer was very sombre when she announced that the number of infected cases in the UK had reached 15 thousand. The death toll was now 2,311. (Day 44 in the UK)

Chapter 18. Julie

11th May

It was late afternoon when my mobile rang. Rose was hysterical. 'Trish has caught it! We've got to get Julie away from Warwick! Come home now so we can get going.'

'Rosie, calm down. You've seen the news bulletins. We wouldn't be allowed through the cordon. Now calm down. I'll get home as soon as I can.'

I looked at Amanda; she nodded.

'I'll be there in about half an hour. We're outside the flats we're calling at so we may as well make the call.'

'To hell with the bloody call,' Rose screamed so loud, I had to hold the phone away from my ear, 'This is our daughter we're talking about. Get the fuck home! Do you hear me!'

The phone went dead.

'Your daughter?' Amanda asked.

'Sounds as if one of her flatmates is showing symptoms.'

'Sorry,' she said quietly.

'Come on, let's make this call.' I needed to be busy.

The tower block had been built in the 1960s. Designed by architects who would never live in them, these vertical ghettos lay at the root of many of the problems we experienced in the classroom; fifteen-floor recipes for social exclusion.

The sheet told us we were looking for Dawn Watkins at number 1012. 'I'll bet that's on the tenth floor,' I said. And I was right; by the time we had climbed the urine reeking stairs, I was puffing through the facemask and perspiring like mad. The door to 1012 was opened by an over-weight, shaven-headed, morose looking man of about 40 years of age. He wore a vest, exposing arms and shoulders covered in tattoos.

'You've taken your fucking time! I phoned yesterday. Thought it was supposed to be an emergency line. Some fucking emergency response. We could all be dead by now for all you lot care.' He reeked of booze.

'Mr Watkins, I take it?'

'You taking the piss, mate?' he glared at me.

'Why don't you take Dr Jarvis to the patient.'

He turned without a word and led us into the dingy flat. A woman was watching television; a boy of about fifteen sprawled on a settee, a can of beer in hand. The woman was coughing, but that could have been caused by the cigarette she was smoking.

'Who's the patient?' Amanda asked.

'I told your lot on the phone. She is,' said the man.

Speaking over the sound of the television, Amanda asked, 'How are you feeling?' She took the woman's pulse and temperature.

'Rotten. Got a sore throat and a blinding headache,' the woman answered still fixated on the television.

Amanda placed an electronic thermometer in the woman's ear. 'You're not running a temperature.' She peered into the woman's eyes with a pencil torch. 'How long have you felt like this?'

'Couple of days.'

'Do you work?'

'Cleanin' ... when I can get it.'

Amanda put her stethoscope to the woman's chest and back, listening intently.

'When are we gonna get masks like that?' the Neanderthal asked, looking at me.

'No idea, but the government expect supplies to be available soon.' I lied.

'Load of bollocks. Won't be for the likes of us. They'll be given to the fucking rich first.'

Amanda looked into the woman's throat then started to put her stethoscope away. 'I'll leave you some of these tablets. Try to rest and call again if you get any worse.'

'Tablets! That all! Aren't taking her in?'

'No point at the moment. She'd be at more risk in hospital than she is here,' Amanda answered.

'So that's it then is it. We wait all day for a couple of aspirins. We've got this fucking plague, and you fob us off with pills. What else you got in there?' he grabbed Amanda's medical bag and tipped its contents onto the table.

Amanda said nervously, 'I'm from the Communicable Disease Surveillance Centre. I don't carry normal medicines. There are no drugs if that's what you're after, nothing that's of any use to you …'

'Yeah, well I'll decide that,' Watkins muttered raking through the pill cases and syringes.

The situation was becoming ugly; I had seen it many times during break periods at school: volatile, unpredictable, and usually ending in violence.

'Come on, Mr Watkins, I know you're worried ... but this is not going to help anyone,' I said, moving towards him.

He was quick. Suddenly he had a breadknife in his hand.

'Back off if you know what's good for you.' he waved the knife around ominously … 'And you can both get those fucking masks and overalls off. We'll have them.'

Now I was alarmed. I glanced at Amanda; she seemed paralysed.

'Take it easy man …' I started to say, but he grabbed Amanda and pointed the knife at her chest.

'Take them off now, before someone gets fucking hurt.' He meant it.

The woman just sat watching, the boy looked concerned.

'I'd do as he says, if I was you, mister. He can get nasty,' the boy said quietly.

'OK, OK …' I slipped my mask off and started to undo my overalls, 'Amanda, just do as he says.'

Watkins pulled the mask roughly from over her head. 'Come on, move, you dozy cow!' He was becoming angrier by the second. She snapped out of her trance and unzipped the coverall.

'Right, now beat it. And if you come back here offering us pills, I'll throw you off the fucking balcony.'

I took Amanda by the arm and led her from the flat. I could hear the man and teenager laughing behind us. We hurried down the stairs and crossed the yard to the car. I congratulated myself that I had had the presence of mind to pocket the car keys, when suddenly Amanda's medical bag thudded down beside us, thrown from the tenth floor. All the medication was gone. We bundled into the car, and I set the central locking system. Amanda was shaking with fright, so I took her hand.

'It's OK, I'll ring the police.' I took out my mobile and dialled 999, and it took some time before the call was answered.

I explained our predicament to the police operator, but she seemed non-committal.

'Doubt we can get anyone round there today, I'm afraid. Pretty stretched at the moment. Sorry.' This was not comforting.

Not wanting to sit outside those awful flats any longer than necessary, I started the car, and we drove off.

When I realised Amanda was crying, I stopped in a lay-by on Wimbledon Common. Eventually, she calmed.

'Sorry,' she said, drying her eyes. 'I've always had a horror of physical violence.'

I was tempted to say that it was probably going to get worse but thought better of it.

'He was a real charmer, wasn't he! Do you think the woman has Brazilian Flu?' I asked.

'Not sure. Very early phase if she does.'

'Do you think we were exposed when that cretin took our masks?'

'Impossible to say. Time will tell. God knows what would have happened if you hadn't been there.'

As we drove back to The Hall, I rang Teague and told him what had happened. He was not surprised; one of the delivery teams had been attacked by a group of people trying to hijack food. It was only when a soldier pointed his rifle at the ringleader that they backed off. Things were starting to turn nasty.

Amanda dropped me at home about an hour after Rosie had rung me. As I walked down the path, I noticed with some disquiet that our car was missing from the drive. The house was empty. There was no note or anything to indicate where Rose was. I tried her mobile several times; it was switched off. I left a message asking her to call me urgently. I tried Julie's mobile, but could not get her either. When I rang Nick, he said Rose had told him about Trish and tried to order him to come home, but she had not mentioned any plans to visit Julie. He said they were all OK up there; no cases had been reported in the village. Then I phoned Nalini next door.

'She rang about Julie,' Nalini said, 'She was distraught, Gerry. I told her to stay calm. Julie's friend may have ordinary flu. Do you think she's gone to Warwick?'

'That's my guess,' I sighed … but God knows how far she'll get with The London Cordon ... and now the curfew. It starts in an hour; the police will stop her.'

Nalini was quiet. Finally, she said, 'Let me know if there's anything we can do. OK!' then she rang off.

I poured myself a whisky, switched on the TV and slumped into an armchair. It had been a bad day.

I must have dozed off and woke with a start when the telephone rang. Assuming it to be Rose, I said, 'So which police station are they holding you in?'

A man's voice answered, 'Is that you, Morris?' It was Colin Jefferson.

'Sorry, I was expecting someone else,' I mumbled.

'Look, I thought I'd better let you know. It seems that three of our pupils have been hospitalised with this wretched Brazilian Flu. One of them is in your group. George Paine.'

'Oh, bloody hell. Who are the others?' He told me the other two names. I knew them only by sight: they did not attend any of my classes.

'And Gwilym Morgan rang me this evening to say that he fears he might have it.' Gwilym was our sports master. I groaned.

'All getting a bit much isn't it,' Jefferson said. 'Looks as if you were right to be worried about this wretched disease. And it's going to play havoc with the exam results this year. Have you been roped in to help at one of these Emergency Centres?'

I brought him up to date; and told him about Julie.

'Sorry to hear that, Gerry.' He sounded genuine, and it was the first time he had ever called me by my Christian name; I did not realise he knew it.

'Look, I'll get off the phone. Let me know if there's anything I can do.'

The bad day had just got worse.

Chapter 19. Roadblock incident

12th May

The police rang at three in the morning. There had been an incident. Rose was in Chase Farm Hospital, Enfield. She was injured, but her condition was not life-threatening. I asked what her injuries were, but the police officer did not know. He gave me the phone number for the hospital. Reminding me about the curfew he suggested I went there when it was lifted at 6 a.m.

I wondered how Rosie had managed to land up in Enfield when she was heading for Warwick! But her sense of direction when driving was idiosyncratic, to say the least.

I rang the hospital immediately and was put through to the ward where the phone rang for ages before it was answered. A harassed and testy nurse told me Rose had been injured in a car crash. When I told her that I was Rose's husband and asked what her injuries were; she said that she had sustained a broken arm and ribs and had concussion. The break had been reset, and she was now sleeping.

When I rang off, I sat pondering how the hell I would get to Enfield. With no car, no public transport and little chance of thumbing a lift now that petrol restriction was biting, it was going to be difficult. In the end, I decided that I would have to get my old bicycle out of the garage. As dawn broke, I was sat worrying about Rosie and Julie and decided to make myself a cup of tea: opening the kitchen door the cold morning air chilled me as I listened to the dawn chorus. Afraid of going to bed in case I overslept, I again lay down on the settee and eventually dozed off again. The phone startled me awake, and I was horrified to see it was nearly half-past seven. It was Nalini asking about Rose. When I told her, she immediately offered one of their cars.

It was half-past nine in the morning when I finally found Chase Farm Hospital. It lay a few miles inside the M25 corridor. Security guards were stopping all traffic trying to enter the car park, thereby producing a queue of about fifty cars that took an hour to get through. I noticed that for most of the vehicles in front of me, the guards handed the occupants a piece of paper and directed them back to the road. When my turn came, I lowered the car window to answer the masked guard.

'You got flu symptoms?' he asked.

'No. My wife was involved in a car accident last night. She's in Nightingale Ward.'

He let me through, telling me to collect a facemask at the table. The hospital complex was a hotchpotch of buildings, some looking as if they had been built a hundred-years-ago. I approached what appeared to be the major building, to find a table situated outside the main door, with a queue of people leading to it. They were queuing for facemasks. Security staff stopped anyone not wearing a mask from entering. The masks were the DIY standard I had been given originally, but better than nothing.

But I was shocked when I did enter the building. It was like something from a Third World hospital. People lay everywhere. In the entrance hall and in every corridor. On trolleys, on mattresses on the floor, even on blankets on the floor. Many of them were in the advanced stages of Brazilian Flu. I must have been staring when a young nurse walked towards me.

'A bit of a shock when you first see it isn't it,' she said, in a strong West Indian accent.

'Bloody Hell, I had no idea!'

'No, it's not something for the news bulletins. Strict orders not to allow TV or film crews in.'

'How long has it been like this?'

'We reached capacity last week. All new flu cases are sent to a big country house called White Webbs. Cleared the building there apparently. Hope to move some of these over there soon.'

'Have all these people got Brazilian Flu?'

'Probably,' she said.

'But there must be hundreds of them …'

'Nearly a thousand at the last count. Are you looking for someone?'

She directed me to Nightingale Ward.

I realised that if this hospital was anything to go by, the government's reports of the number of people infected were grossly understated.

As she walked away from me, I felt humbled by the sheer dedication of that young nurse. Knowing that the very air she breathed was probably lethal, she went about her business with the ideals and commitment that had brought her into the profession. To help people who were sick. And she would do that come hell or high water; she was not one of those who would run away in this crisis even though she knew it may cost her her life.

The corridors on the way to Nightingale Ward were filled with flu victims. Some lay quiet, fully aware of their terrifying surroundings; some were coughing; some held blood-stained cloths to their mouths. Some were bodies with a blanket pulled over their faces. A few had relatives trying to comfort them; everyone looked scared.

I suspected that in normal times Nightingale Ward had been used for post-op surgical patients. But by then, there were also flu patients squeezed in. Rose occupied a bed in a corner. As I neared her, I could see that her eyes were closed, and her head bandaged framing an ashen face; her arm was in plaster. I kissed her forehead, and she opened her eyes.

'Gerry. Thank God, you're here,' she muttered woozily through a parched mouth and a facemask.

'What happened, love?'

It took a while for her to answer, 'I tried to drive through a police roadblock and crashed the car. It's probably a write-off.'

I groaned inwardly but managed to say, 'Well, don't let's worry about that for now, so long as you're OK.'

'You look a bit ruffled. What's the damage?'

She sighed, 'Broken arm, couple of cracked ribs and a cut forehead,' she said, 'And the police have charged me under this new Emergency Powers crap. Attempting to cross an authorised cordon, I think they said. Can you hand me that water, please?'

I almost smiled. 'How far had you got?'

'I hadn't managed to cross the M25 cordon.'

'So where's the car?'

'Just outside Enfield somewhere … last time I saw it.'

'I'll find out from the police. I've kept trying to ring you,' I said.

'I've lost my mobile,' she beckoned me towards her, and whispered, 'Gerry, we've got to get out of here, before we both catch this awful disease, if I haven't already.'

'Steady on. You're in no condition to travel. You'll have to stay here for a few days at least!'

'No, Gerry, absolutely not. I mean it! I can walk; they got me up for the toilet this morning. I am not staying here. Look around you! There are hardly any staff. All these people have this bloody disease. If I stay, I'll get it too. Pull the curtains around, get my clothes out of the locker and help me dress. We're leaving.'

She promptly pulled the saline drip needle out of her hand.

I looked around. Rose was right; the hospital was a breeding ground.

Wearing her blood-stained clothes, I helped her walk out of the hospital. Nobody tried to stop us or even ask where we were going; they had more important things to worry about.

As I drove to Enfield police station, Rosie told me what happened. She had driven north across London planning to avoid all main roads and stick to the smallest country lanes. At about eight o'clock, she parked and waited for dark, reasoning that she would have a better chance of going undetected at night. She started off again at about 11pm but lost her way and decided to ignore all the temporary *"No Entry"* signs erected to enforce the cordon. But just outside Enfield, she saw a roadblock about half a mile ahead. It appeared to be a wooden trestle placed across the road; although it was floodlit, it was not manned. She decided to approach it cautiously to nudge the trestle out of the way with the car. What she had not noticed was the police hut and tractor blocking the road just beyond the barrier and outside the floodlit area. Someone heard her coming and started flashing a spotlight. Panicking, Rosie put her foot down, crashed through the barrier, swerved violently to avoid the tractor, and sent the car through a hedge, down a bank and into a tree. The two Special Police constables who dragged an unconscious Rose from the wreckage were not best pleased.

While Rose sat in the car, I tried to see the Desk Officer at Enfield Police Station to find out where my car had been taken. But the door to the Station was locked, and I found myself standing outside speaking through an intercom.

'It'll be right where your wife left it,' a voice answered tersely, '… breakdown trucks and garages are on an emergency-only basis. And since from what you say, your wife survived the crash, this does not qualify.'

But he told me where the incident had occurred, and I left.

Rose was right about one thing; our Mondeo was a write-off. She had rolled it and damaged the front wheels and suspension. As I stood looking at it, I realised she had been lucky to escape so lightly. And a few thousand pounds would be needed to restore it to its former faded glory. We drove home almost in silence with Rosie in considerable pain. When we finally arrived back at Norwood, the petrol tank was almost empty. We owed Anil and Nalini big time.

After I had put Rose to bed, I rang Teague told him the story and that I would need to look after her for a while. He thanked me but commented snidely that my family seemed to be accident-prone. Stuff you, I thought! Then I rang Amanda, who seemed genuinely pleased to hear Rose was OK. She told me not to worry; she would get another helper, but she would appreciate it if I would join her again when I returned to work. I was quite touched.

Julie was mortified when I rang to tell her of her mother's exploits. I asked how Trish was, and Julie said she had been taken to hospital. All the rest of her flatmates seemed to be OK, she said, so we were not to worry about her. But I detected unease in her voice.

Chapter 20. Julie again

19th May

During the following week, my time was divided between looking after Rose and watching television. After her stay in that highly infectious hospital, we both spent days anxiously waiting to see if either of us developed symptoms. I rang Amanda to confirm the incubation period being five or six days. To our immense relief, the seventh day passed without either of us showing any signs.

The food ration being left on our doorstep was basic, to say the least; a loaf of bread, a tin of food of some sort and a couple of apples.

I wondered how long it would be before the general health of the nation suffered given such frugal fare. Not that we were too bothered thanks to Rosie's pre-emptive strike on Sainsbury's. But we were careful with our supplies, unsure how long they would have to last.

I was hypnotised by news of the spread of the disease. Country after country struggled to contain it, but without success. The government's ministerial broadcasts became a nightly feature. It was never admitted of course, since it might have bad for morale, but I gained the impression the broadcasts were no longer coming from Number 10 but from some biologically safe haven. By mid-May, there were over nine thousand four hundred dead in England and nearly eighty thousand infected. Panic had started to set in.

As the number of cases and deaths rose, the Home Secretary, Ann Freer, tried courageously to paint a hopeful picture, insisting that some areas were virtually disease-free, although she did not say which areas. That was probably just as well since desperate people would have headed for them. Grim though her figures were, I could not forget those nightmarish corridors at Chase Farm Hospital; I knew the real numbers were much higher than she was quoting.

Not surprisingly, Rose suffered delayed shock from her accident and was in pain. She lay in bed, hardly able to move due to the cracked ribs. I tried ringing our doctor but could only get an answering machine that informed me that the doctors would visit genuine emergency cases only. Patients with flu symptoms should contact the NHS's Brazilian Flu Hotline. I left a message explaining our predicament. I even visited the surgery only to find it deserted and locked. A couple of days later, and quite unannounced, one of the GPs in the practice called at home, examined Rose, gave her some strong painkillers. He advised us to stay well away from hospitals. As I saw him to the door, I mentioned my assisting Amanda Jarvis. He said he had met her and had been impressed. When I asked him for an update on the local situation regarding Brazilian Flu, he answered, 'Frightening. I don't know about the rest of the country, but it's certainly not under control locally. Two of my colleagues have already died of it.'

During the next few days, Rose suggested several ways in which I might 'rescue' Julie. None were convincing since they depended on Julie's willingness to leave Warwick Uni. We spoke to her on her mobile each evening, and each time she emphatically rejected any pleas to come home. We even suggested Matt accompany her. But no, she would not have it; she would not leave her friends. And for about a week she reassured us by saying that her remaining flatmates were in good health and spirits.

Nicholas seemed contented at Lindsey's parents. He was in a small village called Brysleigh, about twenty miles north of Manchester. He surprised us by saying that the residents had decided to barricade the village by blocking off the four roads accessing it. The barricades were manned 24/7 by armed villagers. When I asked what the police reaction had been, Nick said that from what he had heard, most of the villages and small towns in the area had done the same thing and that there was tacit approval by the authorities. The drivers of vehicles delivering food left it a hundred yards away, and the villagers collected it once the delivery vehicles had departed. At least Nick seemed to be safe. Perhaps it was these sorts of rural areas that The Home Secretary was referring to. And the lower infection rates made sense. There was simply much less contact with other people than in towns and cities.

Ten days after Rose's accident, a hysterical Julie rang mid-afternoon to tell us that Trish had died. We were horrified. Tearfully she also told us that Matt had slunk off, leaving her a note saying he thought he should be with his parents … in case they needed him. I never did like that little shit.

The good news was that three of Julie's other flatmates had agreed to make their way home to London and to our immense relief she had decided to join them. They were planning to leave as soon as the curfew lifted the next morning. They would try to thumb a lift but would walk if necessary. Needless to say, Rose went frantic, begging me to collect Julie. She insisted that she was fit enough to fend for herself and that I must go alone. Alarmed at the potential hazards facing Julie, I needed little persuading; I must fetch her. But with no public transport and no car, it would be a problem. It was no good asking Nalini again; we had already used all their petrol. I tried ringing a couple of school colleagues, but none had fuel. I tried phoning local car hire firms, but the only one who answered just laughed. The government clampdown had been extremely effective; there was no petrol to be had.

Then I remembered Amanda saying she lived near High Wycombe, so I rang her. Explaining my predicament, I asked if she would give me a lift when she returned home that evening. At least that might get me beyond the M25 cordon. She agreed and said she would pick me up at about six o'clock.

I then spent a hectic hour planning ahead. I am by nature analytical and have always found it useful to make, "Must Do" lists. In the past, these had been the source of much amusement to my family. Maybe now they would think them a good idea.

Since I occasionally cycled to school, I knew that my bike was serviceable. I packed a rucksack with a warm sweater, a few tins of food and a couple of soft drinks, my walking boots and my Berghaus coat: my Swiss army knife I clipped to my belt. With some irritation, I realised that my road atlas was in my car lying in a field just outside Enfield, so I had to resort to an old one I was harbouring in the garage. I rang Julie again and asked what route they planned to take. It soon became apparent they had not given it much thought. Conscious of what Nick had told us, I advised them to stay off main roads and gave them a route mainly on the B4011 that brought them south via villages and small towns that they could detour if they encountered problems. I insisted that they write it down. Bishop's Tachbrook, Gaydon, Warmington, Banbury, then onto the A423 to Alderbury, Deddington, Kidlington, and Oxford. But I expected to be with them long before they reached Oxford. Realising that reliable communication would be critical, I asked Julie how many of her group had mobile phones. They all did so I wrote down their numbers and told her that they must charge the batteries fully before leaving campus. We agreed that they would switch on only one of their phones for five minutes every hour on the hour; that way we could stay in touch but save battery power; and I could plot our combined progress. Finally, I advised them to travel light, to carry only small bags with enough clothes and food to get them through three days. Definitely no suitcases. The rest of their stuff could stay at the campus until the emergency was over.

Gradually I began to feel less anxious. With Amanda dropping me at High Wycombe, given a fair wind and no disasters, I might even reach them by tomorrow evening. When I told her that, Julie suddenly became very tearful, and I sensed her relief in knowing that Dad was coming to help. I did not ask if any of the other parents planned to meet them; I did not much care.

One way or another Julie and I must have rung each other about half a dozen times before Amanda arrived. I had done everything I could for Rosie, placing food, drinks, and toiletries within easy reach. I told Nalini what was afoot, and she said not to worry, she would look in on Rosie.

In the event, Amanda did not collect me until nearly half-past seven. When she did arrive the first thing she did was dump a pile of new protective clothing onto our drive; she then she got back into her Volvo which now had a large red-cross stuck on the side.

'Put those on before you get in,' she called from the car.

I did as she bid then loaded my bicycle and rucksack into the rear of the car.

It felt odd to wear a mask again; I had hardly worn one since I had returned home with Rose.

'How are you?' I asked brightly as I climbed into the car.

Looking at me, she forced a smile. 'What did we used to say; overworked and underpaid. God, if only we'd realised what a doddle it was compared to this.' I sensed fragility in Amanda.

She asked after Rose and Julie, and we made small talk for a while.

'What's it looking like locally?' I asked as we drove towards Streatham.

'Catastrophic. I think we've lost.'

I let that sink in. 'That's a bleak statement!'

'It's changed a lot since you left. People are terrified. We've been ordering them, begging them, bribing them to stay isolated, to self-quarantine, but they're not listening. On lots of visits, I find relatives have fled, leaving the patient to get on with it. The ones who flee are of course, probably just spreading the disease to wherever they end up. And so it goes on. We're behaving like some Third World country.'

I sat, staring out of the car window. There were few pedestrians now, and those all wore some form of facemask. And there was no dawdling; people were conscious of the curfew starting at 8pm. The few vehicles were mainly emergency vehicles of one sort or another but included several white vans emblazoned with that ghastly bio-hazard icon. I assumed these were ferrying confirmed cases to Emergency Stations.

As we passed the public commons at Streatham and Tooting, I saw that they were covered in small brightly coloured tents. I had seen brief shots of them on TV, but the sheer numbers surprised me. I asked Amanda about them.

'Just people who have fled their homes and pitched their tents in the open. Presumably, they feel safer. God knows why; most of them have already been exposed to the virus.'

It was the same on every piece of open ground we passed on our journey across London.

'How are things at The Hall?' I asked.

'Fewer people turn up every day. Teague hasn't shown up since last week, and rumour is that he has the flu. And I haven't seen your teacher friend Carol for a few days.'

I made a mental note to give Carol a ring once back from Warwick.

‘To be honest, I’m surprised more people haven’t tried to leave London,’ I said, ‘I think I would of by now had it not been for the Emergency Team duty … and now Rose of course.’

Amanda stared ahead. ‘Thousands have. The army has been ordered to seal off the cities; nobody is allowed out without a pass. There are several reports of shootings at people who ignored orders to turn back. It’s not being broadcast for obvious reasons. But we live not too far from the cordon. We hear gunfire every night.’

It was clear that the situation was much worse than inferred in the nightly Ministerial Broadcasts, and I began to wonder how Julie and her friends would fare, and myself for that matter. Amanda seemed to read my mind.

‘I am going to drop you at Princes Risborough. That’s well beyond the M25 cordon, so at least you won’t have that to worry about. Then your Emergency Clothing and Pass might help.’

‘I don’t have a Pass.’

‘I’ve been thinking about that. We’ll call in at home, and I’ll give you David’s pass. You’re not unlike him to look at. Nobody’s looking too hard at photographs nowadays.’

‘But won’t he need it?’ I asked.

She was silent for a moment; I turned to look at her.

‘We realised yesterday that David’s infected. He won’t need it anymore.’

‘Oh, Christ, Amanda, I am sorry.’

She shrugged. ‘I’ll probably not go back to The Hall after today. Although David insists I carry on with the emergency work, I’ve decided to look after him. He hasn’t got long, and we both know it. We have a small cottage in Lincolnshire; quite isolated, on the edge of the fens. It would have been nice to get him up there. He was born there.’

I was about to blurt out that David's pass might help them to cross whatever barriers they might encounter on their way to Lincolnshire. But I stopped myself. She knew that. And she realised that in a few days, David would be too ill to face a 200-mile drive. Tears rolled down her cheeks. Feeling utterly inadequate, I put my hand on her shoulder. We drove in silence as we crossed the Thames and headed northwest.

Amanda's house was situated in a pleasant country lane to the north of High Wycombe. Not sumptuous but certainly comfortable.

'Just give me a minute, and I'll get David's pass.'

She was gone about five minutes before coming back and driving on.

'Here, take this.' It was her husband's pass.

'Thanks,' I mumbled, 'How is he?'

'Like everyone else with this fucking disease. Dying.'

Chapter 21. Breaking Curfew

20th May

Following a discussion in the Group last night, it was clear that apart from the military among us, I am the only one who travelled outside the London Cordon during the height of the outbreak. Which means I probably saw and experienced several aspects of how the authorities tried to cope which the others did not. For the sake of my Chronicle, I have decided to describe my experiences more thoroughly than I had previously planned.

By 4 a.m. a faint glow of light had started to appear in the east. The rain trickled down my neck as I looked down at my watch and I wondered if I should ignore the curfew and start cycling. But I decided to wait before chancing it. Thanks to Amanda, everything had gone smoothly so it would be stupid to take risks now.

As promised, she had dropped me on the northern outskirts of Princes Risborough the previous evening. She actually apologised for not being able to take me further because she wanted to get back to David. I tried inadequately to thank her for her exceptional help, and we became quite emotional as we hugged goodbye. She waved me away as she turned to spend the precious last days with her husband. I never saw her again.

Being somewhat apprehensive about being spotted abroad during the curfew even on country lanes, I had waited until dark before I started cycling. Picking up the B4011, I had been travelling for only about 10 minutes when I was startled by the lights of a car in the distance. Hurriedly I dismounted and ducked behind some bushes. It turned out to be two vehicles; the first was a bio-hazard logoed white van; the second an army Land Rover, possibly escorting the van. But the encounter unnerved me, and I began to wonder what would happen if I were to be arrested. That thought did not calm my state of mind! So, a few miles south of Thame, I sheltered for the night in woodland.

Having lived all my life in towns or cities, I found myself genuinely nervous sitting in a dark wood at night. That depth of darkness was alien to me; it seemed suffocating. In Norwood, our bedroom was never dark since the streetlight always penetrated the curtains. Eventually, I moved closer to the road so that I could see the comforting lights of a house about a mile away.

I was cheered, when as planned, Rosie rang me at midnight. She was really pleased when I reported my position; we spoke for only a few minutes to conserve my mobile's battery. As planned, she would then ring Julie to update her. Apart from the drizzle that had fallen steadily for the past hour, things were OK, so I treated myself to half a cup of hot coffee. I must have fallen into a fitful doze from which I awoke with a start, ludicrously convinced that there was a wild animal nearby. I shone my torch around, but there was nothing. By about 5am, I was cold, damp, and stiff, so I decided to start to walk for a while. I reasoned that if a vehicle approached, I would hear it and take cover. When 6am finally arrived, I mounted my bike, knowing I was not breaking the Curfew. Curiously, I still felt that weird sense of invincibility and importance bestowed by my Emergency Team outfit. I cycled through Thame without any delay. Julie rang on schedule at 7am and reported that she and her three friends were about to leave Warwick campus. She sounded a little subdued, but I put that down to anxiety over the journey ahead.

For about an hour or so I made good time. The B4011 was deserted, and I saw few people in the villages I cycled through. They paid no attention to me. But then I reached Bicester. As I approached the town, there was a large hand-painted sign stating;

Turn Back
No visitors allowed in
Bicester during the epidemic

Lorries parked across both lanes ahead blocked the road, so I dismounted and stood staring for a while. Nobody seemed to be around, so after a few minutes, I started to push my bike forward. At about 100 yards, a harsh voice called out.

'That's far enough. Can't you read! What do you want?'

Although distorted by a loudhailer, the voice belonged to a well-spoken man.

'I want to cycle through. I need to get to Warwick.'

'Well, you're not cycling through here. Find another way. Only Emergency Vehicles and food lorries allowed.'

'I just want to come through. I won't be stopping. I'm going to pick up my daughter at Warwick University. I haven't got the disease.'

'Sez you. Anyway, from what you're wearing, you've been in contact with it, so bugger off and find a different way.'

'Look for Chrissake, you can't stop people using the public highway! I have every right to come through,' I said, walking on purposefully.

Three figures stepped out from behind the lorries; one carried the loudhailer, one a shotgun and one a pickaxe handle; all wore facemasks.

'You can try. But I'll tell now that last bloke who tried could hardly crawl back into his car when we'd finished with him. We haven't got the disease in this town, and we're determined to keep it that way. Bicester is a "No Go Area" for the duration. Now beat it.'

I stopped. Surely they were bluffing; surely our stable, comfortable, and secure British society could not have broken down already? Surely not?

'What if I call the police,' I called.

There was a laugh, 'Saying what?'

'That you've blocked the public highway.'

'You think they don't know!'

Just a moment's thought was enough; if this road had been blocked the police definitely would know. And officially or otherwise they must have condoned it. On the other hand, these people could be bluffing. To be on the safe side, I concluded it was time to turn around. Before doing so, I called, 'Can you at least tell me roads that are open which will take me towards Warwick?'

There was a pause as the men conferred.

'Try going via Stratton Audley. That's still open as far as we know. Take the left-hand turn about two miles back.'

'Thanks.'

'Sorry about this chum, but we're just trying to protect ourselves. Good luck finding your daughter,' the voice had mellowed and sounded almost friendly. So a vestige of compassion remained.

Cycling the two miles back towards the Blackthorn – Stratton Audley junction, I reflected on what was happening; how the law-abiding, well educated, citizens of Middle England felt obliged to take their well-being into their own hands. And who could blame them? The steps being taken by the authorities were having only limited success. Why not take all reasonable precautions? I was doing the same thing to protect my daughter. And it did not sound as if wearing my Emergency Team outfit was particularly helpful after all. I stopped, took it off and stuck it in my pannier bag.

Encountering two more roadblocks during the next hour, I decided it was counter-productive to confront the people manning them. At each one, I simply got out my map and plotted a different route. There were more pedestrians about by that time, mainly alone, but some in groups of two or three. They too seemed to be walking with purpose, heading both north and south, presumably having been stranded by the transport ban and now trying to get home. Most wore crude facemasks, and all avoided coming into close proximity to anyone else. I could also see black smoke rising in the distance at two well-separated places and wondered whether the fire brigade had been unable to reach house fires. But they were a long way distant, and I heard no sirens of fire engines.

By mid-day, I had travelled only 18 miles north and was very frustrated. Julie's twelve o'clock call did not help my temper. When I asked her how far they had got, she said, 'Not far. We've only just come through Bishop's Tachbrook onto the B4011. The strap on Louise's sandal has broken, and she's got a blister.'

I saw red. Unbelievable! They wear trainers all the bloody time! Why is that silly cow Louise wearing stupid bloody sandals? She knows she may have to walk miles! These are university students for God sake! One assumes they have a modicum of common sense. But I was careful not to take my frustration out on Julie, so I did not verbalise my thoughts. Julie sounded down, so I told her to keep her chin up and stick to the planned route.

To my dismay by late afternoon, having been forced into making further detours by three more roadblocks, I had only reached Banbury, which to my surprise had unimpeded access.

Stopping only to fill my water bottle at the drinking fountain in the town centre, I cycled on.

I saw the Tesco lorry as I crested the brow of the hill; it was stationary in the valley about a mile ahead. A Ford Transit van was blocking the road just past a sharp bend, and two other Transits were parked behind it. It had been the perfect spot for the ambush. Five men were unloading boxes from the lorry and hurriedly putting them into the three white Transits. I then realised that two men, presumably the Tesco drivers, were holding their hands in the air because a sixth man was pointing a shotgun at them. I crouched close to the hedge and watched. They seemed to have almost finished unloading the lorry when one of the lorry drivers dived at the armed man. There was a brief struggle, the gun went off, and the lorry driver slumped to the ground. The armed man then clubbed the other driver and jumped into one of the Transits, which then sped towards me.

I promptly dived into the ditch, praying that the gang had not spotted me. I must have been in shock because I could not stop trembling. Apart from the odd scuffle in the playground and the encounter with that Neanderthal Dwayne Watkins, I had never before witnessed violence in adult life.

Waiting until I could no longer hear their engines, I re-mounted and freewheeled down to the lorry. One driver was unconscious and bleeding badly from a head injury. To my surprise, the other man wore an army uniform and was clearly dead from a massive chest wound. He was fair-haired, and his blood was spattered all over his face; he looked about nineteen; Julie's age.

After I phoned 999, I tried to make the injured man comfortable. I had some difficulty stating my location precisely and had to keep consulting the map. It seemed an age before the police arrived and another thirty minutes before an ambulance got there. The driver did not regain consciousness before the ambulance took him away. The two policemen took details from me and were particularly interested in my mention of the white Transit vans. But they had flashed past me so quickly that I could furnish no other details.

'That's the third time in two weeks in this area,' one of the policemen said.

'Big money's being made on the Black Market for food. These bastards stop at nothing. Food lorries were given soldiers to ride shotgun about a week ago. Instructions to shoot first and ask questions later. It's cost that poor little sod his life.'

I suddenly noticed that both policemen were wearing pistols.

'Hope you catch them,' I commented, 'Well, I need to get on. Nearly six o'clock. This has delayed me for over an hour.'

'Where you heading?' the second policemen asked.

I told them about Julie.

'Be careful. It's starting to get ugly in the towns.'

As I cycled away from the police, I remember hoping that Julie would be well clear of Warwick by now. I estimated that with any luck, I would probably be only about fifteen miles from them.

But on the scheduled phone call at six o'clock, my world stopped when a frightened Julie said quietly, 'Dad, I've got a sore throat.'

Chapter 22. Rendezvous

20th May

I do not remember cycling those last miles. My mind was numb. Please, God, don't let it be ... Please! Why had I not collected her that first night? Why, why, why? Just because of heavy traffic. Rose had been right; we could have brought Julie home, locked the door, sealed the windows, and rode out the epidemic. God! Rose will never forgive me ...

I seemed to be flying along approaching Gaydon, my heart pounding with the effort. They could not be far now. Then I saw that Gaydon had a roadblock and came skidding to a halt. Shit! If I detour now, I may miss them.

Panting for breath, I forced myself to calm down and think clearly. When I had regained my breath, I rang Julie again to find out precisely where they were. She said they had reached a village called Morton Morrell. I looked at my map. I could see where Morton Morrell was and realised that I would need to backtrack and pick up the road to Kineton. I told her to stay where they were and that I would soon be with them. The problem was the scale of the map did not show smaller side lanes, so I could not tell whether there were any shortcuts. But I turned and rapidly cycled back to the junction that would take me to Kineton.

It took me nearly an hour to find them sitting at the side of the road just to the north of the hamlet of Morton Morrell. Julie was sitting alone and the other three girls about 20 yards away. They all wore basic facemasks.

Julie burst into tears when she saw me, and we hugged close and tight for what seemed like minutes. I could feel the sobs racking her body and knew I had to be strong for her; I did not want her to see me crying.

'It's so good to see you,' I mumbled, 'How are you feeling?' I was dreading her answer.

'My throat feels worse, and I got an awful headache. I'm scared.'

Her body shook as she sobbed hysterically. I fought back my own tears.

'Come on now love, cheer up. You've probably just got a dose of normal flu. There's plenty of it about,' I lied.

'But what if it's not? What if it's this awful Brazilian Flu that Trish died of?' I struggled for an answer.

'Now, now. Let's try looking on the bright side, shall we? Have you taken anything?'

'I took some aspirin before we left and felt better for a while, now it's got worse again.' I felt her forehead with the back of my fingers; her temperature definitely seemed up.

'How are your friends feeling?'

'Rach said she's started to feel a bit fluified. Claire seems OK, and Louise is just a moaner. I told them to keep clear of me just in case I've got it.'

That was typical of Julie. I walked over to them.

'Hi, girls. How're we feeling?' I tried to sound bright.

They all mumbled their greetings through the masks.

'Really glad to see you, Mr Morris,' Rachel said, managing a smile despite the mask.

'Well, there are still a few hours of daylight left, so if you feel up to it, we can start to make our way home.' It sounded totally inept but was the only positive thing I could think of saying.

'I don't think I can walk any further with this blister,' said Louise.

'Wrap something around it or burst it.'

'But it hurts!'

I knew Louise would bring out the worst in me, 'Well, you stay here while the rest of us head home.' She looked shocked.

Rachel and Claire stood up.

'How's Jules feeling?' Claire whispered.

'Not great, but she'll make it.'

The four of us started walking back the way I had come leaving Louise sitting on the grassy bank. After a few minutes, Rachel glanced back.

'Come on, Lou. We're not hanging about for you,' she called.

'Just keep walking,' I said, 'She'll come.'

And when Louise realised I was not kidding, she did. But she resolutely limped along about 30 yards behind us.

We phoned Rosie to tell we had at last linked up; she was, of course, delighted and chatted aimlessly to Julie. To my relief, Julie did not mention feeling unwell, and eventually, they hung up.

'I thought best not to mention it yet, she'll only start to worry. Let's just get home,' she said. But home was a long way away.

As I pushed my bike along, Julie walked beside me, and we talked family talk as if we had not a care in the world. I told her about Rosie and Nick and my eventful day, and she seemed to brighten up. At my bidding, Rachel and Claire walked about 20 yards ahead of us.

I was pleased to learn that Rachel's father was planning to meet her as she neared London although so far, he had been unable to break through the London Cordon. I thanked my lucky stars for Amanda Jarvis and wondered how she and David were faring. By nine o'clock that evening, we were all feeling tired, so I began looking for a place to sleep. We eventually found a hedge that gave us cover from the road, and we shared out food and drink. It was a warm night, and under other circumstances sleeping under the stars may have been a pleasant experience.

As we lay there, I tried to plan for the following day. I estimated we only had enough food and drink for about a day. If Banbury to London was about 70 miles, and if we were forced to walk the whole way, it would take us about four days. But my chief anxiety was Julie. Did she have regular flu or Brazilian? I had seen enough cases in their early stages to know that one simply could not distinguish between the two until about day five. But when exactly had she have been infected?

How long was she with Trish? Julie and I lay close together, and at my insistence, she had the blanket covering her. The other girls lay about 20 yards away, and as they whispered, I gained the distinct impression I had been removed from Louise's Christmas Card list. But after the emotional tension and physical demands of what had seemed a very long day, I fell asleep.

I was woken by Julie, gently shaking my arm. It was five in the morning, and I was amazed I had slept so long.

'Hullo, love. How are you feeling?' I asked.

'Awful. Can we get moving? I think I need a doctor. Rach is feeling worse too.' Another bad day had started.

We headed towards London, making about 3 miles an hour. Before we left, I had relented a little with Louise and inspected her foot, which was indeed severely blistered. But when I again spotted her stupid bloody sandals, my compassion faded, and I brusquely told her to wrap her handkerchief around it.

It was about nine-thirty when we approached Banbury from the north, and I could see that today there was some sort of roadblock. But it seemed to be an official one, not one manned by vigilantes. It was manned by people wearing bio-protection suits. And about 10 yards behind them, also in protective clothing, a couple of armed soldiers stood leaning against the wall, chatting.

On reflection, it is ironic that I experienced a feeling of relief that at last, we would be able to get some medical care for Julie and Rachel before moving on.

There was nobody on the road ahead of us, and as we neared the checkpoint, one of the people manning it pointed a body temperature scanner at each of us. Although I realised what it was, I had not seen these being used in London.

The man held his hand up. 'Stop.'

He moved in closer with his scanner, first to Julie then to Rachel. He then put an electronic thermometer in their ears. He studied it for a moment before taking out a card from which he started to read.

'You are registering a body temperature of 100 degrees, therefore under the powers delegated to me for the duration of the present emergency, I am hereby sending you to an Isolation Centre.'

I was taken aback. 'What! I'm an Emergency Team member. You don't have any such powers.'

'Emergency Power Directive 14 issued two days ago, expressly restricts unauthorised travel by any infected person or person showing a temperature of over 98.6 degrees. Both of these women must, therefore, be detained.'

'You don't know that they've got the disease! Detained where? And for how long?' I asked sharply.

'Until it is established beyond doubt that they are not carrying Brazilian Flu, in other words for 5 days at Selworth Isolation Centre.'

'To hell with that. Come on girls, we'll find another way around Banbury…'

'Hold it,' called one of the soldiers, 'Stay where you are, mate. Like the man says, the ladies have to go to Selworth.

Don’t let’s have any arguments about it. They don’t have a choice. Government Orders. Right?’

Images of Chase Farm Hospital flashed into my mind.

Chapter 23. Selworth Isolation Centre

21st May

We waited hours for transport, and during that time I advised Claire and Louise to push on as quickly as they could. They both looked apprehensive.

'But aren't you coming with us? They're not detaining you,' Louise pleaded.

Did she really think I'd desert my daughter to walk her home!

'I'm going to the Emergency Centre with Julie and Rachel,' I said, patiently.

Both girls tried phoning their parents but had no joy. I suggested they join any other travellers heading south. Within the hour they teamed up with a family of three who seemed glad of their company. Undoubtedly there was still safety in numbers for some aspects of travel.

There were tearful goodbyes, but they eventually walked away. I felt mildly guilty that I could not accompany them and was genuinely anxious about their safety. The last two days had left me in no doubt that the fabric of our society was undergoing profound change. It was no longer wise or safe for two nineteen-year-old women to be walking English roads unescorted.

When the transport finally arrived, Julie and Rachel were ushered aboard, and I tried to follow them.

'Whoa, whoa. Where do you think you're going, matey?' A young soldier stepped in front of me, blocking my way.

'I'm accompanying my daughter to wherever she's going.'

'Not on this truck you're not.'

'Why not? There's plenty of room.' Only four other people were sitting in the Transit van.

'But there won't be by the time it gets to Selworth. This has been picking up people from around Banbury. It's got a lot of stops to make yet.'

'Well, it can take me as far as it can. I'll get out when they need the seat.'

'No. Doesn't say anything in our orders about giving family members a free lift. Infected people only.'

'That's ridiculous. I want to stay with my daughter.'

'Wouldn't mind staying with her myself.'

Although I could not see his face through the mask, I knew he was leering.

'Where's your commanding officer?' I asked sharply.

He stiffened, 'Not within ten miles of here, mate. Now just what d'you think you're going to threaten me with?' He prodded my chest with the muzzle of his rifle. The health officials standing nearby stayed uncomfortably silent. Julie was on the edge of tears.

'So where is this bloody Selworth place?' I snapped at him.

We glared at each other.

'Do you know, my mind goes completely blank when people disrespect the uniform,' he said, enjoying his moment of power.

Suddenly another voice spoke up. 'It's about 10 miles, over towards Buckingham. It's well signposted. You won't miss it. What's your problem, Taylor?'

The awkward bastard rounded to face a corporal who had just appeared.

'You prick, what d'you tell him that for!'

'Because I've got kids. I know how I'd feel if I thought they had this disease! Right. Now get back over there and help Metcalf load that Landrover. Now!' The last word was shouted very loudly, startling everyone nearby.

'These civilian tossers need to be taught a lesson,' Taylor muttered as he slunk off to his task.

An immense feeling of relief swept over me.

'Thanks,' I said to my saviour, 'That was about to get heavy.'

'Yes, well, I'd get on my way if I was you before he decides to play up again,' the corporal said quietly. 'He's been right stroppy the last few days. Crazy talk, the world coming to an end, all sorts of crap. Must be stress. I'd report him, but we need everyone we can get. But we can't let you on the transport, chum. If we took you, everyone's family would want a lift. Sorry.'

'Not your fault.' I turned to Julie, 'I'll make my way there on the bike, love. I'll see you when I get there. Text me to let me know exactly where you are. And don't worry, everything will be alright.'

We hugged. 'Please hurry, Dad.' The van pulled away.

The corporal said, 'I doubt they'll let you into Selworth. It's an isolation camp. They check everyone in and out. Anyway, rather you than me!'

'Well, I'll worry about that once I'm there. I don't have much choice. Thanks again for your help, corporal.'

The Banbury to Buckingham road was almost deserted except for an occasional food lorry. It was a warm summer morning, and the fields had that beautiful sheen on them. I wondered what plans were being made for the harvest. It seemed inconceivable that a foul disease was disrupting this beautiful English summer. It also became evident as I cycled towards Buckingham, that I was getting closer to one of the columns of smoke I had noticed yesterday. And by now, I had an awful feeling that I knew what was producing it.

The soldier had been right. Selworth Isolation Centre was well signposted with those unmistakeable stencilled signs beloved by the military. It had obviously been a small airfield until recently. A windsock hung limply in one corner of the field, and a few light aircraft stood forlornly outside wooden buildings. But the airfield had been transformed by dozens of large army-issue camouflaged tents pitched over a wide area, and I could see people in bio-protection suits moving between them. Apart from having an eight-foot-high chain-link fence around it, the site had no additional signs of security. While still about 200 yards away, I dismounted and watched the procedure at the entrance gate, which appeared to be manned by soldiers in full bio gear. About 20 or 30 people stood patiently outside the entrance gate. All wore facemasks of some sort, and they did not stand close enough to speak to each other. They silently huddled into their makeshift protective clothing.

I knew instinctively that they were relatives or friends of detainees. Various sorts of vehicles were entering or leaving every few minutes. Surely they could not all be carrying people who were running high temperatures.

Suddenly my mobile rang. It was Rose, sounding bright and cheerful.

'Hi love, how far have you got today?'

I had been dreading that moment and wondered if I should delay telling her. But she had to know sooner or later. When I finished, there was a silence at the other end, then a quiet, "Oh, God, no," and I could hear her crying.

'Oh, Gerry, why didn't you pick her up that first night. Why the hell did I allow you to turn back? God, what idiots we were,' all of it rendered through intense sobbing.

'Steady love. We don't know for sure she's got it yet. She just running a temperature …'

'Of course she's got it," was almost screamed down the phone, 'Haven't you understood anything. The whole fucking world's going down with it. People are dying in millions! It's the only subject on TV or radio… A catastrophe for humanity. Our politicians are just not telling us the truth!'

The vehemence of her rebuttal both shocked and silenced me. Eventually Rose said, 'Put Julie on. I want to speak to her.'

'She's been taken to an isolation centre. I've just arrived there. I'll let you know as soon …' but the line went dead.

Rose had rung off, leaving me feeling like a totally inadequate arsehole. Her reaction was a combination of fear, frustration at her immobility, and an unspoken sense of inevitability that pervaded our thinking. I knew that. But the undertone of her despair at my inability to recover Julie was plain and sat corrosively in my mind. I also knew that despite my efforts in overcoming the various obstacles, I was failing them both. I must have sat on that grass verge for about half an hour, and for the first few minutes cried with sheer frustration.

When eventually I recovered, I knew what I must do. Putting on the Emergency Team Suit Amanda had given me I mounted my bicycle and peddled down to the main gate of the Isolation Centre. When one of the guards approached, I said, with some trepidation,

'New Emergency Staff reporting for duty. Who do I report to?'

To my relief, he simply waved me through,

'Dr Cairns. Over in that hut.' I kept peddling.

The walls of the hut were covered in pictures of people standing beside small aircraft and posters advertising flying lessons or insurance. A woman in bio-protection gear sat tapping away at a computer keyboard. She turned as I entered.

'Can I help you?'

'Looking for Dr Cairns.'

'He's just doing his rounds. Be about half an hour if you want to wait.'

'Thanks.' I slumped into an old but very comfortable armchair.

'Looks busy here.'

'Sure is! Where have you been sent from?'

'Oh, Norwood, South London.'

'Is it bad there?'

'Difficult to compare. Everything seems unprecedented.'

'Yup, that's part of the problem. Nobody ever planned for this. And why would they.'

'You a medic normally?'

'Administrator at the John Radcliffe Hospital in Oxford. Got the fascinating job of recording the details of everyone who comes into the camp,' she sighed.

'You a volunteer?'

'Sort of. They were looking for nurses to help and not surprisingly few wanted to. My son was brought here, so I volunteered.'

Her candour had a mind jolting pragmatism about it.

'Sorry to hear that,' I mumbled.

'So was I, 'she said, 'Worried sick or not, I can still type names into a computer.'

After a while, I asked her, 'How long has the camp been open?'

'They started setting it up about a month ago. I've been here for three weeks.'

'How many patients have been treated?'

'Well…' she sighed, 'Not sure I'd call it 'treatment' per se. We just try to make those infected comfortable during their last days. Well over two thousand people have passed through here. We've only had three show any sign of recovery. We sent those to the Radcliffe.'

I looked at her, unable to ask the obvious question.

She looked back at me, sensing my dilemma. 'No, unfortunately, Gordon wasn't one of them. He passed away last week.'

I sat numb for about ten minutes, reflecting on what the woman had told me. Amanda Jarvis's estimate made days-ago seemed to be holding up. Only about one in about a thousand was recovering from the disease. God. Please spare Julie!

Dr Cairns turned out to be equally pragmatic. He asked me into his tiny office and immediately asked, 'What healthcare experience do you have?'

'None, except for the few weeks I spent on the Emergency Team in Norwood. I did visit suspect cases with a doctor, but I'm not pretending to be a medical person. I'll do whatever you want me to do to help out.'

He stared at me for some time.

'Well, God knows we need all the help we can get. We've got very few volunteers. Why are you here?'

I decided to level with him and told him about Julie.

'I see,' he said, 'We don't let relatives in … for obvious reasons.'

'But as I've said, I have had experience dealing with infected people … and the doctor I worked with complimented me on my bedside manner. I'm sure I can make myself useful, and as you said, you need all the help you can get.'

He was silent for a while, before saying, 'If I do let you stay, it's on the strict understanding that you do whatever we need you to do. I cannot allow you to simply nurse your daughter. And we have no room for passengers. Is that understood?'

'Completely, and thanks.'

'OK, let's give it a try and see how things work out for a couple of days. Then we'll review the situation. Agreed?'

'Agreed.'

There was a pause; he was looking through some papers on his table, when without looking up, he said, 'Are you squeamish?'

'Don't think so. But perhaps I've never been tested.'

‘Hmm. What do you think about euthanasia?’

That took the wind out of my sails. I tried to be careful with my answer.

‘Probably merciful when people get really old or incapacitated. I’ve never fancied existing as a cabbage …’ Dr Cairns interrupted me.

‘We’re not talking about some cosy hypothetical moral case. I’m talking about helping the people in those tents die with dignity ... before they reach the agonising stage where their lungs are shedding their linings and disintegrating. Because that’s what we’re reduced to. Do you still want to stay?’

Chapter 24. Duty Roster

21st May – 2nd June

Cairns took me to see the nurse in charge of volunteers. After introducing us and telling her about Julie, he said, 'And make sure he gets a proper face mask and dumps that Mickey Mouse thing.'

'This was issued to my Emergency Team in London,' I said, somewhat put out.

The nurse took my mask and dropped it into a sharps bin. 'I guessed. But one of the problems with the Brazilian Flu virus is its size. It's only about 20 milli-micrometres in diameter, which makes it one of the smallest known. You need bloody effective filtration to stop that getting into your lungs. Here put this on.'

She passed me a mask which covered mouth, nose and eyes and had a tube connected to it.

'And just put this on your back,' she said, handing me a backpack.

'Now you plug this in here and switch this on. Now you have proper filtration to breathe through.' Initially, I found breathing through it a strain; it took a few minutes to get used to.

The nurse then gave me a succinct but unforgettable description of Selworth Isolation Camp.

'It's laid out in Rows. The army insists on calling them Lines, but nobody else does. The earliest intake was put in Row A. That's ten tents with twenty beds to a tent. Two hundred patients. That took three days to fill. The second intake went into Row B and so on down to Row J. Ten rows. Total capacity of two thousand patients. We're now re-filling Row E ... for the third time. Ninety-two per cent of the people admitted to this camp are dead within eleven days: ninety-nine point something per cent within thirteen. We've only had three patients who survived fifteen days and showed signs of recovery. They were

taken to Oxford so that the scientists could try to replicate their antibodies.'

It was all so coldly matter of fact, stated without a hint of compassion.

'So how many people with high temperatures get brought in and turn out not to have Brazilian Flu?' I asked.

'Very few. Trouble is, although we do our best to keep the new intake separated, there's obviously a high risk of becoming infected just by being here. That's the Reception Compound on the other side of the field. We minimise contact in every way possible. It has its own staff and infrastructure. And patients are not transferred to this side until it's confirmed that they have the disease, which may take 4 or 5 days.'

The truth suddenly dawned on me. By pure chance, I had entered the camp but by the wrong gate. I wanted to be working in the Reception Compound so that I could be near Julie.

'Is there work I can be doing in the Reception Compound?'

She looked at me and shrugged, 'Probably, but you'd better be careful of Dr Cairns. If he thinks you're just looking after your daughter, he'll have you out of there in a flash.'

In the event, they gave me the job of helping to check people in at the Reception Compound. As patients got off the transport vehicles, I wrote their details onto a form; name, address, date, and time of entry, next of kin, temperature, could they have been in contact with an infected person? Etc etc. On that first day alone, I must have checked in over a hundred people.

By evening, I was anxious to find Julie, but also weary and hungry. I was taken to a tent on which there hung a sign which stated, 'Medical Staff Tent'. There I was given a bowl of soup and a sandwich. That tent had both positive pressurisation and UV lighting around the entrance area; presumably, it was hoped that the combination of these measures would give us some protection when we removed our masks to eat and drink.

When I asked if there were any hotels or pubs nearby where I could stay, one of the other helpers smiled, 'Pubs and hotels are businesses remember. All closed.'

I felt stupid to have forgotten that. He then told me there was a tented area where staff had to stay; we were not allowed off camp. The fact that nobody had mentioned that minor point before must be a measure of their desperation to get volunteers. But it sounded sensible once one thought about it. And by then, I was determined to locate Julie before phoning Rose. It was about 11pm when, after some searching, I eventually found them. Julie and Rachel lay on flimsy camp beds next to each other in the Reception Compound. Since I was wearing a full bio-protection suit and the appalling facemask, they did not at first recognise me. But when they realised who I was, both were hugely relieved to see me. Both gave big hugs, and both were in tears.

'We didn't think they'd let you in!' Julie said, crying.

'Just try to stop me. How are you both feeling?'

'Not too bad. A nurse gave us some tablets as soon as we arrived, and they took the headache and sore throat away. But apparently, we're both still running a temperature.'

'But so is everyone else in here. They can't all have Brazilian Flu, can they?' Rachel sobbed quietly.

'I shouldn't think so,' I lied.

'Rachel's dad's not managed to get through the London Cordon yet.' Julie said quietly.

'But I bet he's trying like mad. He'll be here as soon as he can, you'll see. Tell you what! I'll leave word at the gate that if a Mr Balcombe turns up, I'll go out and see him ... to let him know how you are.' I said, smiling at Rachel.

We chatted for a few minutes until I noticed one of the staff nurses kept looking our way. So I said, 'Look, now that I know where you are, I'll try to pop along to see you as often as I can. But they've got us working pretty hard here. Great that you're feeling better. OK.'

I put my fingers onto my facemask and made as if I kissed them before touching Julie's forehead.

'Night, love,' I whispered.

'Night, Daddy. Thanks for rescuing us.'

I went outside, found a quiet corner, and cried. Then I phoned Rose.

'Yes, I know where she is,' Rose answered, 'she was good enough to ring me and let me know, which is more than you did!'

She was slurring her words slightly, and I realised she had been drinking. I didn't blame her; I would have welcomed a stiff whisky.

'Well, it's not all bad. I've got a temporary job at the camp so I can be with Julie.'

'So I should hope. But how do I get there?'

I was aghast. I had deliberately withheld things to avoid alarming Rose. Obviously, she had no idea of just how dangerous travel had become. But now I was forced to tell her, and I did. When I had finished, she was silent for a minute before saying, 'Then I'll just have to think of some other way,' she said petulantly.

'Rosie, please don't try to come up here. Don't even think about it. I know you want to be near Julie, but it's just too dangerous … for a lot of different reasons…'

'Can't be that dangerous. You managed it!'

I was becoming irritated 'For God sake, listen to me! There is absolutely nothing you can do here. Besides, they won't let you in. No relatives are allowed. I only managed to con them by pretended to have medical experience. And this place is lethally contagious, just like Chase Farm Hospital was and you know how that freaked you. You couldn't get out quick enough.'

'So what am I supposed to do?' she snapped, 'Just sit here until someone rings me to tell me you're both dead?'

'Let's not be melodramatic. I'm doing everything I can to comfort Julie as well as working a twelve-hour shift in conditions you can't begin to imagine. Now get a grip of yourself and be patient. I will let you know of any changes in Julie's condition. But stay in the house …'

'I should hope so too. It's your fault she's in there.'

A great weariness crept over me; I knew from experience that there was no point in talking to Rose when she was in one of these moods. I rang off.

I spent twelve days at Selworth and despite all that has befallen me since I can honestly say they were the worst days of my life … so far. We slept about four hours each night, then worked long shifts until the evening when we were called for our one 'meal' of the day. This was usually just some soup, bread, potatoes, cabbage, and whatever meat the army cooks were given. Frugal, basic, and very welcome. It was at one of those evening breaks that I met someone who remains clear in my memory, an Anglican priest, Father Arthur Weaver. Father Weaver must have been in his late eighties. Physically slight and giving the appearance of frailty, his mind was as alert as any there. He wore his old clerical collar and moved quietly between the patients lying on the groundsheets. To enable him to hear people and for those who gained comfort from his presence, he wore no form of facemask, nothing at all. He must have realised it would be only a matter of time before he became infected. I spoke to him one mealtime. He told me that he had spent most of his working life at inner-city parishes and had retired from being a full-time parish priest in his early seventies. He now lived with his sister in a village a few miles away, occasionally taking services when asked by colleagues in the nearby parishes. It would have been superfluous and greatly insulting to ask Arthur Weaver what he was doing at Selworth. He was administering to the sick and needy, giving the last rites to those who wanted it and praying privately and unobtrusively for those who were not of his faith. I was tempted to ask him how any God could inflict such suffering on humanity, but I could not; I had no wish to offend this fine old man. Although I had never found solace in religion, Father Weaver's very presence was an icon of its best and most endearing quality, compassion.

As more infected cases arrived, the workload became heavier. Maybe I imagined it, but the number of people staffing the centre seemed to decrease. My right foot began to pain me with all the unaccustomed walking. On our fourth day, Rachel was transferred to the Confirmed Infected Area and Julie on our fifth. There was no trouble getting assigned to work in the Confirmed Infected Area, they were markedly short of helpers; nobody wanted to be there.

During my twelve days at Selworth, I witnessed all the phases of that loathsome disease. From the typical flu symptoms on the fourth day to the start of the coughing phase on the seventh. This was coupled by a seemingly insatiable need to drink water. And so onto that final phase; the blue-purple blotches on the skin, the violent coughing and spitting of blood and mucus as the lining of the lungs sloughed away leaving the patient terrified and in agony as their chests heaved for air. It was particularly heart wrenching watching it happening to children. I witnessed medical staff, who like me, had had to switch off their humane response systems, and gently inject those patients who were in extremis with lethal drugs to end their agony. One night, just before dawn, I was assisting one of the young nurses who had been directed to end the agony of a middle-aged woman. She had found the vein and was just about to give the injection when she stopped, and I could see through her mask that she was sobbing. She wrenched off her facemask and succumbed to the emotions that had been building for a week.

'I can't do this anymore. She reminds me so much of my mother. I just can't. All my training had been to save a life, not take it. I can't do it anymore.'

Feeling helpless, I tried to comfort her; and wary of the syringe she was holding, I took it from her. The patient was having one of the brief periods of lucidity that characterise the final stages of the disease. She looked at me, pleadingly.

'Please,' she whispered, a bubble of bloody mucus at the corner of her mouth. And so I gave her the lethal injection. Sitting holding the hand of the woman as she passed away, I felt a hand on my shoulder and turned to see Father Weaver. He gave me a look by which I knew he was neither admonishing nor condoning; he was simply understanding.

Since then, there have been many nights on which I have woken from the recurring nightmare of Selworth and laid awake, reliving it. I cannot put it from my mind. I Gerald Morris, someone who preferred to catch spiders and moths and put them out of the window rather than kill them, had helped people to die. Yes, I had put an end to suffering; but I had extinguished that unfathomable spark in a fellow human. Fate had me kill.

The time I had been dreading came as Julie entered the final phase on the eighth day. By now all the staff knew she was my daughter and made no fuss as hour by hour I sat beside her bed. When sitting next to her, I removed my facemask so that she could see me, and I could whisper comfort and give her water when she asked for it. Fully aware of the danger it posed, like Father Weaver, I chose to ignore it. Rachel was nearby, and I did my best to minister to her too. She was just as sick and frightened as my Julie.

It was on day nine when, with tears in her eyes, Julie tried to smile as she whispered her last coherent words to me, 'I'm sorry, Daddy.'

'Shush, sorry for what Sweetheart?'

'Sorry I didn't come home when Mum begged me …'

Then the hideous coughing and retching started again. A few minutes later she lapsed into unconsciousness. But being unconscious does not prevent the body from trying to expel the poisons killing it. The coughing went on, hour after hour. On the tenth day, after yet another of the ghastly coughing spasms, I realised someone was standing next to me, watching. It was Dr Cairns. He put his hand on my shoulder and nodded for me to talk with him.

To my surprise, his tone was quiet and intimate.

'I'm sure you know there's no hope now she's got to this stage. We've had no patients recover from it.' He paused and put his hand on my shoulder.

'Would you like me to help her go comfortably?' he asked quietly.

I looked back towards my beautiful daughter. The baby I saw enter the world, that infant whose pudgy hands clasped my fingers so tightly as she took her first steps. My lovely laughing four-year-old who liked to be tickled, who was scared of chickens and fascinated by snow, who was inconsolable when Monty the hamster died. Who would not allow me into her bathroom once she was ten, who whistled out of tune, who always made me laugh when I tried to reprimand her and who now had purple blotches on her skin and bloody mucus trickling from her nose and lips. I nodded. I held her hand and kissed her forehead as he injected her, so gently, and left me holding my Julie as she slipped slowly to peace.

Chapter 25. Pyre

4th – 6th June

By then, I knew the routine. Once the death was recorded, the bodies were collected as quickly as possible and transported to the cremation area. As I had suspected, cremation was being carried out at the sites from which the columns of smoke arose. There were no burials now, no plague pits, no ceremony. Cremation ensured that another carrier of infection was eliminated.

In the early morning light, I helped put Julie's body and the 87 others who had died overnight onto the trucks then climbed aboard to accompany her on her final journey. I had to be with her to ensure she was treated respectfully; such was my guilt and remorse at Rose's accusation that I should have done more.

The nearest column of smoke was about five miles from Selworth, and as we approached it, I could see that it arose from the centre of a large, wooded area. The truck turned off the road and onto a track where armed and bio-suited soldiers manned a barrier. We drove several hundred metres into the wood before it opened into a large clearing that was completely hidden from the road.

I stared in horror at this vision from Dante.

Hundreds of corpses lay piled in rows. Three JCB fork-lift trucks moved slowly around the site, and at first, I thought how incongruous they looked with their bright yellow and black paintwork. I then realised that they were feeding the corpses onto the four rows of fires. Men in silver-coloured fire-proof suits were, in turn, loading bodies onto the fork-lifts. There were piles of logs and old railway sleepers and drums of oil stacked well away from the fires. But it was the fires, crackling away and belching thick smoke that was the focus of that ghastly scene.

As I climbed out of the truck, I was hit by a wave of heat. Although it was midsummer, all the leaves on the trees surrounding the clearing were scorched.

I stayed only long enough to lay my Julie gently onto one of the rows. Then I ran … and ran. I ran down the track we had driven along, ran through the trees, ran past two trucks bringing in more bodies. I am still running from that place of nightmares.

About a quarter of an hour later, as I leaned against a tree at the side of the path having finally finished vomiting, the truck that had taken me pulled up.

'I know how you feel, mate. It shocked me when I first came here,' the driver said.

'How can you know? Did you bring your daughter here?' I muttered wiping my eyes as I climbed aboard.

'Fuck me, you didn't, did you? Christ, that's rough.'

We were silent on the drive back to Selworth. But I sat wondering how many cremation sites there were in England. And how many bodies were being fed into them every day?

I had phoned Rose every day, updating her on Julie's deteriorating condition as gently as I could. Most days, she seemed distant, and I realised that she had hit the bottle big time. When I finally plucked up enough courage to tell her ... through deep sobs ... of our daughter's death, there was an eerie keening cry followed by what must have been her dropping the phone. After that, I had no response to anything I asked. Although I tried ringing several times, each time I got the 'Number Engaged' tone. Perhaps Rosie did not realise she had left the phone off the hook, or maybe she did. Eventually, I rang Nalini and told her what had happened. She was, of course, saddened to hear about Julie, but I could detect a distracted air. When I asked if she would look in to see that Rosie was OK, Nalini was silent before saying,

'Gerry, I don't think I should. I think Anil may have it.'

I remained at Selworth for another day while Rachel clung to life. To have done otherwise would have been another betrayal of Julie. Although by then, I had given the final injections to several sufferers, I could not bring myself to help Rachel die. I had to ask another volunteer to kill her.

My bicycle was still where I had hidden it. I rode away from the site during the night. In addition to the terrible memories, I took two other things from Selworth. Half a dozen of the lethal syringes and the knowledge of how to best administer them. But Selworth will haunt me while I live.

The crow-fly distance from Selworth to Norwood I calculated to be about 80 miles, but those miles proved to be even more tortuous and frustrating than my journey from London. The fabric of British society had changed dramatically during my 12 days at Selworth. By now, virtually every hamlet, village and town had barriers. I concluded they were officially sanctioned. On approaching one small hamlet, a shot was fired over my head with no warning given. After that, I took wide detours across fields and along footpaths and bridleways rather than approach habitation.

It took me nearly two days to travel just 50 of those 80 miles. I was stopped and had my temperature taken on three occasions and held and interrogated by either the police or army on four others. But they were more concerned with people trying to get out of London than with people trying to get into it; they found no reason to detain me, especially when they learned that I had just come from Selworth Isolation Centre. Even so, as I started to see road signs for London, I decided to wear my Emergency Support Team outfit. All except my mask that is. Having spent the three days at Selworth without any facial covering nursing

Julie and Rachel, I had resigned myself that it would be only a few more days before I experienced the first symptoms.

The detours had forced me further west than I would have wished and eventually I found myself near the village of Boarstall close to the M40 motorway. As I sat resting for a while, I realised that there was little traffic using the motorway apart from the occasional food delivery vehicles, army trucks and Red Cross vans. The government measures to stop all road traffic except for officially sanctioned vehicles was undoubtedly effective as far as motorways were concerned. So I decided to chance cycling towards London on the M40 as soon as night fell. After all, there are no corners on motorways and no habitation so there could be no surprise ambushes or roadblocks: they would have been visible from miles away. And by now, I was growing increasingly anxious about Rose. Try as I might, I was unable to make any phone contact. Although I had recharged the battery before leaving Selworth, the Battery Charge indication was gradually reducing as I tried to call. I also began to wonder whether all mobile phone transmitter cells were operational.

I rested until midnight then hauled my bicycle up the embankment and warily started to pedal along the hard shoulder towards London. At some time during my travels, I had picked up a slow puncture, which forced me to stop regularly to re-inflate the front tyre. Even so, I made good time on the M40 and after a few hours passed Beaconsfield.

It was about three in the morning when I started to hear the gunfire. I stopped and listened. Even to my untrained ear, it sounded like automatic weapons fire. And hearing the odd explosion of what may have been grenades or mortars, I was convinced that there was some sort of battle taking place. It seemed to be coming from the general direction of London but was some distance away. It had started to drizzle, so I decided to shelter under a bridge to wait for daylight.

Oddly, I remember feeling hungry as I climbed into my damp sleeping bag and realised that it was the first time in my life that I had ever been hungry! In our previous lives, at the slightest hint of peckishness, one would unconsciously walk to the fridge or reach into a well-stocked fruit bowl without a thought. My God, how incredible that seems now!

I awoke from my fitful doze just after daylight and continued on my way, glad to be active if only to get the blood circulation going again. But remembering the sounds of gunfire the night before, I was cautious. As I approached 'The M25 Cordon' it became evident that this had become the front line for containing the population of London. There was an Armoured Personnel Carrier parked on the hard shoulder at the M40-M25 interchange, and a Challenger tank parked ominously in the middle of the northbound carriageway, its turret pointing towards London. A military helicopter circled overhead. About a mile further down the motorway was a chicane formed by three container lorries. To my surprise and relief, nobody took any notice of me as I cycled slowly towards them wearing my bio protection suit. But as I got beyond the container lorries that formed the chicane, I was in for a shock. I had emerged onto the site of a battle. It appeared that civilian traffic had tried to leave London recently. The shells of burned-out vehicles still smouldered and those in the vanguard were riddled with bullet holes. Some cars still had blackened corpses in them, and other bodies lay on the ground; nobody was making any attempt to clear them. Armed soldiers and police in riot gear stood in small groups talking, and I could see that in the fields on London side of the motorway, soldiers were dug into slit trenches spaced about two hundred metres apart. Dismounting, I began to walk past the wrecked vehicles and the charred occupants, hoping that nobody would notice me. But suddenly an army officer turned around and waving his revolver, ordered me to stop. He asked me where I had been and where I thought I was going. So I told him, carefully and deliberately mentioning Selworth Isolation Centre; his reactive step backwards was hardly perceptible.

'You're heading for trouble continuing down the M40,' he said.

'What's happened here?'

'Another bunch of fools tried to cross The Cordon last night. They never learn. Eighteen more unnecessary deaths. Why the hell can't they just stay put!'

'I guess they're scared, like everyone else.'

After a moment's thought, he said, apologetically, 'Look. The chopper's reporting a crowd waiting about a mile along the road, behind those burned-out trucks.'

He pointed towards London, and sure enough through the early morning mist and smoke from the vehicles, I could see trucks on the road. With some difficulty, he fumbled into the pocket of his protective suit and pulled out a handkerchief. He offered it to me.

'Use this as a flag of truce. Tell them we're under strict orders to hold The Cordon at all costs. We will shoot to kill again if necessary. Tell them not to try to rush us again … or to try creeping through after dark. We have night sights. And even if they take this barricade, I will simply order my men to drop back to our next prepared positions.'

I must have looked shocked.

'Believe me, chum, we don't want to hurt them, but these are government orders. They've been warned repeatedly on TV and radio … but perhaps they thought the government was bluffing. It's not. For God's sake, tell them to stay put until the disease burns itself out. We are British, too, for God sake. I've got relatives in London! We don’t want to kill our own people. But we will carry out orders. Containment is the only hope we have.’

I could not clearly see his face through his mask, but there were genuine remorse and pleading in his voice.

‘But whose survival?’ I asked.

‘Just tell them. Please,’ he said, waving me on, ‘Good luck.’

Chapter 26. Homeward Bound

6th June

I stood with his white handkerchief in my gloved hand, uncertain whether to walk across what was effectively no-man's land, and into the camp of the hostiles, or to go down the bank and try a safer route across the fields. There were trenches a hundred metres in front of me, and on the edge of some woods. A few heaps on the ground looked suspiciously like bodies. It was daunting. The army captain stood watching me.

'I've tried reasoning with them,' he said, almost pleading, 'but they're not listening to people in uniform anymore. They might listen to a civilian.'

I wondered how they would be able to tell I was a civilian since we were both wearing almost identical bio-protection suits, but left it unsaid. For a few moments, I stood in shock, looking at the carnage on the motorway inflicted by the forces of the State; forces directed by politicians elected by the people to serve the people. It would not be smart to walk straight into a group of furious, desperate, and bitter people who were simply trying to move their families to safety. I gave him back his handkerchief.

'Sorry. I'm trying to get home to my wife.'

He shrugged. 'Good luck anyway.'

As I manoeuvred my bike down the embankment and started walking along a footpath towards the small, wooded area, I could feel the eyes of the soldiers staring at my back. I glanced back to see the captain talking into his radio. I hoped he was ordering his men to hold their fire. And I wondered who was watching from the woods, from where I could smell the smoke from a campfire. I sincerely hoped that the bizarre apparition of a jittery man in an Emergency Team suit pushing an old bicycle along a muddy footpath did not look like someone posing a threat!

The refugees in the woods allowed me to get within about fifty metres.

'Hold it right there. There's a shotgun aimed right at your stomach.' My empty stomach turned over, and I stopped.

'Where do you think you're going?'

I could just about see a couple of figures standing in the dark shade among the trees.

'I'm trying to get home to Norwood.'

'You're trying to get *into* London?' There was disbelief in that voice.

'Christ, you must be fucking mad, mate. You got any idea what it's like there?'

I explained about Julie, and they were silent for a few minutes.

'How many men do they have left manning that roadblock?'

I thought for a moment, 'I saw about twenty.'

'What types of weapon did they have?'

I shrugged. 'I know nothing about weapons. They looked like the sort of guns soldiers normally carry.'

'That's bullshit! They used RPG's on us last night …'

'Sorry. I don't know what an RPG is …'

Silence.

'Why did they let you through?'

I told them what the captain had said.

'Bastards,' the first voice said venomously.

'They've already killed and wounded dozens of us. Why won't he let us through?'

'He said he's got his orders.' I shrugged again.

'Yeah, well he may have. But we know that some of the soldiers are deserting. We've spoken to them. They can't stomach killing our own people.'

His revelation was unsurprising.

The second voice chipped in again, 'They'll get their fucking orders when this lot's over. People will insist on a full public enquiry as to why British troops were ordered to fire on their own people. Every one of those bastard politicians will hang in the Tower for treason. I'll be happy to do it personally.'

Silence again.

Then I asked, 'Where are you people heading for?'

'Huh. Anywhere away from London!'

Silence.

'Even when you get through this, there are roadblocks in just about every village.'

'We'll take our chance. It's better than staying in London. People are dropping like flies.'

A blackbird started to sing close by, and I again wondered whether I was trapped in some Kafkaesque nightmare.

'Can I come through?'

Initially, there was some quiet talk among the figures then a few louder exchanges, before the first voice called, 'Go round wide of us. Right over by that other hedge. You might be contaminated.'

Although I sensed other people in that woodland, I have no idea how many there were. Nor do I know if their experience was typical of those trying to escape from cities. Such was their desperation.

I began to realise that during my twelve days at Selworth, I'd had minimal contact with the outside world apart from vehicles bringing in new patients. We had no TV or radio to keep us abreast of developments. We were so busy caring for the dying that we were both physically and emotionally too drained at the end of our shift to take part in idle chitchat. No, the situation had deteriorated significantly since I left Norwood. I wondered how many people in Britain were infected by then?

Having crossed The Cordon, near Fulmer, I took out my battered map to plot my route to Norwood. I decided to go via Hillingdon, Heyes, Hanwell, cross the River Thames at Richmond and across Wimbledon Common. I assumed that my journey across London to Norwood would be tedious but straightforward. In the event, I could not have been more wrong.

Right from the outskirts of London, near Uxbridge, I started to encounter barricaded roads and side streets. It seemed the police and army had been ordered only to ensure that major A-roads were kept clear for emergency and food delivery traffic. It seemed as if the residents of every road, street, crescent, avenue, and cul-de-sac had decided to barricade themselves in. It was as if someone had started a ludicrous rumour that they could stop the Brazilian Flu virus by isolating the streets where they lived. And to some extent, that was true. If minimising personal contact was government policy then logically it extended to village level, street level and even house level. The trouble was, the microscopic yet robust Brazilian Flu virus was airborne.

Much later we discovered many cases of families locking their doors and sealing up all windows and openings. Some of them probably died of suffocation without realising it.

As I manoeuvred my way across London, I saw food lorries unloading rations at the end of streets for residents to collect. This was done in haste as four or five men from the street in question stood protecting the fetchers and carriers. These guards were armed with crude weapons ranging from the occasional shotgun to garden forks, spades, pickaxe handles and whatever else came to hand: one old boy brandished an ancient cricket bat! I surmised that there had been incidents of food being stolen as it was delivered. At several points, I saw corpses had been placed outside the barricade awaiting collection. The centuries-old cry of ‘Bring out your Dead’ echoed again in London.

Clearly, London, England and the World had changed.

The palls of dense smoke rising from the commons and major parks needed no explanation. Although I was gratified to see that all the incineration areas had makeshift hoardings to hide the most gruesome scenes.

It was late on that warm June evening when – eighteen days after I had left home to fetch Julie - that wearily I climbed off my bike. I had at last reached leafy Newbury Crescent where I lived.

And the people manning the barricade refused me entry.

Chapter 27. Quarantine

7th Jun

Three men guarded the barricade. I vaguely recognised one by sight, which was surprising since they all wore the standard-issue Mickey Mouse masks over their noses and mouths, giving them a raffish appearance. But I certainly did not know his name.

I once read that during the dense London smogs of the 1950s, the government issued cheap facemasks to people who were vulnerable to respiratory ailments. When it was pointed out by medical experts that the masks offered no protection from the noxious air, Prime Minister, Harold Macmillan, said, 'I don't suppose they do. But it makes people feel better wearing them ... and it makes it look as if the government is doing something.'

Echoes

The barricade consisted of five cars parked tightly alongside each other with their boots toward the main road. They must have been pushed together since there was certainly not enough room for a driver to climb out. But there was just about enough room between the centre two cars to allow a pedestrian through. As a barricade, it was nothing like as elaborate as some I had seen and would never have withstood any serious assault. Not that it needed to; it was there to make a statement.

'What do you want?' one of the men asked suspiciously.

'I want to come through. I live in the Crescent.'

They looked at each other.

'What number?' he consulted a list.

'Fifty-seven. Name of Morris. Gerald Morris. My wife, Rose, is in the house.'

One of the men said to the others, 'That's next door to fifty-five where that Indian bloke died the other day.' Realising he must have meant Anil, I groaned.

'We don't have you on our list of current residents, Mr Morris. Where have you been?' asked the older man.

One of the others, consulted a different list, said, 'He's on the Electoral Register.'

I noticed that the third man was speaking on his mobile phone.

I sighed: I was weary and hungry and had little patience for their stupid questions.

'I went to collect my daughter from Warwick University.'

'So where is she?'

'She died on the way home,' I said quietly.

After everything I that had passed, I found it painful to have to tell these strangers. It was as if I was betraying an intimate secret. They were silent for a moment, then one of them muttered, 'Sorry to hear that. Were you with her when she died?'

'Yes, I was.'

'Did she die of Brazilian Flu?'

'Yes.'

'And when and where was that, precisely?'

'Look, what the hell has that got to do with anything! I've been travelling for two days, I'm tired, I'm hungry, I need a bath, and I just want to get home.'

The younger one said firmly, 'Quicker you answer the questions, the quicker we decide whether you can come in.'

This was too much. I was becoming totally pissed off.

'You can't keep me away from my home!'

'Government Directive 23 states that anyone who has been in contact with someone suffering from Brazilian Flu must be quarantined for at least five days. You have to have a Clearance Certificate before we let you in.'

I was dumbstruck. 'You're kidding? Quarantined where?'

'Nearest Quarantine Centre is at Crystal Palace Park.'

‘Oh, for Christ sake …’

Standing there, I could see that Government Directive 23 made sense. Once someone had been in contact with the disease, why would you want him wandering about? In fact, as I pedalled home, I had decided that I would not go into the house for some days … until I was certain I wasn’t contagious. The last thing I wanted to do was infect Rose. I had already been on the road for two days since leaving Selworth, so I had planned to spend three or four days in the garden shed in self-imposed quarantine. The confrontation had pre-empted that decision. Not that there was any point really. Brazilian Flu was already in Newbury Crescent. They had already told me Anil had died of it.

I resigned myself to more delays, ‘How many cases have there been in, The Crescent?’

They looked at each other as if unsure, then the elder one said, ‘About twenty-two.’

‘How many deaths?’

‘What’s the difference?’

I was shocked. There were only about a hundred houses in Newbury Crescent: I guessed about two hundred and fifty people.

‘My God. We’ve lost nearly ten per cent of the residents!’

They glared at me as if I had accused them of being responsible.

‘Now you know why we're careful.’

‘What about the family of the chap who died yesterday, Anil Patel? How are they?’ I asked.

The men shrugged. ‘They have to stay inside the house for five days. Those are the rules now.’

More echoes. This time The Plague of 1665.

Two other men were walking quickly down Newbury Crescent towards us. Both carried crude weapons. I suspected they had been summoned by mobile phone. It was clear to me that these five were not going to let a possible new source of infection into Newbury Crescent. And who could blame them?

I sighed. 'Look. The battery on my mobile has run out, and I've been unable to contact my wife. Would one of you at least tell her that I'm back and that I'll contact her as soon as possible from quarantine?'

'Nobody is permitted to visit other people's homes. Government Directive.'

I gave them our phone number, and they grudgingly agreed to ring it.

As I made my way to the Crystal Palace Quarantine Centre, I wondered whether I would ever see Rosie again. I *must* have picked up the disease at Selworth. The first symptoms should manifest themselves at any time. As much as I wanted to get home, reason told me that I would be putting Rose in danger. Perhaps it was best this way.

The Quarantine Centre turned out to be an office block commandeered by the authorities; it was clearly and ominously sign-posted. As with all the other emergency arrangements that had been hastily thrown together, the few people manning the Centre were doing their best in unprecedented circumstances. Who they were and where they came from, I never found out. There were three people in front of me walking down the pathway to the building, and I saw a bio-suited figure standing by the door pointing a body temperature detector at each of us as we approached. He stopped the second person, a woman who looked to be in her sixties. As I passed, I overheard him say that she was already running a temperature and that she should wait to one side and he would arrange for transport to the Dulwich Isolation Centre. She looked scared and shocked.

I remembered how I felt at Banbury and immediately recalled Selworth. Even from the outside, the quarantine building looked drab and rundown, and I hesitated before entering. What were my options? I pondered for a few moments. I was desperate for a meal a bath, and above all, somewhere to sleep. Inside the building, it felt worse. I did not like the ambience of the place one bit; there was a feeling of desperation.

The check-in procedure was the same as Selworth. A bio-suited figure asked a series of questions and typed the answers into a computer.

Name, DoB, Address,

When were you last in contact with a BF sufferer?

Are you experiencing any of the following symptoms? Etc, etc.

I was then given a tag containing all this information with a date on which I could leave, as long as I showed no symptoms. After again having my temperature taken with an ear measurement device, I was allowed in.

To be honest, having not eaten for nearly three days, I was famished and longing for something to eat. But when I asked at the desk, I was told I must wait until 'Food Distribution Time.' (Whatever happened to supper time? Why were people using this peculiar jargon?)

In fact, I lied to my interrogator. I told her that my last contact with Rachel had been four days-ago. That meant that tomorrow, all being well, I could officially be out of quarantine with the appropriate Clearance Certificate declaring me fit to enter Newbury Crescent. That suited me better. I could then go peacefully to my garden shed and indulge in some R&R until I had proved to my own satisfaction that I was clear ... or infected.

To my surprise, there seemed to be only about a hundred people at the Centre. But I soon realised that they were basically in two groups. The first consisted of children and young people who had been orphaned by the disease; the second was elderly and frail people who had been left to fend for themselves when their families or carers had either deserted them or perished. I discovered later that rather than go to an official Quarantine Centre, most adults who had lost loved ones chose to quarantine themselves in their own homes and hope for the best.

I was directed to a shower and afterwards changed into my spare clothes. These had not been washed since Selworth but did not stink as much as the ones I had been wearing. Cycling on a warm summer day is one thing; cycling on a warm summer day wearing a bio-protection suit is quite another. I had sweated like a horse, so I gave my dirtiest clothes a rinse through. That made me feel better, but only slightly. I also managed to re-charge my mobile phone. Food was my next objective.

But I was shocked when 'Food Distribution Time' came. A bio-suited figure walked around, handing each of us a chunk of bread, an apple, and a cup of weak soup. When I asked the man sitting next to me what else there would be, he gave a cynical laugh.

'Blimey, mate. Where you bin? Mars?'

'I might as well have.'

'Haven't you heard? They're having big problems with food deliveries in all the big cities. We're lucky to get this!'

'You mean delivering food to people's homes?'

'Christ. That stopped down my road weeks ago.'

'But they are still making deliveries to the end of the roads. I've seen them.'

'Maybe in some areas. But it's not regular. And anyway, when they did, the Road Committees were responsible for doling it out. So you can guess who got the lions share.'

'Surely, people complained?'

'You must be joking. Who can they complain to nowadays? Their MP?'

The five men I had encountered at the barricade to Newbury Crescent must have been the Road Committee. I wondered who had appointed them.

After the so-called 'meal', I tried again to phone Rose and to my surprise and delight she answered: she actually sounded pleased to hear me.

'They told me you were back,' she said, 'You've had a rotten time.' She sounded apologetic.

'Have you heard from, Nick?'

'Yes. He's phoned most days. They seem to be avoiding the Flu up in Lindsey's village.'

Part of my mind queried why she had answered our son's 'phone calls but not mine, but I didn't want to start anything.

'I heard about Anil.' I said.

'It's awful. Nalini's gone to pieces. I keep ringing her, just to chat.'

Since it was the first time for nearly a week I had been able to talk to a sober Rosie, I told her of my plan to stay in the garden shed for a few days … just to be sure.

'Well, you must be OK once they give you the Clearance Certificate,' she said.

Unfortunately, I was not as convinced as Rosie about how effective the quarantine system was. Anyone who lied about when they had last been in contact with the disease … as I had … was let out while still potentially contagious. It was not fool proof. Rose promised to put food and one of the patio chair mattresses in the shed before I arrived home. I hoped this marked the start of my rehabilitation.

But my stay in the Crystal Palace Quarantine Centre sticks in my mind because of one significant event. It happened to be the night they first broadcast the infamous, Kevles Indictment.

It is another of the programmes that everyone in the Group remembers watching.

Chapter 28. The Kevles Indictment

7th June

A copy of the Kevles document lays on the desk before me. It is, of course, one of the defining records of humanity: one that will be cited every time the history of our species is discussed.

In the short time the chattering classes had to debate such niceties, the 'experts' concluded that Douglas Kevles had gone mad as a result of the tragic accidental death of his family. *While of unbalanced frame of mind* is the polite British legal phrase; the less liberal-minded used more forthright expressions, criminally insane being the politest.

But I am not so sure. I believe that the chilling words in the Indictment prove conclusively that Kevles knew precisely what he was doing. They also state clearly why he did what he did. Since the document is a primary source for why The Catastrophe occurred, I will include it in my Chronicle in its entirety.

The newsreader announced that the BBC had ascertained that Kevles had arranged for the Indictment to be transmitted automatically from several computers.

It had been sent to every government, every major broadcasting organisation, every major newspaper, every major scientific journal, every university and body of higher learning. Every medical research establishment, every drug company, and every religious organisation for which Kevles could find an email address had received it. No government would have been able to hide it. He also had hundreds of personal contacts in the scientific community, and he sent it to them too. He had even set up his own web site carrying the same message. There were literally thousands of addresses to which the Indictment was sent on 5th June. It must have taken Kevles weeks to search out and set up that address list. And his message ended all speculation about how the disease the world called Brazilian Flu had spread so rapidly.

The full text of what has become known as The Kevles Indictment is shown below.

The Indictment of Homo sapiens

By the time this message is sent, I will be dead. I know my mission will have been successfully accomplished because it was so deemed. Why I was chosen to carry out what some of my species will consider the most heinous crime ever committed by one human being, I do not know, but the life force that chose me did me great honour.

Although I have no beliefs that align with any recognised religion, I am a fervent believer in the sanctity of life. By which I mean all forms of life on planet Earth: that myriad of wonder and diversity that every fibre of my being told me has been created by a supreme intelligence totally beyond the comprehension of humans at their current stage of development. But because Homo sapiens are creatures obsessed with naming, I will simply state that from all my studies I had become a devotee of Gaia, the belief that we are all part of a single living organism called, planet Earth.

As a scientist trained in the credo of producing repeatable results through careful experimentation. I submitted to the rigour of the scientific method and for the major part of my working life added to the sum-total of human knowledge via the tenets of science. My work dealt with small and sometimes primitive organisms and how man might modify them, manipulate them … or exterminate them.

But gradually I became convinced that the immense and improbable range and diversity of life on planet Earth cannot have been caused by the random collisions of atoms or of the random intermingling of a ludicrously few

chemicals. There are clearly other forces at work. At one time, I would have attributed my growing beliefs to be the same wishful thinking that is the basis of all human belief systems and of every religion: but no longer.

Suffice to say I believed that the supreme power bestowed on me the facility to reason. And sublime reason told me to act, for the sake of planet Earth.

In any case, it does not matter. What I have done has been done to protect all forms of life on planet Earth from human beings. For it is clear to me that humans are the biggest single threat to the survival of life on planet Earth. Although it has one of the largest cranial capacities compared to body weight and mass of any other creature, Homo sapiens have singularly failed to develop the intellectual capacity, respect, or morality to cherish this beautiful planet Earth.

I came to regard man as an INFESTATION; an INFESTATION that had to be expunged totally if the myriad of life forms on planet Earth is to survive. If the human species cannot be totally eradicated, it should be set back at least a thousand years in its ability to pollute and destroy so many species and habitats through a combination of selfishness, greed, or criminal indifference.

Reason and experience convinced me that man was incapable of listening to cogent argument. The breathing space required to enable planet Earth to recover can only be brought about by eliminating a significant number of humans.

Those of us who are attuned to the natural world and honour Gaia believed that if ever humans approached a point where there was the danger of them destroying planet Earth then forces will be unleashed to prevent that happening.

I am therefore not only a disciple ... but also an instrument of Gaia.

Perhaps during that thousand years breathing space Homo sapiens will find wisdom, tolerance, and the ability to recognise the sanctity of other life forms.

Gaia put me in a unique position. She had deemed that my academic training and personal interests allowed me to understand the problem: she also placed the solution in my hands.

For the record, and so that humanity will realise that the disease is unstoppable, I visited the following twenty-two cities between 25th Feb – 31st March in the sequence shown below.

Sao Paulo
Rio de Janeiro
New York
Mexico City
Los Angeles
San Francisco
Seattle
Manila
Jakarta
Sydney
Tokyo
Singapore
Bangkok
Delhi
Islamabad
Dubai
Riyadh
Cairo
Lagos

Madrid
Paris
Moscow
London

At crowded places in each city, I put on a simple worker's overall and a bio-protection mask. I then used an aerosol spray can labelled deodorant to release quantities of the Anders Nyquist *Variant A, B3 and F1 viruses into the atmosphere. Nobody once stopped me or questioned what I was doing. It was as easy as that; an appalling lesson to the human race on how it had devised such a simple way to ensure mass extermination of its own species. The fact that I did not become infected with the disease was manifestly because Gaia watched over me.*

If in future the human race again fails to recognise the need to be at harmony with the life forces governing planet Earth and finds it is causing irreparable damage to fragile ecosystems or callously destroying irreplaceable life forms to satisfy nothing but its own greed, then either another member of the human species - as foresighted and determined as myself - will be anointed by Gaia to stop it. Either that or ... Gaia will invoke other forces.

Politicians, business, scientific and religious leaders repeatedly proved themselves utterly incapable of ensuring that the correct steps were taken. Democracy proved to be a sham ... and a fundamentally dangerous sham ... that lies at the heart of the problem. Democracy, by its very nature, panders to the lowest common denominator and therefore to the basest human instincts.

Humanity MUST learn to restrict its catastrophic growth. The human population of planet Earth had tripled in my

own lifetime, clearly to the detriment of almost every other species. It had to be stopped.

I pray that in time, the remnants of the species Homo sapiens will accept that the steps I have taken were for the long term good of planet Earth and all the life forms that inhabit it.

I beseech you in the name of Gaia to love life on planet Earth in all its forms.

Douglas Kevles PhD, BSc, MIB

The whole of the text was shown on screen, and a voice read it aloud. When it had ended, I sat numb. Someone near me muttered, 'With a whimper … not a bang.'

As I watched the Special Broadcast that night, some people around me were utterly indifferent to what was said. A few sat chatting, not even bothering to watch. An air of fatalism hung over them. The older man who had told me about food shortages, simply said, 'Well, I s'pose it was bound to 'appen one day. Those barmy scientists always thought they knew everything. Stands to reason they were going to fuck it all up eventually.'

A woman sitting close to me was in tears.

'He had no right to play God. What about all the children and babies? They hadn't done anything to mess up the planet.'

Another woman tried to comfort her.

'It's no good, love. It's happened now. We just have to get through it somehow.'

'But what about my grandchildren?' she wailed, actually wailed.

None of my companions that evening questioned how, for the first time in human history, a single person had acquired the knowledge and resources to wipe out our species. And nobody asked who or what Gaia was: that came later.

During the following days, psychologists, analysts, and every other form of 'know-all' specialist were wheeled on by broadcasters to rake over the entrails of, *The Kevles Indictment*. (All by phone and Skype of course: the days of studio appearances were gone.)

The word structure of the statement and the sterility of the language; the lack of reference to any persons, the lack of compassion, the lack of mention of his family, the seeming obsession with planet Earth (an expression he used thirteen times in a statement of only 1036 words!) and his devotion to Gaia, were all raked over ad nauseam. An American analyst likened the language to that in the letters of the so-called Unabomber in the States.

Every aspect was analysed by a broadcast media obsessed with finding a reason for such insanity. It was not prepared to accept the enormity of the implication that Kevles' actions were just that. Insanity. They could not, would not accept that they were a lucid and reasoned commitment to an ideal beyond their comprehension.

That a member of any species could deliberately sacrifice the greater part of that species ... for the sake of its environment ... was inconceivable. The Darwinians would not accept the premise at all: it was directly opposed to their sacred concept of evolve and survive. Therefore his action must be aberrant: an insane aberration. What the Hell was this Gaia thing anyway? That a single member of a species could effectively decide to commit suicide and take the significant part of the species with it was utterly insane!

But such conjecture was too late ... because that is precisely what had happened.

Few people I have spoken to care about Kevles's reasons. Most feel like me: an intense and irrepressible hatred for the man who killed my family and destroyed our way of life.

Having been out of touch for nearly two weeks, I did not realise that the first and last stories on every news bulletin and Ministerial Broadcasts were the numbers now infected in the UK and the number of deaths. In retrospect, hearing of the infection rate in Newbury Crescent should have warned me. But I was unprepared for the figures announced that evening.

The newscaster stated that it was estimated that nearly half-a-million people were infected in the UK.

But that night, as I lay thinking, I was convinced that to try to retain control and lessen the likelihood of mass panic, the government were constantly understating the number of people infected. Half-a-million represented about 1% of the population. I estimated that it was about five times that figure … at least! But we shall never know.

Chapter 29. The Shed

8th Jun

Getting my Clearance Certificate the next day was a tedious process. It involved a medical examination and an intense Q&A session. Those eligible sat outside the doctor's room in the time-honoured subservience of patients in British surgeries. Some chatted about trivialities, but I was still reflecting on the chilling document revealed the previous evening. When called, I entered the room to find a young man – who surely was hardly older than my college students – looking completely haggard even through his bio-mask. He looked at my notes and asked a few preliminary questions, then frowning he said, 'It says here that you entered this Isolation Centre wearing a bio-protection suit.'

'That's correct,' I answered politely.

'Where did you get it?'

I told him that it had been given to me by Dr Amanda Jarvis.

'Only there have been several cases of Emergency Workers being attacked and their bio suits stolen.'

'It's easy enough to check. Just ring Clayton Teague. He's the Emergency Co-ordinator for the Norwood Area. He'll vouch for me.'

The young man pondered my suggestion and with a shrug satisfied himself that I had not stolen my suit. He then looked again at my notes.

'It says you were last in contact with someone infected five days ago … at Selworth.'

'That's correct.'

'That's not near Selworth Isolation Centre by any chance?'

'I was at Selworth Isolation Centre for twelve days.'

He frowned and stared at me. I told him about Julie … and Rachel.

When I had finished, he muttered his commiserations, then to my surprise asked what I had been doing before that.

'Are you a doctor?' I asked.

'Nope. Second-year med student. Doctors are an almost extinct species.'

He did not need to elaborate.

'In fact,' he said, 'tell me what you've been doing since the Flu outbreak started?'

He leaned back in his chair as if he had all the time in the world.

Over the past few weeks, I had learned that the best way to deal with this sort of interrogation was to answer as swiftly and honestly as possible. And I was becoming increasingly wary in case the 'doctor' had realised that I had lied about the date of my last contact and wanted to detain me longer. But not a bit of it!

I started by telling him about my conscription into the Emergency Medical Team and of accompanying Amanda Jarvis on her rounds of Flu Hot Spots. I then recounted the trip to Enfield and the chaos at Chase Farm Hospital. When I told him about the trip to Warwick to collect Julie and her friends that had caused me to spend the time at Selworth, he asked me to go into more detail. How many cases had I seen? How many had died? Did I get close to them? But his eyes opened very wide when I told him that I had actually removed my mask so that I could talk to Julie during her final hours. I concluded by outlining some of the difficulties of the journey home.

When I had finished, he stared at me. 'Are you taking the piss?' I was not sure what he was getting at.

'Do you really expect me to believe that you've done all that?'

I shrugged, 'I don't much care whether you believe it or not. But I know I've done it … and am still here to tell the tale.'

He continued to stare silently for a few moments; then he seemed to have a bright idea.

'May I take a blood sample?' he asked.

'Why?'

'Because if half of what you say is true, you, Mr Morris, have had more exposure of this fucking Brazilian Flu than anyone I've ever encountered … or even heard of! By rights, you should be dead!'

Which was an encouraging endorsement of all my efforts.

Reluctantly, I agreed to him taking a blood sample, and while he was getting the equipment ready, I asked, 'So are there any signs of the infection slowing down?'

'Nope. In fact, some of the medics at St. George's think that there's more than one strain out there.'

'Isn't that what that Kevles bloke said in his statement on TV last night?'

The young medic sneered, 'I reckon that bloke was either some crank who managed to fool the broadcasters or it's some weird story dreamed up by the PR people in Whitehall to cover their backs.'

'I suspect Kevles exists,' I said. Oddly, I felt reluctant to tell him why I thought that.

'Doesn't really matter now. The damage is done, but the guys from the research labs seem convinced that there's more than one strain. Hold still.'

'Kevles mentioned releasing more than one strain?'

'Could be. Anyway, people seem to forget; simple bacteria can evolve as much in a day as humans can in a thousand years. And viruses mutate even faster.'

'A comforting thought …'

'Just clench your hand a few times.'

I suddenly remembered my ladder accident, causing the broken bones, the subsequent infection and medication I had taken to control it: I mentioned it to the young medic.

That did it! He asked for chapter and verse about my accident, about the treatment, the aftermath infection, and the cocktail of anti-inflammatory and infection depressant drugs I had taken. He made notes all the time.

'Mr Morris, I think your experience may be very important. So I'm going to pass my notes up the line. We have been asked to identify anyone who has had prolonged exposure, and if half of what you claim to have done is true, you sure hold a full house on that score! I think they'll send someone to follow up.'

He then switched tack completely by asking a lot of questions about The London Cordon and conditions in the countryside beyond it. When I asked if he had relatives living there, he said he had not but had become convinced that life in London would soon become untenable – which, at the time, I regarded as a strange phrase. He told me, confidentially, that he was thinking of trying to leave London with his young family.

I felt obliged to tell him about the massacre at the M40/M25 junction.

He did not believe me. 'I never saw any reports on TV,' he said suspiciously.

I shrugged. 'Well, I guess the Government's censoring news reports pretty thoroughly. This stuff is dynamite.'

He was shocked; I think my traveller's tale made him review his plans. I have often wondered whether he made it out of London.

Nobody ever came to follow up on the case notes he took.

Only two of the guards who had barred my entry to Newbury Crescent were on duty when I returned the following afternoon.

But a woman with whom I was on nodding terms, Mrs Keep, accompanied them.

They studied my Clearance Certificate with an air of suspicion - which made me suspect it was the first one they had seen – before grudgingly allowing me to wheel my bicycle through the gap between the cars.

As I walked towards number 57, it seemed as if I had been away for months. When I left, I thought we would be back home after two days: at most. My God, how naive we all were! I subsequently calculated that on my mission to save our daughter, I had been away from home eighteen days.

Rose was as good as her word. She had placed a lounger mattress, blankets, food, drink, and a portable radio in the shed. Since there was an electricity point in there, I would be able to cook hot food for myself. And the fact that Rose was concerned for my welfare was comforting.

I proceeded to empty the shed (which was only 8'x5' feet) of its usual clutter to give myself room. Two lawnmowers, a lawn scarifier, a barbecue stove, assorted garden furniture, a step ladder, garden tools, a pressure washer, two children's bikes, an old roof rack and two car tyres were all unceremoniously dumped behind the shed.

When Rosie saw me, she opened the back door of the house and started to come out, but I waved her back; quickly, I rang her on my mobile.

'No, love. Stay inside, please. As we agreed …'

'I just want a hug,' she said plaintively.

'I know. So do I. But let's leave it for a few more days. We don't want you catching it.'

She was quiet for a moment, then said, 'I'm sorry I lost it when Julie died,' and she burst into tears.

'You couldn't help yourself. It was natural …'

I could hardly distinguish what she was saying through the rending sobs.

'It must have been ghastly for you,' she managed to say at last.

'Yes, it was ... ghastly. But I'm glad I was with her. Rachel died too.'

'Oh, God, Gerry. Where is this going to end? Did you see the thing about Foster's mate, Kevles last night? My God, that bastard was fucking insane!'

'Yup. But with people restricting their contacts so much now, I would guess the number infected is levelling off.'

'But they said over half-a-million!'

I said nothing of my own thoughts about the real numbers: I let Rosie get it all off her chest. Eventually, when she was calmer, she said quietly, 'Nalini thinks she's caught it. She says she got an awful sore throat and headache. They only collected Anil's body yesterday. It had been lying in the house for four days. Gerry, it's horrible. It's like a dreadful nightmare. I keep praying I'll wake up.'

To be on the safe side, I had decided to stay in the shed for three days. To my delight and relief, Nick rang me. He was, of course, devastated about Julie – they had been close – and pressed me for more detail of Selworth. I gave him the sanitised version I had given Rose. There was no point in inflicting my nightmares on them.

Nick told me that things were relatively quiet in Lancashire. There had only been two cases in nearly six hundred people; that was the most encouraging piece of news I had heard for weeks. I concluded that if communities isolated themselves effectively, they had a chance of escaping the disease. And the virus had to burn itself out sometime as it ran out of human hosts.

The second time he rang … a few days later … he sounded less positive.

Apparently, the disease had ravaged a neighbouring village, and a couple who believed they had become infected sent their twelve-year-old son to stay with their in-laws in Nick's village. Knowing that if he tried to enter via the road, he would be stopped at the barricade, the lad had travelled across the fields at night and crept into his aunt's garden in the early hours of the morning. When the aunt discovered him, she took him into her home for shelter. That was all it needed. Nick's village now had several new cases to contend with.

From the shed, I kept in touch with Rose via my mobile and tried to keep her calm, tried to play everything down, pretended it was all blowing over, played up the good news about the village where Nick was. But Rose was no fool. She could see and hear the news bulletins just as well as I could.

Besides which, she kept ringing Nalini. And it was clear that our neighbour had contracted the disease. On Nalini's behalf, I tried ringing the Flu Help Line several times. But I only ever got an answering machine talking me through the options. The sing-songy coldness of the response was bizarre.

'If you are seeking general advice, please press one. If you, or one someone in your household, have contracted Brazilian Flu, and wish to be visited by Emergency Medical Staff, please press two. If Medical Staff have already visited you and confirmed a case of Brazilian Flu and the person infected is waiting to be transferred to an Isolation Centre, please press three.

If the patient has died, and you are waiting for the body to be collected, please press four. If you still need to speak to an operator, please press five. However, due to the unprecedented number of calls, you will be placed in a queue before your call can be answered. If you would like to leave your details on the Emergency Answerphone Service, please press six.'

Not for the first time, I felt our plight Kafkaesque!

I phoned Nalini, who was becoming frantic about baby Sherida, as her conditions worsened. By then, my experience allowed me to conjure all too graphic images of the phases Nalini was about to go through. I did not share the gory details with Rose and absolutely insisted that she did not go into Nalini's house.

It worked for three days. Then Rosie rang me during the night.

She could hear the baby crying. And in the stillness of that warm summer night, so could I. Rose started to cajole and argue, insisting that since neither she nor I had caught the disease when we had been exposed to it at the hospital, we were probably immune. I begged her not to go next door, but she said that she could not bear listening to Sherida crying. She had tried ringing Nalini but got no answer. So very, very reluctantly, and convinced that I was harbouring the disease anyway, I agreed to go into the Patel's house. I wish I hadn't.

We had always held keys to each other's houses, so entry was not a problem. I had again put on my wretched Emergency Bio Suit and mask. Torch in hand, I entered the Patel's. I called Nalini's name, but there was no reply, so I searched the rooms on the ground floor; she was not there. I called louder and heard someone upstairs coughing. With trepidation, I climbed the stairs.

Nalini was lying on the floor in the child's bedroom, and as soon as I saw her, I knew that she was eight or nine days into the infection period: purple blotches were starting to form under the skin, and there were small flecks of blood on the carpet near where her head rested. The bouts of coughing left her exhausted.

I do not think she realised who I was as she begged for water. I had to struggle with her to restrain her from drinking it too fast. Then I collected a pillow from her bedroom and made her as comfortable as I could, but she lapsed into unconsciousness again. I did not try to take her to her own bedroom; she would want to stay close to baby Sherida. After a while, she again entered one of those lucid phases that came to some during the later phase. But she was overcome with grief over the loss of her husband, anxiety over her inability to contact her two older sons – one had been working in America and the other visiting family in India when the disease broke out – and her concerns over her baby. I estimated that Nalini had three or four days to live. She certainly was beyond being able to care for Sherida.

Sherida must have been terrified as a monster in a green bio-suit and mask leaned over her: she screamed as I changed her nappy. I noticed that there were only a few left in the packet. But perhaps she recognised my voice because she gradually calmed as I fed her some formula milk. But touching the child's forehead confirmed my growing fear; she too had a temperature.

After I had rocked the baby to sleep, I went back to the shed to think things through. Yet again I had been in contact with that accursed disease: it would be another five days before I should enter my home or be near my wife.

Rose must have been watching. She rang me, 'How is she?'

I sighed, 'It doesn't look good, Rose. Nalini's at quite an advanced stage…'

'And the baby?'

'Running a temperature … unfortunately. There's nothing we can do for her, love.' There was a sob, then a silence: then Rose rang off.

I lay on my lounger, again feeling totally inadequate. God, I must ask Rose to leave a bottle of Scotch out for me!

It must have been about half-an-hour later when Sherida started to cry again. I lay listening, unsure of what to do for the best. But suddenly I realised that the bedroom light had come on in the Patel's house. Rose had gone in there … and I could no longer protect her from seeing what Julie had suffered during the final phase. And I knew that for the rest of her life she would share the nightmares.

I have often speculated about how much human compassion contributed to the spread of the disease. Like Rose and the aunt in Nick's village, most humans were incapable of standing by and watching other humans suffer without trying to comfort them.

Some in The Group have argued that compassion was one of the qualities that set man apart from beasts. Although I have not voiced the thought, I have become convinced that it played a significant part in The Catastrophe. In the long term, compassion probably proved a significant weakness in our determination to check the disease. And I suspect that compassion proved fatal for millions of people. As it did for Rosie.

As I reluctantly pulled on my bio-suit again, Rose came out of Nalini's house carrying Sherida. I sat down on my lounger and wondered what to do. There was little point in my trying to quarantine myself now. By picking up the baby, Rose had overridden my best efforts. But I decided to don the bio-suit anyway. I ran out the garden hose and sprayed the suit down the best I could. I had no idea whether it would have any effect or whether, simply by wearing the suit, I was taking the accursed virus into our home.

Rose looked startled when, dripping wet, I walked through the back door into the kitchen: Sherida started to scream again as soon as she saw me. Rose looked at me pleadingly, as if she expected me to wrench the child from her and take it back.

'I couldn't just leave her, Gerry.'

'I know, love. It's difficult.'

She was trying to pacify the baby and turned to look at me.

'Is there any point in wearing that thing anymore? You're scaring her … and you're dripping water all over the floor.'

I shrugged, 'It's protected me so far. And now you've brought, Sherida in, well it's probably a good idea. It means I can tend her. You should stay well clear of her.'

I went to pick the child up, but Rose insisted on hugging it to her.

'I couldn't just leave her, Gerry. And what shall we do about Nalini?'

'I'll try ringing again, but I don't hold out much hope for anyone coming.'

'Shall we bring her in here?'

'Absolutely not, Rose. It will do no good, believe me …'

'So what are we going to do? We can't just leave her!' I could see that Rose was frightened, angry with me for being such a Cassandra … and on the edge of hysteria.

'I won't leave her, I promise. I'll make her as comfortable as possible, and I'll pop in there when I can …'

'I'll come with you …' I was becoming exasperated.

'No, Rose, you will stay in here. I will tend her,' I said very firmly.

'But she's my friend. I can look after her!'

'No, you can't. She's beyond your help … or anyone else's.'

'You don't know that for sure …'

'I do, believe me. I do …'

'Well, at least I can feed her …'

'Rose, for God sake! Haven't you got it yet? Nobody recovers once they're infected. Nalini will be dead in three days! Absolutely guaranteed. If you want to die of this fucking disease too, then go in and sit with her!'

My shouting made the baby cry again.

Feeling defeated, I walked to the sink and started to fill the kettle with water: I was dying for a decent cup of tea. Rose was quiet for a while, fussing with Sherida.

'There's a tin of evaporated milk in the fridge,' she said, trying to placate me: she knew I disliked black tea. I went to the refrigerator and took out the can, but then hesitated.

'We might need that for the baby.' I put the tin back.

'Do you really think Sherida's got it?'

Beyond pretending, I nodded my head.

After a frugal meal that evening, at Rose's request, I again recounted my sanitised version my last days with Julie. Naturally, we both broke down at the thought of our beautiful daughter suffering that obscene affliction. When we had calmed a little, I went to pour us brandies, and to my amazement discovered all our spirits bottles were empty.

'I think I must have drunk it all while you were away,' she said semi-apologetically. I was amazed. Seven bottles stood empty.

Rose brought me up to date with what had been happening in The Crescent. She believed that several families had left London.

'What makes you say that?' I asked.

'I haven't seen them around for several days.'

'They are probably doing just what the government ordered and staying locked up until the flu burns itself out.'

'Nobody's leaving rations outside their doors.'

That sounded ominous.

Before I turned in that night, although I was exhausted, I decided to log on to the internet and google Gaia. I had occasionally come across the name in my reading. Still, perfunctory scans of the articles had indicated that they were of no interest to me: I had regarded them as the output of some 'way out' scientific minds hypothesising and veering unscientifically towards the religious. But that night when I typed the word Gaia, the search engine came back with over four-million references.

Chapter 30. Mounds in the gardens

9th Jun to mid-Oct

Nobody responded to my phone messages about Nalini. Three days after returning home, I put on my mask and ventured out to the barricade to ask one the men manning it if he knew how to get help for the sick.

He shrugged. 'Getting anything takes longer and longer. We had a very sick kiddie in number eighty last week. We called the bloody Emergency Services time after time, but nobody came. Nothing we could do to help poor little sod. They still haven't collected his body! Everything's gone to bloody pot.'

'What about food deliveries?'

He snorted, 'Good question! What about them? We haven't seen a bloody food lorry for days. People are starting to get desperate. All very well the bloody authorities saying, 'stay indoors and the disease will burn itself out'. People must eat. We've got several families saying they've got no bloody food left! And of course, the un-emptied dustbins and piles of rubbish are a bloody health hazard. You should see the size of the rats nowadays.'

I told him about Nalini and Sherida. He wrote it down in a notebook.

He sighed. 'OK, thanks for letting us know. We'll paint a sign on the gate.'

And that was the only action the Committee for Newbury Crescent took. More echoes of The Plague.

I walked back to the house, thinking about the food problem. I was convinced that the government had taken the correct … and only feasible … steps in the circumstances. The strategy had been to reduce interpersonal contact using every means possible. It had ordered all non-essential business life to close-down, stopped all public transport, stopped delivery of vehicle fuel, and banned all activities where people gathered. But that had left the problem of food. By curtailing regular retail business, they had radically altered the way food was distributed. The overall strategy was a huge gamble: it was a gamble that would only pay off if the spread of the Brazilian Flu virus could be halted quickly. And that had not happened. Governments still had to obtain and distribute food. Since over half the food consumed in the UK was grown and processed overseas, it left our government with severe logistical problems. The first was how to unload the foreign food needed to feed the population in the first instance. Supply ships were floating at anchor with crews quarantined. There had probably been enough food in warehouses of retailers to sustain the UK for a month when the outbreak started, that must now be running out since it was not being replenished.

The second problem was of how to distribute the food it did have while still minimising interpersonal contact. Deliveries to people's doorsteps made perfect sense. The only problem was that it appeared to have ceased.

I thought guiltily about the cache Rosie had squirrelled away before this disease had escalated and toyed with the idea of doing the decent thing by offering to share it out. But I decided against it … for the moment at least. Perhaps later if anyone became desperate.

Occasionally I had caught the odd waft of a sweet unpleasantly cloying smell and dreaded its implications. But by the middle of that hot June summer, the pungent odour of death and decomposition had started to assault our senses for real. If we needed one, the swarms of flies and bluebottles were a reminder of what lay in our gardens and houses. I wondered if the flies could spread the disease. The smell of death grew more obnoxious with each passing day. And I grew ever more convinced that nobody would be coming to collect Nalini's body.

After another few days, it was apparent we would have to act. I wrapped Nalini's corpse in a bedsheet and buried her in her back garden. A few days after that, I uncovered the grave and lay baby Sherida and her teddy bear next to her mother. Deeply distressed, I had chickened out of helping the child to die. Rose was distraught.

From our bedroom window, we had a fine view of London as the ground dropped away towards Streatham. We could see into about twenty back gardens, and after a few days, I noticed that several other families had followed my example and had taken the same ghastly measures. Mounds of earth started to appear under the flowering cherries, magnolias and Leylandii; next to swimming pools, patios and climbing frames, near barbeque areas, trampolines and in flowerbeds. Few were marked with crosses: religious belief seemed hollow during those bleak days. We had no option but to bury the dead. I suspected that few of the bodies were buried deeper than a few feet and it may have been that people thought … against all the evidence … that in a few weeks the disease would have burned itself out: that social norms would be re-established and life return to normal. I wondered how people in tower blocks were coping; their plight did not bear thinking about.

I stood for hours looking out over the panorama of London during those humid days and nights, speculating on our fate. Very few people were moving about. An area in the west of London lost power for several days, and I wondered if it would ever be restored: it was eventually. Then there was a big fire in the West End. Neither of those incidents was mentioned on the nightly news bulletins. One night as we lay in bed, I thought I heard gunfire not far away. I asked Rose if she'd heard it, but she mumbled something in her sleep and turned over.

The nightly news bulletins brought no comfort. The number infected continued to rise, and I no longer recognised the person purporting to speak on behalf of the government. I could not recall an MP of that name. He offered no encouraging or gung-ho statements anymore: just a series of government edicts and communiqués. One that sticks in my mind was that three looters had been shot dead by the army. Clearly … and understandably … the situation was virtually out of control. No government anywhere on the globe had faced a catastrophe on this scale.

Sometimes when we sit around the fire remembering that dreadful time, people in The Group criticise the actions the government took. Occasionally I have asked them what they would have done had they been in power. The only answers I have received have been in the form of ranting and raving; nothing coherent; no ideas that might have made any difference.

News from around the world had grown sketchier to the point where I began to wonder whether the media were simply making it up. When not showing news updates, the TV schedules were filled with a mixture of films, comedy, and pornography, presumably all designed to keep people glued to their TV's: to take their minds from the reality of what was lying in neighbouring houses.

Three days after burying Sherida, my worse fear was realised. Rose complained of a sore throat. I did everything I could to comfort her and sat with her during the whole course of the illness. Towards the end, when she begged for water, when the coughing and retching had become unbearable to watch and when the blotches had started to form and blood, and mucus trickled from her mouth, I decided to end her agony. I let her drift into a comatose state then … in tears … I kissed her forehead and gently injected her with the contents of one of the phials from Selworth.

On the 11th of July, I buried my beloved Rosie next to her favourite azalea, Sapho, and as I knelt crying by her makeshift grave, I took out my last remaining lethal phial. But, to my shame, I was too much of a coward to use it.

As I re-read the above, I know I have not done justice to my lovely and courageous Rose. Perhaps I will return to her later.

Despite all I had experienced, it came as quite a shock when, a few days after burying Rose, I awoke with a sore throat and feeling hot. I went to the bathroom, stuck a thermometer under my tongue and saw that it registered just over 101 degrees.

Just like everyone else, I immediately wondered whether I had ordinary flu … or a bad cold. But all my senses told me that, after having been exposed to that accursed virus in one way or the other for several weeks, my nine lives had run out. I knew for sure that I had full-on Brazilian-fucking-Flu.

After the initial shock, I drifted into a mental state that was curiously calm and analytical. It was as if part of me was relieved that my turn had finally come. I can honestly say that at that point, I did not feel afraid, although I did not relish the prospects of facing the latter stages alone.

I dosed myself with aspirin, made myself a cup of coffee and sat down to try to work out how to cope with the coming days. I recall making the following aide memoir.

1. Ring Nick
2. Leave letter for Nick
3. Tell Emergency Services
4. Tell Road Committee
5. Steal more Scotch from Anil's
6. Put water by settee (For some reason I visualised myself ending my days on the settee in the lounge rather than in bed!)

7. Place notebook and pen by settee (Although I knew that others would already have done the same for clinical purposes, somewhat obtusely, I wished to record how the disease affected me. I have no idea why except to wonder whether this desire was induced by the strange psychological state I had entered.)

8. Place the last syringe by the settee

9. Put out the remaining birdseed for Rose's birds

10. Put a notice on the gate saying that there is food in the house for anyone who wants it. (In fact, I later scratched that one out. I did not fancy strangers wandering in while I was in my death throes.)

11. Say adieu to Rose

I tried ringing Nick dozens of times ... and emailing ... and texting ... but although his mobile appeared to be ringing, nobody answered. Naturally, I feared that the virus had finally entered Lindsey's home. It looked as if the whole Morris family were to be eliminated by the lunatic Douglas Kevles. I hated that name with an intensity I had never before possessed. What right had Kevles to play God?

Chapter 31. Infected

The state of calm left me on the third day. I was hit by a blinding headache. My body was on fire, and I ached all over. Suddenly I was terrified … and oddly as angry as hell: anger that seemed to consume me.

I recall trying to phone the Emergency Help Line only to get that banal answering service advising me of my options. Incensed, I yelled obscenities into the handset and tried to hurl the stupid thing across the room. Unfortunately, the coiled cable brought it back sharply to hit me in the mouth and split my lip. I sobbed like a child wanting to be comforted by its mother.

Recording my symptoms in my notebook, I wondered whether this heightened psychological state was normal for Brazilian Flu? If it was, I had never observed it in any of the sufferers I'd seen. And by then I must have seen hundreds … if not thousands! I began to wonder whether I had caught one of the newly evolved strains that the young medic at the Quarantine Centre had mentioned.

Slowly the headache and other symptoms subsided, and a wave of relief swept over me. Now I was sure I had only limited time. Not having advised the Road Committee of my condition and knowing I would be confined to the house once I told them, I decided not to. Somewhat rebelliously, I decided to have a final walk around Crystal Palace Park while I was still able.

It was another hot day. Donning a cheap mask to cover my mouth and nose … more to limit people asking awkward questions than for any other reason … I walked boldly out of Newbury Crescent. Mrs Keep and the man on duty at the barricade asked no questions, nor did they try to stop me.

It was a walk Rose, and I had taken regularly during summer evenings, and I missed her being beside me. We would admire the gardens, comment on healthy shrubs or displays of annuals, and chat with people tending their borders.

Entering Crystal Palace Park and wandering through our old haunts was like embarking on a final pilgrimage. Staring at the concrete dinosaurs that Julie and Nick had played on as kids brought such potent memories, it brought tears to my eyes. No children laughed and played on the models that day. In fact, I had seen no pedestrians since leaving home: just an occasional Emergency vehicle. But I could hear heavy engines working somewhere and idly walked towards the sound. As I exited a gap in the trees, I was confronted by a high wooden fence that carried a badly stencilled sign:

KEEP OUT: BURIALS IN PROGRESS

There were no tell-tale columns of smoke this time but finding a tiny gap in the fence I peered through. Tractors and bulldozers were scrapping deep and wide trenches on the park and beside them lay piles of corpses: several hundred at least. A few bio-suited individuals monitored progress as one of the tractors turned towards the bodies and … as if they were rag dolls … began shoving them towards the mass graves. It did not have the Dantesque fiery impact of Selworth … but I remember thinking that Stanley Spencer would have done the scene justice. What was shockingly grotesque was that it was happening in a London suburb and not in some remote spot distant from public view. Clearly, there was no longer time or resources to haul the corpses out to rural locations for mass cremation. They had to be buried quickly. I wondered if these were the dead from the flats and tower blocks: the dead of families without gardens. But what would be the long-term impact of burying the virus in the soil?

I turned away, relieved that Rosie, Nalini and Sherida had their own quiet spots. Seeing that mass burial site, I decided not to advise the authorities that yet another nobody was infected with the disease. How many in authority were left to care anyway?

As my head again began to ache, I took a route home past a small parade of shops. As I approached, I was amazed to see someone emerge from one of them furtively clutching a bag and walk rapidly away.

Intrigued, I wanted to see what was going on. It was a shop I knew well; a newsagent and grocery shop run by a man in his late sixties, Arthur Sanderson. For many years they had delivered our daily newspaper. I had taught his son, Dale, at college. There were no lights on, but I could see through the window that Mr Sanderson stood behind the counter just as he always had. But unlike former times, he wore a facemask.

'Hullo, there. I didn't realise any shops had reopened.'

Sanderson looked a little abashed. 'I'd be out of business if I obeyed all these stupid new rules, Mr Morris.'

'Must be tough for businesses.'

'They don't know the half of it. I was just arranging to sell this shop. Got a good price for it too. Then this bloody Flu breaks out, and everything's gone on hold. This was my pension. I'll never get a decent price for it now.'

'I hadn't realised they'd lifted the ban on shops opening.'

'They haven't. But there's a few opened again if you know where to look. Even a couple on the High Street.'

I paused, 'Well, won't you get into trouble if someone tells the council?'

He scoffed, 'They have enough on their plate to worry too much about shop owners like me. Anyway, the local police know I'm open. They've been in a couple of times to buy cigarettes,' I could sense that he was smiling beneath his mask.

'I don't know whether I'd chance it.'

He gave a derisive laugh, 'So what will they do? Summons me?' He laughed again, 'Last time I had a summons, it took two months for the case to get in front of a magistrate! You got any plans for two-months-time?'

I smiled at his everyman logic. He had calculated the odds and was betting things would work to his advantage.

'Well, at least you appear to have avoided the disease.'

Even as I said it, I sensed I had made a mistake.

'My Margaret's gone,' his voice trembled as he said it. Mrs Sanderson had been a large jolly lady who always had a smile.

'Oh, sorry to hear that,' I paused wondering whether I was ready to share my own loss, 'Is Dale OK?'

'He was working at my brother's factory in Devon when they stopped the trains. I've told him to stay there. He'll be OK there.'

'My wife's gone too,' I said after a pause.

He did not reciprocate directly but eventually said, 'I thought you didn't look too good. It's no consolation to you or me, but a lot are dying around here.'

We stood awkwardly for a moment, two lost souls, joined briefly by shared grief. I could think of nothing comforting to say. I realised suddenly that Arthur Sanderson was the first person I had spoken to since Rosie's death, but grief was the only thing we had in common.

'I've just been up to the Park. Looks like they're turning it into a mass cemetery.'

'Yup, I can see them from my upstairs window. Tragic. But what else can they do?'

I decided to change tack and glanced around the shelves. They were nowhere near as full of goods as they used to be, but there were still tins and packets of food left. And to my surprise, sweets.

'I'm amazed you've still got anything to sell!'

'I only reopened two-days-ago. But the word's getting out.'

'Are you getting any deliveries?'

'Nope. Once it's gone, that's it. None of my suppliers are answering their phones.'

Staring at the shelves, I realised I had not tasted chocolate for months. And suddenly I fancied a Mars Bar.

'I'll take a couple of these, please.' I said, picking up two bars.

'That'll be ten pounds,'

'Pardon!'

'Ten pounds I'm afraid, Mr Morris.'

I looked at him in amazement. The retail price before the outbreak was forty pence a bar. So much for the brotherhood of grief.

'That's a bit steep, isn't it?'

'Know anywhere else you can buy them?'

He had a point. I put one bar back on the shelf.

'I'll just take the one.'

'Put your money in the bowl.'

I had not realised the significance of a bowl of greenish looking liquid standing on the counter. I thought that Sanderson was cleaning.

'I've only got a fiver,' I said, offering him a five-pound note.

'That'll do. Just dump it in there. It's a strong disinfectant.'

'Ah, wise man.'

'Once they've had a few hours in there, I hang notes on the line to dry. No bloody viruses are going to survive what's in that bowl.

As I walked home, eating the Mars Bar, I felt irritated and bemused by my own behaviour. Why had I refused to pay the asking price for two Mars Bars? I had enough money with me! In a few days, I would be beyond caring about a piece of paper with £5 stamped on it, yet I had denied myself the pleasure of additional luxury. Why? Was it merely a refusal to pay the man his exorbitant mark-up? I concluded that it was: old habits die-hard.

I wondered how many other small traders were open. Sanderson was right in a way: life had to go on. The government's big gamble had not paid off. The spread of the disease had not been halted, but people still had to live and survive the best they could. His bowl of disinfectant would probably prevent the virus from being passed on.

In retrospect, that visit to Sanderson's Newsagents marked a significant milestone for me. It was the last time I purchased anything with money.

On reaching home, the headache turned into a monster. It needed six aspirin to quell it. Catching sight of myself in the bathroom mirror, I looked like a tramp. No wonder Sanderson said I did not look too good! Since Rose died, I had lapsed into what she would have called 'despicable slovenliness', a condition she would never have tolerated. When I remembered to eat anything, it was either straight from the tin or packet because I had dirtied all our crockery. That now lay around the kitchen, attracting flies. I had not changed my clothes for days, not shaved, washed, combed my hair, or cleaned my teeth. I slept on the settee in the lounge because I could not be arsed with all the palaver of changing into pyjamas. I had lost my self-respect and did not give a damn.

Even after consuming half-a-bottle of the Scotch liberated from Anil Patel's house, I had difficulty getting to sleep that night. I had taken to reading old favourite books to lull me and had finally dozed off reading the dearest of all, 'Wind in the Willows', messing about in boats with Mole and Ratty. But at three in the morning, I was woken by the sound of police sirens close by. I lay awake and tense: Suddenly there was the definite crackle of gunfire, and this time, it was not a short sharp exchange. This was very close … possibly in the next road … and the sporadic firing lasted about ten minutes. Then there was the sound of men shouting and running past my house. I dare not switch on the light. But after what seemed a long time, I crept to the window and peered out. Everything looked normal. The quiet of night had returned to Newbury Crescent.

I ached all over, and my clothes were sodden with sweat, I opened the patio door to let in the cooler night air, but instead caught a whiff of decomposing humanity. The six aspirin had not eased my headache … perhaps the Scotch had not helped … so I took four more: there seemed little point in worrying about liver damage. By my estimate, I had only a few days left during which I would be able to fend for myself.

Just after dawn, I walked to the end of the Crescent. The men on barricade duty looked cold in the grey light.

'What was all the activity last night?'

'Looters as usual. Police chased three blokes down Kirkwall Road. Then they doubled back down here. They shot one dead. He's laying over there.' He gestured towards a figure laying spread-eagled next to a pile of rubbish. Unattended and uncared for as if he too were part of the rubbish.

'I think one of the coppers was wounded. We kept our heads down and stayed out of sight. They can keep all that.'

Our leafy, suburban, comfortable Norwood was sliding further toward chaos: and there was not a thing anyone could do about it. As we stood talking, I was suddenly overcome with a feeling of nausea and realised that I needed to return home quickly. I could sense the men watching me as I walked away. And as I walked, I started to cough. Although I made it to the house without vomiting, I lay on the settee exhausted after that first spasm of coughing and retching. Later I scribbled in my note pad.

‘Feel like shit already. God knows what I’ll feel like in a few days’ time!’

On the fifth day, the headache and nausea kicked in with a vengeance. Certain I would never leave the house again; I began to make my final arrangements.

I wrote a letter to Nicholas and placed it in an envelope on the telephone table, the place where in former times all family messages were left. I told him of the death of his Mum and that I now had flu symptoms. And, of course, I told him how much we had loved him and Julie and how proud we were of them. And I told him how much I hoped that he would have a good life. In my heart, I did not expect he would ever read it, but I wrote it anyway. A cathartic act, I suppose.

Placing the coffee table next to the settee that had become my bed, I remembered how victims dehydrated during the final phase, so I put several bottles of water within easy reach. On the table, I set my favourite picture of Rose and me… taken on a holiday in France … as well as a photo of the whole family taken on a beach in Devon when the kids were young. Besides the pictures stood Anil’s last bottle of vodka. Finally, I placed my remaining lethal syringe.

Somewhat groggily, I wandered into the garden … all the time hearing Rosie lambasting me over the state of the lawn. Picking all the best flowers, I placed them on her grave. As I was putting the final touches to the flowers, I again became nauseous and dizzy. I had to cling onto the fence to make my unsteady way back to the settee. As I sat down, I felt terribly thirsty.

Later that evening, feeling slightly less ill, I switched on the TV and found to my surprise that only the BBC was broadcasting. I could find none of the satellite channels.

Yet another strange face presented the Ministerial Broadcast, and the news was unremittingly bad. I scribbled in my notebook the number of cases in the UK: I have the notebook in front of me but can hardly recognise my own handwriting. I think it says millions infected, hundreds of thousands dead. Scribbling those figures is the last thing I remember doing. Blurred and incoherent images occasionally come unbidden none of them comforting. I remember nothing of the following days with certainty ... or clarity. But I will write down what I do recall, for the sake of completeness.

Many days must have passed because, by the time I have any firm memories, there were autumn leaves! I must have eaten, slept and boozed because I stayed alive! But I cannot in honesty give any coherent account of how the world fared. Then, one morning in early October, I found myself lying in someone's garden, freezing cold and with an empty whisky bottle by my side. Light rain was falling, and a sycamore leaf had landed on my face. I had no idea where I was.

Chapter 32. Black Hole

Mid October

Feeling weak, I crawled to a wall to pull myself to my feet; an exertion that made me nauseous and dizzy. I had to lean against it for some time trying to recover. As the dizziness cleared, I looked around, trying to make out where I was. One thing I did know; I was not in my own garden. God knows whose garden I was in, but nobody came to chase me away. Eventually, I found a garden rake and used it as a support to walk … unsteadily. Reaching the end of the road, I realised with relief I could see the mast of the Crystal Palace TV transmitter and established my bearings. In my delirious state, I had wandered at least a mile from home. More alarmingly my watch told me it was mid-October ... which meant I had been 'out of it' for over two weeks!

Every member of The Group reports having suffered similar memory loss once infected. For some, it was a total wipe-out, others retain just fragments of memories from that time. We call it the 'Black Hole'. The only difference between individuals is the length of time it lasted; some say they have no recollection of a few days; some say they lost many. In my case, I believe it lasted a few weeks: Jane is the extreme case: she says there are four or five weeks, of which she has no recall. To a greater or lesser extent, we must all have gone about the fundamental business of surviving like automata. People have suggested that we reverted to a primitive animal state. I prefer automata.

My own fragments of memory are an incoherent blur. Initially, I recall trying to settle in with old friends, Huck Fin and Big Jim. But by then, the headache and nausea were relentless and resistant to any painkillers in our bathroom cabinet. I'm sure I had left all the lights on, but I awoke in darkness. Then it was daylight, and someone was backing out of the room ... with their hand over their mouth. My throat was parched, and I ached all over: I begged him to give me water ... but he was gone. Perhaps I dreamt him.

The coughing spasms came and went, leaving me a little weaker each time. After each episode, I looked for blood in my sputum, but none came, which even at the time, I found odd.

Then nothing! How I ended up a mile away two weeks later remains a mystery.

Walking back to Newbury Crescent, I did not encounter a soul, and no vehicles passed me. Where was everyone? Had they at last taken the government seriously and were staying indoors? I was mystified. I did see bodies, though. Two were in the remains of a car that had smashed into a lamppost and caught fire. The blackened state of the car told me there was no point in inspecting it too closely; besides, it looked as if the accident had occurred days before. A cloying sweet stench pervaded the area. As I walked on, I saw a group of three dogs standing staring at me: one was a collie, one a black Labrador, the third an Alsatian; they looked well fed. Not wishing to let my thoughts dwell on that, I quickly walked on just occasionally looking back to see whether they were following. Thankfully, they lost interest; in my final glance, they were trotting towards the car wreck.

There was one other disturbing thing I recall about that journey home ... it obviously had an impact on me; the eerie quiet. Quiet enough to hear the drips of rain and the sound of the wind in the autumn trees: I don't even recall any birdsong. As someone who had lived in a city, one was accustomed to noise: noise from every conceivable source. Voices, vehicles, trains, aircraft, TV, radio, phones, home appliances: the ambient clamour was incessant. But on that walk home, only my own footsteps disturbed the silence.

There was no Road Committee to impede me entering Newbury Crescent, although the cars blocking it were still in place. As I entered my house, an unpleasant smell assailed me. Whatever was causing it would have to wait because I was ravenously hungry. But when I opened the refrigerator door, the source of the smell hit me full on. The food inside it was rotten and stinking. The fridge must have broken down. Even that did not deter me from food.

Opening a tin of sausage and beans and another of boiled potatoes, I tried to ignite the gas stove, but it would not light. That was when I discovered there was no electricity. Unconcerned at this inconvenience I opened the back door, sat on the garden bench, and ate the food straight from the tins. Only much later did I learn of the abrupt crashes. First, the gas supply followed a few days after by the end of electrical power: it had happened during my Black Hole period. They both ceased through a lack of experienced healthy people to keep them running.

My God, the things we took for granted in those golden days. What wouldn't we give for them now! I never saw mains power in London after that.

And no power meant no TV ... or radio ... and no mobile phone networks.

But my biggest shock that day came when I caught sight of myself in the hall mirror. I looked even more like a tramp; filthy, bearded and with matted hair. And I had lost two stone.

After devouring two more tins of food, I felt sated, but my starved body thought I was too greedy because, within half-an-hour, I'd vomited it all up again. But re-established in my own home, I felt safe. Slumping onto the couch, I drifted into a deep untroubled sleep.

It was a grey dawn when I woke, cold and bursting for a pee. Only then did I try to assemble my thoughts and take stock of my situation. Remembering the old camping-stove we kept in the garage, I was pleased to find it had a full canister of propane alongside it. At least I would be able to make myself a cup of tea. I had a rough shave and wash in tepid water and as I did so realised that I had been infected with Brazilian Flu, endured it ... and survived!

How? And more to the point, why had I survived? It did not make sense.

That shock realisation helped me snap myself out of my mawkish and slovenly state. I should let the medical authorities know. Urgently! I must be carrying anti-bodies that might prove helpful in the search for a vaccine. But before I went anywhere, I decided to clean up the pigsty I had made of Rosie's pride and joy of a home. And that was what I spent the morning doing. Then at lunchtime, I boiled a can of soup and ate it together with a packet of stale crisps. Old habits die hard.

The day deteriorated in the afternoon. Since I was still prone to occasional bouts of weakness, I decided to ride my bike the few miles back to the Crystal Palace Quarantine Centre reasoning it would expend less energy. It was while cycling there a couple of curious things happened. Firstly, I saw only two people; secondly, they both ran off when they spotted me. I tried calling after the second one, but he disappeared into a house slamming the door behind him. Feeling starved of news of what had transpired during my Black Hole period, and willing to re-assure anyone who would listen that I was living proof that the Brazilian Flu was survivable, I felt irritated.

My next shock was to find the Quarantine Centre completely deserted. The front door stood half open and on it was pinned a hand-written note hardly distinguishable after the ravages of rain.

This Quarantine Centre is closed.
I advise you to stay isolated from other people as long as possible.

May your God go with you ... whoever you are.

Signed: Dr J. Hafees

In retrospect, the reluctance of the few people I encountered that day is now entirely understandable. Having lived through the previous few weeks, they were far more aware than I that our cosy and comfortable existence had collapsed under the onslaught of the virus. Humanity and compassion were in their death throes. But one final thing distressed me that day: a pack of dogs running across the park. They were not chasing around for fun. The smallest of the pack was Collie sized; there were a couple of Alsatians, a Doberman, a mastiff and three or four Labradors of different shades. To my horror, I realised they were chasing a Poodle. And when they caught it ... they tore it apart.

Chapter 33. Shortwave

Those dogs unnerved me, and for some days, I was afraid to leave the house. I moped around feeling anxious and frustrated by the lack of news. But it forced me to slow down and gradually regain my strength. As I did so, I reverted to my old analytical self. Gerry Morris, the anally retentive schoolmaster, began making lists again. I made a list of what remained of the food Rose had hoarded ... and another of what else I possessed that might help me survive. In one particularly inspired moment, I remembered Nick buying a powerful airgun in his early teens. I found it in the loft with a half-full box of pellets and cleaned it up.

Occasionally during the daytime, I watched the windows of houses in The Crescent for another human face; even the twitch of a curtain would have been a comfort. But there was nothing, and no flickering lights appeared at night. On several evenings, I stood at our bedroom window with my binoculars looking out over London. Purged of car exhaust fumes and smoke from chimneys, the air was sparkling. I could clearly see the rising ground of Hampstead Heath to the north. On moonlit nights, the city stretched out as never before, but dark and brooding. Occasionally I saw flashing blue lights in the distance which I took to be emergency vehicles. Here and there the binoculars would pick out occasional faint flickering glows, a few hours bought with priceless candles, torch batteries and oil lamps; people like me, who knew that their meagre emergency supplies were dwindling.

Standing in that room looking out over our back garden, I could see Rosie's grave and every time I did, she filled my thoughts. More than once, I found myself in tears just thinking of the life we had shared, her love and her dry, chiding humour. I recalled her saying she had a bad feeling about Brazilian Flu, and I remembered ridiculing her Mother of All shopping sprees. With a heavy heart, I recalled her wrecking our car in her desperation to bring home Julie. My God, her fey gift had undoubtedly saved my life.

In analytical mode, I estimated that with care, I had enough food to last me through winter. Water should not be a problem: although no mains water came from the taps, there was plenty in the loft storage tanks in every house in the Crescent.

Peering across London depressed me. I felt that humanity had been hurled back to a medieval age where people went to bed at dusk and rose with the sun. More to the point, our species was being eliminated by an insentient organism unaware of humanity's stupendous achievements. Homo sapiens could be facing extinction! We were grappling with forces comparable with those that caused mass exterminations of species over hundreds of millions of years, forces utterly beyond man's control. Thinking such thoughts, my anger rose. For in this case the force had been deliberately unleashed by one man. If Douglas Kevles had been in that room, I would happily have killed him with my bare hands.

Surely civilisation endured somewhere! Perhaps in isolated towns: perhaps in Australia ... or America ... or Russia ... or China. The remote tribes in the Amazon were probably best placed. It was utterly frustrating not to know the current world situation.

One morning, after about a week indoors, I was listing the contents of a cupboard in my study when I came across a priceless item I had completely forgotten. A small portable radio-cum-torch with a wind-up power facility! I had purchased it in Robert Dyas for about eight pounds some years previously but forgotten it. Rose had teased me for buying it to which my rapier-like response had been, well, you never know!

Immediately I switched it on only to have it make a slight sigh before the battery discharged. I stood turning the dynamo handle furiously for some minutes before turning the radio on again. At once, a hissing sound filled the room. I literally squealed with joy. Placing it on a table, I moved the station dial slowly through its complete AM range picking up a couple of very faint signals barely distinguishable through the static. Neither broadcasts sounded as if they were in English; the strongest might have been Arabic. Impatiently I switched to FM; nothing. Alas, the little set possessed no Short-Wave capability, and I reasoned that the government would not be using any fancy DAB technology because fewer people had appropriate receivers. If any emergency transmissions were being made, they would surely be on a commonly used frequency. Placing my ear to the receiver, I tried the faint AM signals again. Yes, there was certainly something there, but the static rendered it unintelligible. I sat back and stared at the device; my feeling of elation deflated.

Then I had a thought. What if, to save power, broadcasts occurred only at specified times! My watch told me it was 11:33. Perhaps they only broadcast on the hour ... or half-hour. But if so, which frequency would they be on? Surely one of those most commonly used: Radio 4 probably. Pressing the pre-set button for Radio 4, I sat back and waited.

And sure enough on the stroke of twelve, a much stronger signal flooded in; still not the pristine clarity of old but clear enough to hear. What I was not prepared for was the Call Sign they were using: I had heard it before on recordings of wartime broadcasts. The opening to Beethoven's 5th Symphony ... Doom doom doom dooom. The voice spoke with a slight Birmingham accent.

'This is BBC broadcasting the UK Emergency Administration news bulletin for 19th of October.

The number of reported cases of Brazilian Flu has decreased regionally. Fewer cases have been reported in the south and west and marginally so in the midlands.

I wondered whether that was due to so many being dead or in their final throes ...

Urban conurbations, however, remain highly infectious, and residents of all major cities are ordered to stay indoors until the virus burns itself out completely. It is estimated that over seven hundred thousand people remain alive in London ...

Had I misheard? London was a city of over eight million people. Seven hundred thousand! A ghastly mistake, surely.

... and approximately two hundred thousand in Birmingham.

An Administration spokesman said today that the slowdown is welcome news and shows that the policy of containment is effective. But there will be no relaxing the measures currently in force. These same measures have been taken by civilised communities world-wide.

There have been no further communiqués from Tel Aviv where a nuclear weapon obliterated the heart of the city a week ago. The retaliatory strikes by the Allies on Damascus, Tehran and Islamabad have increased levels of radioactivity in the atmosphere.

In a broadcast to the American people, President-Elect Graham said the USA had repeatedly warned against any warlike actions against their ally Israel yet still the pre-emptive and unprovoked attacks had been carried out. He said that the Iranian, Syrian, and Pakistani people must blame their own leaders for the agony they are now suffering.

Citizens are reminded in the strongest terms that Martial Law remains in force. Security Forces will summarily execute anyone caught looting.

The next news bulletin will be broadcast on this frequency at the same time tomorrow. Remember to switch off your radio to conserve power.

I must have sat an hour in that chair trying to take it all in. Only seven hundred thousand people alive in London! That meant that about only one person in ten had survived: a Mortality Rate of 90%. I simply couldn't get my head around it. Nine people out of every ten had died! Those figures had hit me like a physical blow.

Was it the same in rural areas?

And what was all that about the Middle East? And who were these Allies? Didn't humanity have enough on its plate without some egomaniac starting a war! Jesus. It was unbelievable.

Except that when I lay down to sleep that night thinking things through, I concluded it was totally believable. The Islamic world had longed to eradicate Israel. Only the threat of American retaliation had prevented it. So what better time to strike than when American forces were being withdrawn from their global policing role to help combat Brazilian Flu at home. Not a strategy of Machiavellian subtlety, but effective none-the-less. I doubted it would end there. What next? What new tyrant would emerge from the ruins of human civilisation?

But to hell with all that. I turned over and snuggled under the duvet, wondering what the winter would bring.

Chapter 34. Winter

The daily news broadcast grew unremittingly depressing; I found myself switching off in disgust at the end of each bulletin. But, as mid-day approached, I was drawn to the radio, hoping for better news. None came. I wondered how those preparing it and reading it were coping; was there no good news to report? And even though the news was dire, was it even worse than they were telling us?

Over the winter months, the Mortality Rate increased relentlessly. From one in ten ... to one in twenty ... then one in fifty ... and then in mid-December, that awful announcement; only one person in every hundred that had lived in London before the outbreak was still alive; a mere eighty-thousand people; the virus had reached 99% mortality

To add to our woes, the Weather Gods had noticed that man had stopped sending all kinds of shit into the atmosphere. Humanity's demise seemed to act as a massive stimulus to the weather system comparable with a shock hitting a mechanical system or a pulse input to an electrical system; the result was a damped oscillation with weather swinging to extremes.

Whatever meteorologists were still alive must have had a field day as the weather swung unpredictably. Whether the Jet Stream had shifted, I do not know. Early November saw prolonged torrential rain then on the last day, arctic conditions descended bringing sub-zero temperatures and a snowstorm that lasted a week. When it abated, over three feet of snow lay in the garden. Since the weather had been normal since the start of the epidemic, I wondered if freezing conditions would finally kill off the virus.

Glancing at my watch one day I realised it was Christmas Eve. Rosie had taken a childlike delight in Christmas, buying, and dressing a tree and decorating our lounge. But there was nothing I wanted to celebrate that year.

I had never seen such snow as I gazed out across London; it looked magical. But of all the houses I overlooked, few had wisps of smoke rising from their chimneys. And it was bitterly cold: so much so that I spent most of my time huddled under the bedcovers like a pathetic hibernating animal. It occurred to me that the lack of proper food and the Arctic weather could act as a scourge on its own. Hypothermia was lethal to the elderly and vulnerable, and possibly the very young.

Inevitably, with no heating in the house, the water pipes froze. No matter, for the moment there was plenty of snow to melt for the little water I needed.

One night I woke and for a moment lay tense; something had disturbed me. Always a light sleeper, any unusual noise in the house can wake me. Then I heard it; it was not a noise in the house, they were deep thumps and rumbling sounds some distance away. Wrapped in the duvet, I made my way upstairs and picked up my binoculars. I was right. Across the snow-scape, intermittent flashes and the rumble of explosions seemed to be coming from the M25 cordon towards West London. I stood watching for about half an hour until finally, they subsided. What had it been? Were people still trying to break through the cordon? Even if they were, the military was unlikely to resort to artillery to stop them. No, I must be wrong. They must have been demolishing some virus-infested building or something.

But there was one aspect of humanity's death-throes that enchanted me: the crystal-clear nights. Since man-made atmospheric pollution had ceased, the air took on a gin-like clarity, both by day and by night. And it was the nights that benefited most. On cloudless and moonless nights, I swear one could have found one's way around by starlight. It was awesome. The Milky Way glowed with an intensity I had never seen. Such was the attraction that I climbed into the loft and found the telescope I had bought as a teenager. When the nights were right, I bundled myself with clothes and stood on the patio peering through my puny scope at the night sky. Stunning ... awesome ... breath-taking ... and intimidating! Why wasn't it always like this? And pollution was not the only thing missing from the skies; I had not seen an aircraft for months.

But my main concern was my diminishing food stock. Although I had reduced my intake to what I regarded as survival level, by mid-February my stash was sorely depleted. Despite the daily announcements about how many people had been executed for looting, I began considering raiding neighbouring houses. For I had seen no lights at night and no sign of movement during the day; nobody had left their homes for the snow lay virgin on the paths and pavements. I was forced to conclude that I was the only person still alive in the Crescent. And the loneliness was taking its toll. I began talking to myself. Thus, it came as a considerable shock when late one snowbound evening in February the front doorbell rang.

I was so startled I dropped the cup I was holding. I was upstairs and immediately switched off my head-torch. Creeping towards the window, and hoping I was unseen, I looked down at the front door. Yes, there were footprints in the snow on my front path.

The figure standing there was partially concealed in the porch.

The bell rang again: I was transfixed.

A voice called, 'I know you're in there. I've been watching your light.'

Shocked, I drew back even further, my mind in a whirl.

'Can you hear me?'

I could not tell whether the voice belonged to a man or a woman.

'Can you spare a little food?'

I stood hardly breathing, so startled was I at the unexpected sound of another voice.

'I need food ... for a child. Please!'

It was a woman's voice. I stood paralysed.

'Please. You must help me. I beg you. Yours is the only other house where I know someone's alive.'

'Have you had the Flu?' I called eventually.

The answer was hesitant, 'I think I must have ... but I'm all confused. The child has.'

'How old is the child?'

'About eight.'

'Is she your daughter?'

'No. I found her wandering alone weeks ago. We are starving. And I don't think either of us is contagious.'

'Where do you live?'

'Walmer Lane.'

It was a few roads away; some of its houses could be seen from our front upstairs windows; that must have been how she had seen my feeble lights.

What the hell should I do? Was it smart to be exposed again ... possibly to a mutated strain? And in truth, I hardly had food to spare. I was wracked with indecision for what seemed an age.

Eventually, I mustered, 'Go back to the end of the road. I'll put a couple of tins out ... then you can come and collect them. Be silly to risk contact.'

'God bless you!' I watched as the figure, bundled in layers of clothing, shambled away. She almost slipped on the ice but regained her balance. She must have been freezing standing there.

Collecting a few tins of the food I liked least, I opened the front door. The woman was standing thirty yards away. I could just make out the silhouette of a child beside her. I placed the tins in the middle of the road, all the time anxious that I might be attacked.

'God bless you!' she called.

I hurried inside and locked the door. Then I watched from the upstairs window as the woman hurried down to collect the tins.

I could not stop thinking of that encounter; my first human contact since God knows when; in fact, since meeting the parsimonious, Sanderson. And I had blown it. And the more I thought about it, the more ashamed I felt. She must have been desperate to take such a risk! Anything might have happened. My response had been utterly selfish. I was appalled. What if it had been Rosie forced to beg from a stranger ... or Julie? What had got into me? Had compassion and decency deserted me entirely? I decided to make amends the next day.

My outdoor thermometer showed minus seven degrees centigrade when I left home, so I had wrapped up well. An icy crust had re-formed over the snow overnight, making it lethally slippery. My progress to Walmer Lane was slow for I clung to every fence and wall knowing that to fall and break a bone in these times could be fatal. The woman said she had been watching my lights so earlier that morning from my own upstairs windows, I had identified the three houses whose windows I could see; she must live in one of them. Eventually, I reached them and knocked on the first door. In the utter silence, the noise of that rat-a-tat sounded like a thunderclap. There was no answer, so I knocked again; nothing. But as I walked up the path to the next house, the door opened slightly, and a woman's face peered out.

‘It’s me,’ I said lamely, ‘From Newbury Crescent. I’ve brought you some more food. Sorry about last night. Took me by surprise.’

She looked astonished. I held up the plastic bag holding six tins. ‘My God ... you’re our angel! I can’t thank you enough ...’

I placed the bag on the icy path and backed away.

‘No wait,’ she called, ‘don’t go. Stay and talk.’

I hesitated, wondering how close it was safe to get.

‘Do you know what’s happening?’ she asked.

I shrugged, ‘Only what the mid-day broadcasts tell me.’

‘What mid-day broadcasts? There’s no power. My television and radio won’t work!’

I felt oddly smug, ‘I’ve got one of those little wind-up radios. There’s a broadcast every day at mid-day.’

‘When will they start food deliveries again? We’re totally out. That’s why I came sponging last night.’

Uncomfortably I said, ‘I doubt there'll be any more food deliveries. I suspect that life as we knew it has ended. As far as I can make out, the whole social infrastructure has become ... well ... unravelled.’

The woman emerged into her porch-way; she wore a balaclava and was still bundled up in an assortment of clothing. And I could see she held a carving knife in one hand. She saw me staring.

‘Sorry,’ she said, ‘Can’t be too careful. It’s all I’ve got.’

‘Don’t blame you.’ A child came from the passageway to stand beside her: it too was swathed in an assortment of clothing.

The woman moved forward and picked up the bag of food. ‘Thank you, Mister ... I’m sorry, I don’t know your name,’ she said.

Uncertainly I said, ‘Morris. It’s Gerry Morris.’

‘Cassandra Metcalf. And this is Julie.’

Chapter 35. Forager

February

In retrospect, it was a defining moment. Had the woman said the girl's name was Kate ... or Gillian ... or Stephanie ... or anything else, I might have simply grunted and walked away. But to hear that the girl had the same name as my own daughter, Julie, well, it hooked me. I could not turn my back.

We stood for some moments in silence in that Arctic chill.

'So what's the latest?' she asked. And for several minutes I told her what I had learned from the broadcasts. She put her hand to her mouth when I told her the most recent mortality rate. By then only one person in about two-hundred and fifty had survived.

'At least, that's what they're admitting. But I don't know how much I believe in government statistics ... '

'Oh, my God' she whispered.

Seeing I had shocked her, I struggled to find something more upbeat to say. 'They say it isn't as bad in the rural areas ...'

'That's it, isn't it! Nobody in London is going to survive.'

'No, some will,' I tried to raise her spirits. 'All three of us seem to have survived for a start.'

'But if there're no more food handouts … we'll starve.'

'Not necessarily. There must be tons of food scattered about the place.'

'Where? People around here started fighting over the deliveries weeks-ago. Have you been down to the High Street lately? It's a shambles. Every shop has been ransacked. Not only food shops, everything's gutted.'

'You've been down there!'

'I had to. We've nothing left. Surely the government ought to be doing something by now!'

I shrugged. 'Like I said, those times are over, at least for our generation. From what they're saying on the bulletins, the strategy is still to let the disease burn itself out. That means sealing off the most densely populated areas ... the cities and towns.'

She frowned, 'You sound as if you approve.'

I shrugged, 'I can see their reasoning. If there's no cure to hand, it's the logical thing to do.'

'I thought governments were elected to protect people; not let them die.'

'This is uncharted territory. Apparently, every country is doing the same.'

'But they can't just let us die!'

'I fear it's beyond anyone's control. And my guess is it's like this worldwide.'

The pinched face that looked out of that absurd balaclava was pleading, 'So can you help ... Julie and me, Mister ... Morris?'

For reasons I could not explain, I found that contact with Cassie Metcalf disturbing. I left them standing on their doorstep with a non-committal wave. It would have been wrong for me to commit to 'helping' them long-term. So I had been my usual evasive self and muttered I would give them whatever I could spare. She had not been impressed. There seemed to be a tacit inference that as a male, I should protect them. I did not like the feeling it generated in me. But she had been right on one topic; if all the food shops had been gutted, then we would have to forage to survive. At least until the government got its act together and reclaimed the cities.

That afternoon I searched my toolbox and steeled myself to start looting my neighbour's houses. And since our next-door neighbours the Brabourns had never returned from the world-wide cruise, theirs would be first.

Despite knowing they were absent, on that first foray, I was a bag of nerves; I expected to be apprehended at any moment. I even knocked on Brabourn's front door first! Only when there was no answer did I resort to my crowbar. Food-wise that first forage was disappointing. The smell told me there was no point in opening the fridge or freezer. And Marjorie ... being a great promoter of the best and freshest ingredients ... stored few tins and packets. Nevertheless, I took them.

Alec's drinks cabinet was a different matter. It took me two trips to repatriate it entirely; although as I did, I decided not to indulge in any more benders. But that foray into Alec and Marjorie Brabourn's home marked a sea change in my life. Up until that point I had been a conforming, law-abiding, tax-paying schoolteacher who had never dreamt of stepping out of line. That afternoon, for the first time, I had stepped across that undefined line: I had robbed the house of my neighbour. I had broken the law. Despite the extraordinary circumstances prevailing, that troubled me.

Later I left two tins of the Brabourn's food outside Cassie Metcalf's house, knocked on the door and was at the end of the road before I heard the woman calling her thanks.

Next day I burgled Noel Augustus's bungalow opposite. I had now convinced myself that being discovered looting was unlikely. No vehicle tracks or footprints except my own and the woman's had disturbed the snow on any of the roads nearby; ergo, no vehicles and no police had ventured into our neighbourhood for at least four weeks.

Whereas I knew the Brabourn's house had been empty, with the Augustus's, I was more nervous about what I would find. And if there had been in any doubt in my mind, the smell of decomposing humanity that hit me as I opened the front door confirmed that there were bodies; the stench was overwhelming. So bad was it, that I decided to open the door wide and retreat to my own house for an hour simply to let the air clear. Only reluctantly did I return.

The pyjama-clad remains of Noel Augustus lay near the kitchen sink, an empty bottle beside him. Remembering the unquenchable thirst of victims in that final phase, I suspect he had been trying to fill the bottle with water. From the sight of his face, Noel had reached the haemorrhagic phase, so I concluded that somewhere in the bungalow his wife had too. But I did not bother to find the remains of Therese. My only interest was in any food I could steal ... or anything else that might be useful to the living.

That was the first residence where it looked as if the occupants had consumed almost everything edible: a few bottles of sauce were all that remained in their larder. But my forced entry was not entirely wasted; in their garage, I bagged three canisters of propane gas, which meant I could have hot meals for a while longer.

Those burglaries lay the foundations of my looting strategy: open the door, retreat home, and let the stink clear ... at least partially. But it took a while to quell the revulsion of seeing the bodies; in fact, I never have overcome it.

On one of the milder days during that period, I use the term loosely for the temperature never rose above zero, the thought struck me that if the stink of the corpses was that bad in winter, what in God's name would it be like as the temperature rose? And it was worse if a pet had died in the house; the stink of a dead cat is the most nauseous imaginable. At some time during that period, I started collecting any tins of pet food I came across. Some were surprisingly tasty when cooked for long enough.

There was another item I searched for in every house I burgled; an item that made me ransack every garage. An item that might have made a difference to my declining lifestyle; a petrol-driven power generator. I had seen such machines in DIY stores before the epidemic and occasionally toyed with the thought of buying one. But mainly because Rose deemed such a purchase unnecessary and ridiculous, I never had.

I got into the habit of leaving something outside the Metcalf house on most days. And it was while approaching late one afternoon that I realised I could hear music; the closer I got to Cassie Metcalf's house the louder it became until standing at her front door, I knew that the sound came from inside. Although I claim to know little of classical music, I recognised the piece being played; it was the Bruch violin concerto, and its haunting melancholy nearly reduced me to tears. When would I ever hear such a sound again? But gradually the sound grew quieter until finally, it faded altogether. Almost as though I had broken a spell, I knocked on Cassie's door.

She opened the door a little and peered at me through the crack.

'Oh, Mr Morris!'

'I brought a few tins,' I said, offering her a plastic bag.

'Oh, this is so good of you to do this. Julie and I would have perished but for you.'

I could see the child standing behind her in the hallway.

'Did I hear music?' I queried.

She hesitated, 'Yes ... but the battery in my player has finally run out ... so that'll have to be it for a while.'

'The Bruch, wasn't it?'

'Yes, one of my favourites.' There was just the hint of a smile.

To take the tins, she had to free up her hands, and as she did so, she placed something on the hall floor. To my astonishment, it was a violin.

'Was that you ... actually playing?' I asked incredulously.

She nodded.

'But ... I thought I heard an orchestra.'

'You did. It was a backing track ... allowed me to practise with an orchestra.'

'Wow! I'm impressed.'

'Don't be. I never made the front row. But I so wanted to play the Bruch one last time.'

Her face looked thin and pinched. It suddenly occurred to me that in former times, Cassie Metcalf was probably an attractive woman. Now her hair was lank and greasy; she looked half-starved and near collapse.

My thoughts jumbled, I said, 'Are you able to heat up food?'

'Only when I can get the lounge fire to light. But I'm running out of matches ... and it's harder to find firewood now. Thank you again, Mr Morris. Goodbye.'

And so saying, she closed the door.

Maybe it was the absence of other sounds, but the strains of the Bruch stayed with me for hours.

A few days later I found them a camping stove and a couple of canisters of propane. Cassie Metcalf twice asked me to eat with them; to share some of the food I had brought; but on each occasion, I declined. I was never sure why; I do not think it was fear of infection; more that I did not want to become involved. I felt emotionally drained by the last few months.

I was not sure what Cassie's motives were, but I did not want her to become dependent on me. Probably she only wanted adult company. At least she had the child to talk to. Whereas I only had Dog.

Chapter 36. Dog

It was waiting outside a house I had looted. Up to his ears in snow, Dog was a starving, wretched-looking mutt. Initially, I looked around anxiously, fearful that other dogs were nearby; I had not forgotten that pack tearing the poodle apart. But there was only this bedraggled mongrel. Not being a dog-lover, I had no idea what breed he was, and I doubted whether pedigree had figured in his ancestry.

It so happened that I had retrieved some tins of pet food from the house so may have been feeling benevolent. Inevitably it followed me home, struggling through snow deeper than he was. On my way, it occurred to me that having a guard dog around might be a good thing. Not that Dog in any way resembled a guard dog; it was a mongrel. But it appeared to be an intelligent mongrel.

For a start, he had been canny enough to stay out of the jaws of that ravaging pack. Smart Dog. And I was smart enough to sense that once I had given him that first tin of food, his loyalty was ensured; we would sink or swim together. At least it would be company.

One morning in early March, I was again startled when my front doorbell rang. Cassie Metcalf and Julie stood there. It had begun to thaw; not a rapid thaw as was usual but gradually, the temperature only a few degrees above freezing.

Without preamble, she said, 'My pipes are leaking. Can you help us?'

'Sorry, I know nothing about plumbing.'

'What am I going to do? You're the only man around! At least have a look. Please. It's dripping through the bedroom ceiling.'

This was just the sort of situation I wanted to avoid, but I bottled out. Grudgingly I collected a few tools and followed them back to Walmer Lane.

I had never been inside her house and could not help noticing that despite everything, it was clean and tidy: much more so than my own! And the plumbing problem was obvious; a pipe in the loft had sprung a joint. It could have been worse: at least the pipe had not split.

The loft tank had nearly emptied though Cassie's ceiling. The good news was that it would soon be empty and unable to do more damage. The bad news was the tank was being refilled by only an occasional drip of water. After some puffing and blowing, I managed to get the pipe back into the joint and tighten it. Climbing down from the loft I said, 'I've tightened it up so it should be OK now. But there's not much left in your tank.'

She looked blank, 'Why not?'

'Because there's no mains water now.'

She blinked, 'I don't understand.'

'Our mains water was fed from large storage tanks. These were filled by electric pumps that pumped the water from major reservoirs. All dependent on electric power ... which has failed. So our water supply is no more. Kaput!'

'Are you saying we'll have no water!' It was almost an accusation.

'It won't be a problem for a while because there are hundreds possibly thousands of gallons stored in the loft tanks in Walmer Lane. But eventually, it will run out.'

'But ... can't you do something?' she pleaded.

'Like what?'

'I don't know ... like getting it restored!'

I shook my head and simply walked away.

Cassandra Metcalf was a life-long city-dweller. She had no conception whatsoever of the fragile infrastructure that had supported her lifestyle; knowing such things had always been somebody else's problem ... some lackey at the end of a phone line. But from now on, there would be no lackeys.

I was in a sombre mood as I walked home. It was not her posture of female helplessness that had irked me; in that respect, she was no different to most women; it was the realisation that by now thousands of London houses probably had burst pipes. Water would keep gushing from those bursts until the reservoirs ran dry. It may take months ... or years ... but eventually, it would happen. Then there would be no water from taps. It was a sobering thought.

Despite not wishing to become involved, I continued making deliveries to Walmer Lane. As the weather warmed, it was interesting to see Cassie Metcalf and Julie emerge from their cocoons. Mrs Metcalf still wore her wedding ring ... and turned out to be a slender athletic-looking woman whom I guessed to be in her early forties. I made a point of not enquiring after her spouse; for some reason, I did not wish to know. Neither did Mrs Metcalf enquire after mine. Perhaps relating our recent past was too raw. But I was certain they could not be surviving only on the meagre supplies I left them; they must also have been foraging on their own account.

Mrs Metcalf had been right about the local shops. As soon as it was less treacherous underfoot, I ventured down the hill only to find that not only food shops, but every shop had been ransacked. The wreckage was strewn everywhere. How in God’s name were we ever going to rebuild any kind of civil society amid all that mess? I returned home, utterly depressed.

Over the following few weeks, I 'explored' all the houses in Newbury Crescent. If nothing else, it confirmed that nobody else had survived there. Few houses produced any food to speak of, so it became necessary to widen my foraging area. Only then did I begin to encounter a few other people. The first man ... who appeared to be carrying a sack ... spotted me just as I spotted him and darted down a side road despite me calling after him; he must have thought I was the law. The next was a boy in his teens; surly, wretched, and spotty he gave me the finger when I tried to talk with him. But who could blame any of us for our reticence?

On another occasion, the sound of banging led me to a third person; the only one I saw that day prepared to stand and talk, if only from the opposite side of the road. He looked to be in his forties, unshaven and dishevelled. He was using a club hammer to knock the palings out of a fence and pile them onto shopping trolley; I assumed he would use them as firewood.

'Seen many others about?' he called.

'Only a few. You?'

'You're only the fifth this week. And I've wandered all around Streatham and Thornton Heath.'

'Pretty grim, eh.'

'You can fuckin' say that again, mate. What with the plague, no food and this freezing cold it's a wonder there's any of us left.'

'Seen any still infected?'

'God knows. If I see any bastard who even looks slightly odd, I'm gone.'

'D'you think it's dying out?'

'Must be. There's hardly anyone left!'

'That's something I suppose.'

I was about to move away when he called, 'What d'you reckon about Feltham?'

'Feltham! What about it?'

'Christ! Haven't you heard? Big battle there. Sounds like a breakout at last. It's been on the radio for a couple of days now.'

I frowned, 'I haven't heard any mention of Feltham ... and I listen to the midday bulletin every day.'

'No, not that government crap! They're just a bunch of lying bastards. No, you try listening to Radio Free London. They're telling a totally different story.'

Astonished, I said, 'Radio Free London! What frequency is that on?'

'Don't ask me. On my radio, it's up a bit on the dial from the government station. But much weaker of course. They don't come on at any fixed time. And they move around, naturally. Those government arseholes have shut them down twice. But someone new seems to pop up. You try listening to them. You get a totally different angle from the government crap.'

And with that, he proceeded to push his trolley down the road.

It took many patient hours of tuning with my ear hard against the speaker before finally, I found Radio Free London. It was two in the morning ... and I could hardly believe what I heard.

Chapter 37. Radio Free London

Faint through the crackling static, the voice was already speaking when I found it.

... the fascist regime of George Colville continues to attack and oppress the people of all major cities in England. I again appeal to all those in uniform who obey this savage oppression to lay down their arms and join their fellow English men and women who are fighting for our right to live. We are your brothers, your sisters, and your cousins! We are your parents and your children! We have the right to live, just as you have. If you join us, you will not ... as Colville and his clique say ... be deserters and traitors. You will prove yourself decent, compassionate human beings.

The man speaking was no professional newsreader.

For those who continue to prevent their fellow countrymen from leaving these plague-infested cities, I have a message; a message we give to you and the so-called government that issues its diktats. Listen well. When this epidemic is over, you will be hunted down and brought to account for your monstrous and inhuman behaviour. Perhaps I should remind you that virtually everyone in the cities has now been exposed to the virus; most have died. But many have contracted the flu and survived; some seem to have been immune. You, on the other hand, have been protected in your bio-suits and airlocks. But someday you too will be exposed ... and then it will be your turn to face that hideous death. If you stay with Colville's despicable army ... once we do catch you ... you will be given an injection of blood taken from a Plague victim. That is a promise.

I felt my hair stand on end.

We know all about your cosy lair near Oxford. Those who have shown compassion and rejoined their families have told us all about you. So we know about you stopping food supplies to starve the virus of victims. Oh yes, fuck the common people, as long as you kill off the virus. One thing you may be sure of when we catch you, you will be shown the same mercy you have shown us.

The passion in his delivery ... the words ... the raised voice ... the venom in his style shocked me.

Fellow Londoners, last night another attempted break through the M25 Cordon was brutally suppressed. This was near Dartford. Ever since the defeat of fascist forces at Feltham, the self-elected regime of the tyrant Commander Colville has re-enforced its efforts to kettle the population of London ... condemning everyone in it to death by the plague. Our organisation, led by Evan Hakim ...

The signal stopped abruptly.

Frustrated, I fiddled with the tuning but to no avail. I did not find RFL again that night.

I slumped back in the chair, my mind spinning at the implications of what I had heard. Who the hell is George Colville? I had never heard the name ... and did he call him Commander Colville ... is he a politician ... or someone in the military ... and what is Radio Free London ... who does it represent? And what did he say: *Our organisation led by Evan Hakim*; who was he? And what was that accusation about starving the inhabitants to death to kill off hosts for the virus! That was chilling. And who occupies their HQ at Oxford ... and how many of them were there? And why had the broadcast stopped mid-sentence? The questions were endless, and I felt utterly frustrated at losing the signal. I was both intrigued and perplexed. For it sounded as if I had been so wrapped up in my own survival, that a civil war had broken out! And I knew nothing about it. I was desperate to learn more.

The thaw continued, and the next morning, I walked back to where I had spoken with the man breaking the fence, but it was a long shot. He was nowhere to be seen. However, I did encounter two other people who were prepared to exchange a few words ... from a distance. Neither had heard of Radio Free London or the Battle of Feltham. Obviously, I was not alone in my ignorance.

The mounds I had noticed on the snow-covered roads turned out to be what I feared; bodies of frail or starving people forced to leave their homes in search of food only to perish in the sub-zero conditions. They were left where they had fallen; there were no civic authorities to clear away the remains.

Each night I tried to find RFL on the radio; once I thought I may have it, but it was indistinct and soon faded away. The only other broadcasts I found occasionally were all foreign language stations; mainly Arabic speaking or so it sounded.

One day I realised that it was in mid-March last year that we first heard of the accursed Brazilian Flu. Just one year! Our world had been turned upside down in one year. My God, it was laughable how our much-vaunted superior species had been so utterly trounced by a microscopic virus. Would Homo sapiens ever dare feel so mighty again ... always assuming it survived ... or would we join the list of 'extinct' species we were so fond of listing? If Homo sapiens is to be wiped out, I wondered when on Planet Earth the next species might arise capable of compiling a list!

Dog earned his keep during that period. On more than one occasion I awoke to hear him barking. When I peeked out of the window, it was to see someone slinking off. But the biggest surprise he gave me was that he was a good ratter. His method was short and sharp; he would corner the rat, grab it by the scruff of the neck and shake it violently. Dog probably disposed of as many rats as I did with my airgun.

The last of the snow melted in the third week in March, and for the latter part of that week, we were treated to a few days of sun that would have graced July. But it was an ill-wind for the warm weather brought back the stench of decaying humanity. During those freezing winter months, that side of our predicament had been suppressed; the dead had been refrigerated. Now the reminder was all-pervasive; there was no escaping it. Although every window in the house was shut tight, I was forced to drench my face mask in disinfectant when venturing out. And soon there were flies and bluebottles everywhere. The potential for the spread of other diseases had increased dramatically.

Since I had not seen them for a few days, I went to see Mrs Metcalf and Julie. I found them lugging buckets of water from a house in Walmer Lane that still had some in its loft storage tank.

'It would be easier to move in there,' I suggested as I walked toward them.

The woman looked at me, 'It wouldn't be right, surely.'

I shrugged, 'You can take your pick. Nobody's going to stop you. Sorry, gallows humour unintended.'

Cassie Metcalf smiled, she actually smiled. I wondered how long ago it was I had last seen anyone smile.

'David was always saying things like that.'

'Your husband?'

The smile faded, 'Yes.'

'Well, seriously if you want to move, move!'

'What about the ... dead bodies?'

'Choose a house ... and I'll help drag out the bodies.'

There was a momentary pause, 'No. I'd rather stay where we are. We're comfortable where we are. Aren't we, Julie?'

The child nodded. She was bent over, silently scratching Dog behind his ear. I realised I had not heard her speak.

'How are you for food?' I asked.

Mrs Metcalf shrugged, 'Living from day-to-day. It's getting harder. Lots of the packet food show signs of vermin damage.'

'Yes, rats are on the increase. By the way, keep an eye out for dogs when you're out foraging. They're roaming in packs now ... and I wouldn't fancy getting caught by one.'

'It's the fresh food I'm missing. No vegetables or fruit. We're in danger of developing scurvy. And to think I used to be a vegetarian. And I so miss a slice of nice bread and butter.'

'You could bake your own.'

'Huh, I was never good at cooking.'

There was an awkward silence between us before I ventured, 'Were you a full-time musician?'

'Good lord, no. Just the Croydon Symphony.'

'Really. We went to see it a couple of times. They are very good!'

'Were, ' she corrected me, 'I'll never have that joy again.'

She hesitated; we both sensed that this was personal territory; an area studiously avoided to date. Had I made a mistake? It was Cassie who made the decision to reveal a little of herself.

'My full-time work was in an advertising agency.'

I felt an odd sense of relief. 'Not much call for that nowadays.'

'That's for sure. You?'

'School teacher.'

'Huh. Likewise.'

We stood for a moment as a blackbird began singing in a nearby cherry tree.

'Do you fancy some soup?' she asked.

The day was bright and warm; the only reminder of our dire situation was the occasional waft of decomposition. Her question was so unexpected it caught me off guard. I gave in.

'Why not!'

The embers of a fire glowed in the grate, and a pot stood on the camping gas stove I had given them.

'This looks commendably practical.' I said.

'You think!'

The soup was good. I did not ask what was in it.

'Do you know what's happening in the big wide world?' she asked when we had finished.

I told her about the RFL broadcast.

'Doesn't surprise me. I always regarded politicians as a bunch of self-serving shits.'

'I couldn't make out whether this Colville was a politician. Being a commander, he could have been a navy man ... or even a policeman.'

We sat in silence for some time; Julie lay on the sofa, mute. Dog lay beside her. I decided to address her directly.

'That was nice soup, wasn't it, Julie.'

We both sat looking at the child expectantly for a few moments.

'She hasn't spoken since we found each other, have you love. But she will, one day ... when this nightmare is over.'

Feeling embarrassed for not realising, I asked, 'Where did you find her?'

'To be honest, I'm not sure! There's a period for which my memory is very confused ... if it exists at all. Then one day, I found myself a few roads away, and she was walking alongside me. I don't know her real name. I just called her Julie.'

How odd that such a coincidence should have had such repercussions.

'She was traumatised by her experience, I suppose,' I said quietly.

'I couldn't just leave her to fend for herself, could I!'

'Of course not. But I imagine there are kids of her age doing just that. Or going under.'

Cassie nodded. 'What a shitty hand these kids have been dealt. It's so unfair.'

'I used to teach at a school of six hundred kids. I wonder how many of them are still alive.'

'Did you have kids?'

I nodded but only said, 'You?'

She shook her head. 'No, thank God. David and I both had careers we wanted to pursue. It wouldn't have been fair.'

We sat for some time in silence, before she said, 'Can you see any silver-linings?'

I shook my head slowly. 'Not one.'

She smiled a wry smile, 'You don't think the American Cavalry will come galloping over the hill to save us all; like in the films?'

'Regrettably not. I guess they have exactly the same problems.'

Wistfully she said, 'So sad. I liked America. We lived in New York for a while. So much energy.'

Carefully placing a couple of sticks on the fire, Cassie said, 'So what do you think will happen now?'

I had been puzzling over that question increasingly over the past days. My conclusion was that living in London was rapidly becoming untenable.

Chapter 38. Options

April was a real zephyr month; the trouble was that these were not balmy Chaucerian zephyrs, these were further evidence of an unstable global meteorological system following the abrupt removal of man's toxic output. The winds whipped up to speeds of 80-90 mph uprooting trees and damaging roofs. Nonetheless, with my store of food in constant need of replenishment, I had no option but to forage. And it was while foraging that several incidents occurred that mark April indelibly in my memory.

Loath as I am to reprise such memories when starting this Chronicle, I vowed to describe to the best of my ability the horrific nature of humanity's decline, distasteful though they may be. So here goes.

As my forage area widened, it was inevitable that I encountered many bodies. To my shame, I became quite detached when seeing them. Some had definitely died of the disease; some looked as if they starved; some had probably frozen to death. The one thing I had to steel myself against was the rat damage; especially gruesome when they had fed on children ... particularly babies. Rat numbers seemed to have increased in proportion to the rate of humanity's decrease. So when time and opportunity presented itself, I became deadly at dispatching rats with the air-rifle.

On one occasion, I was startled out of my wits. As I forced open a front door, a pack of rats ran out. I did not bother further with that house.

Another incident that shocked me was my first encounter with cannibalism. There was no doubt about it; by then, I was used to seeing rat damage. But what had happened to that man's leg was not rat damage. The woman appeared to have expired from the virus but must have succumbed to it late in the epidemic. And rather than starve to death, she had chosen to devour her dead partner.

On another occasion, I discovered a woman who had hanged herself from the bannister. Her face was blue and hideously swollen, and a pool of putrescence lay beneath the corpse. A kitchen stool lay overturned near her. But the disconcerting thing was, I had a strong sense that in the moment of kicking the stool away and beginning to choke, she had changed her mind. For her fingers were caught inside the noose in a vain attempt to release it. I backed out of the house trembling and empty-handed.

That evening I realised I needed to 'man-up', to use an expression bandied about by my erstwhile students. I had thought I had seen it all at the Selworth, so could be further shocked. I was wrong. Gruesome sights would be an everyday occurrence from now on; being squeamish and leaving empty-handed would not help my chance of survival. In former times our actions would have been called ghoulish ... and that we were grave robbers. But those bygone times were a golden age.

An incident occurred in the third week in April. That one was altogether different. I was foraging about a mile downhill. There had been no answer to my knock, and I had broken in. While I was rifling through the kitchen cupboards, Dog growled. And I turned to see an old man leaning against the door frame. He wore pyjamas and from the blotches on his face I could tell instantly that he was in the eighth or ninth day after contagion. He tried to speak, but as he did his strength gave out and in slow motion ... he slid down the wall.

I stood frozen to the spot. This meant that the old man had only contracted the flu in the last few weeks! And all the time I had been assuming it had virtually burned itself out in the Croydon area. In fact, it was still lethal!

Almost as if I were trying to make amends for my trespass, I tried to make the old man comfortable on his sofa and left him water near to hand. But I did not loot ... and I did not linger ... for I could not be certain that he was not carrying a newly mutated strain.

But it was another incident that disturbed me most. I had knocked on the first house on a road I had not plundered before. There was no reply, so I was crow-baring my way in when there was a shout behind me; two men emerged from a house opposite.

'What the fuck d' you think you're up to!'

The spokesman was a burly unshaven lout who I took to be in his mid-twenties: he held what looked like a baseball bat in his hand. An older man behind him held an Alsatian on a chain. Seeing the Alsatian, Dog cowered at my heel.

'Searching for food,' I answered timorously.

'Not in this fuckin' road you ain't, pal. This is our patch.'

'I didn't know there were patches ...'

'Well, you fuckin' do now. Got it!'

This was ominous; I was only two roads away from Newbury Crescent.

'So where does your patch ... begin and end?'

'Anywhere we say it does,' the other man said. He held a crowbar similar to my own and had a large rucksack slung over one shoulder. The Alsatian strained at the chain.

The burly lout found his companion's remark amusing. 'Good one, Jacko!'

I put up my hands as a gesture of peace and started to walk down the path towards them. The burly one stepped forward, blocking my way.

'Where you from?'

'Just up the hill.'

'Well, from now on, you stay up the hill ...'

'Otherwise, you'll be over the hill,' the comedian chipped in.

'Another good one, Jacko.'

I fleetingly considered a sharp riposte but decided that discretion was the order of the day.

'What you got in that bag?'

'A couple of tins of dog food.'

'Good. Hand ‘em over.'

'What!'

Jacko said, 'Consider them a fine ... like the old Congestion Charge.'

Both men found this hilarious.

When I made no move to hand the tins over; they stopped laughing.

'I said, hand them over!'

'But my dog's hungry ...'

'So's ours. Or would you like him to eat your dog!'

'You are on a roll today, Jacko, my son!'

'Nice to be appreciated, Degsie.'

I took the tins out of the bag and handed them over.

'Smart man,' the burly one muttered, 'Now, stay smart ... and stay away from our patch.'

They let me pass, but when I was about twenty yards down the road, they must have done something to make the Alsatian bark. It was very, very loud. Startled out of my skin, I turned to see Jacko fiddling with the dog's collar apparently about to release it. At which point I ran as I had ever run before, the sound of their laughter ringing humiliatingly in my ears.

I know why that incident disturbed me most. It was the sheer mindless thuggery ... the intimidation ... and the knowledge that this sub-class would become dominant given the current situation. As a schoolmaster, I had encountered many Degsies. They are to be found in every school; the bastard sub-culture that bullies and threatens the decent kids; always just out of sight and reach of authority; brought to book only when a kid feared the teachers more than the bully. Now, the rule of law had vanished: that thin veneer of civilisation that kept such an underclass at bay, a distant memory. Sanctions were gone.

But the more I thought about it afterwards, the most disturbing aspect was Jacko's voice. It was not that of some South London pond-life; his voice was that of a well-spoken man. For the sake of survival, he had thrown in his lot with an obnoxious thug like Degsie.

Lying awake that night, I began wondering where one should go to give oneself the best chance of surviving the coming years. Although I had understood the government's strategy of isolation and rationing to lessen personal contact, that strategy had failed. And there had been no food deliveries for months. Was it true what the man on RFL had said, that the initial tactic of rationing had evolved into one of starving the virus by denying it living hosts? That could only be done by starving the population; logically, to death. Is that what was happening? Is that what the authorities had resorted to? Not a comforting thought.

I reasoned that although it may be, months ... or even years ... before all the food squirrelled away in London's houses would be consumed ... that day would come. Then what?

And the more I thought it through, the more convinced I became that staying in a city was a bad long-term prospect. Presumably, the people trying to break through the M25 cordon had reached the same conclusion. But the powers that be, whoever they were, in this case, the better armed, had decided that the starvation strategy was the only feasible one since it offered the chance of survival for the maximum number of people. I was not entirely convinced that it did, but that did not matter. This was a case of Might Is Right if ever there was one.

So how could I get out? Clearly, there were government forces still manning the M25 cordon, but simple maths told me they must be thinly stretched. The London orbital is approximately 130 miles long! The UK simply did not have that enough armed forces to quarantine every city. That being so, it must be possible to find a sparsely guarded part of the cordon ... and slip through under cover of darkness.

But a note of caution raised itself. If it were that simple, why were there battles being reported along the M25 cordon?

After much deliberation, I decided that the only way to be reassured was to find out myself. So the next morning, I liberated a decent looking bicycle from a nearby shed and headed south. Rose and I used to picnic on a hill that afforded a good view of several miles of the M25 motorway.

The dozen or so vehicles I saw on that bike ride were police and emergency services, but there were also a few military trucks. Nobody stopped me. It was a pleasant morning, but I saw very few pedestrians as I cycled. Those I did see stared as if I were from another planet.

Chapter 39. Obstructions

April

Whether it was my general unfitness or a lack of energy due to poor nourishment, I was pretty knackered by the time I reached the M25. My ride had not been only to get in the general vicinity of the motorway; no, I had taken a specific route.

Hiding the bicycle in bushes, I climbed the hill to look down on the east and westbound carriageways. Through binoculars, I could see in the distance that both lanes of the M25 had chicanes formed by container lorries, just as the M40 had on my journey from Warwick. No vehicle was going to negotiate these without slowing almost to a standstill and thus become an easy target. But the burned-out wrecks of a few cars were evidence that people had been desperate enough to try it ... and suffered the consequences. I sat for some minutes watching and was able to confirm my previous speculation; there were very few soldiers manning the roadblocks, although the ones that did, still wore biological protection suits.

However, I had not come to see the motorway. Obviously, the motorways and A-roads would be blocked. But what obstructions were there on the B-roads ... the B2220 towards Reigate in particular. Because that passed under the motorway. But on reaching it, I found it too was blocked by lorries, although I could see only two soldiers idling nearby.

Shit!

That at least proved that the B-roads were also hazards. So what about minor roads? Cycling east and checking the map regularly I observed each minor road as it passed under the motorway. For some reason, I wanted one that went *under* rather than *over* since that sounded safer ... less exposed. Eventually, I found what I was looking for; a road that ran under the M25 towards the village of Headley. Looking down on it from the North Downs, I could see that it had only a pole as a barrier and an army tent pitched close by. A soldier leaned against the post on which the pole hinged, and he was not wearing a full bio-suit, only a light-weight face mask. Nor were there any army vehicles nearby. I assumed that a truck dropped off the guards at the start of a shift then picked them up when it brought their replacements. I spent a pleasant half-an-hour watching the activity, or lack of it, gradually growing more curious as I did so. Since during that time, the lone soldier did not move. I decided to get closer to him and edged my way down the hill ending up about one hundred metres from his post.

Still, he did not move. I moved closer and called out. No response. I walked even closer. Still no response. When I was ten metres away, my suspicions were confirmed. It was a dummy! I stood for some time, staring before looking in the tent.

Empty. Then it hit me. This was a ruse like the desert fort in Beau Geste; that was the only logical explanation. The military did not have enough troops to adequately man the cordon!

That being so, the Headley crossing, as I began calling it subconsciously, would be perfect. Just the Achilles Heel I was looking for. If and when I decided the time was right to leave London, this is where I would breach the cordon. But for the time being, I would keep it to myself.

It took me several hours to cycle back to Norwood, and I did not arrive there before it was dark. Once home, I fell into a deep and well-earned sleep.

April gave way to May, and the situation did not improve; the stench remained, but I had a nasty suspicion I had become used to it. The government broadcasts spoke of the army setting up food distribution centres where one could collect rations. The nearest one to Norwood was at Caterham, and I realised that all the locations mentioned were close to the M25 cordon. The army had no intention of venturing towards the centre of London to distribute food; perhaps for fear of being attacked.

It was soon after that announcement that I found RFL on my radio again. Not surprisingly it was excoriating the government's puny efforts, although I found myself more interested in what they said about the health of military personnel. It was the voice of the man I had heard previously.

'And we are pleased to announce that more and more of the rude soldiery are falling victims to the virus. So there is some justice after all! Let's hope that the den of vipers at Oxford has also been contaminated. Thus, are the mighty fallen.

And for those at Oxford ... and elsewhere ... who avoided contamination, well, you should not be thanking your lucky stars. Be in no doubt that the people are coming for you. You will be arraigned before a People's Court to answer for your crimes against humanity ... and you will not be spared. We will ensure that your deaths are as painful and obscene as those of the citizens you betrayed.'

With his blood-thirsty announcements, the man sounded more like the spokesman for an extremist faction. Depressed by his tone, I switched off.

In case she had not heard, I went to tell Cassie Metcalf the news about food. We were having tea in Cassie's back garden, giving every appearance that the world had not changed one iota. I did not enquire where the tea and biscuits had come from; I simply wanted to enjoy the moment.

'But how the Hell is anyone expected to get to Caterham!' she groaned, 'I've hardly enough energy to walk to the end of the road.'

'It's no more than a gesture. Maybe scared of what will happen when the virus does finally burn itself out.'

'Trying to cover their arses you mean.'

'Definitely. But I doubt it will do any good. The RFL are whipping up lynch mobs.'

'Good! The way they abandoned us; I'd be happy to string up those government bastards!'

'And they're starting to bang on about programmes to concentrate British effort.'

'What does that mean?'

'No idea. But I'm not keen on the sound of it.'

'Why?'

'Because I suspect it will entail gathering everyone up to live in kibbutzes where their energies can be channelled for the common good.'

'Do they have the power to do that? Sounds all a bit like 1984, doesn't it?'

'In this ... Alice in Wonderland environment ... they'll grant themselves whatever powers they deem appropriate. Who's going to stop them?'

'But they've no mandate for such draconian measures ...'

'I'm only speculating, of course.'

She smiled, 'You're a real Job's comforter, you are!'

I sat for a while thinking about how best to break my news to her; eventually, I said, 'I'm thinking of getting out.'

She looked shocked. 'Really! Why? Things seem to be settling down.'

'I don't think we should kid ourselves. Life will never go back to the way it was. Not when only one person in a thousand has survived. Not for generations, it won't.'

Cassie looked concerned; perhaps it was the prospect of losing her only ally.

I continued, 'Besides, I don't fancy another winter in London. And the food has pretty much gone. I haven't had a decent haul all week. And the scarcer the food gets, the fiercer the competition will get.'

'You can say that again! I had a real set-to with a woman today. All over a wretched tin of rice.'

'It'll get worse. You mark my words.'

I told her about my experience with Jacko and Degsie and warned her to avoid them.

'I think I may have already seen them. They were down the hill from me, but they were demanding that some old man give them his haul.'

'That sounds like them.'

We sat listening to a thrush for some minutes, 'Won't it be dangerous trying to get out?'

'I'll take my chances.' It sounded more macho than I intended.

'Where will you go?'

I shrugged, 'Not sure yet. Somewhere rural. Grow my own food, keep a few chickens, perhaps a pig or a goat.'

'You seem to have worked it all out. When are you leaving?'

'Don’t know. Sooner rather than later. I'd like to get settled in before winter.'

In retrospect, I believe I wanted Cassie Metcalf to ask if she and Julie could come too; that she was prepared to team up with me. But she did not.

Of course, I could never have imagined how I would actually leave London.

Chapter 40. Chimes

I was dreaming, and as usual, during my afternoon nap, that accursed sound dragged me back to consciousness.

'Oh, oh Antonio he's gone away

Left me alonio, all one my ownio ...'

So incongruous ... so nostalgic ... a forlorn dream. Awakened, I stared at the ceiling for a few moments before again, closing my eyes. But it came again; closer, more distinct.

'Oh, oh Antonio he's gone away

Left me aloneo, all on my ownio ...'

This was no dream; that sound was utterly familiar. Jumping up, I hurried to the window, threw it open and stood holding my breath. For one minute ... two ... three.

Then it came again. The sound I had heard and cursed a thousand times as it had disturbed my Sunday afternoon naps.

The chimes from an ice-cream van.

Turning my head this way and that, I tried to locate where it came from. I estimated it to be anything between a mile and two miles away; although since there was no other sound, there was an impression of the chimes bouncing around the walls making accurate location difficult. I concluded it probably emanated down the hill near Thornton Heath,

Who in God's name was doing it? I ran to the end of Crescent and held my breath waiting for that melancholy sound to echo again: for several minutes I heard only the sound of the breeze in the trees. I turned to go back to the house, but the chimes rang out again, although this time definitely further away.

Feeling disappointed, I concluded that someone had 'acquired' the ice cream van and was playing the chimes for a laugh. But I had been surprised at my elation at hearing it, so reminiscent of happier times. It invoked Julie and Nick and memories of their delight at the sound of the Ice Cream Man even though Rosie kept plenty of ice cream in the freezer.

I was therefore astonished when at approximately the same time the following day, the chimes came again. And again the day after that. This time I was halfway down the hill before they began to fade. On the fourth day, I was waiting at the bottom of the hill; and there they were, right on time ... and probably only a half-mile away. Hurrying towards the sound I was just in time to see the back of the ice-cream van as it drove away. But I was not surprised to see several people in the square; the largest gathering I had seen for months. And they were standing outside a police station, looking at a poster on the notice board.

'Who was in the ice cream van?' I asked.

The man nearest me shrugged, 'No idea, mate. Some nutter if you ask me. But they've been round here every day this week.'

'Yes, I've heard them. But what are they doing?'

'Well, according to that poster, they're looking for volunteers.'

Frowning, I walked over to the poster: it read,

My name is Martin Fuller.

I have had Brazilian Flu and am completely recovered.

I am convinced that London is no longer a healthy place to live ... and will not be for many years to come, certainly not in my lifetime.

Our so-called government wishes us to remain bottled up in cities so that the virus can burn itself out although how many will be left in these charnel houses before that happens is anyone's guess. Millions of lives have already been sacrificed to this insane policy.

But I, for one, am not prepared to wait to see. I intend to leave London in August.

I do not expect an easy ride. There will be obstacles to overcome before reaching my goal so we will, therefore, be ready for any contingencies.

My objective is to leave London and start a new life somewhere in the countryside. Being city born I have never lived in the countryside, so I am not entirely sure what I am letting myself in for. But whatever it is, it will be better than starving to death ... or being left to rot ... in London. The more I have thought about it, the more it offers the possibility of discarding the puerile values that made our previous existences so hollow. As a result of the Kevles catastrophe, humanity has been given a unique opportunity to evolve a society with more meaningful values.

I, therefore, wish to meet like-minded people to start a new self-reliant, self-sufficient community.

To this end, I will be carrying out interviews at this location starting at 2:30pm on Monday next ... 4th June.

Anyone interested in joining my venture is welcome to come along and hear my proposal.

What impressed me most was the fact that the poster was printed: which meant that Martin Fuller, whoever he was, had access to electricity. And that he had the wit to use a device that would arouse the curiosity of anybody left alive, a simple Ice Cream Van. Inspired!

This was someone after my own heart; someone unwilling to cower to misfortune. As I walked back to lonely Newbury Crescent, I knew I would be at the Square on Monday at 2:30 waiting to throw in my lot with him. And I decided Cassie Metcalf should hear of this promising development.

But she did not show much enthusiasm. 'Don't you think that sounds a bit odd?' she said.

'Odd! How?'

'Well, the fact that he's carrying out interviews.'

I frowned but shrugged. 'Not particularly. My guess is he doesn't want to find himself saddled with lowlifes ... like Degsie and Jacko. You wouldn't fancy having them on your team, would you?'

'I suppose not. But you make it sound like some hippy commune.'

I felt hurt; I had tried to convey not just the text but how much that poster had lifted my spirits. We sat in awkward silence for some moments.

For some reason, I wanted her to see this as an opportunity. 'You see, I agree with this Martin Fuller. I don't think city life is going to be tenable for years.'

'But you told me yourself the government's starting to bring food in again.' She displayed a childlike wish to believe.

Shaking my head, I said, 'If they were serious about delivering food again, they'd be bringing it into the city centre ... not leaving it seven miles away. Anyway, I'm not convinced that there's any viable infrastructure to do it. Even if only one person in five hundred has survived, it means there are only about one hundred thousand people still alive in England. And apart from the military most of them are at their wit's end just trying to survive.'

'And we will. I'm sure we will ...'

'Not without food ... clean water ... and sanitation we won't. I foresee the cities sliding into barbarity ...'

'Now you're being hysterical ...'

'Cassie, for God sake. Think! Look around us. It's already becoming dog eat dog. Come down with me and let's find out what this man Fuller is offering. We've nothing to lose.'

She was not convinced. 'The trouble is ... '

'What?'

'I don't like the countryside. Never have.'

On Monday, 4th June at 2 pm, I was in the Square, waiting. For some inexplicable reason, I had tried to smarten myself up; it reminded me of going for a job interview. I had been there for about fifteen minutes, interested to see how many others would turn up. I had heard the chimes from a distance of a mile and wondered how many people had lived within a mile radius of the Square before the catastrophe. It was difficult to estimate; perhaps five thousand people ... ten thousand ... more? Not that it mattered now. For scattered about the Square stood just eleven people. Nobody stood close to anyone else: we all eyed each other; all wondering whether the person closest was still contagious. But only three wore any form of face masks, indicating that by then most of us were fatalistic.

By any standards, we looked a bedraggled and motley bunch, but one or two facts stood out. There were seven men and four women. Two of the men were of negro ancestry, one Asian or Middle Eastern. They mainly looked to be thirty to fifty years old, although there was one teenage boy; maybe the one I had encountered foraging. As I had surmised, the events of the past year had been brutal to the old and the young. They looked shabby; some little better than tramps; both fatalistic and devoid of self-respect.

I was startled by a tap on the shoulder; it was Cassandra Metcalf; Julie stood beside her.

I smiled, 'Changed your mind?'

'Like you said, can't do any harm to find out what he plans.'

'Exactly.'

'Is this all there are? I expected more people.'

'Hmm. A bit grim, isn't it.'

At that point, we heard the sound of an approaching vehicle.

In fact, two vehicles pulled into the Square and parked. The first was a Land Rover. The second a mobile home! But the thing that registered most in my mind was the Land Rover; it was a military vehicle painted in army camouflage.

A man and a woman climbed out of the Land Rover. The woman wore a red fleece and dark slacks; the man was black and wore an army uniform. The woman glanced around the square, counting how many had assembled. When the man took a military issue rifle from the vehicle, two people promptly left the Square. The woman then reached in and took out a megaphone. I have described these actions in some detail because although each movement was entirely innocent, each seemed to have an air of menace about them.

Through the megaphone, the woman said, 'Hello. My name is Jessica Trehearn, and this is Corporal Taplin. We are here to interview people who wish to join the Martin Fuller Group in making a new life away from London. The interviews will be carried out in the mobile home. The corporal will call each of you in turn and ask you to approach the vehicle. Please do not approach before invited. As you approach, he will measure your temperature using a remote sensor. If your temperature is abnormally high, you will be told to stop and leave the vicinity. I'm sure you all know why ... and none of us wants to risk coming into contact with the disease again. When we're sure you're O.K. you will be invited for the interview, which will be conducted with you individually.'

The level of forethought impressed me.

For a few moments, the man and woman spoke quietly to each other, then someone from across the Square called out, 'I thought we were going to meet this Martin Fuller bloke.'

'Only those chosen for an interview.'

Someone called, 'Aren't you taking everyone?'

The woman again shook her head, 'Unfortunately not. But if you wish to leave London, nothing is stopping you from forming your own group. That's Martin at the door of the caravan by the way.'

Chapter 41. Martin

My first impression of Martin Fuller was how young he looked. For some reason, I had expected a man in his fifties. In fact, he appeared to be in his early thirties. Whereas everybody around me was dishevelled, he was entirely the reverse. Clean-shaven with longish dark hair, he wore a lightweight sweater and jeans. It was as if the catastrophe had entirely passed him by. As the woman introduced him, he waved his hand in friendly greeting after which he withdrew back into the mobile home.

The corporal beckoned the first onlooker forward and as he approached, took his temperature with the remote sensor. As the man drew closer Corporal Taplin muttered something and gestured for the man to stop.

The woman said, 'Sorry. You're running a temperature. You'll have to leave.'

The man tried to protest, 'I know I've got a cold. But it's not Brazilian Flu, that's for sure. I've had that, so I know it's not.'

The woman said, 'But you might be incubating a mutant strain. We're not taking any chances. Sorry.'

'Christ! That's not fair. Can't I at least talk to Mr Fuller?'

The soldier growled, 'On your way, pal.'

The man stood glaring for a moment; but when the corporal unslung the rifle from his shoulder, he slouched off muttering to himself.

Cassie whispered, 'Christ. What is this! Some bizarre beauty contest?'

The next person, a man of West Indian descent, was then waved forward, and no hand tried to stop him. When he reached Jessica Trehearne, she quietly asked a few questions and wrote his answer on a form. She passed him the form and waved him into the mobile home.

'What do you think they're asking?' Cassie muttered.

'A bit of background, I would guess. They're selecting the right candidates.'

'A load of old rigmarole.'

'I wonder how many he's taking?'

It was several minutes before the first man emerged from the mobile home, and when he did, he moved back to where he had stood originally. I was tempted to go over and ask how he had fared but decided not to. Two more men were allowed an interview, but the next person, a woman, was turned away. By that time, a few more people had joined those waiting. The corporal seemed to be going clockwise around the Square, which meant we were next. When the corporal pointed at us, I walked forward.

Jessica Trehearne asked the questions and noted the answers on a form.

'Name?'

'Gerald Morris,'

'Age?'

'Forty-six,' ... but it suddenly hit me that I'd had a birthday in February, 'No, forty-seven.'

She sighed and altered the entry.

'Occupation?'

'School teacher.'

She hardly looked at me: she simply wrote down my answers.

'Have you had Brazilian Flu, Mr Morris?'

'Yes. And recovered.'

'Are you taking any medication?'

'No.'

'Have you lost any members of your household to the flu?'

'My wife and daughter ... and probably my son.'

'Why probably ... is he still infected?'

'He was with his girlfriend in Lancashire when the travel clampdown was imposed. Then the village got infected. I've not heard from him since.'

She seemed disinterested, 'When did your wife and daughter succumb?'

'About six months ago,' My God, was that all it was!

'And were you in close contact with them?'

'Yes.'

She scrutinised me for a few moments, 'Well, you look fit enough now. Go on in.'

Martin Fuller stood up and offered his hand. He took the document and sat down, gesturing for me to do the same. Then he glanced at the form.

'So, Gerald ... what subjects did you teach?'

'Science mainly but occasionally history ... as a stand-in.'

Martin smiled, 'Science might be useful, history less so in our current situation. What other skills can you bring to the party?'

I frowned, 'I'm reasonably handy at DIY and a pretty good organiser ... '

'Could you kill a pig?'

For a moment, I thought he was joking, but when our eyes met, I realised he was not. 'Yes, I probably could if necessary ...'

'Because you see, Gerald, I plan to find an abandoned farm and to become self-sufficient.'

'Highly commendable. I'm all for it ...'

'What do you know about farming?'

I hesitated, 'Very little.'

There was a slightly cynical smile, 'Hmm. We won't survive if the party doesn't have the appropriate skills. And knowing who won the Battle of Hastings is no longer relevant. Wouldn't you agree?'

'I take your point, but you'll need someone to teach the future generation some basic education ...'

'What, the three Rs? I would imagine any of us could do that. Not that such knowledge will be needed much for a few generations.'

'Possibly but ...'

'You see, I believe that although Douglas Kevles has set Western Civilization back at least a thousand years, he has also offered us an opportunity to rethink certain values. It will be many generations before we crawl our way back to the present level of so-called technological sophistication. That's if we ever want to. And I for one, don't.'

I hesitated, 'What would you prefer to see instead?'

'Almost anything. Wouldn't you?'

I shrugged, 'Undoubtedly there were shortcomings ...'

'It was a society driven entirely corporate enterprises creating a culture of greed and shallow materialism.'

'Huh, one can't argue with that. I'd add aided and abetted by shallow, gutless and morally corrupt politicians ...'

He laughed aloud, 'Now, on that we do agree.'

'It will be good to get away from London.'

'Yes, won't it. Any other skills you could add to the list? Any hobbies?'

'Well, I never was one for sports. But I enjoyed gardening. Mainly vegetables.'

'Did you now. Well, that could be useful,'

To my surprise, he wrote something on my form.

There was silence for a few moments, before I asked, 'How many are you taking?'

Martin Fuller leaned back on his seat and put the tip of his pen to his lips, 'How many would you take, Gerald?'

'Not too many. Food will be a huge problem initially. You've got more chance of surviving as a small group than as a large ...'

'My thoughts exactly. So how many?'

I shook my head, 'About twenty. Thirty, maximum.'

'Good man!'

'And in the longer term ideally, you'd need a range of ages.'

'You've thought about this, haven't you.'?

I felt gratified, 'Hasn't everyone!'

'I've been amazed at how few have. Most seem paralysed by the past year.'

'Hardly surprising. Where will you head?'

'Not sure yet. West Country probably. At least for the first community.'

'The first community! You intend to have more than one?'

'If I can find the right sort of people. Ideally, I'd like to establish communities spaced about twenty to thirty miles apart. Adds a measure of isolation but close enough to mix the gene pool.'

I nodded, 'Seems sensible. Do you have any idea what's going on in the rest of the country?'

'It's not good regardless of what you may hear. Neither is the rest of the world. We listen on Short Wave radio. The French are struggling with a nuclear reactor that's running amok.'

'Christ. Whereabouts?'

'Golfech, between Agen and Toulouse.'

'At least it's well south.'

'And things have turned really nasty in the Middle East.'

'You'd have thought they'd have enough to think about.'

'Well, it appears that the Middle East hasn't been as badly affected by Brazilian Flu as the rest of the world. Nobody knows why.'

'So who is this Evan Hakim Radio Free London keep mentioning?'

'Oh, Hakim's leading a bunch of hot-heads. Largely testosterone driven. Seems intent on stirring up trouble. He and his lot are best avoided.'

I nodded, 'So when do we go?'

'Whoo! Let's not get ahead of ourselves. I intend interviewing a hundred or so people. Thanks for coming, Gerald. Please wait outside. We'll let everyone know whether they've been shortlisted by the end of the afternoon.'

Startled by this abrupt termination, I said, 'Am I in with a chance?'

Martin Fuller looked pensive for a moment, 'I'd certainly place you among the first reserves.'

As I walked back to my spot, I felt dazed. It had all happened so fast. I had half expected that he would welcome anyone semi-intelligent who was not halt or lame. To find so well-conceived a proposal had wrong-footed me. And I was shocked at my summary dismissal. I thought the interview had gone well and that Martin and I were on the same wavelength. To be so abruptly shown the door took the wind out of my sails. Although I had to admit to being slightly thrown by some of Martin's questions, I had the impression I had not been able to offer sufficient skills to cement a place.

When I came out, Cassie and Julie were standing next to Jessica Trehearne who waved them in the second I exited. I walked back to my waiting place, feeling ill at ease. But comforted by the thought that if I did not have the right skills, someone like Cassie Metcalf had no chance.

Later that afternoon, Martin Fuller stood on the steps of his mobile home and read out the list of seven people shortlisted to join him. Cassie and Julie's names were called out; mine was not!

I was gobsmacked. When I looked across at Cassie, she also seemed astonished.

The watchers began drifting away, but as I stood stunned, Cassie walked across to Martin Fuller and quietly spoke to him.

He glanced up at me and shook his head. She spoke again, which caused him to ponder.

Then he shrugged his shoulders and called across, 'You're on the list, Mr Morris.'

As we walked back up the hill towards Newbury Crescent, Cassie said, smiling, 'You looked flabbergasted.'

'Totally mystified ...'

'Why, because Martin chose me but not you?'

'I thought he was looking for specific skills.'

'How do you know I don't possess any?'

'I don't! You're obviously a dark horse.'

'Maybe. Although we hardly know each other.'

'True.'

We walked in silence for a while, and it was clear she was not going to tell me, so I said, 'OK, what the hell did you say to him to make him change his mind?'

'I told him we are partners. And if you didn't go ... then neither did I.'

'You're kidding!'

'Don't go jumping to any conclusions. It doesn't mean anything. It's just that, after what you've done for us, I didn't fancy the thought of leaving you in the lurch. It was entirely spontaneous.'

I struggled for words. 'Well, my turn to say thanks.'

'To be honest, I didn't think he warmed to me at all, although he asked a lot about Julie. Then one question seemed to turn it around. And for the life of me, I'm not sure how he latched onto it.'

'Onto what?'

'He was totally dismissive of my musical background. Almost rudely so. Then he suddenly asked where I'd gone to university ... and what I'd read.'

'And?'
'Well, before I switched to music, I read medicine for a year.'

Chapter 42. Filtering

On a sunny July morning, a week later, Cassie, Julie and I walked down to the Square. I felt decidedly upbeat at what the day would bring. Julie walked ahead of us leading Dog on a string.

Cassie said quietly, 'Julie was talking in her sleep last night. So at least we know there's nothing physically wrong.'

'Oh, that's good to hear! Let's hope there's a few kids her age making this trip.'

'Fingers crossed.'

I counted over thirty people scattered around the Square; more than I had expected. But I was comforted to see a couple of children about Julie's age standing together.

When Martin Fuller climbed onto the back of a flatbed truck, the hum of conversation subsided. Jessica Trehearne handed him a microphone and Corporal Taplin, still in khaki, stood close by. There was also another man in army fatigues; this time, there were no weapons on display. Again, I was struck by how young, and clean-cut Martin looked: he wore a short-sleeved blue shirt and as he leaned forward a quiff of dark brown hair dropped across one eye; he ran his hand through it to sweep it back.

'Good morning, thank you for coming. Well, I'm sure you'll agree this is a pretty important day for all of us.' He smiled, 'After all, it's not every day we have the opportunity to completely alter our lives. We all know why we're here, and I don't intend wasting time talking about the recent past, tragic though it is. Let’s focus on the future. Our future, together.'

A few people muttered their approval.

'Everyone here is a volunteer. Nobody has been coerced. Most of us are no doubt, apprehensive. That's understandable. Because we are taking a step into the unknown. Literally, since

I, for one, have no idea where we will end up. We will undoubtedly meet obstacles, even before we reach our destination. And we're a group of people who have never met each other before. That will sort itself out as we go along. But I do want to state a few ground rules. If you can't accept them ... wholeheartedly ... you should seriously consider whether this venture is for you. Seriously, you must, for your own sake and the sake of everyone else in this square. Success requires our full commitment.'

A man behind me muttered, 'Here we go.'

Martin paused and looked at the expectant faces. 'For a start, I do not intend to contaminate our new society with race, religion or politics.'

A murmur of unease rippled through the crowd as this startling comment sank in; Cassie whispered, 'Wow. A big ask.'

He waited for silence before continuing. 'I am simply not prepared to inflict any form of religion on our community. If you cannot live without whatever religious beliefs you hold, then please leave now. You are not welcome.'

I was told later that a couple of people near the back walked away at that point.

'Neither will I allow racial intolerance. If you are unable to live peaceably with your fellow men and women regardless of the colour of their skin, then our group is not for you.'

Most people glanced around, wondering who this aspect would flush out.

One man standing near us sneered and walked away, muttering, 'A load of old bollocks. Thinks he some fucking Messiah.'

To my surprise, it turned out to be Degsie! The thing that really surprised me was how he had got through Martin's first filter, but perhaps he had not; maybe he had simply turned up.

Martin continued, 'Anyone who exhibits racial intolerance in any form will be banished from the group. Is that accepted?'

There was a general murmur of agreement. I glanced around me; there were at least five or six black faces and about the same number of Asian or Eastern origin. I wondered what they made of such a radical proposal.

Martin nodded, 'Good. And lastly, politics. There will be no politics as we have previously understood them. The major shortcoming of democracy was that it pandered to humanity's basest instincts. And by that principle alone it proved itself utterly flawed.'

Several people whispered to each other; Martin looked at them.

'Does anyone here believe that the politicians we trusted have acted in our interests this past year?'

A woman's voice cried, 'They want stringing up ...'

Martin ploughed on. 'I'm sure there are people present who would agree with you. No, our group will be run by myself and a few people I choose as advisers. They will be people who have the future of our community at heart ... and not their personal ambitions. They will not be elected because they cling to some outdated political dogma.'

I whispered to Cassie, 'He's making it sound like some sort of Utopia.'

Someone asked, 'What happens before you choose these ... advisers?'

'Well, since you're happy to follow me out of London, I shall lead the group in consultation with whoever I deem appropriate.'

Martin let his eyes range over the crowd; nobody challenged him. 'You have all been invited today because you possess skills needed in a fledgeling community. In some of us, these skills may have been learned in the past but have lain dormant. In those cases, the group will expect you to work vigorously at re-learning and updating yourselves on those skills. For instance, as you can probably imagine, virtually the whole of the medical profession has been wiped out. After interviewing nearly a hundred and twenty people, I have found only one person who claims to have even the most basic knowledge of medicine ... and we are lucky to have found her. That person will be the cornerstone of our medical team.'

I felt Cassie stiffen beside me and whisper, 'Oh, my God!'

'One man was a builder's labourer. He is the only one among us who has any knowledge of building. His knowledge will be invaluable. Another young man was a garage mechanic. These are all vital skills; skills we will need. I have tried to weed out accountants ... lawyers ... bookmakers ... anyone who worked in the media ... estate agents ... or telesales workers ... unless that is, they possess compensatory skills. In fact, none of the parasites of the previous society is welcome. In the future we face together, their experience is valueless.'

A woman's voice from the rear called, 'What did you do, Mr Fuller?'

Martin Fuller paused and smiled slowly; a broad welcoming smile which I guessed made some women swoon.

'I spent my life preparing for this day.'

Various people around me smiled. But the voice persisted. 'No, come on, fair's fair. You know all about us. What about you?'

After a short pause, he said, 'I was studying for a doctorate in psychology.'

The voice persisted, 'And will that be of value in this Brave New World of yours?'

Martin Fuller drew a deep breath, 'It has given me the insight ... the nous ... the ability ... to gather together thirty strangers in the hope that I can lead them to a new life. Could any of you have done that?'

Nobody answered.

Martin continued, 'The conditions I've outlined will put some off. And that's as it should be and best confronted now and not in a month’s time when the chips are down. If you are one of those people, please feel free to leave us. I wish you luck in whatever the future holds. In fact, you might be interested in throwing your lot in with Evan Hakim. He's looking for people to join his group. They are slowly coming together in Islington. And as far as I can gather, he's placing no restrictions on who joins him.'

I glanced around to see several small groups talking with each other quietly. A few more drifted away.

Cassie whispered, 'I hope to God he didn't mean me when he talked about medical experience. That was eighteen years ago!'

'He may have been. Surely you don't object. It will be a vital role.'

'Anyone thinking I have genuine medical knowledge is very mistaken.'

I tried to reassure her, 'We'll be fine.'

Martin spoke again, 'I'm sure there are questions you want to ask.'

Someone called, 'When do we go ... and where are we heading?'

'We leave next week. It's important to get established before autumn sets in. As for where we're heading, my only thought is to head southwest. Ideally, find a small, deserted village to make our own.'

'Then what?'

'Then we set about learning skills few of us possess. Skills that our previous sybaritic society had allowed to fade away. As far as we can tell not one of us here today knows anything about farming ... although one or two claim to grow their own vegetables ... so that's a start. If there are any garden centres nearby where we can collect seed potatoes ... or vegetable seeds of any sort, go and get them.'

Without thinking I raised my hand, 'I've already started to do that, Martin.'

'Good! Someone with initiative.'

That brought a few less than friendly glances.

Martin continued. 'But I must warn you now. The success of our venture cannot be guaranteed. The odds against us may be too high ...'

A whiney voice said, 'The radio says the government will start bringing food again soon. Wouldn't it be better to wait?'

'That's entirely your choice, friend.'

Someone else asked, 'How much stuff will we be able to take with us?'

'I was coming to that. There will only be enough space for essentials. By essentials, I mean warm clothing, sleeping bags, boots, wellingtons, outdoor gear, tools, torches, batteries, and any food you have left. And weapons. If anyone has any weapons, bring them. We may need them.'

This too brought a murmur of unease from those assembled.

A woman at the front raised her hand,

'I'm almost out of food, Mr Fuller. What can I do?'

'We've already assembled a cache of food. But it won't last long. Bring all the food you can forage.'

The man standing next to me said, 'Do you want us to bring our own cars? Only I'm out of petrol.'

'Up to you. But we have commandeered some trucks ... courtesy of our military friends. Not the most comfortable vehicles I've ever travelled in, but functional.'

'What about pets?'

'If they can fend for themselves, fine. But we can't spare food.'

I glanced down at Dog, 'Don't worry, boy. I'll look after you.'

A man from the back called, 'You mentioned weapons, Mr Fuller. Are you expecting trouble?'

'We've already reconnoitred the best way through the M25 cordon. Again thanks to our army friends. But you never know. Some towns and villages have constructed formidable defences, and many are armed. Not that I intend to try storming any barricades. We're not looking for trouble, so we'll always try to find a way around them. But we must be able to defend ourselves and our food and equipment. Others will want to take them.'

A few more people slipped away.

Martin went on, 'It may be that once we're settled, we can come back and collect other belongings. But we can't take them now. Next question?'

Eventually, the questions petered out; by then, there were only twenty-seven people left in the Square. It had not been entirely comfortable listening. But in my opinion, everything Martin Fuller said was measured and reasonable. He was not offering a joyride; he pulled no punches; he told it like it was. And I for one was totally convinced. I would be ready to leave in six days.

Cassandra Metcalf was less convinced.

Chapter 43. Exodus

Early August

Those final days were frantically busy. I re-scoured the local garden centres and gathered every packet of vegetable seed I could find. On visiting the local libraries and bookshops, I was shocked at the destruction. Presumably, some of the contents had been plundered for fuel during that harsh winter. But I collected every book on farming and smallholding that remained. Not that there were many such books in the libraries around Norwood. But the very process made me think again; so I went back and collected everything they had on natural remedies. Having satisfied myself on these topics, I started a new quest; to find my weapon of choice. But in that, I was disappointed.

On the last day, I rewrote the letter for Nick and propped it against the telephone, adding that I was leaving London with a group led by Martin Fuller and that we were heading south-west. But mainly the letter expressed how proud Rosie and I had been of him and Julie and how much we loved them. Not that I held out any hope of Nick seeing it; it was merely a substitute for the Rite of Passage; my eulogy to my son.

Cutting all the roses in bloom, I placed them on my Rose's grave and cried my goodbyes to her too. Ludicrously I found myself locking my front door as I left the house.

As I pushed my laden wheelbarrow towards the end of Newbury Crescent, Cassie Metcalf and Julie were waiting for me. Cassie looked puffy around the eyes. She pushed two large aluminium cases with wheels.

I raised my eyebrows, 'No, violin?'

'Hidden in this case. Didn't want anyone deciding it's surplus to requirements.'

'I'm sure there'll be times when we need to lift our spirits.'

She was half smiling as she stared at my load, 'What the hell do you want with a wheelbarrow? Surely to God, we can find one of those.'

'It's not the barrow. It's the boxes in it.'

'Which hold?'

'Books mainly. Come on. Time to go. Can you take Dog, Julie?'

The child nodded and smiled.

Three Land Rovers were waiting in the Square: one of them in military camouflage. There were also three trucks, two of which bore army markings; some people were already aboard two of the trucks. By the time of our scheduled departure, I counted only twenty-six people. And I was encouraged when a girl in her early teens come over and speak to Julie; the girl did not seem deterred when Cassie told her that Julie had not spoken since we had known her.

Cassie nudged me and nodded her head in the direction a young Asian woman nursing a baby; it appeared to be no more than a few months old.

Quietly she said, 'Jesus. Can you imagine going through childbirth over the past few months? It must have been horrendous.'

'I wonder if she delivered it herself?'

Jessica Trehearne came over and put a tick against our names on her list.

'You're all in truck number two. This is Philip, your driver.'

Philip looked to be of Asian descent and wore a camouflage jacket; he nodded but remained silent.

Jessica continued, 'Put your luggage in there. Stick to the same truck. It makes roll-call easier. Understood?'

Without waiting for an answer, she moved on to someone else.

'Why do I get the feeling that woman doesn't like me?' Cassie whispered.

'Don't worry about it. I get the same vibes. Possibly she's still traumatised.'

Martin came across and shook our hands. 'So glad you're both coming. We've got a fine day for it.'

'I managed to get quite a lot of vegetable seeds, Martin. It's all in my luggage.'

'Brilliant! Good man. Gerald isn't it?'

'That's right. Although I prefer Gerry.'

'Gerry it is then. '

'And I plundered the local libraries for everything I could find on agriculture ... and medicine ... and any veterinary books.'

'Excellent. Good thinking! We've already assembled quite a few. But yours will add to the collection.' I felt slightly deflated.

'And how about you, Cassandra. Up for it?' Martin asked.

'A few butterflies.'

'Yes, it's all a bit overwhelming, isn't it. We'll all feel better once we're underway.'

Martin bent down and stroked Dog. 'And what about you, boy? Are you about to be left behind?'

I intervened quickly, 'He's with us, Martin. He's proved himself an alert guard dog … and a bloody good ratter. I'm more than happy to share my food with him.'

Martin Fuller stood up and looked me in the eye. 'Well, as long as that's understood. No special helpings. We can't afford passengers.'

Cassandra and Julie looked relieved.

Corporal Taplin came over, 'Their gear's all loaded up, sir.'

'Are we all present and correct?'

'Waiting for three latecomers, sir.'

'Tony, it's not sir: it's Martin … or Mr Fuller if you must. OK?'

It was evident that the corporal was trained to address all adults as sir and looked uncomfortable at the thought of doing otherwise. 'OK', he muttered.

'Good. Let's give them another five minutes. If they've not turned up by then, we'll go.'

'Sir.' The corporal walked over to our driver Philip, and they began talking quietly.

Martin smiled and shook his head.

'Where did the army lads come from?' I asked.

Martin hesitated momentarily, 'Oh, they turned up with a truck full of supplies one day. Said they'd deserted; that they were sick of killing people trying to get away from London. Told us quite a bit about how the military was faring.'

'Which is?'

'Not too good by the sound of it. Despite their bio-protection, it seems that the virus eventually catches up with them. I guess they have to take their masks off some time.'

'Difficult to have much sympathy.'

'I guess the poor sods are just obeying orders.'

We stood for a few moments watching people load their belongings onto the trucks.

'What route do you intend to take?' I asked.

'Well, as of a few days ago our army friends had found a nice quiet route through the M25 cordon near Leatherhead. Let's hope it's still unguarded.'

The way the corporal had addressed Martin gave me a vague feeling of unease. After five minutes, only one further person turned up, so without further ado, we set off. There were no speeches and no waving crowds. On that bright sunny morning, we simply abandoned our past lives.

Martin was right about one thing; an army truck is not a comfortable mode of transport. Every bump in the road jarred the body. Just enough room had been left in the back for eight subdued and pensive people and their luggage. We were squeezed between assorted boxes, crates, and jerry cans. Although there had been the odd nod on eye contact, nobody had tried to introduce themselves. Now with the truck moving, the noise level did not allow for polite conversation. Perhaps they all felt as I did, that this day was a waymark in our lives. For me, leaving the neighbourhood I had lived in for so long invoked powerful memories of family life and everything I had lost. Again, I cursed Douglas Kevles, as I had vowed to for the rest of my life.

On that first ride, the vehicles in our convoy took up the positions they would maintain for the rest of the journey. The army Land Rover in front, followed by Martin in the second Land Rover about a quarter of a mile behind, followed by the three trucks, also spaced about a quarter of a mile apart, loaded with people and supplies … and hope. The third Land Rover brought up the rear. As we passed through areas containing shops, the signs of looting were visible; none had escaped.

I saw only one pedestrian as we headed south, and she tried to wave us down as we sped past. Julie waved to her as she faded into the distance. But progress was slow because we encountered several barricaded roads. At each one, the leading Land Rover stopped and reversed before finding an alternative route. To my relief, no shots or warnings were exchanged, and some roadblocks appeared to be unmanned.

Apart from the detours, things went smoothly, and the convoy did not stop until we approached Leatherhead. Our drivers seemed to know the routine; no vehicle halted within a hundred yards of another. Eventually, the convoy slowed to a stop, and someone from the front shouted, ‘Five-minute comfort break!’

As we climbed down to stretch our legs, I offered a hand to some of our fellow passengers. Standing and stretching, I decided to break the ice.

'I guess we're going to get to know each other pretty well soon. So let's make a start. My name's Gerry Morris ... this is Cassie Metcalf ... this is Julie. We don't know her surname.'

A man thrust his hand in mine, as if in relief, 'Trevor Beamish.'

The woman next to him said timidly, 'Wendy Fraiser.'

The next woman said, 'Jane Passfield. It's so good to have someone to talk to at last. I'm bursting for a pee. Anyone else?' The ladies hurried off.

A heavily built black man offered his hand, 'Michael Southern. I remember seeing you at the Lambeth Council Centre when the flu started. You were attached to the doctor. I forget her name.'

'God, that seems an eternity ago.'

'Fifteen months,' he sighed.

'Do you know if any of the others survived?'

He shook his head, 'You're the first one I've seen.'

We stood in awkward silence for a few moments, probably both thinking of the number of people who had crowded into that dingy hall. Suddenly he said, 'Well, at least we're doing something positive. Getting out of that stinking trap.'

'Amen to that.'

Corporal Taplin walked up to us; his rifle slung over his shoulder. 'The lead Rover is going to recce the road we want to use. It's a bit narrow, so we want to take it at a lick. Everyone else will stay put. And keep your eyes peeled. OK? We don't want to get bounced by a bunch of locals.'

'OK.' I said. He walked off towards the next truck.

'Officious bugger,' Trevor Beamish muttered once the corporal was out of earshot.

'The deadly silent type,' I smiled trying to make light of it, 'But definitely an acquired taste.'

Another man offered his hand, and we all shook it. 'Dan Tucker. Used to be a carpenter.'

'Good to meet you, Dan. Useful man to have around.'

'Looks like you and me might be the oldest blokes,' he said, smiling. My mouth opened to refute such a slur, but to my amazement, I realised he might be right. Jesus, that was an uncomfortable thought. Perhaps that was why I had not been selected initially.

As if offering a grain of comfort, he added, 'Although I did see one old biddy being helped onto the other truck.'

The reconnoitring Land Rover returned after about ten minutes and the convoy restarted. As the corporal promised, we took the next section through narrow lanes at speed. But we passed under the M25 without a hitch and were soon skirting Leatherhead, all the time on minor roads. The roads into Leatherhead itself were barricaded, reminding me of that fraught journey to Warwick. Whoever had planned this route had been careful to avoid all towns and as many villages as possible. Soon we were negotiating the lanes around East Clandon, and I watched for signs of habitation in this rural area. The government bulletins had insisted that the mortality rate was less in the countryside but the further we went the more I became convinced that had been another lie. Fields lay unattended, and I saw no farm animals. The position of the sun told me that we had started to head southwest, and I became quite hypnotised by the sun flickering through trees as we passed through woodland.

The screech of brakes as the truck swerved violently threw some of us from our seats. Then it rapidly reversed. Having backed about one hundred yards, it stopped.

When Philip jumped down from the driving cab, I was alarmed to see him carrying a rifle.

'Stay in the truck and keep your heads down,' he called.

'What's happened?' I called.

'The lead vehicle's in trouble.'

Chapter 44. Ambush

Leaning my head outside the truck, I looked down the lane. Cassie tugged my arm, 'He said keep your head down!'

By now the first truck had also backed and was stationary about one hundred yards in front of us. About half a mile ahead the lane curved into woodland. The barricade had been laid just beyond the bend. The driver of the first vehicle would have been on top of it before he saw it. Philip had vaulted over a gate and was stealthily making his way forward screened by a thick hedge. Out of sheer curiosity, I decided to follow him.

As we got closer, I could see Martin Fuller and another man walking towards the barricade; they appeared to be wearing flak-jackets. Philip seemed irritated to see me and impatiently gestured for me to stay low, so I did; but gradually, shielded by the hedge, we inched forward. Putting my hand onto stinging nettles, I almost swore.

There appeared to be three people manning the barricade, and initially, I wondered why we had not adopted our usual tactic of backing-up and finding an alternative route. But then it became apparent; there must have been others I could not see because a couple of logs had been dragged behind the leading Land Rover making it impossible for it to reverse. Its occupants were trapped. By then, Philip and I were close enough to see the men at the barricade. To my dismay, they were soldiers.

Martin called, 'Captain Fuller of the Norfolks. On government orders, we're carrying civilians to establish a community. They've all been checked, and none of us is infected. Here are my orders.'

He waved a sheet of paper at the barricade.

It was a few moments before an answer came, ' What supplies you carrying?'

'Just enough for them to survive for ... a few weeks.'

'Good. Leave half here. Then we'll let you pass.'

In a perfectly calm voice, Martin called, 'Fetch your CO.'

'Died two months-ago. It's every fucking man for himself now, mate.'

'Then fetch your senior NCO!' Martin's voice was sharper, more assertive now.

'You're talking to him.'

'Right. Get this barrier shifted ... or suffer the consequences.'

'Not 'til you unload half your supplies.'

Martin seemed to sigh ... then he dropped the sheet of paper he was holding.

Two cracks rang out, one close by. One of the figures behind the barricade jerked backwards and slumped to the ground.

Only then did I realise that Philip was lying on the ground and had fired one of the shots.

The men behind the barricade began to return fire and bullets whizzed through the hedge next to me. I closed my eyes tight and covered my head with my arms.

I heard Philip mutter, 'Shit. One of our blokes has been hit.' Taking careful aim, he fired a short burst. Another man behind the barricade was thrown backwards as bullets struck their targets. The third man turned and ran into the woods.

Martin shouted and waved to us, 'Man down. Tony! Covering fire. Quickly. Get him to the truck.'

Two men rushed over and helped drag the wounded man to the first truck.

'And get this log cleared. Quickly, before that bastard gets reinforcements!'

I stood paralysed by what I had witnessed.

Philip sprang up and shouted at me, 'You heard what the officer said. Move it for fuck sake!'

It took four of us to haul both logs out of the road, by which time I was bathed in sweat.

Calmly Martin said, 'Now back to the vehicles, sharpish. Let's get out of here.'

I turned to go with Philip when I heard Martin say, 'Gerry, a word please.' It was an order rather than a request. As we walked rapidly back to the vehicles, he said, 'For the time being it would be best if you didn't say too much about what's just happened. We don't want our people getting the wrong impression.'

'Are you army?' I asked panting.

'I was. But I didn't like what was happening and decided to get out. Some of my men came too. Now we're civilians, just like you, Gerry. But the training comes in useful when we need it. I'll tell everyone when the time's right, but not yet. Let's get somewhere safe first. OK?'

'Christ. Is this what it's going to be like ... killing people just to get through roadblocks? Couldn't we have negotiated with them?'

'We could have tried. But all the time they'd have been assessing our strength and calling up reinforcements. Then they'd have taken all your supplies … and kept the women. The men would be invited to walk away or join them. Say no to either option ... and they'd have shot you.'

'Jesus! How do you know?'

'Because that's what it's come down to. They weren't soldiers by the way. Just civvies with shotguns wearing camo gear. Lots of disparate groups around now. Food's become really scarce. Now get back in your vehicle and, Gerry ... keep shtum.'

Uncertain how much the other people in my truck had seen, I was reticent about answering questions. Cassie and the others asked, but my silence soon caused them to desist. Perhaps I looked too shocked to respond. For the first time, I found myself anxious at what sort of group we had joined.

Giving Guildford a wide berth, we continued our way south-west. But when we stopped mid-afternoon for a comfort break, I saw Martin, Tony, Philip talking seriously. I guessed they were discussing the ambush; for undoubtedly, that was what it had been; both an ambush and a lucky escape. Having calmed from the short sharp action, I concluded we had been fortunate in joining Martin and his men. What would have happened if it had been just Cassie, Julie, and I, did not bear thinking about. I had been naive about how conditions had deteriorated: I needed to toughen up. There might be many such ordeals ahead.

My reverie was interrupted when Martin walked over to Cassie, 'Would you have a look at the wounded man, doctor.'

Cassie's jaw dropped, 'I'm not a doctor ...'

'Mrs Metcalf, you studied medicine for a year. That's a year more than anyone else in the group. So from now on, you're our doctor. And let's not lose any more time. We've been unable to stop the bleeding.'

She looked horrified, but Martin gently took her by the arm, 'Please, Mrs Metcalf.'

I felt obliged to go with her, but they would not allow me up into the truck; I could only gauge the severity of the situation by the look on Cassie's face when she saw the wounded man. I could see she felt helpless, but she appeared to pull herself together.

I lost sight of her when she bent down to inspect the wound, and at that point, I felt nothing but admiration. When ten minutes or so later I helped her down from the truck, she was pale and trembling. We walked away from everyone, and I let her compose herself; I was afraid she would throw up.

Then she looked at me, 'My God, Gerry, what are we doing here? This is crazy. Did you know these men were soldiers?'

'Of course not. But we're lucky to be with them. I doubt we'd have survived long without them.' Cassie wasn't listening.

'It's madness to think I can treat wounds like that. I only completed the first year! Along with dentists and vets. We hardly covered basic anatomy, let alone trauma. Eighteen years-ago for Christ's sake. And what if anyone needs an operation?'

'Will he survive?'

'I've no idea whatsoever. His pulse is feeble and irregular ... and he's lost a lot of blood. It's all over the truck floor.'

'Is he conscious?'

'Just about ...'

Martin came over. 'Well done, doc. I know how difficult that was for you. You did your best.'

An hour later and still winding our way through country lanes, I saw a signpost indicating that Alton was five miles.

Trevor Beamish tapped me on the shoulder, and said quietly, 'Have you noticed how scruffy most of the fields look, Gerry. Full of grass and stubble. Doesn't look as if much has been planted.'

He was right. Few fields looked as if they had crops worth harvesting, and it occurred to me that they must have been planted in spring.

'And I don't think I've seen many animals either, just a few sheep and cows. There was a field back there with pig enclosures, but there was not a pig in sight. And absolutely no horses. Where have they all gone?'

'Probably slaughtered for food.'

The lead Land Rover stopped again and reversed rapidly. The following vehicles in our small convoy did the same. Once we had retreated about half a mile, the drivers climbed out, carrying their weapons. A few people climbed down and hurried behind the hedge to relieve themselves. When Philip came back, he said, 'There's a couple of burnt-out cars on the road ahead. We can't tell if it's recent, so we're not taking any chances. We're going to turn around and find another route. Everyone back on board.'

An hour later, we had not progressed much further, and it started to rain. We negotiated our way through a couple of deserted and unbarricaded villages; Oakley, Steventon and Wonston being among them. A signpost told us that Winchester was ten miles south. But the number of unguarded villages seemed to have increased significantly, which gave me a feeling of security and I began to relax a little. By early evening we were travelling on the old A30 toward Stockbridge when the vehicles ahead slowed and pulled into a lay-by.

Martin climbed out of his vehicle and beckoned us to gather around. His boyish smile was reassuring. 'Well. I'm sure you'll all agree, this has been a pretty eventful day. But so far, so good. I think we deserve a brew up. All those in favour say aye.'

Those were the most comforting words I had heard all day, and the muted cheer told me everyone felt the same.

Martin continued, 'The good news is that we're well away from London now. But unfortunately, we've taken our first casualty. One of our party, Gavin Brennan, was wounded. Our medic, Mrs Metcalf, is tending him. But I want to find somewhere to lie up for a few days, to help him recover.'

The news of someone being wounded caused whispers of anxiety.

'Now, I don't know how many of you have brought food. But we have some K-rations, courtesy of the army, that you're welcome to. They're not the tastiest food ever, but it's nourishing and safer to eat than most things we've seen laying around. Pass some out, Tony?

A woman asked nervously, 'Where will we spend the night, Mr Fuller?'

Martin pondered for a moment, 'Well, for tonight, I think it'll be safer if we bunk down in the trucks. And we'll post a guard.

We might as well get into the habit. And everyone except for the children will take a turn. At least two people per truck at all times. Understood?'

So it was that we spent that first night away from London; in trucks spaced fifty yards apart parked in a lay-by somewhere near Stockbridge in Hampshire.

And it was while standing guard in the rain at two in the morning that I remembered a place Rose and I had once visited. And if memory served me correctly, it was not far away.

Chapter 45. The Abbey

At first light the next morning, I told Martin about the place.

'As far as I recall, it's an old manor somewhere between Stockbridge and Romsey. But I can't remember the name of it.'

Martin went back to his Range Rover and returned with an Ordnance Survey map. 'Show me on this.'

In the half-light, it took me a few minutes, but eventually, I pointed to it, 'I think that must be it. Mottisfont Abbey. Look, that small group of houses. And it shows an Abbey Farm too.'

Martin studied it for a few moments. 'National Trust property ... so it's probably in reasonable nick. And close to a river. Might fit the bill for a few days.'

Running my finger down the map, I said, 'Looks as if the most direct route is down that road. The A3057.'

He pondered for a few moments, before saying, 'If Gavin Brennan is to have any chance at all, he has to lay up for a few days to try to stop the bleeding. Give our medic a chance to work her magic.'

Martin called the Group together and made the announcement as we sipped hot tea. 'Gerry remembers a place nearby where we can rest for a few days. It's only about five miles away, so we're going to recce it.'

A few heads turn towards me; I was not sure I wanted responsibility for this diversion.

'He will travel in the lead Land Rover with Tony to show us the way.'

By then, I definitely regretted my suggestion. Without the OS map, I had no idea of the way. I had only been to the place once; several years before when Rose and I spent a weekend with her aunt in Andover. We had visited Mottisfont to see an al-fresco performance of a Shakespeare play.

One of the trucks had not been running smoothly, and Tony wanted to look at the ignition. Martin agreed; we did not want it stalling in an emergency. During those hours of waiting, no other vehicle or person passed by. It was mid-morning before our convoy finally got underway. Driving to the edge of Stockbridge, we then followed the sign to Romsey.

This was my first experience of being in the lead vehicle, and I was aware of its vulnerability. If anything nasty were to happen, we would get it first. In my nervous state, I tried chatting with Tony but stopped me.

'Do me a favour, mate. Just concentrate on keeping your eyes peeled. If anything looks suspicious, shout.'

Admonished, I stayed silent but watchful.

It was just a couple of miles further on when Tony slowed the vehicle to walking pace. We were heading downhill, and there was a bend in the road beyond which we could not see. My mouth felt parched. Tony stopped and backed up a hundred yards or so, and wary of another ambush, muttered, 'Don't like the look of this,' he called up Martin on the walkie-talkie.

Martin and another soldier climbed out of the second vehicle and, staying close to the hedge, disappeared round the bend. I realised I was holding my breath. After about five minutes, he reappeared and waved us forward. As we rounded the bend and cruised slowly downhill, we passed a signpost stating we were entering King's Somborne.

There was nothing remarkable about the village per se, houses, a pub, a church, and a school. But the villagers had erected a barricade, and it was the remnants of it that shocked me. For the cars, vans and tractor used to form it had been destroyed. Something large and powerful had simply bulldozed its way through. It was not just the barricade that had been destroyed; two other cars were gutted by fire, and thin wisps of smoke rose from them; another was simply crushed beyond recognition.

Large letters had been sprayed over one white-walled house.

This is SDF Territory

Three bodies lay nearby; Martin knelt to examine one. Some of the nearby houses were burned out; no flames, but despite a night of rain, thin smoke was still rising. One building had a ragged hole in the front wall.

Tony muttered, 'That's RPG damage.'

But a worse sight awaited; the body of a man hung from a lamppost. I stared in shocked silence; the face was pale blue, and his tongue protruded from his mouth.

A sign hung around its neck.

He defied the SDF

Tony muttered, 'Fuck me.'

Martin walked briskly over to us. 'Keep going, Tony. My guess is this happened a few days ago. Let's not stick around.'

Although I had seen battle damage on my trip to Warwick, the carnage and destruction at King's Somborne unnerved me. I glanced back at the other vehicles but could see only a few pale faces.

After a few more miles, a brown sign pointing to the right read, *Mottisfont Abbey*. Our convoy halted, still widely spread. Martin laid the OS map on the bonnet of our Land Rover.

'It's a few hundred yards down there; across those two rivers. But it’s a narrow lane ... little room for manoeuvre if anyone's waiting. Just in case whoever caused that carnage at King’s Somborne has taken a fancy to Gerry's country house, we need to stay sharp. We'll recce it on foot. Philip and Tony with me. Gerry, you come too since you know what we're looking for. Craig, you're in charge here. If the shit hits the fan, get the hell out of here quickly. Let the others know what's happening. Let's go.'

Craig muttered, 'Good luck.'

I was oddly disconcerted to see "Craig" to be given any semblance of responsibility. Because Craig was none other than Degsie's partner in crime, Jacko.

In previous times, this would have been an idyllic English country lane to wander down. A pretty cottage, tall hedges, the smells of summer and a peaceful river. But no longer. We were all jittery. Perhaps we had all been spooked by King's Somborne; I know I had. And I was the only one unarmed.

Martin was right to be wary, for as soon as we turned the bend in the narrow lane we saw a bridge over the River Test. On the far side of the bridge stood a National Trust Land Rover completely blocking the road. Keeping undercover, we bent low. Martin took out binoculars to see who was manning this makeshift barricade. After a few minutes, he muttered, 'Can't see anyone. Let's get a bit closer.' When we were about twenty-five metres away, he called out. There was no reply.

'We are going to be totally exposed as we cross that bridge, so we'll do it one at a time. Tony go first.' Without hesitation, Tony moved forward, at a crouched run, rifle at the ready. To my relief, he crossed the bridge without being challenged.

Martin said, 'OK, I'll go next. Wait for me to get across, then you, Gerry. Then Phil.'

So saying he was gone. There was no sign of anyone manning that barricade, but we were all conscious of being exposed targets if anyone was watching. We pushed on. I had no recollection of how we had approached the place all those years ago, so I had no idea what to expect. Eventually, we came to an entrance to the car park for Mottisfont Abbey.

A chain was draped across two wooden entrance posts upon which hung a hand-made sign that read,

In accordance with Government Directive 3,
the Abbey is closed for the duration of the emergency.

The building looked smaller than I remembered and more dilapidated. That may have been because what had been well-manicured lawns were now a riot of weeds. No special security measures had been put in place, and we gained entry by Philip putting his shoulder to a small side door. On Martin's orders, we then systematically searched each room. Mottisfont Abbey was deserted; whoever had worked here had chosen not to die here.

As we stood on the top floor, Martin and the others seemed to visibly unwind; they smiled at each other and gave high-fives. 'I think you've done us proud here, Gerry! We can relax here for a few days. Added to which, this place is defendable. Look at it. Clear views and fields-of-fire in all directions.'

He was right; it was a sturdy Georgian building built on the foundations of a medieval Franciscan abbey.

'What's more, there were some useful looking kitchens downstairs. Phil, I think it's safe to get the others. Let's see if we can rustle up a meal. I'm famished. While Phil does that, we three will have a look around the village, just to see if anyone's about.'

Mottisfont Village turned out to be small; about two dozen houses clustered around the outside wall of the Abbey. I guessed some of those residents would have worked there. We shouted and forced a few doors but found nobody alive, only their nauseous remains. By the time we were back to the Abbey, the other vehicles were parked, and the Group were milling about taking their bearings.

Cassie was talking to a man who was smiling broadly. I was disconcerted to see it was Craig Jackson. As I approached, he nodded to her before sidling off.

Cassie looked relieved to see me. ‘Glad to see you’re safe.’ She peered up at the building. 'This looks nice, Gerry.'

'Yeah. A bit faded now, but I imagine it’s seen plenty of life in its time.'

'This is quite a coup for you. Everyone's relieved ... and impressed.'

'Just luck that I'd been here before.'

'So what's the plan? Are we going to stay in the house?'

'Nobody's said. I guess we'll have a meeting sometime. Thrash things out. In the meantime, Martin's suggested we treat ourselves to a meal.'

'I'd better go see Gavin Brennan. Catch you later.'

As she walked away, holding Julie’s hand, I felt pleased that Cassie was starting to embrace her new role; God knows we needed someone with an iota of medical knowledge. Remembering I was only with the Group because she had told Martin we were partners, without a doubt, I was indebted.

The first 'formal' meeting of the full Group since leaving London took place that evening. We had gathered in the largest room, and for the first time, we were together. It was also the first time I was able to make an accurate count of our number. There were twenty-six of us that night, although Gavin Brennan was in another room. Everyone seemed light-hearted; euphoria brought on by the sheer release of tension and having eaten a frugal but welcome meal. We felt safe for a few days at least.

Martin had positioned himself in an ornate armchair, and everyone else sat around in varying degrees of comfort. He had that air of boyish charm again; this was Martin as we had first seen him, not Martin, the no-nonsense army officer.

'Well, apart from the wound to Gavin, so far so good. What's the update on the patient, doctor?'

I sensed Cassie's discomfort with the title; nevertheless, she replied. 'He's more comfortable now he can lay still. He's lost a lot of blood, but mercifully, the bleeding seems to have stopped.'

'Excellent news. For all those who do not know, I'll start the proceedings by introducing Cassandra Metcalf. Cassie spent a year training to be a doctor. As you can imagine, the survival rate for any health professional was virtually zero. Their constant exposure to the Flu was catastrophic. So we are fortunate to have found Mrs Metcalf.'

There was a general murmur of agreement around the room.

Cassie was pale; her face had a look I had not seen before. She promptly stood and nervously said, 'Before anyone gets the wrong idea, I did just one year of medicine before dropping out. I'd decided medicine wasn't for me. And that was eighteen years ago. What little medical knowledge I may have absorbed ... has well and truly gone. I am not a doctor, and it would be a serious mistake to regard me as one.'

The room fell silent.

Martin said quietly. 'But I am sure you will do all you can to brush up your skills, Cassandra. We've collected several medical books of one sort or another.'

Cassie was trembling.

He continued, 'And I suspect that over the coming months until things stabilise, we'll all find ourselves doing things we'd never dreamed of doing.'

The atmosphere in the room had started to slide, and Martin sensed it.

'Now I think it's time we got to know one another. I was going to leave it until we reached our final destination. But let's do it now. Let’s go around the room ... with everyone spending a few minutes telling us about themselves.'

He hesitated, 'Look, I know that for most of us these last fifteen months have been a nightmare we don't want to relive. Myself included. But I think it may have a cathartic effect. So why don't I start the ball rolling? And while we're doing so, I'm going to tell you why each person was invited to join us.'

At which point, I began to feel uneasy.

Chapter 46. The Group

'I'm Martin Fuller. I'm 27 years old, and until about three months ago I was a captain in the Norfolk Regiment. My wife and I, and our three-year-old son, lived in married-quarters at Norwich Barracks. When the balloon went up, my unit was posted to Birmingham with orders to prevent civilians from leaving the city,' he paused.

'What I found myself doing ... sickened me. We were firing on our own people. Unbelievable. So I left. Deserted if you like. Definitely, a court-martial offence if ever things go back to pre-plague times. Which they never will. Not in my lifetime, anyway. Before I got back to Norwich, Nicole, my wife, and Daniel had caught the flu. They died as I nursed them. I probably got the virus from them. I remember being ill and thinking I was going to die; it's all a bit of a blur. But one day I suddenly realised I'd survived. That's when I decided to try to collect some decent people together and start afresh. I fear that few of the skills I was taught at Sandhurst or while serving will be much use for the future ...'

A man's voice from my left called, 'Why didn't you tell us you were army when we were still in London?'

Martin paused; I sensed tension.

'Many people have … understandably ... developed what I call ... a jaundiced view of the military over the past months. Seem to think we're all born killers. We're not. We were simply carrying out orders as we had been trained to do. When I deserted, I decided to select a bunch of decent-minded people whose views of us are not tainted.'

There was another pause before a woman's voice called from across the room, 'Mr Fuller, it's thanks to your leadership skills we're all sitting here this evening.'

There were murmurs of, 'Hear, hear.'

'Thank you, Mrs Westonby. Why don't you go next?'

The woman walked to stand beside Martin setting a pattern that everyone afterwards followed. Alice Westonby is the oldest person in The Group. Sharp featured and with grey hair tied into an unflattering old-fashioned bun. She is in no way a mother-figure, although, at one time or another, most of us have confided in her or sought her advice.

'Alice Westonby. I was a civil servant in the Treasury. Unmarried, no living relatives, so probably spared some of the emotional trauma most of you experienced. But I lost my partner and dearest friend.'

There was just a hint of a tremble in her voice.

'Like Mr Fuller, I seemed to have survived a bout of the flu. Special skills, well, I was a senior strategic planner, so some background of seeing the bigger picture. Read PPE at Oxford. Got my PhD in Strategic Planning. What else? Hobbies? Enjoyed bridge and my weekly badminton evenings; neither of which will be of value here. Alas, none of my friends survived. I think that's all for now.'

Before she could walk back to her seat, Martin glanced at the clipboard he held. 'Well, I doubt I need to say more about Alice. She has a quality of mind we'll find invaluable as we begin to evolve our future strategy. OK, who's next?'

Another woman stepped up; it was the one who had helped Martin with the recruiting.

Cassie whispered, 'I knew she wouldn't be slow coming forward.'

'Jessica Trehearne. I was the PA of the MD of a manufacturing company. We made lighting ... especially the large neon signs. You'll have all seen our products.' She paused, and her breezy nature seemed to fade. 'I lost my partner. We'd been together for six years and were talking about getting married. Too late, alas. Special skills, well, I'm a good organiser and not afraid of long hours. As soon as I heard Martin speak, I knew that this would be the best thing to do. The cities were turning into death-traps. Is that enough, Martin?'

'It'll do for now. So why, Jess? Energy, enthusiasm, and organisational skills. Who's next. Tony, how about you.'

The corporal stepped forward. 'Tony Taplin. I'm 24. I was in the Norfolks like Captain Fuller. I didn't like what we were doing either, so I got out with him. I had a girlfriend in Colchester, but she's gone. Skills? Well, soldiering mainly. Did a couple of tours of Iraq and Afghanistan. Did a few training courses that might come in useful. M.T. mainly ... oh, and a bit of pioneer corps stuff. You never know.'

'Thanks, Tony. Why Tony? Completely reliable. A good, thinking soldier. Next.'

Jacko stepped up. 'Craig Jackson. I'm thirty-nine. First of all, and on behalf of everyone, I'd like to thank you for getting us here, Mr Fuller. None of us would have escaped from London without you.' There was another murmur of agreement.'

Martin simply nodded.

Jackson hesitated. 'I may as well just say it ... get it over with. Both my kids caught it early ... and died. After that, Sandra, my wife committed suicide,' he took a deep breath, 'And I nearly did too ... but was too much of a coward. I definitely had the disease for a while, and I seem to have no memory of quite a longish period. Just flashbacks.'

Having a sceptical nature, I was dubious. I muttered to Cassie, 'I wonder if his flashbacks involve Degsie and an Alsatian dog.'

Jacko continued, 'Skills and hobbies. Well, I was a manager ... so organising staff. Not much time for hobbies. Golf mainly for what it's worth. A bit of DIY, nothing fancy. That's about it.'

Martin frowned, 'And what did you do for a living?'

'Oh yes, I ran a firm that sold electrical goods.'

Martin looked at his clipboard, 'You said you were an electrician!'

Jackson looked flustered, 'Well, yeah, I know a bit about it.'

'So not a real hands-on electrician?'

'Well, no, not as such. But I'm sure I can turn my hand to it ...'

Martin did not look pleased. 'Let's hope you can for your sake. That’s why you were selected.'

Craig Jackson returned to his seat, smirking slightly; he did not look at all embarrassed. Martin, however, was frowning.

I muttered to Cassie, ‘Electrician my arse. He’s no more an electrician than I am.’

'Next. How about you, Wendy isn't it?’ Martin said.

A young, thin woman stood up hesitantly. Compared with the previous speakers, she looked decidedly nervous.

'I'm Wendy. Wendy Fraiser. I'm twenty-four. Born in Scotland. Me and my boyfriend worked in Aldi. Then the plague broke out. And one day he stopped ringing. When I went round to his place, he wouldn't let me in. Called out he thought he'd caught it. They took him away. I never saw him again. Don't have any special skills. Just an ordinary shop worker.'

Consulting his clipboard, Martin said, 'But Wendy used to enjoy riding, so she's probably good with animals. Thank you, Wendy. Who's next?'

A woman near the front stood up and turned to face us. 'Jane Passfield. Wife and mother. Lost my whole family to this fucking disease. Husband, kids, parents, the lot. I'm determined to survive, and I think this is our best chance.' As she stood glaring at us, defying anyone to challenge her, a tear ran down her cheek.

Martin glanced again at his notes and said gently, 'Jane's 34. She omitted to mention the major skill she brings to the party. She was a school cook! And I'm sure we all appreciated her effort this afternoon ... albeit with limited ingredients available. Well done, Jane.'

There was a muttered round of congratulations.

Cassie whispered, 'She's on a knife-edge. I thought so this afternoon when I was helping in the kitchen.'

A man who had been in our truck stood up.

'Trevor Beamish, Mr Fuller. Wife died of it seven months-ago. I nursed 'er till the end. But I never caught it meself. Funny that ...'

Martin interrupted. 'You never had it at all, Trevor?'

'Well, nothin' like you others describe. I thought I'd caught it, but it turned out to ordinary flu. No loss of memory, nothing like that.'

'Interesting. Carry on.'

'Used to work for the council. Household Waste Operative was the poncy name they gave us. Everyone else called us Bin Men. Not much of a one for 'obbies. 'Cept football of course. Big fan of The Palace. Season ticket 'older me. Even went to some of their away games. Big fan.'

Martin smiled, 'Canaries man myself. Thanks, Trevor. Good to have you with us.'

He cast his eye around. 'How about you, Toya isn't it?'

A young black woman stood up; she looked to be about twenty. I gained the impression that a year or so ago, she had been twice her current weight.

'Toya Eaton, from Tooting. I was learning ... to be a beautician. Not much use now. Didn't have no hobbies. Just used to hang out with my friends. Loved music. Brought all my music collection with me. On a memory stick. '

Embarrassed Toya shrugged, 'That's all.'

Martin smiled at her, 'Toya, I'm sure that after a few years we're all going to need your beautician skills.'

Watching Toya, I remembered the kids at my school. Like so many with her background, she had low self-esteem; she had probably been indolent and lacking in ambition. How would they fare in this new world order?

I whispered to Cassie, 'Odd choice, considering all the others available.'

A haggard, unshaven man stood up. 'I am Goran Petrovik ... from Poland. I come to England to work three years ago. I am stranded when travel ban came. My family are in Poznan ... I do not know if they alive. Nobody has been able to contact Poland. Oh, I'm twenty-five ... same age as my wife.'

Martin glanced at his clipboard. 'And your job, Goran?'

'I was fitter. I fit replacement boilers in houses.'

'So, Goran has skills at handling gas, electricity and water. A useful man to have around. Even though there is unlikely to be gas or electricity on tap for the foreseeable future.' But Goran had not finished, 'One day I go back to Poland. But for now, cities, not good places to be.'

'Thanks, Goran. How about you, Mike?'

The West Indian who said he remembered me from the Distribution Centre stood up.

'OK. I'm Michael Southern; I'm thirty-six. I came to the UK as a baby, so I've spent pretty much my whole life here. I was a prison officer at Brixton Prison. My story's the same as all yours. My wife was a nurse, so the family got infected early on. None of them survived. Same as all you, I had it ... and did survive. God knows how or why! But I'm thankful to be among like-minded people. If we pull together with Martin leading us ... we can make this work. That's about it for now.'

Martin gave a gentle reminder, 'Nothing else you'd like people to know?'

Michael Southern hesitated, then gave a deep sigh. 'In my spare time, I was a deacon at my local Baptist church. But no more. The thought of a generous and compassionate God is ... anathema to me now.' The room was silent for some moments.

'Your turn, Gerry.'

Suddenly nervous, I said my piece but name rank and number only, all the time fearing that when I had finished, Martin would tell the Group the only reason I was there was because Cassandra Metcalf had insisted. But he did not. Other than that, my story was the same as everyone else's.

'How about, you. Jinta isn't it?'

The thin Asian woman stood up, still holding her baby, which was looking around the room. Her accent was strong; probably Punjabi, I could not tell.

'We came to England five years ago. My husband's brother had an Indian restaurant ... and we worked there. Then sickness started, and it closed. But Sunil had caught it. Before he died ... I found I was pregnant.' The poor girl looked embarrassed at having to make such a confession to strangers.

'My son, Vijay, was born seven months ago.'

She looked pleadingly at Martin.

'Thank you, Jinta. Vijay is the youngest member of our group. It's good that we have a baby with us. He's our mascot of hope. Now, who haven't we heard from?'

'Me, Mr Fuller. Daniel Tucker. I'm one of the old codgers ... forty-four. Lost all my lot too. And everyone else in my tower-bock as far as I could make out. But I left there months ago. Had to; the stink was awful. Been a carpenter ever since I left school. On building sites mainly. Always workin' for someone else. As for hobbies, well, that's easy. I loved me allotment. Me and the missus spent many an 'appy 'our down there. Grew all our own veg, right through summer and into autumn. Even stopped goin' on 'olidays because everything was beginnin' to ripen ... and we wanted to 'arvest it when it was at its best. You can't beat it.'

'And that makes you an important member of the group, Danny. Welcome. Anyone we've missed out?'

A young man of Asian ancestry hesitantly put up his hand.

Martin nodded, 'Yes, Euan, isn't it?'

'Euan Miles, Mr Fuller ... from Wales. Our village got the flu ... and my Dad went down with it. Mum sent me to stay with relatives in Thornton Heath. Wasn't easy ... I walked most of the way. My parents must be dead now. They didn't answer their phone about a month after I left. And I got no replies from anyone I texted in the village. I never had a job. I was still at college ... studying accountancy.'

A few people, including Martin and myself, smiled. Martin said, 'Hopefully there's going to be little need for that in our community. Right, who's next?'

A thin young woman hesitantly raised her hand; she was in tears. Martin glanced at his clipboard.

'Raisa Kovaks, right?'

She nodded. 'I come to England to be au-pair ... for lawyer's family. They were good to me. But all died, and I was left alone. I wish only to go home to my family. Back to Bratislava.'

And she burst into tears. The mood plunged again. I felt so sorry for those of us stranded far from home; perhaps that had been how Nick felt, among strangers.

Martin said gently, 'I have to say, Raisa, that at this point, the prospect of you returning home looks unlikely. I know this sounds strange, but we are all your family now. The Group is the family all of us have lost.'

Several people nodded their heads; some smiled at each other. Quietly they began to chat.

Then the young girl who had befriended Julie walked over to Martin. She said something that I could not catch; Martin smiled and nodded. The girl turned to face us, and we fell silent.

She stood pale, gaunt, and determined. ‘I’ve listened to all of you. So I want you to know my story. My name’s Lynne Filton, and I’m nearly thirteen. We lived in Croydon. Then my Mum got sick. They took her away, and we didn’t know where. Dad went to try to find her … and didn’t come back. So I had to look after my little brother, Peter, who was six. Then he died. So I tried to bury him in our garden like I’d seen other people do. But I couldn’t dig deep enough ‘cos the ground was too hard. And a pack of dogs dug him up … and ate him.’

There was a gasp around the room.

Cassie was not the only one to put her hand across her mouth.

The child’s eyes looked pleading, ‘I couldn’t stop them! I tried … but one of them turned on me … and bit me. I had to run into the house. But I tried. Honestly!’

We looked on in silence, contemplating her appalling ordeal.

‘That’s all. I just wanted someone to know.’ She wiped her eyes, before walking back to where she had been sitting; Jane Passfield put her arm around her.

Even Martin looked shocked. Then he cleared his throat, ‘Well, all I can say is … if we have people as brave as Lynne in our company … we have a promising future.’

Several women went over to Lynne to pat her back and give her a hug.

Martin composed himself, ‘Anyone else want to speak tonight?’

Nobody responded although I was sure not everyone had spoken. Gradually people began to chat quietly. The release of tension was palpable.

It was some minutes before Martin stood and stretched himself, 'Well, I don't know about the rest of you, but I feel whacked. We'll have a guard rota again tonight and every night from now on. We don't want to be jumped by anyone.'

Alice Westonby chimed in. 'Can I suggest, Mr Fuller, that for added security, and until things sort themselves out, that we all bed down in this house rather than the trucks. Men and women in separate rooms, of course.'

Chapter 47. Proposal

As we filed out of that room, I felt elated. The adrenalin was flowing. Perhaps because after sixteen months of trauma, we had reached some kind of sanctuary. It was only eight-thirty and the evening was pleasant if overcast. I invited Cassie for a stroll around the grounds before dusk. We walked alongside what looked to be a man-made river about fifty yards from the house. Julie threw sticks for Dog to fetch. The air had a damp feel to it; autumn approached.

'What do you think of our fellow travellers?' Cassie asked.

'Wow, there's a phrase with other connotations. But a pretty mixed bag. Not sure why Martin chose some of them. Especially some of the women. Didn't seem to have any particular skills.'

'I wondered about that. And I think I've guessed why.'

'What?'

'CBH'

I frowned, 'CBH? What's that?'

'An acronym we used to use in the orchestra. CBH ... Child-Bearing Hips.'

'You're kidding!'

'I'm not actually. Apart from Alice Westonby, all the females are of child-bearing age.'

'Hmm, I hadn't noticed.' Then I recalled that first conversation I had with Martin Fuller.

'But you're probably right.'

'Well, if he thinks I'm a breed-mare he's got another think coming.'

I thought it politic not to reply.

Cassie stared ahead, 'My God, that poor kid, Lynne. Watching your brother being eaten by dogs. God. Horrific experience at any time, but at twelve-years-old! I'm sure it'll stop me sleeping tonight.'

'The kid has guts, that's for sure. What a shitty experience.'

We walked for some time in silence.

I sensed Cassie shiver before she said, 'Everything's changed, hasn't it. Listening to us describe our past lives drove it home. Whatever we were ... whatever we did ... is irrelevant. It's never coming back, is it? The cavalry is not going to come charging over the hill. It's Brave New World time.'

'It sure is. But it could have been worse.'

'How in God's name do you make that out!'

'We could be survivors from a nuclear war wandering around a devastated country, waiting to die of radiation sickness. As it is, the infrastructure's intact, mainly. We've just got to rebuild human society.'

'Huh, just he says. In my opinion, *just* is a four-letter word.'

We walked for a while, enjoying the evening air.

She seemed pensive, 'All the rules have changed, haven't they? Everything.'

I simply nodded.

Then, to my surprise, Cassandra took my hand. 'Gerry, now we're safely out of London, why don't we try to make it on our own. Just the three of us.'

I sighed, 'Cass, I honestly think we have more chance of survival in a group. We saw examples of what we've been reduced to on the journey down. It's not going to improve anytime soon. There's safety in numbers. Especially having a few soldiers around.'

'You make it sound so easy!'

'Huh! That's the last thing I think. Townies like us are so far removed from even rudimentary self-sufficiency that the next few years are going to be an uphill struggle. We're going to have to re-learn a lot of old skills to have any chance at all.

We're going to have to grow our own food ... make our own bread ... make candles ... husband our own animals ... and slaughter them ... concoct our own medicines. What little fuel there is to run engines will soon run out. Kevles has set humanity back a thousand years ... at least. What's to worry about!'

'Oddly, it's the thought of delivering babies that terrifies me.'

I reached out and squeezed her hand, 'Everyone I've spoken to is so grateful you're with us. Some of the other women have given birth; it'll be OK.'

We walked about twenty yards with only the silky murmur of the river and the cawing of rooks and jackdaws breaking the silence.

'Do you think there are other groups like us?' she asked.

'Sure to be ... somewhere.'

'Coming through that village today with the burned-out cars and that hanging man ... really frightened me. The violence seemed so casual. So unnecessary.'

'That's why there's safety in numbers. My God, look at the size of those fish!'

I was amazed at the dark shapes lying await in the river.

'Wow! That must weigh about four pounds. Look ... another ... and another. There are loads of them.'

'What are they?'

'Trout probably. Perhaps it's a fish supper tomorrow. I'll mention it to Martin.'

We slowly wandered along the overgrown paths. Pausing at a narrow bridge, I noticed that at some time in the past this man-made tributary of the River Test had been channelled to flow between low walls, now reduced to ground level. But the water ran through at a fair rate. Which made me wonder if a mill had stood there in the past. Soon after that, we discovered the spring, with crystal-clear water welling up vigorously. A

National Trust notice stated that it was probably the presence of the natural spring which had caused the Franciscan monks to build Mottisfont Abbey here. In retrospect, perhaps it was that sign that seeded my idea.

I woke early the next morning and lay thinking about where our caravan had rested. And I decided to reconnoitre the site more thoroughly. An idea had started to germinate.

So, in a chilly dawn with mist hanging over the river, and clutching a notepad, I began my lone exploration.

Mottisfont Abbey is not a stately home in the grand style, but it surely had been a comfortable family home for the lord of the manor at some time. The centre section looked to be a solid red-brick Georgian construction built on medieval foundations; the wings were a made of dull grey stone. In fact, the original cellars were exposed at ground level and were being used for storage. Part of the ground floor level had been converted into a restaurant by the National Trust with a modern kitchen capable of feeding dozens of visitors, albeit using gas and electricity. There were pantries and larders dating from before refrigeration. The first floor contained the social rooms and the upper floors many bedrooms. Some had obviously been servant's quarters.

Standing apart from the main building was a stable and storage area which the National Trust had converted into tea-rooms and a gift shop; so the buildings were sound and weatherproof. Across a grassed area stood a large walled garden that had become a tangle of overgrown roses, shrubs, and weeds. It was only later when we found old brochures, did we realise that the walled garden had once held the National Collection of old English roses. In addition, there were buildings which may have been estate offices.

The area at the front of the house had been a laid to lawn, presumably to give the owners in Georgian times a fashionable vista. To the back of the house was more lawn but also a parterre garden leading the eye to an open field that now had a nondescript crop of rotting cereal in it. I rubbed some of the cereal heads in my hands; they felt dry and hard. I doubted it had been planted this spring; it may have been gleanings from last year, hence its bedraggled appearance. But it was apparent even to my city eye that this was good, fertile land.

Walking back along the lane we had used the previous day I saw what I assumed must be water meadows; dried cowpats indicated that this pasture had been used for grazing although, there were no cattle visible now.

Apart from one, the road approaches to Mottisfont village were via three narrow lanes; the exception being what appeared to have sometime been intended as a grand approach to the Abbey; it took the form of a dead straight road that ran west for about half a mile.

During my exploration, my germ of an idea had taken root.

It was mid-morning before I went to find Martin to present my thinking. He was talking with Cassandra. Initially, I assumed they were discussing Gavin Brennan, but she was laughing and walked off before I reached them. He stood watching her go. Undeterred I told him my thoughts.

'You mean, stay here!'

'Well, I'm not sure how much further west you intended to go.'

'I was flexible. As far away from any major conurbation as possible. Dorset or Devon possibly.'

'Well, this must be about seventy miles from London. Southampton is, oh, say ten miles south. That's the nearest major city. Salisbury and Winchester are much smaller; I've visited them.'

Martin was pensive for a while, and he looked dubious. He needed persuading.

'I've not come to this view lightly. It would be clearer if I walked you through it?'

He stood staring at me for a few moments. Then he called to Tony, 'Gerry and I are going to beat the bounds. Keep us company.'

Tony immediately collected his rifle.

'Right,' said Martin, 'Give me the grand tour ... and convince me.'

It took nearly two-hours to retrace my tracks and cover all pros and cons for remaining at Mottisfont. Then we made a more detailed tour of the houses in the village.

Tony asked, 'Can the Abbey be seen from the main road we came in on?'

'Good point. We need to check that out.'

'I'll do it, sir,' Tony replied.

Martin hardly spoke but was taking it all in. Eventually, I had said everything I wanted to say. Nodding, he said, 'I underestimated you, Gerry. You're a useful man to have around. There's merit in your suggestion. So I'm going to get you to make your pitch to the whole Group this evening. Let's hear what they think.'

He smiled, 'Now you've pointed them out, I think this place has capabilities!'

I spent the rest of the afternoon retracing my steps and making sure of my facts. I wanted to use Cassie as a sounding-board, but to my surprise found her talking with Craig Jackson; although, at second glance, it was Jacko doing most of the talking. I left them to it. When later I managed to find her alone, although she saw some merit in my proposals, I sensed she had reservations.

Late in the afternoon, it began to rain, and people moped around, listlessly.

I said to Cassie, 'Why don't they find something useful to do?'

'They're not all driven like you, Gerry. They're probably missing media gratification. It's the youngsters who'll struggle most. They were addicted. I noticed the young, coloured girl, Toya is it? Still has her iPhone dangling around her neck ... like an amulet ... probably hoping it will suddenly burst into life! Poor kid can't accept it's all gone.'

'Christ, that all ended a year ago. It was valueless anyway! Useless and parasitical.'

'Not to their generation.'

After another frugal meal, Martin said he wanted everyone to assemble in the Meeting Room. When we did, he took his position in the ornate chair.

Without preamble, he said, 'Gerry has a proposal to make, and I want you all to hear him out. The floor's yours.'

For someone who had spent his life addressing pupils, I felt very nervous. But once I had started, enthusiasm crept into my delivery. Spelling out the big problems, I emphasised that the tasks facing us would be the same, no matter where we put down roots.

'Priority One. Food! Plain and simple. We *have to* become self-sufficient very quickly. We may have just about enough food to see us through the coming winter, although I hope to God, it's not as hard as the last one. But there's little leeway. I propose we gradually clear the whole of the walled-garden area to plant vegetables. Then dig up the front lawn and do the same there. The soil's good, and it's protected from the wind. Then there's water. A reliable water supply ended about a year ago in the cities; and we are going to need clean, fresh, water. And Mottisfont has one; a free-flowing supply of spring water which has supplied this place since Norman times ... probably longer.'

Wendy remarked, 'Yes. I saw that sign. Looks OK!'

'Also, we need to scour the countryside to find supplies of grain; otherwise, no bread. In fact, we need cereals of every kind. And seed-potatoes. We need those urgently before they rot. We may strike lucky at nearby farms. Fortunately, there's a tractor in a barn at the far end of the grounds. Let's hope it has fuel. Otherwise, it's ploughing and sowing and reaping and hoeing by hand, just as they did three-hundred years-ago.'

Alice Westonby asked quietly, 'How much land will we need to feed us all?'

'Good question. Books on self-sufficiency generally reckon you need at least an acre to feed a family of two. There are twenty-six of us, so about thirteen acres. Clearly, we have vastly more acreage than that within the estate walls. The critical step is getting it cleared and planted.'

'Then what?'

'Find farm animals. Every type: cows, sheep, pigs, horses, goats, chickens, geese, you name it; we could even keep rabbits. And as anyone who has looked at the river can see, there are fish galore. So we have the option of a fish farm ...'

A woman's quiet voice said, 'Sounds like you want to make same mistakes again! Repeat all the wrongs Kevles condemned ... make the death of all our loved ones in vain.'

It was the Slovakian girl, Raisa Kovaks. I was taken aback, 'What do you propose we do?'

Her gaze was piercing. 'Become vegetarian. No more brutality to animals. Respect life. Don't let humans control earth again. Allow Gaia to ... flourish.'

The room was silent.

I tried to respond logically, 'Well, we are going to need plenty of calories to see us through, Raisa. We're going to have to get accustomed to hard, manual labour again. I doubt a vegetarian diet would give us enough energy to do that.'

'But, please, no more factory farms ... or battery chickens ... no fish farms ... no calves for veal. Respect life! Please.'

'I doubt there will be anything like that again in our lifetime.'

To my surprise, Trevor Beamish said, 'He's right. But who the hell wants to live on beans!'

Jane Passfield called out, 'But you said we were heading for the West Country, Mr Fuller. After what we saw as we came through that village yesterday ... surely it's not safe here.'

Martin shook his head, 'No, I said I didn't know where we'd end up ... as long as it was away from a city. Gerry spelt out what we need to do wherever we end up. And the more one thinks about it, the more this place has going for it. And another point is it's much more defendable from attack than a typical farmhouse.'

'And it can't be seen from the main road, I checked. At least not at this time of year when the leaves are on the trees. Might be different in winter,' Tony said.

Martin continued, 'As for what happened at King's Somborne, well, I fear such occurrences are probably common now. Tony, Philip and I have seen similar ... outrages.'

'Do you expect us to be attacked?'

'Can't overlook the possibility.'

'What did that sign mean, SDF Territory?'

'No idea. But my guess is a bunch of thugs who have ganged up to rule the area.'

'Will they come back?'

'Probably, sometime. You all saw what we encountered getting this far. There are desperate and violent people about. Once we start to become self-sufficient, we'll have to defend what we've grown. Is there anything more you want to say, Gerry?'

'No, I've had my say. Thanks.'

'So, what do others think about this place?'

Craig Jackson had a cynical smile, 'I think he's gilded the lily. It's not all doom and gloom.'

Martin frowned, 'What makes you say that?'

'Well, all this bucolic Archers stuff. None of us has a clue about growing food! Besides, there must still be tons of it laying around for the taking, if we knew where to look.'

Martin watched him intently, 'Possibly. How do you plan to get it?'

'We just take it from anyone who has it! Same as that lot tried with us a couple of days ago.'

'So sink to their level?'

Jacko shrugged and smiled, 'Survival of the toughest nowadays. We've already seen that. Perhaps that SDF bunch have the right idea.'

'You fancy joining them?'

'I never said that.'

Martin stared at Craig Jackson for a few moments. I hoped his thoughts were the same as mine; it was a mistake inviting that one; the proverbial rotten apple.

'Well, I suggest we all sleep on it tonight. Then tomorrow morning I would encourage you all to have a good look round bearing in mind what Gerry has said. After that, I'll take soundings. Then I'll decide whether we stay at Mottisfont or push on. My objective was to stick together as a group for safety. Hopefully, we can still do that. But I don't intend to force anyone to do anything. In the meantime, I've posted the guard rota for tonight on the restaurant notice board. It'll be dark soon, so I suggest we turn in. Since we're not entirely sure who else is in this area, let's not go flashing any lights around.'

As on the previous evening, Cassie and I went outside to take the air.

'I think it's brilliant you remembering this place. I can see it working. Do you think many will want to travel further?'

'Difficult to say.'

'Craig Jackson can go as far as he likes. What an arsehole.'

'An acquired taste for sure.'

'I'm glad you answered that European girl the way you did. I never liked the idea of factory farms either. All just for profit.'

'Yes, that was interesting. Kevles' manifesto clearly touched a nerve with some people.'

We walked for a while, before Cassie said, 'Gerry, I've been giving a lot of thought to something. Something we need to decide.'

'What's that?'

'Whether you and I become ... partners. Real partners, I mean.'

Had I misheard? I turned to look at her, 'Are you serious?'

'Of course! People will pair off. It's going to happen. And I've already had ... overtures ... from one or two men. If you're interested ... well, you need to put down a marker.'

Perhaps I smiled, 'It had never even occurred to me.'

'Obviously not. My God why are men so slow! Or have you got your eye on someone else?

'Not at all!'

'So that's agreed.'

Bemused, perhaps I hesitated, 'This is all very sudden.'

Cassie cocked her head slightly; she had a wry smile that reminded me of Rose.

Hesitantly I said, 'When you say ... partnership ...'

She stopped and took my hand, 'Jesus! Look, Gerry. I don't know if ... or when ... there’ll be time for romance in future. But from where I'm standing, in the given circumstances ... well, you look like a pretty good catch. You're smart, intelligent ...

and well, resourceful and caring. So by partnership ... I mean ... like husband and wife. Full on.'

Perhaps I stood dumbstruck because that was when Cassandra Metcalf pulled my head down and kissed me as if she meant it. It was not unpleasant.

When I came up for air, she said brightly, 'Good. That's agreed. From now on, we're an item.'

As I lay in my sleeping bag that night, I could not help thinking about Cassie's proposal. I was under no illusion as to what it was about; it was merely an attempt on her part to gain an iota of security in our chaotic new world. I did not blame her. Perhaps she had made the same proposal to Martin and Jacko. But I was not sure I wanted that level of responsibility. And the more I considered it, the less enthusiastic I became. Everything was too chaotic. It would be better to defer any such thoughts until things were more settled. I resolved to let her down gently the next day.

Chapter 48. Decision

Considering it was such a momentous decision, Martin's announcement, which happened at mid-day, was an anti-climax.

We were having soup when he stood and said, 'I've consulted all the adults this morning and found out how you all feel. I'll be honest, there's not a unanimous wish to stay here; some think we're still too close to major cities. Southampton is only about ten miles away. But on balance I think this place has a lot going for it. The difficulties we may face with outsiders will be the same wherever we end up. So I've decided we will stay at Mottisfont. We stay. That's my decision. Anyone who doesn't like it is free to travel on. But without our transport or supplies of course. Any questions?'

Nobody answered.

Cassie whispered, 'He doesn't beat about the bush, does he.'

'A man of action,'

She squeezed my arm.

Someone said hesitantly, 'So will we all live in this house, Mr Fuller?'

'I think it would be best ... until we know the lay-of-the-land.'

Danny Tucker chipped in, 'Well, I think this is a great place. We can really do something with all this land.'

But Martin had not finished, 'There's one other thing. Before we left London, I told you I would lead the expedition and that I would eventually appoint a couple of advisors. Well, I've decided that Alice Westonby and Gerry Morris are best suited for those roles.'

I was astonished; there had been no consultation.

'Their first task will be to plan what needs to be done. We don't have time for buggering about so rough and ready will do. Refinements will come later. Gerry, what should they start doing first?'

Taken by surprise, I said hesitantly, 'Well, clearing that old walled garden would be a good start. Then we can get seeds planted ...'

'Good. Let's do so. Danny, you organise that. Jane has agreed to be in charge of the kitchen, so I've told her to select a couple of helpers. Everyone else will help Danny. And I mean everyone. We won't be carrying any shirkers. Meanwhile, Tony, Philip and I will recce the surrounding area ...'

Unprompted I said, 'Keep an eye out for any farm animals ... and any fruit still on the trees.'

As the group started to break up, Cassie stood up called out, 'Before you all go, I've got an announcement too. Gerry and I ... have decided to become man and wife. Best get it out in the open.'

There was silence for a moment. Then Martin smiled and said, 'Good for you! Congratulations. And we must see about a celebration in due course. Good for morale.'

When people gathered round to congratulate us, I found myself tongue-tied and blushing.

Before she left, Cassie gave me a hug and whispered, 'Special Advisor! I knew I'd picked the right bloke.'

Eventually, only Alice Westonby and I remained in the room. Smiling, she offered her hand. 'You've had quite a morning, Mr Morris. Announcing your nuptials *and* being given a place in the inner-circle.'

'Is that what it is?'

'That's what we must make it. Martin was right; you and I are the obvious candidates. Now, where shall we work?'

Chapter 49. Epilogue

Thus, our motley collection of people began its life at Mottisfont Abbey; damaged survivors of the greatest catastrophe our species has ever encountered; individuals that would coalesce into The Group.

My concentration had drifted. I was watching the smoke curling up from the logs, the dying flames reflected on the Group's faces, when at the end of the Sunday meeting, Martin suddenly said, 'Oh, and I want someone to be recorder for the Group, keep our diary. Gerry should do it.'

This then has been the start of my Mottisfont Chronicle. The story of how and why we arrived at the Abbey. It has been months in the writing, often by candlelight on frosty nights as Cassie lay sleeping. Written in pencil on treasured paper. Looking up, I see a coal-black night sky festooned with stars. Last week as the moon faded, I wondered when humans would again walk on it. If ever!

Gavin Brennan's wound became infected and gangrene set in. He died a few weeks after we settled here. We buried him under one of the huge London Plane trees growing in the grounds. Cassie was devastated; his death severely undermined what little confidence she had. Despite her protests, Martin insisted she continues as our medic.

One intriguing thing happened after Gavin's funeral. Next morning, we found that a wooden cross had been placed at the head of his grave. Martin was not best pleased. He said it showed someone still harboured 'nonsensical religious beliefs … even though he had made it clear from the outset that all form of religion was banned.' Unsurprisingly, nobody owned up.

Working with Alice Westonby has been a revelation. She is a cagy soul with a dry wit, keen powers of observation and a phenomenal memory; one of the most intelligent people I have ever met. And she has a fund of priceless anecdotal information. She is also sensitive to the feelings and moods of individuals and seems able to sense when people are approaching breaking point.

At a recent Sunday evening meeting, several people griped about one thing or the other. Next day Alice said, 'We must not allow this to slide into a dystopian society, Gerry. That could happen as the stress levels rise.'

But recently she really surprised me and made me uneasy. We were standing at our office window when she saw Martin, Tony, and Philip walking towards one of the vehicles, when Alice muttered, 'There walks Caesar with his Praetorian Guard.'

I laughed, then realised she was serious.

'Haven't you noticed, Gerry,' she said, 'Wherever Martin goes, one of them is always with him. And they are always armed.'

'Doesn't want to be caught by a surprise attack.'

'Hmm. I'm not sure. I can't quite make out what he's doing here. It all smacks of too much of Plato's Benevolent Dictatorship.'

I did not comment.

'He's always on the prowl; like a caged animal. Waiting to pounce, or escape.'

'He's got a lot of responsibility …'

'And considering the fuss he made about everyone working, no exceptions, he and his guards don't do a stroke. Just swan around doing reconnaissance. God knows what they expect to find.'

She has a point. It has been bothering me ever since.

When Martin insisted that Cassie and I hold a wedding ceremony to formalise our relationship since it would be good for morale it was Alice who suggested we revive the custom of the happy couple jumping over the broomstick. I protested and was in danger of being regarded as a stick-in-the-mud, but Cassandra was up for it and eventually persuaded me. We were married outdoors on the first Sunday in October; a sparkling autumn day. Michael Southern officiated in a non-religious but dignified ceremony. Booze had been liberated from one of the local houses and Jane Passfield, and her team had prepared a minor feast. I felt incredibly privileged and touched that virtual strangers had gone to such lengths. Although in fact, they are all part of our extended family now. Besides, everyone welcomed having something to celebrate after so much gloom and doom. When in November, Goran and Raisa formalised their relationship by 'jumping-the-broomstick', we realised a tradition had been established.

There is one other thing I should record here. People address me as Mr Morris, Cassie as Doctor Morris, and Alice as Miss Westonby. Martin is addressed as Mr Fuller. I was mystified by this since everyone else is called by their first names. When I expressed my curiosity, Alice told me Martin had suggested those titles be used because it underwrites status and a chain-of-command. I suppose it reflects his military background. I am not convinced but have gradually grown accustomed to it.

If anything, this winter seems even harsher than last. Thick snow again covers the fields. I fear that after all our hard work in clearing the walled garden, few of the seeds we planted as a winter crop will germinate; it is so cold. Luckily, there is plenty of wood for fuel.

When they deserted, Martin and his men liberated several useful items. In addition to an assortment of weapons, were a

2kw petrol-fuelled generator and a short-wave radio. So following the Sunday evening Group meetings, we start the generator and listen to the radio to hear what is happening in the world. But the reception is poor and what little we have picked-up fades in and out badly. Goran thinks we need a proper aerial so that may account for it; but since none of us knows what a proper aerial looks like, we are stymied. However, we do indulge ourselves on Sundays. We play a DVD of a film; that is the sum-total of our entertainment for the week.

What we have heard on the radio is of little comfort. There have been no 'official' BBC-like broadcasts since shortly after we arrived here. We assume that all pretence of government has collapsed.

Despite the Middle East faring better than the rest of the world as far as deaths from Brazilian Flu was concerned, there appears to have been a short sharp war between the Arabs and Israel in which nuclear weapons were used. Nothing more was heard from Israel after that. One can only speculate. In one weak transmission, it was inferred that Mecca, Medina and Riyadh had been obliterated. By whom we do not know. But by then probably only the USA had that capability. There has been no mention of it by the American Radio Ham we picked up. It is frustrating not being able to transmit; thus, a transceiver is on the list of items sought whenever Martin recces further afield.

On one of their early reconnaissance trips, Martin and Tony found a cow and its calf on the edge of nearby woodland; it took four of us all afternoon to herd the beasts back to the Abbey. A few weeks later, they brought back a couple of sheep; but ewes only; no ram.

A helicopter passed close by last week, about three miles to the north so now we keep all our vehicles under cover. We have deliberately isolated ourselves at Mottisfont in the hope we stay clear of any mutations of the virus; time will tell.

We have had only two would-be visitors; an old man and a young woman who asked if they could join us. Both looked starving. We would not allow them into the grounds, so Martin, Alice and I interviewed them from twenty feet away. Martin was prepared to accept the woman if she served ten days quarantine on the edge of the village, but he did not think the old man possessed any skills we needed so would not be allowed in. But the young woman refused to abandon the man; we never found out what their relationship was. We left a small portion of food for them to collect, and eventually, they drifted away. When later I told Cassie, she asked wistfully, 'Was the woman of child-bearing age?'

'Probably, although undernourished.'

'Hmm. I'm surprised our alpha male let her go.'

Given such comments from Alice and Cassie, there seems to be something about Martin that makes women wary, but which I do not detect. Interesting.

A few weeks ago, almost due south, there was a huge column of black smoke that lasted for several days. It looked denser than a funeral pyre. As Martin, Alice, Tony, and I stood on the Abbey roof watching, Martin lined up the smoke on an OS map and concluded that its source may be Fawley Oil Refinery. He is of a mind to drive there, but we are careful with fuel usage. Although there may be fuel to be had there, there are risks.

I have urged us to try to become entirely dependent on our own resources; to use old-fashioned methods wherever possible. We need draught animals for muscle-power, but to date, none have been found.

Our attempts at self-sufficiency have brought a stinging dose of reality. With severely reduced diets, everyone has lost weight. It will be dangerous to lose too much; otherwise, even human muscle power will be depleted. Alice and I have also been considering allocating food according to the amount of physical work an individual does. But we have not yet discussed this strategy with anyone else. There will be uproar if ever we are forced into it.

The lack of even rudimentary knowledge of agriculture and horticulture has proved alarming. After our initial euphoria at escaping from London, everybody now knows survival will not be easy. In fact, some have grown increasingly despondent about staying at Mottisfont. Why they think it might be easier elsewhere baffles me.

Our future is ... at best ... uncertain.

I wonder what London is like now.

This has been my story ... our story ... until now. In some ways, I feel we are colonists in a foreign land so much being in doubt. But as I lay my pencil down at year-end, looking out at the mist rising from the river, I have to acknowledge it has been an incredible and tumultuous year for humanity.

I know I have not done justice to the experiences of the rest of The Group. Perhaps I will find time in the future to record them.

P.S. Irony of ironies. On his most recent recce, Martin discovered we have planted our flag about ten miles from Porton Down!